I0600359

The Isle across Acheron

ALSO BY THE AUTHOR

Dear Kate—Dear Dad,
The Slip through Time

DENALI MAJESTO'S

THE ISLE ACROSS ACHERON

The Isle across Acheron
Copyright © 2024 by Denali Majesto
Paperback edition first published in 2024

Title also available as a Kindle eBook.

Cover Design: J. Alder Buckthorne
Interior Design: Ansel Muir

Requests for information should be addressed to Chelsey Hanel via email at chelsey@denalimajesto.com.

All rights reserved. No part of this book may be reproduced in any manner whatsoever, or stored in a retrieval system, or transmitted in any form by any means, electronic, mechanical, photocopying, recording, or otherwise, without written permission. Exceptions made in the case of short quotations published in articles and reviews.

The characters and events portrayed in this book are fictitious. Any similarity to real persons, living or dead, is coincidental and not intended by the author.

To inquire further or learn more about the library of Denali Majesto, please visit www.denalimajesto.com.

ISBN 9798992803808

To my children, for their many reminders to slow down and play once in a while.

May 18, 1954 – 9:08 a.m.

IT IS HERESY, REALLY. Not the kind of heresy which creates zealots and ends with burnt corpses tied upright to stakes. This heresy is of a lesser caliber, like drinking bourbon made in Virginia or baking Christmas cookies with a recipe other than your gramma's. It is the sort which rankles something in the very marrow of your bones, awakening dormant prejudices grafted into your genetic makeup.

Like a stiff jab to the nose, the acrid plumes of diesel exhaust sting my nostrils and bring tears to my eyes. But their offense runs far deeper than some fleeting olfactory discomfort. They are a slap in my very family's face.

After all, the Luthers are coal people. That black bounty of the earth was both our livelihood and that of our town. It was as much a part of our biology as the red blood coursing through our veins. We pulled it up from its ancient burial places, refined it, parceled it, and shared it with a nation. We used it to heat our homes, create electricity, and power machines to win a war in Europe.

And, throughout my younger years, it was coal which fueled our locomotives. Great trains—one, two, five miles long—crisscrossed our blossoming country. They hauled California gold to New York jewelers, and Minnesota lumber to Texas ranches.

It was coal which poured the foundation of our nation. Our world.

Then diesel took over. One by one, its steady burn consumed the coal engines of yesteryear. As other forms of fuel conquered our kitchens, our homes, and our machines of war, coal became all but forgotten. A relic of the past.

But I have not let go so easily. My heart contains too many memories which are inextricably linked to my young life as a coal proprietor's son. To excavate and discard them would mean nothing less than a denial of my own history. Thus anthracite, and my loyalty to it, will remain woven into the fabric of my being until the day I die.

And, as coal's unwanted successor, diesel shall forever remain the great infidel.

Yet here I am, riding cross country in the iron belly of a diesel-powered train. Propelled toward my destination by the very thing I condemn. So who am I to judge?

Along with coal, betrayal is another element inherent in my personal makeup. Always has been.

A glass of lukewarm water sits on the table in front of me, rippling to the rhythm of the train's tireless wheels. I pick it up and swallow a mouthful. As I do, I stare out the window, hoping to distract myself from the disagreeable fumes in the passing countryside.

Beyond the confines of the passenger car, I rediscover a land painted almost entirely in shades of green. First are the low, dandelion-dusted hills of central Pennsylvania, home to thousands of sheep and cattle. Rising behind them, emerald carpets of primeval forestland blanket the rounded peaks of the Allegheny Mountains. Although they are too distant to identify specific trees, I know well what I would find there: gnarled oaks, both white and red; sugar maples, which will set the forest afire come autumn; American beech and assorted birches; a prickly variety of conifers.

I know they are there, because those trees once belonged to me. To us.

Twenty years gone, and I am back again. I hear the ancient words of Odysseus, spoken in my father's voice.

Suddenly uncomfortable, I squirm in my seat.

Like forlorn and tormented spirits, an ensemble of memories grows audible within me. Their voices are relentless, and I know I cannot avoid them long.

But this morning I am not ready. Hardly a day has passed since I received the unexpected phone call that sent me barreling northeast from Wichita on a thousand-mile series of tracks. An unavoidable confrontation with my past is mere hours away. My reckoning can wait patiently until then.

The Pennsylvania landscape has failed as a distraction—I will attempt a second. After a moment's fumbling in my jacket pocket, my fingers retrieve a long-stemmed pipe. I unzip a cracked leather pouch and hastily stuff a pinch of black Cavendish pipe tobacco into the polished rosewood bowl.

I'm about to strike a match when a timid voice breaks the silence.

"I'm terribly sorry, sir, but would you mind smoking somewhere else?"

I turn in my seat, and my blood runs cold. I'm staring at a ghost.

Behind me and across the aisle sits a young woman no older than thirty. Sharp, caramel irises gaze at me through springy curls of strawberry blond. Her arm rests around the shoulders of a child, a boy not yet of school age.

"My son has terrible allergies," the caring mother explains, apologetic yet assertive. "Especially to tobacco smoke."

It takes a moment for my sluggish mind to catch up with reality. This woman is flesh and blood and no ghost.

Two other boys sit across from her. These are older than the first, but not by more than a few years. A table, identical to the one in front of me, divides the two halves of the family.

A mother and three boys. All approximately the same ages as ...

I shake my head and try not to give in. But the howling memories are growing louder.

"Are you alright? Sir?" the young woman asks with concern.

I glance at the match in my fingers, still poised to strike, and flash a grin. With a lightning-quick wink at the boy beneath his mother's protecting arm, I remember her request and reply, "Yes. Of course. It can wait until the next stop."

"Thank you," she says pleasantly.

"It's no problem at all. Enjoy your trip."

But I can see that she will not. Something about her demeanor strikes me as broken, defeated. I have learned to recognize sorrow, and an obvious one hangs upon her. She does not carry it in a display of open and teary grief. Hers is of a deeper sort, settled like a fog that will never lift, because the sun will not rise to melt it away.

The realization hits me: no husband. Another backward glance reveals a missing wedding ring on her left hand.

In the wake of the Korean War, it's easy to guess why.

There is nothing I can do, so I settle back into my seat. But I can't settle my mind. I'm uneasy. Disturbed. As the train's vibrations agitate the water in my glass, so my brief encounter with the three boys and their mother has rattled me down to my viscera.

Deep within, the cacophony of voices rises into a dissonant chorus. Each jostles for position among the rest, and I know my attempts to keep them at bay have failed.

Some voices whisper of brotherly love, of motherly love, of friendship and loyalty. Others bring memories of childhood, of wonder, of imagination.

Of magic.

There are memories of verdant lawns, of pipe smoke and whiskey, of clear lake waters and cerulean skies. Of a treehouse and cottage.

A few of the louder voices shout of sickness and loss. Of a father's failure, a brother's recklessness, a deep betrayal.

A blooming family, whose five petals were plucked to become three.

But there is a solitary voice which stands prominently among the rest. At first it is little more than a hum, a child's absentminded playtime song. Soon its intensity swells, marginally at first, then in increments. The hum evolves into words, a song clear and strong, whose deafening melody drowns out all else.

This haunting lullaby sings of hope's golden rays, which seeped into the cracks of my family's darkest hour and flooded our grieving hearts with its light.

I close my eyes and let the memories—and diesel fumes—swallow me whole.

ONE

The Flu

I WAS NINE YEARS AND TWO WEEKS old when the first whispers of The Flu reached my young ears. They came from the lips of Pastor Wainwright during the Great Easter Sunday Prayer of 1918. The chancel creaked under his ample form as he stood, black-gowned before the altar of St. Matthew's Lutheran Church, and pleaded that God might spare the lives of those infected. This he followed with petitions, beseechments, and implorings that the illness neither extend its reach nor result in further loss of life.

When the prayer had been offered—and, presumably, received by God—the triumphal Resurrection service continued with the Lord's Supper. I watched impatiently as the older members of each family approached the communion rail, knelt, ingested the body and blood of Christ, and returned to their seats, only to be replaced by the next sinner in an endless cavalcade of churchgoers, most of whom I hadn't seen there since Christmas.

There were the teary-eyed Millers, Michael and Jane, a middle-aged couple looking especially forward to the resurrection since the loss of their oldest son at the hands of the Germans. Caleb Lasseter, a foreman at Daddy's mine, approached the rail alone. His wife died long ago giving birth to Jeremiah, a beefy kid who also happened to be the most obnoxious person ever to clap erasers at Pierre Primary School. There was Mr. Rakowski, the lifelong Polish bachelor who owned the lumber yard; the Brunners with their eleven children; Tom and Katherine Schroeder, who ran the general store; the flaxen-haired Anne Carrington, our schoolteacher. On and on they came. Solemn, reverent, and in the mind of an antsy boy, infinite. The "Eternal Supper" would've been a more apt name for it. Too bad God didn't take comment cards.

Sitting next to me, John Luther—better known as "Daddy" to me and my brothers—must have sensed my restlessness. He winked an ice-blue eye and whispered, "It'll be over soon, Peter. Be patient."

Sure. No problem. Next he would command the sky to turn pink or an owl to twitter a happy song at sunrise. Sitting still went against the nature of any boy in any church at any time. Being one such boy, I was at the end of my fuse and ready to explode.

A leftward glance told me my brothers were suffering a similar malaise. Walter, fourteen months my elder, absentmindedly scuffed his toe over a knothole in the wood flooring, while little Pip chewed lazily on the last morsels of whatever snack he had snuck into church.

The head usher at St. Matthew's that morning was a grim-faced widower named Hans Albrecht. Whatever he took from those services, I don't know, because he didn't speak an article of English. But I suppose that's what made him such a fine usher. He needed no words to do his job. A curt nod was understood by all to mean it was your turn to approach the altar.

When Daddy finally stood, his Teutonic frame dwarfed everybody in the church. But—stature and blue eyes notwithstanding—there was little else German about him, which was fortunate considering the current events in Europe. Due likely to a healthy dose of Jewish blood on his mother's side, his other features were rather dark. He sported wavy brown hair and the bronze skin of an Italian seaman. When you added to these his prominent cheekbones, cleft chin, and strong nose, everything about John Luther's appearance commanded the attention of others.

Including my mother's.

Her name was Rosalie, and she was the human embodiment of the sun. Wherever she went, she radiated warmth to those around her. Even during the darkest months of winter, she glowed with an infectious joy that shed hope's light upon all. And, like the sun, her touch imparted life. Quickened by her hands, her gardens blossomed, then bloomed into their polychronic array each spring, long before any others in town.

Certainly she was the source of life for the Luthers, and not merely in the biological way. For my brothers and Daddy and me, her resplendent presence was the difference between gloom and mirth, lost and found, faith and apostasy.

That sunny Easter morning, my heart lifted as I watched her rippling waves of strawberry-blond hair, adorned with dainty white ribbons, bounce to the front of church. Upon her return to the pew, her gold-flecked eyes caught mine, and I deciphered in them a message, the promise of some planned mischief which would make me forget all about this ninety-minute exercise in forbearance called "church."

After the final communicants had returned to their seats, the sweet mercy known as the Closing Hymn began blaring from the pipe organ. Mama belted it with operatic gusto—she had a beautiful voice to match her beautiful everything else—while Daddy closed his eyes and sang softly, sweetly. He treated each note as a delicacy, a choice morsel. Strung together, one after the other from beginning to end, these became a feast for his very soul to consume.

When the final note's reverberations had subsided, Pastor Wainwright wiped his beading brow with a hanky and issued a handful of announcements. There was something about an upcoming church cleanup day and a congratulatory birthday notice—I didn't pay close attention.

But his final announcement pricked my ears.

"We will also collect a special offering next week," he said, "for the members of a sister church in New York. They're experiencing a breakout there of some aggressive form of The Flu. From what I last heard, dozens of people are sick, and a couple have already passed away to be with the Lord."

There it was again. A whisper of that mysterious illness. Even over this sun-kissed day of life called Easter, the cloud of Death draped its shadow.

But only momentarily. After an obligatory moment of somber reverence, the parishioners of St. Matthew's resumed their spirited gossip. The sunshine of eternal life had returned. Pastor Wainwright bade us all a blessed Easter, then strode past the pews and out the front door to greet his flock as they exited.

It was the only time in my life I wished I was a pastor. He was outside, enjoying the sunshine, while I had to sit and wait for our turn to leave. Since my family was sitting near the back of the narrow sanctuary—and since on holidays, church greeting lines moved like snails through molasses—the saga of my impatience was receiving an epilogue. Inwardly, I screamed. Outwardly, I groaned quietly and hoped Daddy wouldn't hear.

If he did, it was Walter's question that saved me from a reprimand.

"Mama, what's this *Flu* that Pastor Wainwright was talking about?"

She gazed down at him. Her cream-and-honey face, sprinkled with light freckles, seemed to age with concern as she replied, "Nothing a ten-year-old boy needs to worry himself with."

"But Pastor Wainwright said people're dying from it," said Walter.

Mama ran her fingers through his thick brown hair. "Yes, some. But they're a long, *long* way from here."

"So we're gonna be okay?" Walter posed his question with every confidence that Mama's answer would constitute the gospel truth of the matter.

She chuckled and poked him playfully in the ribs. "I'd sooner die than let anything happen to my boys. So quit your worrying, Wahwie!"

Wahwie—that was the moniker I had bestowed upon him when I was a toddler. Boys of two have difficulty pronouncing their words, and my attempts to call him by name had sounded like "Wahwie" to Mama and Daddy. Seven years later, it was still glued to him like binding on a book. No matter how much it annoyed him, he couldn't escape it.

Of course, he blamed me tremendously for this misfortune.

But I suppose that was fitting. Walter and I were fire and ice, complete opposites. And, in cliché sibling fashion, secret rivals. He was outspoken and daring. I was reserved and a bit timid. The other kids at school felt his presence the moment he entered a room, whereas I had a distinct penchant for melting into the background. Walter was adventurous, resourceful, and tough. I was none of those things. The only area in which I excelled above Walter was that of schoolwork, but being the class bookworm didn't exactly win me many friends.

Even in physical appearance, we were as different as dachshunds and Dobermans. I was spindly and sparse, envious of my brother's natural bulk, and my white-blond hair and sallow complexion couldn't have evoked the jealousy of a ghost. Walter, on the other hand, took after Daddy. Even in deepest winter he was a figure of godlike bronze.

No matter how hard I tried, Walter was always three inches taller than me, in stature and in personality.

How I hated it.

Delivering a stroke of mercy after my drawn-out torture, Hans Albrecht finally approached our row and issued a flinty nod. Like convicts during a jailbreak, we pushed and shoved each other as we followed Daddy into the center aisle. There we stopped and respectfully waited for Mama to shuffle past and lead us out the church doors.

The midmorning sunlight on the other side was blinding, but the loss of my sight was a fair trade for freedom.

"He is risen!" exclaimed Pastor Wainwright. His smile stretched from bushy sideburn to bushy sideburn as he took Mama's outstretched hand in both his own.

"He is risen indeed," Mama responded, echoing what all the other parishioners had said before her. "I assume you're still planning to swing by the house later?"

"As long as the chocolate cake and bourbon John promised are there, so am I!" he confirmed. "I'll phone you from the Schroeders' before I head over. They're having me over for Easter ham."

"Are you so sure you *aren't* the Easter ham, Fred?" joked Daddy. He patted the pastor's protruding tummy before shaking his hand.

Few congregants would have been bold enough to speak to their spiritual father with such insolence, but Daddy got away with it. After all, Friedrich Wainwright—who went by "Fred"—was his closest friend.

"Sure, I've put on a few pounds," Pastor Wainwright admitted. "But when you're my age—"

"Oh, *Quatsch,*" retorted Daddy, daring to utter a German curse word on Easter. "I'm two years older than you, and you know it."

Pastor Wainwright laughed with his whole belly and shoved my father along. "I'll see you later, you old sinner. I've got decent folks yet to greet."

I wasn't allowed to drink bourbon, of course, but Mama's utterance of an inbound cake was enough to put some giddyap in my gait as we circled to the backside of the simple, whitewashed church. There we found our transportation home exactly as we had left it before the service. A meager team of two, Castor and Pollux wouldn't have impressed many Colorado cowboys, but the chestnut stallions did a fine job hauling our buckboard wagon to and from town.

My brothers and I clambered into the cart's rear, while Mama and Daddy perched themselves on the bench behind Castor and Pollux. With the reins in his hands, Daddy flicked his wrists, and the horses heaved us forward. We rolled over the matted swath of grass between the church building and St. Matthew's Cemetery, then turned west onto the endless dirt road which connected Pierre, Pennsylvania, to the rest of the world.

As happened every time we set off upon our rickety wagon, a shade of disappointment flickered across Mama's face.

"Something wrong, Freckles?" Daddy asked, using his longtime pet name for her.

Like wheels through a well-worn rut, the ensuing conversation followed a familiar track.

"You know perfectly well what's wrong, John!" Mama retorted with faux outrage. "How long will you keep driving us around in this splintery old cart?"

Daddy chewed on his answer, then said, as he always did, "At least one time longer than you ask that question."

Mama rolled her eyes at his predictable response. She crossed her arms like a petulant child and said, "We have the money, and you know it."

"The money for what, my love?"

"A *carriage*. A real, proper *carriage*. With doors and cushioned seats and curtains and a roof to keep out the rain."

Daddy smirked and stretched out his hand, palm up, to check the weather. "I wasn't aware it was raining."

Mama elbowed him in the ribs hard enough to elicit a wince and said, "You know what I mean, John Luther."

With an appealing nod toward the horses pulling our wagon, Daddy said, "Poor old Castor and Pollux wouldn't know what to do with themselves if we hitched 'em to a carriage. It'd be so much heavier than they're used to."

"Then we get a couple more!" Mama replied brightly. She adored our horses, and a pair more would only give her more to love.

"That's twice the feed, twice the shoes, twice the caring for. And all for what? To save your pretty rear from a few splinters?" Under his breath, he added, "You know I don't mind helping you find those."

"A few *hundred* splinters," said Mama, ignoring his suggestive comment. "And each with a bruise to match it."

As if he'd just discovered the brilliant compromise, Daddy exclaimed, "Well then, I'll start saving up to buy you a nice cushion for your birthday. Sounds like that'll solve all your problems, and it'll save me the purchase price of an entire carriage!"

"You know it's more than that," Mama growled, even as a serene expression brightened her face. "It'd be just like living in a story by Charles Dickens or Victor Hugo. The people in Paris and London are always riding around in carriages. Why can't we?"

"Because this is rural Pennsylvania," Daddy reminded her. "If we rode around like fairy-tale characters, everyone would think we're snobs."

"Oh, let them think what they want. Besides, it won't matter to me anyway. When I ride past them like Cinderella on her way to the Prince's ball, I can cover up their condescending faces with my velvet curtains."

"So now you're Cinderella?"

"Mmm-hmm. Still waiting for my prince, though."

Daddy laughed fully—a sound like music to my young ears—and said, "I'll make you a deal. Whenever there's a fuel station near enough to make the purchase worthwhile, I'll buy you one of Henry Ford's new automobiles. How 'bout that?"

Mama's scowl gave her clear reply: She would *not* be accepting Daddy's proposal anytime soon.

Then a radiant grin broke out upon her lips. She kissed Daddy on his cheek, leaned her head contentedly on his shoulder, and said no more about it.

TWO

A Tale of Two Families

MAMA WAS RIGHT. We needed a carriage. Hell, I would've given up half my upcoming summer vacation for one of Daddy's proposed cushions.

St. Matthew's lay only a quarter mile east of downtown Pierre, but by the time we approached the cluster of tightly packed buildings bordering Main Street, my rear was as tender as a filet mignon—and possibly as raw as one. Each pebble crushed beneath the wagon's wheels would mean a fresh bruise in the morning, to say nothing of those inflicted by my brothers' elbows, knees, and other bodily protrusions.

As we made our way along the main drag, I cast languid glances at the various shops, parlors, and offices lining both sides of the street. Faces of red brick, almost as bored as I was, stared back. On weekdays the storefronts' dark mouths yawned open to consume Pierre's consumers, but every Sunday those doors of commerce stood shut and barred. Except for a handful of scattered pedestrians upon the cobblestone sidewalks, homeward bound from their respective church services, Pierre rested along with its residents on the Sabbath.

Among all this downtown monotony, there was but a single point of interest for me. Each Sunday, when we approached the intersection of 4th Street and Main, I'd sit up straight and try in vain to flatten the stubborn cowlick in my hair, and my stomach would experience the same queasy sensation as when Walter dared me to drink our goat Maisie's week-old milk.

That's because from here I could catch a glimpse of the Jansen residence one block north. It was the home of my father's longtime business partner Jacob, who lived within its white-trimmed, slate-blue walls with his wife and four children.

Of course, my thrill in seeing the house had nothing to do with some odd, premature affinity for Victorian architecture.

It had everything to do with Hattie. A few months older than me, and a few younger than Walter, she was my number-one ally in mischief and merriment. We were best friends, Hattie and me, and had been for as far back as my memory stretched.

But lately, a change I couldn't explain had settled over our friendship. Every time I saw her, or even thought about her, I felt uneasy and uncertain of myself. I worried over every word before I spoke it, and once I did speak, I only worried more. Her reaction to everything I said and did was the noose upon which I daily hung. A smile or laugh was like cool water in a desert, while the slightest shrug of indifference had the power to lock me away in a prison of gloom.

As we passed through the intersection that morning, my eyes flickered from window to window, but all was dark at the Jansen house. The raised porch, with its wicker chairs and bench swing, also sat uninhabited. The only sign of life came from the old maple in their front yard, whose arms waved apologetically in the lazy breeze.

Hello. Sorry. She's not home.

I slouched, disappointed, and resumed my previous activity of avoiding collisions with Pip and Walter.

As it turned out, I had merely been looking the wrong direction.

"Howdy, Jansens!" Mama hollered.

Daddy slowed the wagon in response.

I shot upright, and my heart leaped in my chest like John the Baptist in his mama's womb.

All six Jansens, likewise on their way home from church, approached us on foot. Jacob, whose first name might as well have been "Mister" to me and my brothers, led his family. Grim and austere, he was seldom seen without a cloud of pipe smoke obscuring his face, and today was no different. Beside him, and a little behind, was his wife Hannah. With her curly hair and striking green eyes, she was probably pretty once, but these days her features drooped with the weight of an untold burden.

The firstborn Jansen, also named Jacob, flanked his namesake's other side. Like his father, he wore a woolen, pinstripe suit that looked far too stifling for such a warm morning. Prim and prissy Arlene, the butt of many a Luther boy joke, walked beside her older brother. With her pointed nose aimed skyward, it was a wonder she could see where she was going at all.

Finally, taking up the troop's rear, Hattie dragged two-year-old Constance along by her chubby fingers.

Jacob waited to return Mama's greeting until they had drawn nearer.

"Happy Easter to you, Luthers," he said, tipping the brim of his bowler hat briskly but courteously. He offered a thin-lipped grin from within his trimmed, rusty beard, but his gray eyes did not smile with it. Behind the oval lenses of his wire-rimmed glasses, they remained icy and stoic.

Hannah Jansen was the sort of wife for whom interrupting a man was as scandalous as intercourse with one. Only when she was sure her husband was finished speaking did she finally say, "Happy Easter, Rosalie. Headed home from St. Matthew's?"

The Jansens went to First Reformed Church every Sunday, and I was justifiably jealous of them. First Reformed was on the west side of town, and I could have shaved a good ten minutes off my Sunday commute if allowed to attend services there. But the Jansens were Dutch, and I wasn't. Cursed with Lutheranness by my Germanness, I was doomed all my days to St. Matthew's the Distant.

About the continued exchange of pleasantries among the adults, I couldn't have cared less. My sights were set on the girl now pushing her way between her parents. The one I had looked for in the windows. The one whose coiled, cinnamon-blond hair bounced like springs, and whose bright smile was darkened by two gaps where her baby teeth had popped loose.

I jumped off the wagon and met her beside it.

"Hey, Hattie."

"Hi, Peter," she said cheerily. Even as she spoke to me, her eyes wandered up to my brother. "Hi, Walter."

"Hey," he grunted, showing his trademark indifference toward her. He hadn't even bothered to climb down from the cart.

Pip's beaming face suddenly appeared over the wagon's low rail. "Hattieeee!"

My little brother harbored a public—and quite shameless—crush on my best friend.

Hattie giggled and held out her arms. Pip almost knocked her over as he jumped into them.

"Happy Easter, Pippie," she said, planting a kiss on his dirty cheek. She set him on the ground, and he stood beside her, quietly holding her hand.

She turned her attention not to me, but to Walter, as she asked, "What're you doing today?"

He shrugged. "Not sure. Abigail's making dinner. And Gramma and Grampa are coming over from Castleton too."

Walter didn't reciprocate her question, so I did.

"What about you?"

"Nothing, really," she said. "I know Mother is making dinner, but that's it."

"You think you could come over later?" I asked, perhaps a bit eagerly. Coolly, I added, "If you want."

"I don't know. Maybe. What do you want to do?"

I stared down at my feet and scuffed the toe of my shoe against a stone, dislodging it from the crust of dirt. "I don't know. Whatever you want."

"We could build a treehouse!" Hattie suggested brightly. She looked again to Walter. "You told me we could next time I came over."

"I guess we could," he said. "*If* we have time. But I've been making a map of the woods around our house and want to do that first."

"But you promised!"

"Yeah. But it's already late. Plus, Gramma and Grampa are coming over. We wouldn't get much done anyway."

Hattie scowled. She continued staring at him, even as I spoke.

"We could start on a treehouse maybe," I said. "But first, you should ask your mother if you can come."

"Ok, I will. Hold on."

Mama had been eavesdropping on our conversation. Before Hattie could say a word, Mama took command of the situation and asked, "Would Hattie be able to come over this afternoon? I planned something fun to do with the boys, and I know she would enjoy it too."

Mrs. Jansen glanced nervously at her husband. "Well, I don't know. What do you think, Jacob?"

Mr. Jansen seemed mildly irritated at the interruption in his conversation with Daddy. "What do I think about what?"

"Rosalie wants Hattie to come by this afternoon."

"Arlene is welcome too, of course," Mama added, though she certainly knew the senior Jansen girl would decline the invitation.

Arlene was two years older than Walter. When she was younger, she used to play with us all the time. As she had grown in years, she had also grown in her snobbery. She no longer had time to spend with "little kids" such as ourselves.

Mr. Jansen's answer was like a dark cloud over the rays of my hope. "I don't think so. Not today, Rosa. It's Easter. We should spend it as a family."

"Well," Mama replied, the gears of improvisation grinding in her creative mind, "what if she came over to play for a while, and then you all joined us later for dessert and a drink? My parents and Pastor Wainwright will be there too. The more the merrier, I say!"

Mr. Jansen took a steely draw from his pipe as he sized up Mama's determination. Finally, he said, "Very well. We'll send Hattie along after dinner. And the rest of us will be by at six o'clock sharp."

Beside me, Pip was unable to contain his squeak of victory. An afternoon with Hattie gave him something more to celebrate even than the Resurrection of the Dead.

For his part, Daddy laughed merrily and said, "Excellent! I already bought a bottle of Labrot & Graham's finest bourbon to celebrate the occasion, and you look like you could use a drink or two."

"Remember that we have work tomorrow, John. Let's not have a repeat of the morning after Christmas."

"I made it in!" Daddy exclaimed defensively.

"Yes. At *ten*."

Daddy laughed again. "Oh, lighten up, will you? A little fun never killed anyone, and two hours late to work never killed a business. But don't worry. We'll send you on your way well before your bedtime, and with a nightcap that'll put you straight to sleep."

Mr. Jansen rolled his eyes, but his grin was authentic as he said, "Very well then. We'll see you this evening."

And with that farewell, he ushered his family along.

Hattie waved an excited goodbye over her shoulder as she skipped along behind them.

"Barrel of laughs, that man," Mama muttered under her breath, once the Jansens were out of earshot. "How you ever got mixed up with him is beyond me."

Jacob Jansen was one of the few people on planet Earth who truly got under her skin. They were as incompatible as storm clouds and the sun.

"I know he comes across as severe," Daddy replied, as Pip and I clambered back into the wagon, "but he's always been good to me. Once you dive below his icy surface, you'll see."

"I don't think I can hold my breath that long," said Mama. "But if you say so, I'll keep trying."

Daddy kissed her cheek. "I do say so."

Then he snapped the reins, and we continued homeward.

As Castor and Pollux pulled the wagon away, I turned to watch the Jansens through the dust cloud our horses left behind us.

Two well-dressed parents. Four obedient children in tow. To any outside observer, they looked like the perfect family walking home from church together.

Then again, I suppose everyone passing my family that Sunday might have said the same thing about the Luthers.

We were a pair of well-to-do households, respectable and successful, influential among the people of Pierre, Pennsylvania. I daresay a good portion of the townsfolk likely harbored secret jealousies against our two families.

But it was all a delusion. One that even we had fallen unwittingly into.

The truth was that we were all broken in many ways. Some of the cracks were ones we had managed to paint over. Others we simply hadn't discovered yet.

But the next months would teach us. In ways we would never forget and could never escape, the remaining days of 1918—and beyond—would teach us not only how broken we *were*.

They also taught us how broken we might *become*.

THREE

The Lincolns of Asphodel Glade

TWO MILES BEYOND THE WESTERN EDGE of town and a half mile south, imprinted deep in the verdant forestlands and striated hills of Pennsylvanian Appalachia, there is a lake. It was deposited there when the glaciers retreated at the end of North America's last ice age. For thousands of years afterward, its waters gave life to myriad fish, turtles, frogs, and birds. Natives camped around its banks and plumbed the depths of its waters. They drank from it to revive their thirsting bodies. In time they were displaced by white men and women, who brought violence from their cities to the lake's sapphire shores. Around it they felled trees, taming the land as they beat back its forests, built their homesteads, and raised their families.

Ultimately, the history of Lake Acheron also included the Luthers. Following the successful advent of his mining business, Daddy purchased a long ribbon of property along the lake's northern bank. Thick forests, mainly of oak and birch and pine, blanketed most of the land's thousand acres.

But at a certain point along the road between Pierre and Castleton, a cart path turned south, slicing through the army of trees. The great forest eventually yielded to a magnificent lawn, a chartreuse sea stretching nearly half a mile to Acheron's azure waters.

It was here, to Asphodel Glade, where we came at last that late Easter morning.

A quaint caretakers' cottage was situated at the north end of the spacious clearing. As we passed by it, Mama raised an arm and waved a greeting to the sweat-drenched man chopping wood beside it.

His name was Eli Lincoln. He was the oldest resident of Asphodel Glade, and not only in the sense that he was born before the rest of us. He had also lived there the longest. Before the first shots of the Civil War were ever fired at Fort Sumter, Eli had come screaming into the world on these very grounds. Back then, Asphodel was still owned by the Vandenbergs, the same family who had built and named it, and from whom Daddy eventually bought it. Born into a free black family, Eli could have left any time he wanted. Yet he had chosen to remain here, living every day of it in the same cottage and working the same grounds.

As I knew would happen, Eli did not return Mama's greeting. If anything, he seemed to swing his axe with a renewed vigor, as if he were personally sentencing and executing each log he split. In a single swift stroke, he would hack one in half, then pick up both pieces and limp to the growing woodpile, where he deposited them.

Daddy snickered and shook his head. He knew better than to take Eli's disdain personally.

"Sure doesn't care for us, does he," Daddy muttered sideways to Mama.

"Not yet," she said. "Maybe tomorrow."

That must have been the day Eli's distaste for us finally registered in my three-year-old brother's mind, because Pip asked, "Why doesn't he like us? Why's he so mean?"

"It's complicated, Pippie," Mama answered. "And it's a long story. Let's just say that white people like us haven't treated black people like Eli very well in the past."

"Or the present," added Daddy.

Pip rose indignantly where he sat, as if wondering what threads of darkness might dwell in their hearts' fibers. "What did you do to him?"

"Not us personally!" Mama assured him. "It's hard to explain, and you're a little young to understand. But if Eli seems mean to you, just remember that people have been way meaner to him. Okay?"

"And no matter what," added Daddy, "you must always treat Mister Lincoln with respect. Understood?"

Pip nodded, thus ending his brief line of questioning.

Our wagon rolled along, passing the large vegetable patch and orchard which Eli cultivated and maintained. Together, these provided Asphodel's residents with all the fresh produce we could ask for, from spinach in May to apples in October.

Not far past the orchard, our wagon crested the rise of a low hill, and the rest of Asphodel Glade filled my field of vision. Left of the path stood a modest yellow barn, whose peeling paint reminded me of birch bark curls. This served as a home for Castor, Pollux, and our goat Maisie. There was also a workshop in the barn's rear where Eli spent much of his time. Directly downhill from the barn were a stone smokehouse and bustling chicken coop, from which Eli's sister Abigail, who lived in the cottage with him, gathered eggs each morning.

And, at the end of the path, with its windows open to greet us, stood our Castle Home. Its official name was Asphodel Hall, and that's what Daddy called it. But Mama found the name stuffy and old, so she began to call it our Castle Home instead and raised her boys to do likewise.

Admittedly, it did not truly fit the definition of any *castle*. Rather, it was a roomy colonial home built in the 1840s. Constructed with stones pulled directly from Lake Acheron, its multicolored walls did indeed look like those of an old European castle, but that was where the similarities ended. No castle I was aware of had a wide, covered porch wrapped around three-quarters of its lower level. Nor did our house contain towers or turrets or battlements or defensive weapons for repelling enemy invaders—much to the disappointment of the three boys living there.

Still, if Mama called it our castle, then our castle it was, and it did indeed feel like one to me and my brothers. Inside our home, with Mama and Daddy watching over us, we were safe. Let the world's problems rage where they might! We were impervious. Untouchable. Within our fortress's walls, we had protection from every imaginable sorrow or evil.

Finally, at the far end of our tiny kingdom, creating a magical backdrop of shimmering mercury under the noonday sun, was our lake.

"Daddy," piped Pip with another of his endless questions, "why is it called Lake *Acheron?* What does *Acheron* mean?"

I already knew the answer, but at the opportunity to explain its meaning to another of his boys, Daddy's eyes lit up.

Mama rolled hers. She knew what was coming.

"Great question, Pip!" Daddy exclaimed. "I suppose there are *two* answers, one that's boring and one that's much more interesting. The first answer is that our lake is named after a river in a faraway country called Greece. It's also called Acheron."

"And now for the *boring* answer," Mama mumbled.

Daddy shoved her playfully and went on. "But in Greek mythology—those're their folktales—Acheron was one of the five rivers of the Underworld. When someone died, they crossed over Acheron on a ferry. That was how they passed from the living world to the land of the dead. Some people called it the 'river of woe' because of all the sadness caused by death. But Acheron was also known as a river of healing, because when people crossed it, they were cleansed of their sins.

They left the sorrows of earth behind and could embrace their truer selves in the Underworld."

"You and your stuffy old Classics," Mama teased. "It's a wonder even the Greeks tolerated them! I'd rather boil my own head than read *The Odyssey* again."

"And I suppose you think Twain and Stevenson will be around two thousand years from now?" countered Daddy, putting a pair of Mama's favorite authors on the stand.

"Whether they are or they aren't," Mama parried, "at least they know how to write something with a bit of excitement!"

"And Odysseus outwitting a bloodthirsty Cyclops doesn't count as exciting?"

"Maybe it would be, if the whole thing weren't written in *poetry*."

I'm sure the jocular banter would have continued if it hadn't been for Maisie. The goat was busy helping herself to a snack from the flowerbed in front of our porch.

"*Scheisse,*" muttered Daddy, for which he received his second Easter elbowing from Mama. "How does that goat keep breaking free? Between me and Eli, we've checked her stall latch at least a dozen times."

"You'd be wise to take her door off and let her roam free," retorted Mama, "like I've said at least a dozen times."

"I know she wouldn't wander too far," said Daddy. "But if she eats too many of those tulips she's currently butchering, it'll be hell for her stomach."

We were approaching the end of the cart path, so Daddy slowed the horses. When the wagon had come to a full stop, he swung his legs over the side and lowered himself to the ground.

"Everybody off!" he ordered, then raised a hand to assist Mama down from the bench. "Pip, you get to help me with the horses, and then we'll see to Maisie."

"Hooray!" my younger brother exclaimed. It never did take much to excite him.

But before my other brother and I could escape unscathed, Daddy continued with further instructions. "Walter, Peter, you run along inside and change, then see whether Abigail needs any help in the kitchen. Gramma and Grampa will be here within the hour, and the sooner they're fed, the sooner they're gone."

Mama shot him a look which contained enough venom to kill ten men.

"Just kidding of course!" Daddy said with a feeble chuckle. Then, under his breath to Pip, he whispered, "It's only Gramma we need to get rid of."

Ignoring him, Mama said, "I'll be in the garden if anybody needs me. I want to cut a bouquet for the dinner table."

Mama's famous flower gardens stretched all the way from our sunset porch down to the embankments just above the lakeshore. They were so vibrant and full, you could've spotted them even if you were standing on the Moon. I didn't know the names of most of the flowers she grew there—my time in the gardens was mostly spent pulling weeds—but they came in every shape, color, and variety my young brain could have imagined. Guests at Asphodel Glade gawked at and marveled over them. They sought tips from Mama, hoping their own gardens might see even a fraction of her success.

And Mama wasn't stingy. She helped as best she was able. But Mama never shared her most important secret.

She simply loved them. They weren't a chore. They weren't something to accomplish. They were her joy, and caring for them was her pleasure.

Mine and Walter's pleasure, however, would soonest be found in changing out of our stuffy church clothes. Once off the wagon, we tore past Mama, bounded up the front steps, and shot through the front door. Walter beat me, of course. Even in something as insignificant as an unofficial race into the house, he always bested me.

As soon as we entered the cavernous Great Room beyond the threshold, the aroma of buttery garlic and roasted potatoes hailed their enthusiastic greeting. Buried beneath that potent bouquet were the subtler scents of stewed lamb, fresh herbs, and crisp greens.

Abigail had been busy. On a normal day her cuisine stood without peer, but it was holidays when she truly let loose her inner gourmand.

Soon I would reap the fruits of her labor, but first, I needed to change and contribute some labor of my own.

A wide staircase hugged the western wall of the Great Room. Walter charged up it, and I followed. At the top, we hung a sharp right and burst through the door of our shared bedroom.

Walter scrambled immediately onto his bed. The top-right corner of his Yellowstone Falls poster was flapping freely in the breeze, and he retacked it to the wall. It was one of a half-dozen posters which hung over his bed, each of them depicting a natural wonder of America's national parks. We had learned about them in school a few months earlier, and Walter had become obsessed. Daddy was even talking about a family trip out West so we could visit them during the upcoming summer.

"Stupid thing keeps coming down," Walter muttered. "It's 'cause you leave your damn window open. The wind rips it off."

We had recently learned the wicked thrill of cursing, but were wise enough to know how dearly we would pay if any adults heard us.

"I was hot last night," I replied stubbornly. "If you want it shut, you do it. I'm not going to."

He didn't bother. Whenever his initial attempt to needle me failed, Walter usually let it go, and I was too excited about what lay ahead that afternoon to let him get my goat.

Chocolate cake. And *Hattie.*

Walter and I stripped out of our stiff, stifling church attire and changed into our playclothes. Mama had personally altered these for us so that our pant legs gathered above the knees, and our shirtsleeves above the elbows. Even on warm days, we could run around outside and barely break a sweat.

Once fully changed, we headed downstairs to see how we might help Abigail, as per Daddy's instructions. We skirted past the scattered couches, overstuffed chairs, and gold-framed oil paintings of the Great Room, toward the kitchen which lay at its opposite end.

There we found Abigail exactly as expected, hunched over a sizzling pan of something-or-other, her back turned to the kitchen doorway.

"Hi, Abigail," we hailed in near unison.

Her strong arms froze. The sinews in her neck tightened as she glanced sideways over her shoulder. Those dark eyes, always in search of some hint of mischief, studied us briefly before returning to the stovetop.

"Even on Easter," she said, her tone deep and her rhythm evenly measured, "you boys'll have hell to pay if your Daddy hears you call me anything other than *Miss Lincoln.*"

It was true. Daddy insisted we address all adults respectfully. Title-plus-last-name was our only option. Even though Abigail worked for our family, and personally preferred that we use her first name, she insisted we obey Daddy's wishes whenever he was home.

"He's outside still, putting up the horses with Pip," Walter said in our defense. "Do you need help with anything?"

Abigail balanced her wooden spoon on the lip of a pot and turned to face us fully. An almost regal quality hid behind her stained blouse and grease-spackled apron. With her high cheekbones and pointed features, she possessed a severe sort of beauty, like that of a distinguished queen. She was lean and hard, as if God had carved her from a knotty old oak. Calluses graced her hands, elbows, and knees, the honorable badges she wore for her many years of hard labor.

But whenever she smiled, it was as if all those years of hardening melted away. In a moment, she shed twenty years, and the soft beauty of her younger self bubbled to the surface.

It was one of those smiles she gave us now, as she said, "Aren't you a fine pair of gentlemen, coming to help a poor old woman like me! I'm sure it was all your idea too."

"Well ... no," Walter admitted. "Daddy told us to."

Abigail, who obviously knew this to be the case, said, "Then if your Daddy wants you to work, work you shall! Walter, you can start by setting the table, just the way I taught you."

My brother scurried to the bulky maple hutch at the far end of the kitchen and began collecting from it the appropriate dinnerware.

"As for you, Little Mister Luther," said Abigail, addressing me with the long-time nickname she used interchangeably with all Luther siblings, "I've got a job right next to me. You're nine now, and it's high time you learned the proper way to use a knife."

"Okay," I replied uncertainly.

"Open up your hands."

I did. Into one, Abigail placed the hilt of a small paring knife. Into the other, a knobby brown root that looked like a quite-unappetizing, mutant potato.

"That's called *ginger*," she explained after seeing my look of disgust. "I'm using it in the salad dressing. And a good idea too, considering the news I heard about this Flu! A little ginger'll cure most every sickness under the sun. That's what my mama always told me, anyway, and she was healthy every day of her life— leastwise, until the one she died on."

"Really?" I asked, mystified that such an ugly thing could do something so wonderful.

Abigail chuckled. "'Course, that's just an old wives' tale. But old wives didn't grow to be so old for no reason!"

I didn't know much about these "old wives' tales," but they sounded reliable enough to me.

Rotating the ginger root uncertainly in my hand, I asked, "What do you want me to do with it?"

"First thing is to peel off that brown skin, same way you do an apple. Thumb on the back of the blade and shave it away from your body. Yes, just like that— Easy with those dishes!"

That last bit was hollered at Walter, following a particularly raucous clamoring of china dinner plates.

Once I had successfully removed the skin from the ginger, Abigail inspected my work and said, "Now you can get to mincing it. Hold one end between your fingers, then start chopping the other end. Use the cutting board, Peter. No, not straight down like that. Keep your knife point on the counter while you do it, and slide the ginger underneath the blade as you move it up and down. Like this." She demonstrated for me with the carrot she was slicing. "Now you try."

Abigail supervised as I butchered the remaining ginger with all the precision of an inebriated galley chef cooking in a hurricane.

"Good," she lied when I was finished. "Now you need to cut those slices into the tiniest pieces you can. That's the real mincing of it. Best way to do it is to rock your knife back and forth over your little pile. Keep your other palm flat on the back of the blade while you do it. Then rock it back and forth, nice and easy. Like your seesaw at school."

The grisly image of schoolchildren seesawing on a giant knife had just formed in my mind's eye when Mama stepped into the kitchen doorway. After her trip to the garden, she had changed into her own playclothes. She now wore a light-weight, silky yellow dress, tied around her waist with a periwinkle sash. Like our shirts, it was a design of her own making. Its high hem rose all the way to her knees and flowed freely about them, allowing her legs unrestricted movement. In town, people would have called such a dress "indecent," but here in our secluded glade, it made for perfectly sensible attire.

"I'm setting the table, Mama!" Walter announced proudly, as he carried a pre-cariously high stack of dinner and salad plates through the kitchen's far door into the dining room.

"That's wonderful, Wahwie!" Mama exclaimed, beaming at him. "Just be sure to put everything in the proper places. Gramma won't let you hear the end of it otherwise."

Abigail dropped a pinch of salt into her stew and said, "I thought I told you I wasn't gonna be cooking for that woman anymore. Henry I don't mind, but that Opal's a different story. She could find fault with the Lord Jesus himself. Prob'ly tell him he didn't rise early enough if she'd been at the first Easter."

Even though Abigail had insulted her mother, Mama was unable to stifle a laugh. "It's like I told you before: she's all bark. Show her your teeth, and she'll back off with her tail tucked between her legs."

"I didn't know ogres had tails," quipped Abigail, "but I take your point."

Mama chuckled again and said, "They're liable to walk in the door any minute now, so you'd best keep those comments to yourself from here on. Or whisper them to me *reeeeeal* quietly!"

Still wearing her radiant smile, Mama absconded from the kitchen.

She did love Gramma Opal. I have no doubt about that. But Mama sure didn't *like* Gramma Opal much. Their personalities were exact opposites, as far apart from one other as penguins from polar bears. Where Mama saw black, Gramma saw white. If Mama laughed, Gramma scowled. They disagreed on almost everything, and neither was afraid to air those conflicting views in front of their family.

"Your Gramma might be the one ailment this ginger *can't* keep away," Abigail murmured to me with a wink. Her gnarled fingers scooped my ginger pile off the counter and into her palm. "Beautiful mincing, Peter. With knife skills like that, you're bound to be a chef someday."

I watched her mix the ginger into a small bowl, but only for a moment before Walter hurried back into the kitchen.

His two words were enough to make my heart stop.

"She's here!"

FOUR

Gramma, Grampa, and a Goblin

"ARE YOU DEAF?" CRIED WALTER, clutching my upper arm. "Gramma's coming up the path! Come on, let's escape out the back. Quick!"

With all the speed of a praying mantis snatching its unfortunate victim, Abigail seized each of us by a shoulder.

"No way," she said. "No running off for you two. If I gotta be here, you're suffering with me. Besides, you know the Commandment to honor your elders. Now, go get the door for your Gramma so I don't have to. Scoot!"

Walter and I dragged our feet with such melodrama, we left shallow grooves in the floorboards as we went. Nevertheless, we obeyed Abigail—and the Commandments—and opened the front door for Gramma.

Wearing her perpetual, thin-lipped frown, she clomped across the creaking threshold. With the flat face and sagging jowls of an English bulldog, she may have been incapable of smiling even if she wanted to.

"Happy Easter, Walter. Peter." Gramma's sharp, barking voice only added to her bulldoggishness.

"Happy Easter, Gramma," we mumbled in reply.

She glowered down at us. Our dearth of enthusiasm hadn't gone unnoticed, and she disapproved. A frown twitched at the corners of her gray lips.

"Is something the matter?" she demanded.

I tried to form a response but couldn't. All I could think about was how the navy, square-necked dress stretched around her pumpkin torso gave her the appearance of a ready-to-pop blueberry.

Walter and I were saved by the sudden appearance of Mama on the stairs.

"Hi, Mama," our mother said, her tone lacking its normal electricity. "Happy Easter."

"Happy Easter, Rosalie," Gramma replied. She met Mama at the bottom of the stairs and enveloped her in a smothering hug. "I see you're wearing another of your bawdy homemade dresses."

"It's more comfortable for playing with the boys. Besides, it isn't like I wear it around town."

Gramma grunted her objection anyway.

"Where's Dad?" asked Mama.

"Putting up the horses. And undoubtedly having a sip of something with John. I'm sure you *Lutherans* still enjoy your whiskeys, even on Easter."

There was little else in this world Gramma loved more than pointing out Daddy's faults. He was eight years older than Mama. He was raised in the "wicked city" of Philadelphia. He frequently enjoyed the company of a few drinks. While his success in business and dedication to family had merited Gramma's absolution for most of his flaws, there was one sin which would remain forever unforgivable in her eyes.

Daddy had converted her Catholic daughter into a Lutheran.

"Please," Mama retorted. "Don't act like you've never had a glass of wine on the Sabbath."

Gramma flushed red and decided to steer the conversation toward another of her favorite subjects. "I suppose your Abigail hasn't gotten dinner ready on time. Again."

"It's not even noon yet." Mama's patience was wearing thin.

"You said dinner would be on the table at eleven-thirty."

"Yes, and good thing it wasn't, otherwise it would've been cold by the time you arrived."

"I know how lazy she is. That's why we took our time."

Mama's jaw jutted forward and froze there. Pink anger rose to her cheeks as she said, "That's quite enough. You will not speak that way about her. Not in my house."

Each woman's stony stare bore into the other, as if both were trying to win an optical tug-o'-war.

Walter and I exchanged our own furtive glances. We were curious to see who would triumph in this battle of wills.

Sadly, we weren't able to witness any decisive victory. Grampa Henry's raucous guffaws sounded from the porch, and a moment later, he was throwing the front door open for Daddy, Pip, and himself.

Like butter in July, Gramma's glare melted into an insincere smile. I suppose it was her subtle way of making nice with Mama, as she hugged Daddy, kissed his cheek, and said, "Happy Easter, John. And thank you for inviting us to dinner."

The gesture of friendliness caught Daddy by surprise. He returned the embrace and said, "Happy Easter to you as well. We're happy you made it."

These faux pleasantries were interrupted by Grampa. The moment his baby blues caught sight of Mama through his thick eyeglasses, he bellowed, "Rosa, my little girl!"

In a flash he scooped her up in his arms, lifted her high off the ground, and spun her around like she was five years old.

Mama also giggled like she was five. Once her feet were safely back on the ground, she planted a spirited kiss just outside his graying bush of a mustache.

"Hi, Daddy! I've missed you!"

"Castleton's only a few miles down the road, you know. Why don't you visit more often?"

Walter and I snickered. We knew one *big* reason why, and she was presently standing in our Great Room.

"We'll come more in summer," Mama promised. "It's hard during the school year."

"Well, when you do, I'll have to take the boys to the movie theater. There's a new one going up downtown, and I bet that Tarzan film will still be playing then."

"That would be wonderful, Daddy."

It did indeed sound wonderful. Visiting Gramma and Grampa was mostly a chore and a bore, but whenever Grampa took us into town by himself, we had more fun than a puppy in a chicken coop. Without Gramma looking over his shoulder, he wasn't afraid to lighten his wallet in the name of our good time.

Now, in the Great Room, Grampa turned to size us up. With one arm each for me and Walter, he pulled us snugly against his charcoal-gray suit. Grampa had such a distinctive scent, someone could have named a pipe-smoke-and-butterscotch perfume after him, the latter of which he nearly always carried in candy form.

But that Easter, he had something bulkier in his jacket pocket. As he let us go, he reached inside it and produced a wrinkled brown bag.

"Here you are, boys," he said, handing Walter the waxy sack. "All the finest saltwater taffies you could hope for, delivered fresh to the store Friday morning."

Grampa owned Castleton's largest general store. He had begun his career there in the 1870s, working first as a manager for his aging uncle. When the childless miser passed away two years later, the store went to Grampa. It was there that the dark-haired proprietor met a young woman named Opal Kastens, a cantankerous but talented young baker who occasionally stopped by to stock his shelves with fresh breads and pastries. They tied the knot in 1879. Gramma took over running the store, and Grampa started working for her—at least, that's how *he* explained it.

Two generations later, plentiful in both years and candies, Grampa was showering the rewards of store ownership upon me and my brothers. The only perceivable fault the generous man had was the woman attached to him, but as long as the taffy deliveries endured, we would also endure her.

"Something smells divine in here, Miss Abigail!" Grampa hollered toward the kitchen.

"Well, I'm glad to hear someone saying so, Mr. Vos," Abigail replied, appearing momentarily in the kitchen entryway. "And your timing couldn't've been any perfecter. I've got one dish left to bring to the table, and then dinner'll be all set."

"Just *wonderful*," Grampa exclaimed to the family gathered around him. He comically patted his stomach and licked his lips. "Let's eat."

THE CLINKING CHORUS OF FORKS and knives had already arrived at its finale, but dinner tables come with unwritten rules, and one of those rules is that little boys can't vacate their seats until the first adult does. Unfortunately, everyone at the dining room table had stuffed themselves so full of Abigail's culinary masterpieces, it was unlikely the grownups would budge any sooner than next morning's breakfast.

Grampa ran his finger across his salad plate to coat it in dressing, then licked it clean and said, "Deeeeelicious."

"I helped make it," I told him proudly. "Well, I chopped the ginger Abigail put in. She says ginger's good for keeping sickness away. Says it's good for us to eat it with the new Flu going around."

To my surprise, Grampa bristled visibly at my comment. The constant gleam in his blue eyes flickered and faded. Suddenly, they looked gray and heavy, like the drizzly late-winter rains that clung to our lake each year.

"That was a good thought of hers," he mumbled absently, as if his consciousness had flown to the far side of the moon. "Let's pray that The Flu and all such illnesses stay far away, yes?"

Trying to resurrect his lost cheer, I said, "Mama told us we'll be okay here."

Sitting across the table, my parents had tuned in to our conversation, but neither spoke.

"I wish that were—" Grampa appeared ready to contradict me, then thought better of it. "I'm sure your Mama is right, Peter. Mamas almost always are."

He readopted his characteristic grin, but it seemed forced, like those of the bereaved at a funeral.

"Well, Henry," Daddy interrupted, breaking the tension, "what would you say about joining me on the lakeside porch for a post-dinner pipe?"

"I'd say nothing could sound better." Grampa pushed his chair backward. "I had a fresh batch of Prince Albert delivered last week, and I've been waiting 'til today for my first bowl."

"Lies," grunted Gramma. "You've already gone through a can of it, or I'm the Pope himself."

"My first bowl from *this* tin, anyway," Grampa corrected himself with a wink.

Abigail entered the dining hall as the men were standing to leave it.

"Another delightful dinner," Grampa told her. "Every time I think you couldn't possibly outdo yourself, you prove again how foolish I am."

"My pleasure, Mr. Vos," Abigail replied, beaming.

As the men disappeared out the back door, Gramma slid her chair away from the table. She waved a hand at the dinnerware scattered across the sturdy maple tabletop and said, "We're finished here, Abigail. You can begin your tidying now."

Earlier, the call to dinner had created an informal truce between Mama and Gramma. Now the conflict reignited, though this time behind the thin veil of feigned geniality.

"Actually," said Mama, laying her fingers gently on Abigail's arm, "I was thinking you might like the rest of the afternoon off. The boys and I will clear the table and wash up."

Walter emitted an audible groan. It wasn't the first time we had become casualties in the longstanding feud.

Abigail stared at Gramma with something akin to gloating and said, "Why, that sounds quite nice, Missus Luther. Think I'll sit in my garden and read through a few more chapters of *Ethan Frome*."

Mama beamed victoriously. "You enjoy yourself."

The moment Abigail left the dining hall, Gramma popped up from her chair like it was on fire. With a haughty grunt, she said, "Enjoy your dishes then. I'll be upstairs, napping in the guest room. You may wake me whenever you're ready to be civil again."

As Gramma huffed away, Mama chuckled and said, "In that case, she'll be sleeping 'til *next* Easter."

She poked Pip in the ribs until he giggled, then rose from her seat and began removing dishes from the table. Walter eagerly followed suit, his initial despair replaced by an unquenchable desire to make Mama proud.

Once the table had been cleared, we all lined up at the kitchen sink. Daddy had updated it a couple years back to remove the old hand-pump faucet. All Mama had to do now was twist a knob, and clean water filled the basin.

As we worked—scrubbing, drying, putting away—Grampa's strange reaction to my comment about The Flu lingered upon my mind. Never in my life had I seen his perennial mirth drain from him as it had at the dinner table. Why did my mere mention of it disturb him so much?

The question eventually became too much for me, so I looked up at Mama and asked, "Is Grampa scared of The Flu?"

She cast me a sideways glance. In it I caught a shadow of the gloom I had seen in Grampa earlier.

"He's a little scared, yes," she answered.

"Why?"

"Well, you might not have known this before, but when I was a little girl, I actually had a brother and *two* sisters."

"It wasn't just Uncle Andy and Aunt Louise?" Walter interjected, looking like he'd accidentally swallowed a fly as he spoke the latter's name. To put it simply, Mama's oldest sibling was the apple that hadn't fallen far from the Gramma tree.

Mama handed me a wet plate. "No. I also had a younger sister, Henrietta. But when she was only three, she got the Scarlet Fever and passed away. Grampa was very sad for a long time after that. We all were. I'm sure he's worried about The Flu because he's scared he might lose someone else he loves."

"But you said we're gonna be okay, right?" Walter asked, revisiting their earlier church-pew conversation.

"Absolutely," said Mama, beaming her most reassuring smile. "We're all strong and healthy. These sorts of diseases like to prey upon people who are already weak or sick, or very old or young."

"Too bad for you, Pip!" Walter teased, elbowing him playfully. All concern had fled at Mama's reassuring word.

In typical baby-brother fashion, Pip began to whine a complaint against Walter, but Mama promptly defused the situation with a distracting change of subject.

"I haven't told you about my special surprise yet, have I!" she exclaimed.

Our attention was hers. Surprises of the "Mama" variety never failed to deliver.

"What is it?" Walter asked excitedly.

"Before I tell you *what* it is," Mama said, lowering her voice to a secretive whisper, "first I have to tell you *where* it came from."

"Where? Where?" cried Pip.

Mama's eyes narrowed. She glanced around the kitchen to make sure we were indeed alone, then leaned in close.

"It came from ... a *goblin*."

FIVE

Chocolate Explosion Cake

"A GOBLIN?" PIP WHISPERED, MYSTIFIED.

"A goblin," Mama repeated confidently.

Walter and I weren't idiots. We were old enough to understand that Mama's games involved plenty of make-believe. Still, we always played along. We knew whatever fun Mama had concocted would be well worth the temporary suspension of our disbelief.

"What did the goblin give you?" Walter asked.

"Well, he didn't exactly *give* me anything," admitted Mama. "I bought it from an old peddler woman in town the other day."

"What did you buy? What did you buy?" demanded Pip. His patience was in short supply.

Mama ignored his question and instead launched into a well-rehearsed narrative.

"This old woman claimed—and I don't know how true it is—that when her great-grandmother was a little girl, she got terribly lost in the Black Forest. That's in Germany. She wandered around for two whole days before she stumbled upon an old cottage. But this was no ordinary cottage. It was much smaller, like it had been built for children to live in. She knocked on the door, but no one answered, so she went inside. There, on a dining room table that only came up to her belly-button, sat the most delicious-looking chocolate cake she had ever seen. She was so hungry after two days without food that she ate the entire thing at once! It was only after she was finished that she saw a brown cloth next to the empty cake platter. And do you know what was written on it?"

"What? What?" cried Pip, riveted to Mama's story.

"It was the recipe for the very cake she had just eaten. Before anyone could return and catch her, she stuffed the cloth into her pocket and ran back into the forest. Not long afterward, her parents found her. When she returned home, she tucked away the cake recipe in her sock drawer, and even though she used that recipe to make a new chocolate cake every day, she thought no more about the little cabin in the woods. But a year later, something strange began to happen. One by one, her things started to go missing. First it was only little things: a sock, an earring, a hairpin. Once the little things had all been taken, the bigger things started to disappear as well: her shoe, her lantern, a jewelry box. And each time, in place of the missing item, she would find a simple note with a simple message:

> *Give me back what is mine,*
> *And I'll return what is thine.*
> *— Dis-affectionately yours,*
> *Gurgan the Goblin*

"But the stubborn girl wouldn't—*couldn't*—give up what had become her greatest treasure, so she hid it away where no one would ever find it. As the years went on, Gurgan eventually took everything else she owned. Finally, in order to escape the thieving goblin once and for all, she boarded a boat and came to America. At last, she was free. But when she was a very old woman and near death, she passed that cake recipe down to her daughter, who passed it on to her daughter, who passed it on to her daughter—none other than the old peddler woman herself."

At this point in her spellbinding tale, Mama opened a nearby cabinet and rose to her tiptoes. From the top shelf, she removed a wrinkled brown rag and held it up for my brothers and I to see. Scrawled in capital letters across the top were the words *CHOCOLATE EXPLOSION CAKE*.

"And now," she whispered excitedly, "that ancient recipe belongs to us."

Pip reached for it as if someone were handing him the Holy Grail.

"Of course," said Mama, "you can't eat a recipe, and we've got about a dozen people counting on us for Easter dessert. Are you ready to get to work?"

Pip and I hollered our agreement, as Walter said, "I'll read off all the ingredients!"

Even though I was the far better reader between the two of us, Walter liked showing off to Mama how far he had come in school. Without waiting for anyone's approval, he began listing everything we needed to bake the imaginary goblin's Chocolate Explosion Cake. As Walter named each item, the rest of us scampered around the kitchen, fetching and placing them on the table. Over time, this had evolved to become our unofficial procedure whenever we baked with Mama. Before we got around to any of the measuring, stirring, or beating, we first gathered all the recipe's required ingredients.

Of course, this was exactly how Mama knew it would go. She had, in fact, been counting on this kitchen ritual of ours.

So when Walter called out for the sugar, Mama hurried to the cupboard where we kept it.

But after opening the cupboard door and peering inside, she groaned, "Oh dear."

"What's wrong?" I asked.

"The sugar crock—it's gone!"

"It is? Maybe Abigail moved it," Walter suggested.

Mama shook her head. "I don't think so. Look at this."

She reached into the empty space normally occupied by the sugar crock and withdrew a creased, yellow piece of paper.

I was closest, so she handed it to me, but Walter snatched it away. Before I could protest, he read:

> "Give me back what is mine,
> And I'll return what is thine.
> —Dis-affectionately yours,
>   Gurgan the Goblin."

In a show of shock and disbelief, Mama clasped her hands to her open mouth and gasped. "I can't believe it! He tracked us down? All the way from the Black Forest? My, he is one determined goblin! But then again, I suppose that's what all goblins are like."

"He ... stole our sugar?" asked Pip, struggling to connect the dots.

"It would appear so," Mama answered.

"Wait! There's something on the back!" I cried. Now I grabbed the page from Walter and flipped it around.

Mama clapped her hands delightedly and said, "If there are two things I know about goblins, it's that they are very determined creatures *and* very stupid ones. He's left us a map to his hideout!"

"That's a map?" Walter asked doubtfully.

I was with him. It looked more like stanzas of poetry than a map.

"Well, not a map so much as *directions*," Mama clarified. "He must have written them down so he wouldn't get lost, but he accidentally wrote them on the back of the note he left us. It'll probably take him a long time to find his hideout without them. If we hurry, we might catch up to him before he eats all the sugar himself!"

Walter jabbed a finger at the first set of lines. "What's it say?"

I read them aloud:

> *"Where sits the sitter of back-and-forth sitting?*
> *Where stings the stinger of those who fear stinging?*
> *There is the place I must make my beginning."*

"Hmmm," Mama mused. "Old Gurgan's not gonna make this easy on us. What do my brilliant boys make of it?"

I scratched my head. "People sit on chairs. And sofas."

"And swings!" suggested Walter. "*And* swings go back and forth! I bet we have to start from the old swing on the front porch!"

"But what about the middle line?" asked Mama, pouring cold water on his idea. "What does the porch swing have to do with *stingers stinging?* You have to consider every part of these riddles."

Walter frowned. Mama had rebuffed his proposed solution, and he took the failure personally.

"What do you know of that stings, Pip?" Mama asked my little brother. She always made sure to seek his help even when the game went over his head.

"Wasps? And ... bees?"

"Good answers!" she said, scooping him up and kissing the top of his head.

"I'm always afraid of getting stung in Abigail's—er, *Miss Lincoln's*—garden," I said. "There's bees everywhere there! Last time Daddy made me help her weed it, I got stung *twice.*"

Walter's face lit up with a second revelation. "And she always sits out there in her rocking chair! She told me she's not afraid of getting stung because she's friends with the bees."

"I think Abigail's garden sounds like a great place to start," said Mama. Since she was the game's creator, her approval was a sound indication we were moving the right direction.

On foot, the trek to Abigail and Eli's cottage took a few minutes. Instead of wasting our travel time, we began working out the second stanza of Gurgan's directions:

From here march toward the mixed-up THORN.
Find ancient father of acorn
Upon which Gurgan's mark be borne.

"It doesn't make any sense," moaned Walter. He became easily frustrated whenever his intellect felt challenged. "The thorns are *already* in Abigail's garden. Or in yours, Mama. But why would Gurgan send us right back where we came from?"

"Keep thinking about it while we walk," Mama encouraged cheerily. "You'll find your answer one way or another."

As we approached the cottage, we saw Abigail sitting outside, reading in her swelling garden. Back and forth she rocked, amid a sea of whites and yellows and purples, while the friendly bees zipped to and fro, from one bloom to the next, as merry as the sunlit Easter afternoon.

Abigail noticed us approaching and placed the book facedown on her lap. She was very proud that she knew how to read and considered it a rare privilege. Even in a more progressive state like Pennsylvania, most black women her age were illiterate in those days, and she had no qualms about showing off her skill. Her father Ezekiel had often borrowed books from the expansive Vandenberg library. He didn't have their permission to do so, and he certainly wouldn't have received it had he asked. But two or three books out of their thousands escaped notice easily, and thus posed little risk. After teaching himself the basics of reading and writing, Zeke shared his newfound knowledge with his children.

The result, according to Abigail, was that she had become the most educated black lady between Philadelphia and Pittsburgh. And, as far as I could tell, it was the truth. She was one of the smartest people I knew, with a sneaky sort of intelligence that flew under everyone's radar, right up until the moment she'd use it to make a damned fool out of you.

"What brings you up here this afternoon?" she now asked Mama. "Boys breaking too many dishes? Need me to come finish the rest?"

Mama giggled. "No, nothing like that. We're on a quest to find our sugar so we can make Chocolate Explosion Cake. It was stolen by a goblin—if you believe that sort of thing."

"Again?" said Abigail. "And I was planning to set more goblin traps tomorrow! Well, I'll just get him next time, I suppose."

"But he left us directions," Pip informed her. "That's why we came up here, and now we have to figure out what the next clue means."

"Bring it here and let me take a look," said Abigail.

She reached out a hand, and I gave her the yellow page of riddles. Like one of the many passing bees, she hummed thoughtfully as she read.

"Any ideas?" Mama asked.

"Well," Abigail replied, "I personally think you did right in following the first lines up here. But this next one sure is a stumper."

She returned the paper to me, then reached into her pocket and withdrew a dingy tin box. This she handed to Walter, and upon closer inspection, we saw that it was a well-worn but functional compass.

"Found it when I was watering my plants this morning," she informed us. "Looks like someone might've dropped it. Think it's a clue?"

"Probably," I answered, "but I don't know what it means."

Mama didn't offer her assistance this time. She could be eternally patient when she wanted us to figure something out ourselves.

I don't know how long we hemmed and hawed over the solution to that second riddle—to Abigail's great annoyance, I'm sure—but it probably came as a relief even to Mama when we spotted Hattie meandering down the cart path.

"Over here!" I called to her.

Hattie had changed out of her Easter best since our Main Street meeting. She now wore a dress and matching ribbon of robin's-egg blue. The fabric wasn't as light and flowy as Mama's play dress, but it still appeared less stifling than the carpet her mother had wrestled her into for church that morning.

"You couldn't have come at a better time," Mama told her. "The boys could use a strong extra brain."

"What's the game?" Hattie asked brightly.

Mama protested the question itself. "No game. A matter of life or death! Well, of cake or no cake, anyway. Our sugar's been stolen, and we're following these directions to get it back. The only problem is, they're all written in riddles."

I passed Gurgan's note to Hattie.

"We're on the second one," I told her. "I figured out the first one."

Hattie read the three lines of riddling poetry out loud:

> *"From here march toward the mixed-up THORN.*
> *Find ancient father of acorn*
> *Upon which Gurgan's mark be borne."*

When finished, she asked, "Who's Gurgan?"

"The nasty goblin that stole our sugar!" Pip replied indignantly. "He doesn't want us to make chocolate cake."

Hattie knew she was missing key elements of a long backstory, but instead of asking for further details, she said, "I don't know about any goblins, but I *do* know the answer to the riddle. It's easy!"

I noticed as she spoke that she aimed her words subtly at Walter. Something about it set a gnawing sensation at work in my gut.

"So? What is it?" Walter demanded. He wouldn't be impressed until proof of her claims sat in his hands.

"We have to go north and find an oak tree," she answered.

He remained skeptical. "How do you figure?"

"The riddle says it's a 'mixed-up THORN.' The word *THORN* is the only one that's all capital letters, which must mean we're supposed to think about it differently. And if you mix up the letters in *THORN,* you can also make the word *NORTH.*"

"And the other part is easy," I interjected, stealing some credit for myself, "because an oak is kind of like the father of an acorn."

"It's a good thing Gurgan dropped his compass," Mama commented. "Now we can follow it straight north to the tree!"

As we tramped away from her garden, Abigail hollered, "You have fun now! And make sure you save me a slice of that chocolate cake!"

SIX

The Isle across Acheron

HOLDING THE COMPASS FLAT UPON his palm, Walter led us due north. The edge of the forest wasn't far, and we soon found ourselves beneath the merciful shade of a gnarled red oak. The tree had endured many harsh winters and did appear, as per Gurgan's riddle, "ancient."

"The mark! The mark!" Pip shouted triumphantly as he pointed at the trunk.

Sure enough, the old oak sported a carved capital *G* etched into its lichened skin. But there was something more. Beneath Gurgan's mark, hanging upon a shiny nail, was a small, silvery object.

"It's a key," muttered Hattie. She reached up and removed it from the nail. "I wonder what it opens."

"Maybe the next riddle will help," Mama suggested, giving me a nudge.

I unfolded the paper and read aloud:

> *"A home for things where swimmers swim*
> *Put key to lock and locked within*
> *Like feet of fowl, long and wooden."*

"My! Gurgan's rhymes are starting to look a little sloppy," lamented Mama. "It's like I told you boys before. Goblins can be very stupid."

Hattie attempted to retake control. "Swimming has to be down by the lake, but I don't know—"

"Of course it is," Walter rudely interrupted. After Hattie's solving of the previous riddle, he needed to reassert his authority over the group. "And I know right where we have to go."

Hattie flashed him a sour expression. "Then where?—if you're so smart!"

"The storage shed by our swimming beach," Walter replied, wearing a proud smirk. "A shed is a 'home for things,' you know."

Mama must have sensed the mounting tension between them. In order to move things along—and ward off their impending blowup—she remarked, "I do remember Daddy saying he saw a funny little creature down by the lake yesterday. Let's head that direction, and we'll check the shed first."

Walter and I took point position in our caravan as we paraded down the hill toward house and lake. After us came Pip, while Hattie sulked in the rear. She always brooded like that when Walter insisted on belittling her. Knowing this, Mama hung back to encourage her before the next leg of our quest.

For our entire lives—and much longer—the decrepit shed had stood a mere stone's throw from the lakeshore. Here the land sloped gently downward until it met the water and melted into a small bay. For whatever reason, this was where Acheron's muted currents chose to deposit their carried contents of silt and sand. Over years uncounted, the result was the formation of a meager but sandy beach. During the sizzling days of summer, and even on warm afternoons, this was where Acheron's cool waters provided our relief.

Or, as the riddle put it, "where swimmers swim."

By the time we reached the shed, Mama had sufficiently rallied Hattie's morale. Walter assumed since he had solved the riddle, the job of opening the padlocked door rightly belonged to him, but Mama objected.

"If Hattie's holding the key," she said, "then Hattie gets to open it."

Even Mama's rebukes were gracious. Usually, anyway. But Walter knew our sunshiny mother could turn into a hurricane when pushed, and he showed the good sense to back down.

Hattie sneered at him as she inserted the key into the padlock. It turned and clicked, and the lock sprung loose. Hattie pulled open the weathered door, then stepped back so we could all peer inside.

Slanted lines of sunlight illuminated the shed's contents. Mostly it was filled with old tools, many of them bygone relics of the Vandenberg era. Among them was strewn a hodgepodge of cobweb-guarded odds and ends, while a half-dozen disintegrating wicker chairs formed a disorderly heap in the middle of the floor.

And, propped up against them, was the answer to Gurgan's third riddle.

The pair of oars, "long and wooden," shone with newness against their time-worn backdrop. With broad, flat blades beneath the slender shafts, the oars did indeed resemble the webbed feet of waterfowl.

Walter liberated them from their musty prison, carrying them victoriously in both arms into the daylight's bountiful warmth.

A moment later, our inflated sense of victory popped. We had oars, but no idea what they were for.

"Let's look at the next clue," Mama suggested. She unfolded the yellow paper and read the fourth—and second-to-last—riddle:

> *"Across the waters I must go.*
> *To southern isle my arms must row.*
> *There hides my secret bungalow."*

Hattie, Walter, and I exchanged puzzled glances. The solution to the riddle itself was easy. A vast island lay some unknown distance southward across Acheron's waters. We had gazed upon it often, dreaming we might turn it into our personal playground someday. Clearly this was the island where, according to the poem, we needed to go next.

The problem was the *how* of the matter. Eli kept an old canoe propped against the back wall of his cottage, but even if hell froze over and he let us borrow it, only three could fit inside. Besides that, the oars we had found were much longer than canoe paddles. They were the sort Grampa used for his rowboat, only we didn't have one of those.

"What're we supposed to do with them?" Walter asked Mama.

She shrugged. "I imagine Gurgan must have some kind of boat hidden nearby. And lucky us! If his oars are still here, it must mean we're ahead of him."

At the sound of the word *boat,* our flighty resolve instantly returned.

"Let's split up and look," Walter suggested. "We'll cover more ground. Hattie, you take Pip and go that way. Peter, you can come with me."

Hattie appeared as pleased as a poked hornet over her team relegation, but she didn't protest.

"Come on, Pippie," she said, holding out a hand. "If we find that boat first, we'll just sail off and leave them behind."

Walter propped the oars against the shed, where they remained under Mama's careful supervision as he and I sauntered westward along the shore.

As silly as it might sound, I was elated that Walter had picked me. Such an occurrence was rarer than a perfect score on one of his spelling tests. Despite the walls of resentment I had built up against my older brother, I still had a strange but incessant need for his approval, and I would take it whenever and however I could.

We hadn't gone far before Walter stopped suddenly. He raised a finger, pointing at something a short distance along the bank.

A *large* something, which had not been there before.

To three energetic boys like us Luther kids, Asphodel Glade's vast woodlands were an explorer's paradise that would have made Daniel Boone jealous. Even during late fall and early spring, when temperatures rose as high above freezing as a timid gopher's head from its hidey hole, our days were spent scouting and mapping as much of our little kingdom as we could. While our thousand-acre wood certainly held plenty of undiscovered secrets, there was no way anything so bulky and near our house could have escaped our attention for more than a day or two.

Yet we both saw it. Only a few feet from the water's edge was a low mound where there used to be none. Even more curious were the branches piled on top to camouflage it. Their leaves were still plentiful and green, meaning that whoever put them there did so recently.

With a self-satisfied grin, Walter remarked, "I think we found the boat."

Even as we ran toward it, I called back to the others, "Over here! We found it!"

Walter and I were stripping away the branch camouflage when Mama, Hattie, and Pip arrived.

"Dilly!" cried Pip. "A boat!"

How Mama managed to sneak that rowboat into Asphodel Glade without our knowing was a beautiful mystery I didn't want to solve. With pointed bow and level stern, its hull was the rich yellow of freshly churned butter, both inside and out, while the gunwales that ran along its length were painted a bright blue. This rowboat was smaller than most others I had seen, but to me and my brothers, it was the *Mayflower,* our mighty ship which would bring us to new lands.

"This proves we're still a step ahead of Gurgan," Mama remarked. Once she started a game, she never failed to keep the act going. "I suppose he'll have to swim for it this time, because we're taking this boat for ourselves!"

We cheered our agreement, then assisted Mama in dragging the rowboat down to the water. Once we were seated inside, Mama fitted the oars into the metal rings which held them in place. As one does in a rowboat, she faced the craft's rear and began to row, heaving us away from the shore.

"Someone will have to navigate so I don't have to keep turning around," she said. "Make sure we stay pointed at the island."

Walter volunteered immediately for the job. He took it quite seriously too, waiting no more than a dozen seconds between each cry of "A little left," "A little right," or "You're still straight!" In each short interim, he studied Mama intently. He watched the way her arms and back and bottom and legs all worked in rhythmic motion, circulating the oars forward into the water, then back toward the stern, then up into the open air again.

A strange light glimmered in his eyes as he watched her, some gleam of admiration or love or fascination or newfound knowledge—perhaps all four. Mama had that effect on Walter, and he always yearned for more of her. Not in some perverted, Oedipal sense, but as a boy who needed his mother to feel truly complete. Just as all people experience satisfaction and fulfillment in the presence of certain friends or loves, Walter found these chiefly in Mama.

I don't know how far the island was from Asphodel's shoreline—boys of nine tend to measure in minutes and hours rather than distance—but by the time we reached the island, the sun was halfway between its noon zenith and the western horizon.

Red-cheeked and sweat-soaked, yet somehow still glowing with her effortless grace, Mama navigated us between two rocky spits. When the hull bumped against the shore, she instructed Walter to climb out and tie off the boat to an adolescent pine growing out over the water. The rest of us took turns disembarking, until all stood firmly upon the needle-strewn ground.

The thrill of discovery fluttered between my heart and stomach. I was Christopher Columbus, Vasco de Gama, Ferdinand Magellan, stepping for the first time upon new and strange soil. Gurgan's isle was *terra incognita*, a wild land to be scouted and charted and tamed.

I didn't realize it at the time, but the woods and glades of this island held far more in store for me. It would become, in due time, the most treasured and hallowed place I would ever know.

But on that last day of March, the Isle—for that's what we would come to call it—was merely a playground for childhood games.

"Big mistake ... not bringing ... any water," huffed Mama. She worked her tongue around her lips, trying in vain to moisten them. "Let's read ... that last clue."

She handed me the page, and I read it aloud for the group:

> *"Upon the crown of Emerald Hill*
> *In wall of green with pink-dappled frill*
> *I'll sit and eat my sugary fill."*

Hattie was the first to offer an idea. "When we were still a long way off, I remember seeing a big grassy hill. I don't think it was far from here. Do you think maybe that's the 'Emerald Hill' he's talking about?"

Mama's unquenchable spirit must have been tamed by her unquenched thirst, because she straightaway said, "I bet that's exactly where we need to go."

Walter led us as we picked our way along the rocky shoreline. When this dropped off sharply into the water, he selected a higher route through patches of dense brush choked with pine. It wasn't long before the woods gave way to a bright and open clearing, the base of the very hill Hattie had spotted during our voyage across Lake Acheron.

"Where's the crown?" asked Pip, glancing around. "Is it gold, do you think?"

Mama giggled. "*Crown* means the top of the hill. We have to climb it."

Like fronds of emerald anemones, long tendrils of grass crept up around our shins as we scaled the lofty hill. White bunches of buttercups and the pink buds of young Virginia bluebells dotted the sea of green. These were the early risers of the growing season, yet they seemed more vibrant and plentiful than normal in these first days of spring. Every manner of nectar-loving insect buzzed, flitted, and hovered about the knoll, eager to spread the pollens and create even more wildflowers wherever they might.

Walter alone appeared unaffected by the afternoon's sapping heat. While the rest of us lagged behind, he hurried to the summit and, when he reached it, cried, "There's the wall of green! It's those bushes with the pink flowers."

"Do you know what they're called?" quizzed Mama.

She stepped past him and approached the woody stand of rubbery-leafed bushes. With their bright, poly-stamened blooms, they did indeed give the appearance of a "green wall with pink-dappled frill."

As delicately as if she were stroking a newborn's face, Mama brushed her fingertips against one of the pentagonal blossoms. "This is mountain laurel. I've never heard of it blooming so early. You're all seeing something very special right now."

"And the goblin's hideout is behind it?" Hattie asked. She cared less about Mama's botany lesson and more about finishing the game.

Mama's moment of transcendence shattered. She grinned affably at Hattie's impatience and replied, "Easier said than done. Some people call thick stands of laurel like this 'laurel hell' because they're almost impossible to pass through. Even a tiny goblin would have trouble, so there must be an opening somewhere. Let's look around and see if we can find one."

"Can't we just go around?" Walter wondered.

"I don't think so," said Hattie, jumping in with her own answer. "The riddle says *in* the wall, not *past* it. There must be some kind of clearing in the middle."

"I'm gonna try anyway," Walter asserted gruffly.

To my irritation, his stubbornness proved valuable. As he began making his way around the laurel, he discovered a breach in its defensive perimeter.

"Over here!" he shouted.

We hurried to join him. Like the cramped space between two walls of a house, a gap no wider than my shoulders divided the laurel stronghold. We peered in, but too many errant leaves and flowers made it impossible to determine where the path led or what lay at the end of it.

Mama ushered us forward. "Go on. I'll wait here."

Walter, ever the fearless captain, led the expedition once more. Like boxers with fists in the defensive position, we guarded our heads with our arms and hands, swatting away the foliage which threatened our eyes and faces. The gap widened as we plowed forward, until we at last found ourselves in a surprisingly ample clearing. Overhead, the afternoon sun filtered through the laurel canopy, leaving us awash in an otherworldly glow of gold and green.

Upon the carpet of fallen leaves and petals sat our sugar crock. Pinned between jar and lid was a note bearing hastily scribbled words.

Hattie knelt and read it:

> *"For your cleverness, wit, and determination*
> *I grudgingly give you my congratulations.*
> *But know this, dear children, with no reservation:*
> *From enemies I must demand reparations.*
> *The battle is yours, not the whole altercation;*
> *You'll be punished soon for your rude violations.*
> *Return to me now and without hesitation*
> *My recipe—best out of all my creations!*
> *If still you insist on your unjust predation*
> *You'll taste soon the wrath of my heart's lamentations.*
> *—With the utmost of dis-affection,*
>   *Gurgan the Goblin."*

"We did it!" yelled Pip, and he wasted no time before rewarding himself with a handful of sugar.

"Okay, okay," murmured Walter, pushing Pip away from the crock. "You'll hurt your tummy eating it like that."

Careful not to let any sugar spill out the top, Walter heaved the heavy crock off the ground. This time he took up the rearguard as I led us back through the laurel, until we once again breathed the free air of the hilltop.

Mama was sitting in the grass, barefooted and facing away from us, her knees drawn close to her chest. The breeze tugged at the riffled hem of her dress, which she had drawn scandalously back to her thighs. Down the hill and past the lake's cool waters, even over the roof of our Castle Home and Asphodel Glade itself, she stared, like someone peering beyond Time and into Eternity. It was as if her mind had become lost there, and she was unable to find her way back to the very hilltop where her body sat.

In a way, Mama never quite belonged in this world. Something about her seemed greater, more evolved than the rest of us, as though she were a higher life form than the people she lived among. Some days, Daddy said he half-expected her to sprout wings and soar upward to a home among the clouds, where she would wait an eon or two for the rest of mortal mankind to catch up.

But that afternoon, when she heard us returning with the sugar crock, she simply giggled and jumped up onto her shoeless feet.

"You found it!" she cried. "Was Gurgan there too?"

"Just a note," answered Pip. "But I didn't know a lot of the big words."

"I can explain later," said Mama. "He must have barely beat you there. I imagine he was hiding somewhere on the boat, or maybe dangling off the back. It's the only way he could have crossed the lake so quickly. Anyway, we have our sugar, so we should probably hurry home. That Chocolate Explosion Cake isn't going to bake itself!"

SEVEN

Red River Valley

LIKE ANCIENT THREADS OF MOSS clinging to stones in a brook, myriad random and inconsequential memories trail within the streams of consciousness, many unforgotten even from my youngest years. Like parasites unwilling to let go of their host, they hold their places, growing ever bigger and bolder with the passage of time. Countless visions become stored there in the mind's eye and, I am convinced, will remain there until I die.

Yet the mind of memory does not have only an eye. It also has a tongue, so that an old man might taste the homemade bread his mother used to bake. And the mind of memory possesses a nose, so that a whiff of attic might transport someone to the dank upstairs of her grandparents' farmhouse.

Likewise, memory has an ear. Two of them, maybe. And no matter how many years might pass, I will never forget the way my Daddy moaned with pleasure when he ate one of Mama's famous desserts. The man had a sweet tooth longer than a walrus's tusks. Whether by pies, puddings, crumbles, or cakes, her desserts always elicited from him those low tones of ecstasy.

It was no different that Easter night in the Great Room as Daddy devoured her Chocolate Explosion Cake. In front of Gramma and Grampa, Pastor Wainwright, all six Jansens, his boys and their Mama, Daddy shamelessly moaned his approval. When he had tucked away his first generous slice, he helped himself to an even ampler second.

After Daddy had finished picking every speck and crumb from his plate, Mama said, "Instead of a third piece, how 'bout you get your violin and play something for us?"

Warm light flickered in his glacier-blue irises. He played his violin almost every night, though usually behind the closed door of his den and for an audience of one.

"I never knew you fiddled, John!" Mrs. Jansen exclaimed. "Do you know 'Yellow Rose of Texas'?"

Mr. Jansen shot his wife a look, expressing his clear disapproval of such secular tunes.

"*Bestimmt,*" Daddy answered in bourbon-rinsed German. "Though special requests cost a penny apiece. You can pay my secretary directly." He nudged Mama.

"Call me that again," she said, "and you're the one who's going to pay, John Luther. Now, run off and do whatever it is you do with your violin to get ready. Hannah, would you mind helping me clear the dishes to the kitchen?"

Mrs. Jansen obliged, and the two began gathering the plates, forks, and cups which had been emptied of their cake-chasing milk. Since my glass was still half full when Mrs. Jansen came around to me, I gave her only my plate and fork. It didn't take me long to finish my milk, and when I did, I slid off the sofa and hurried toward the kitchen.

There is an unusual ability I have possessed even from my early days, a superpower that has served as my frequent ally. While some people are great athletes or orators or military masterminds, I am a phenomenal eavesdropper, and largely attribute this strange skill to an uncanny ability for hiding in plain sight. I can stand exposed in the middle of an open room, yet go entirely unnoticed by those present. In my younger years, this peculiar ability made me audience to many conversations not meant for my ears. Nor could I land myself in hot water for eavesdropping if someone did eventually notice me. You simply can't accuse somebody of snooping when they've been standing out in the open all along.

When I approached the kitchen that evening and heard voices, low and secretive, I decided to put my skill to good use. Mama and Mrs. Jansen stood at the sink, facing away from the open door as I slipped inside.

There I stopped and listened.

"I don't feel like I can apologize enough for him," Mrs. Jansen mumbled. "For the way he is."

"What do you mean?" Mama asked. She saw that her friend was upset and embarrassed, and she laid a comforting hand between Mrs. Jansen's shoulders.

"I can tell you don't like him."

"Why do you think that? I like Jacob just fine."

I had been on our wagon earlier. I knew Mama was lying.

So did Mrs. Jansen. "No, you don't. And I don't blame you. Most days I don't much care for him myself."

Well, this was certainly a different woman than the one I had known since birth. Mrs. Jansen had always come across as one of those ever-devoted, subject-to-her-husband types.

"I'm very sorry for giving you that impression," said Mama. "And I suppose it's true that Jacob isn't my *favorite* person to be around. But I think it's mostly a difference in personalities. I know he's a good man, and John has tremendous respect for him."

Mrs. Jansen hung her head in silence, then said, "Are you ... happy, Rosa?"

The question caught Mama by surprise, but before she could answer, Mrs. Jansen went on. "I never really saw myself as a housewife growing up. I was going to own and run my own store. Lots of them, if I could manage it. I loved business, and I had the mind for it. By the time I was fifteen, my mama and papa left me in charge of all the finances at our farm. We were some of the most successful tobacco growers in all of Pennsylvania, and it wasn't because we had better dirt."

"So are you saying *you're* not happy?" Mama asked.

Mrs. Jansen shrugged. "I don't know. Some days I am. Most days I feel ... incomplete. Or like part of me is being suffocated. Or is maybe already dead."

"Not dead," said Mama, hugging Mrs. Jansen close to her side. "Lost, maybe, but not dead. And anything that's lost can also be found again."

Mrs. Jansen sighed. "Thanks for that. And I don't want you to misunderstand me—I love my children, and I love Jacob too. Some days, anyway. They just aren't *everything* to me."

"I suppose I can't relate to that exactly. I might have been a top-notch florist when I first met John, but my four boys *are* everything to me. Becoming a mother was the best thing that's happened to me, and I look forward to every single minute I get to spend with them. And, to be honest, it's exactly what I was hoping for in life. But I suppose, in a strange way, it *does* help me understand how you feel. Because if my boys were ever taken away from me, I'd feel incomplete too."

Good thing Mama didn't see me. I was blushing like a rose. Of course, I felt the same way about her, but nine-year-old boys generally don't make a habit of sharing such things about their mamas out loud.

The humming of violin strings sounded from the Great Room. Startled by the noise, Mama and Mrs. Jansen turned around. When they did, they saw me standing beside the door.

"Peter!" Mama exclaimed in surprise. "How long have you—?"

I cut her off. Thinking quickly, I held up my empty glass and said, "I finished my milk. Can I put my glass in the sink?"

"Oh!" said Mama, stepping aside. "Yes. Sorry. You scared me is all. I didn't see you standing there."

As I deposited my glass on top of the other dirty dishes, Mrs. Jansen, sounding suddenly uncomfortable, said, "That must be John tuning his violin. We should rejoin the party."

Without another word, she hurried from the kitchen.

Hoping to avoid any further questioning from Mama about my eavesdropping, I followed close upon Mrs. Jansen's heels.

Back in the Great Room, Daddy's violin was balanced upon his left shoulder, and he was sawing a scale to ensure that everything was correctly tuned. Each time he drew his bow across those four plain strings, an electric resonance filled the Great Room's cavernous chamber, as if he were Zeus, and the music his lightning.

Ahead of me, Mrs. Jansen returned to the empty seat between her husband and little Constance. Since Pip had stolen my place next to Hattie, I was relegated to a disappointing berth on the bench beside Walter. Though we had been brief allies earlier that afternoon, it was with a groan of annoyance that he now slid aside to make room for me.

"Ladies and gentlemen," Daddy announced, in the fashion of a circus ringmaster revving up his audience, "I give you 'The Yellow Rose of Texas.'"

He played the first two notes of Mrs. Jansen's requested song comically slow. But the moment he hit the third note, he fell into a tempo so rapid, it would have given a professional tap dancer a heart attack. He bounced cheerfully in rhythm to the music he played, becoming livelier with each step until he was outright dancing.

The somber conversation in the kitchen forgotten, Mrs. Jansen jumped up as if bitten by the sofa cushion. She offered her hand not to Jacob, who certainly would have refused her anyway. Instead, she pulled Constance up from her seat, and mother and daughter hopped haphazardly but joyously about the hardwood floor, trying—and failing—to keep up with Daddy's *vivace* cadence. Before long, she was adding lyrics to Daddy's melody, so that voice and instrument rose together to the rafters.

Next to join in were Mama and Pastor Wainwright, whose well-executed twostep brought a degree of coordination to the dance floor. Grampa even managed to coax Gramma onto her bloated feet, and they too entered the revelry.

A moment later I found my view obscured by Hattie. Seeking her own dance partner, she extended a hand.

But not toward me. Toward my brother.

"Come on, Walter! Dance with me!" she exclaimed hopefully.

There must have been something wrong with that Chocolate Explosion Cake, because I was immediately overcome with nausea.

"Nah," Walter responded with indifference. "I just want to watch."

Hattie's cheeks reddened, and her eyes smoldered with ire. But instead of fighting with him, she turned to me. "Fine. What about you, Peter?"

Apparently I was little more than an afterthought to my best friend. Still, I accepted the invitation, and Hattie yanked me off the bench. Hand in hand, we skipped amid the frolicking fracas of dancers to the fiddle's festive beat. When "Yellow Rose" ended, I feared our dance would end too, but as Daddy transitioned seamlessly into a jig unknown to me, Hattie and I transitioned with him.

As previously stated, the mind of memory has not only an eye, but an ear and a nose. It tastes and it feels. That evening, as I danced with Hattie, my mind's five senses cataloged it all. The fresh scent of her recently laundered clothes. The high-pitched giggles each time I messed up and stepped on her toes. Her soft fingers interlaced with mine. The metallic taste of cotton mouth, parched by my own nervousness.

Hattie's eyes, as green as Asphodel's lawn, staring gaily into my own.

My heart swelled as I danced with Hattie that evening, until I managed to forget that I had been her *second* choice. And when I saw Walter and Mama capering merrily to Daddy's rendition of "The Pretty Ploughboy," another odd wave of comfort washed over me. As it turned out, my brother was happy to dance—just not with Hattie.

At Daddy's greased-lightning pace, it didn't take much to wear everyone out. Except for the fiddler himself, all the dancers were soon sitters again, each of us catching our breath and wiping the sweat from our eyes.

Grampa was the first to return to his feet, but not to dance. He pushed himself laboriously up from the plush loveseat and said, "Well! I'm more beat than a stubborn mule. Carry me up the stairs, will you, Opal, my dear?"

Gramma scowled and rolled her eyes. With her back to Grampa, she issued a stern "goodnight" to the rest of the room, then plodded to and up the staircase.

"Speaking of stubborn mules ..." Grampa muttered with a sly wink at me. He spread his arms wide, addressing the rest of us dramatically as he offered his benediction. "May God give you all a restful sleep and cake-filled dreams. Goodnight!"

Even as Mama returned Grampa's farewell, her bewitched gaze never left Daddy. But it wasn't drowsiness which lay heavy upon her eyelids. No, she had fallen beneath the druglike influence of deep affection for the man holding the violin.

"Will you play 'Red River Valley' for me, John?" she requested, already knowing what his answer would be.

Even if he found it much too depressing for his own tastes, Daddy never denied Mama her favorite. She loved the folk song because, in her words, "Even pain can be lovely, if only given the chance." To her, "Red River Valley" embodied such an idea, both in lyrics and melody.

"I'll play it," Daddy said. "But like I told Hannah before, you have to pay for requests."

"Oh, I'll pay quite handsomely," was her suggestive reply. "Extra, if you sing it too."

Daddy didn't hesitate. Once more he sawed the bow upon its strings, and the clear notes of his own melodic tones joined with them in perfect pitch:

> *"From this valley they say you are going,*
> *I shall miss your bright eyes and sweet smile,*
> *For alas you take with you the sunshine*
> *That has brightened my pathway awhile."*

Even when Jacob checked his watch and announced that the Jansen clan must also call it a night, Daddy continued playing and singing into the song's refrain:

> *"Come and sit by my side if you love me;*
> *Do not hasten to bid me adieu.*
> *But remember the Red River Valley*
> *And the man who has loved you so true."*

Mr. and Mrs. Jansen both thanked Daddy for his Easter hospitality. He nodded and grinned politely back to them, yet still did not break his musical stride. By his way of seeing things, to do so would have been something akin to God taking a break while forming Adam from the clay of the ground. So, on he went:

> *"Won't you think of this valley you're leaving?*
> *Oh, how lonely, how sad it will be!*
> *Oh, think of the fond heart you're breaking*
> *And the grief you are causing to me."*

I waved goodbye to Hattie, and she to me. She did not wave likewise to Walter. Until the door closed behind her, I soaked in every image my eyes and memory could record of her.

Strange behavior from one friend toward another. Even as a boy of only nine, I realized as she left that something had changed between us. Whether for better or for worse was yet to be determined. All I knew was that I suddenly couldn't get enough of her, and that I wanted her in my life forever.

By the time Daddy arrived at the song's final, mournful notes, Pip was asleep with his head on Mama's lap. The strings' reverberations filled the Great Room once more, then faded and disappeared.

And, along with them, the electricity from Daddy's eyes.

Pastor Wainwright, our one remaining guest, was the first to speak following the song's conclusion. "And you won't play in church? Real shame, John. Real shame. A gift like that is meant to be shared."

His guilt trip complete, he hoisted his bulk from the chair and extended a meaty hand to Daddy. "Thank you for the bourbon and the music," he said. Then, to Mama: "And thank *you* for the cake and the dance!"

Although the hour was late, I could have mistaken Mama's face for the sun as she beamed and said, "Our pleasure having you here. Next year, tell those Schroeders where they can stick that Easter ham. Then you'll be able to join us for the whole day."

Pastor Wainwright secured his black, wide-brimmed hat upon his head and replied, "Oh, I don't know if I can do that. You clearly haven't tried her ham. Goodnight, all!"

After our spiritual shepherd's departure, Daddy glanced at Mama. He grinned, but there was something now missing in his smile.

"I'd better go to bed," he said. "You heard Jacob. Can't be late tomorrow. Equipment troubles *and* problems with unbalanced books. All the things that make life worth living."

Mama glanced at the mahogany clock sitting upon the fireplace mantle. It had belonged to Daddy's daddy before he died, and now it faithfully ticked away the seconds of our lives as well. Each hour, it tolled loud and long to remind us we were sixty minutes closer to the grave.

"It's only half past nine," she pointed out, "and I haven't spent a single moment alone with you today. Besides, you're part owner in the company. What'll Jacob do if you *are* late? Dismiss you? Plus, there's the small matter of my payment. You did play my song, after all."

That seemed to put a little sparkle back in Daddy's eyes.

Cradling Pip in her arms, Mama stood to address me and Walter. "Off to bed, boys. It's Daddy's turn to take a spin on the rowboat."

We groaned but were otherwise too exhausted to put up much protest. Obediently, we made our way toward the stairs, and Mama followed us with Pip's limp form over her shoulder. After depositing him in the nursery, she came to tuck us into bed as well.

By the time most boys reached my age, they had abandoned the security blankets they carried around as toddlers. Not me. My "bibby" was my prized possession, and I slept curled up with it every night. After nine years of constant use, it was little more than a shabby rag. Nonetheless, it remained my constant bedtime companion. Most nights I fell asleep with it pressed against my nose and mouth, as I inhaled its musty but familiar scent.

Now, when Mama leaned over to kiss me goodnight, she slid my bibby gently aside to make room for her lips.

"I had a wonderful day with you," she whispered. "Sleep sweet. I love you."

After repeating this at Walter's bedside, Mama turned out the light and left us in the dark.

It never took more than a minute for my older brother to fall asleep, and I soon heard his rhythmic breathing from the adjacent wall. As in everything, where Walter was blessed, I found myself cursed. Most nights I tossed and turned for thirty, forty minutes before falling asleep. Sometimes longer.

I did find small comfort on those sleepless nights, especially when the moon was full and round, that the best view in Asphodel Hall belonged to me. My bed sat below a casement window on the south-facing wall of the house. From here, I had a perfect vantage point to look out over our broad lake and the forests beyond.

Since the unseasonably warm Easter had left the Castle Home's upstairs feeling a touch muggy, I knelt in bed and slid open my window. As the crisp air cascaded in upon me, I laid down again and snuggled beneath my cozy blankets.

That night, with my bedroom window open to Acheron, I learned how clearly voices carry across the surface of a calm lake.

It was Mama I heard first. I had almost fallen asleep when her peals of laughter startled me. I sat up and peered out my window, but she was nowhere to be seen.

So instead of looking, I did what I was best at. I listened.

"I sure do love it when you play, you know that?" said Mama.

"What can I say, Freckles? My father taught me well," Daddy replied. "I sure wish you'd gotten to know him before he died."

"If he raised you, he must have been alright."

"Back at our little apartment in Philadelphia, he used to play his violin every morning at the breakfast table. It didn't make him very popular with the neighbors, but *meine Mutti* and I sure loved it." A pause. "I'm glad he took the time to teach me. When I play his violin, sometimes I feel like he's right next to me. Looking down at me with that big, proud smile on his face."

Such a long silence followed this, I wondered whether they had returned indoors. I had even laid my head back upon my pillow before their voices startled me a second time.

"Where did you learn to row like that?" Daddy asked.

That's when I realized they were out on the lake. It puzzled me how they could sound so near, as if they were directly below my window.

"Your daddy's not the only one who taught his kid something," Mama answered. "I was only seven or eight. I loved being out on the water, and since he couldn't always take me, he showed me how to do it myself."

There was another silence. Then Mama asked, "What's wrong, John?"

"Nothing."

"Liar. I know you're not happy. Not completely, anyway. Tell me."

"No, really. It's nothing. I'm just tired, that's all."

"If you don't want to tell me, fine. Keep your secrets. But try to remember that you have a thriving business, a fine home, three beautiful boys who worship you, and a wife who loves you to death. You could do a lot worse, John Luther."

"I know, Rosa. I *am* happy."

"If you say so. And even if you're not, you'll have one very good reason to be happy in about two minutes."

"Oh-ho!" laughed Daddy. "That's right! I forgot about the little matter of your payment."

Mama giggled. "The moon'll be blushing for a week when I'm through with you."

I suspected Mama must have brought along another piece of Chocolate Explosion Cake as her payment, because it was the chorus of their pleasureful moans which finally lulled me to sleep that night.

I also suspect that I did so with a contented grin upon my own moonlit face. Easter 1918 was, perhaps, the last perfect day of my young life.

May 18, 1954 – 11:48 a.m.

ONCE UPON A TIME, MAGNIFICENT TRAINS, laden with car after car of anthracite, whistled through here, many of them directly from Luther & Jansen Coal. Newly refined and ready for use, our black gold slid across the steel river of these tracks, before it was divided upon a thousand tributaries throughout the eastern United States.

In days that now exist only in memory, the Pierre Train Depot was a frenzied hive of activity. Pointsmen and porters, railway gangs and station agents, engineers and inspectors, servicemen and businessmen, comers and goers alike—all jostled around and past and beside one another in a writhing waltz. Here the odor of circus elephants, enroute to their next performance, mixed and mingled with the Parisian perfumes of Philadelphia's upper crust, either beginning or ending a vacation to the American West. The depot was a circus in its own right, an amalgam of industry and technology and humanity in raucous celebration.

As I approach the train's open door, I smell it on the air. A faint whiff of what it used to be—Pierre's heyday ended long ago—but still there. And not only the train depot's familiar bouquet. Assaulting my nostrils right along with it is the pungent reek of the processing plant.

That rotten-egg stench doesn't come from the coal itself, I know. Raw anthracite doesn't really smell like much of anything. But coal, like everything else we pull out of the ground, comes up with friends, and one of its very best friends is sulfur.

On certain days of my childhood, when the sulfur content was particularly high and the wind just right—or wrong, I suppose—all of Pierre would find itself submerged in a bath of rotten egg. Most of our residents understood that the process of purifying the coal was vital to the life of the plant, and that the plant was vital to the life of the town. While Daddy and Mr. Jansen certainly received a few complaints over the years, most had the good sense to pinch their noses and bear it.

They knew it was the smell of success. A thriving mine meant a thriving Pierre. It doesn't smell as successful as it used to.

I step out onto the dilapidated depot platform and am reminded anew that such days sank beneath the rear horizon long ago. Handrails that were once bright and polished, I now avoid. Rust has consumed them, and I am long overdue for a tetanus shot. Carefully, I choose my steps across the platform. The last thing I need today is a sudden drop through a trapdoor of wood rot.

Only a handful of passengers depart the train with me. Most remain onboard and on their way to more glamorous destinations. Those who did disembark hurry ahead of me, eager to conduct whatever business they have so that they might leave as soon as possible.

I can't help but wonder if some might be on their way to the old mine. It may not be what it was in the glory days, but its output is still among the highest in Pennsylvania.

Jacob Jansen knew business. So did his wife. They did well with it after my father's time was up.

I tighten my grip on the suitcase hanging at my side and make for the platform stairs. My single piece of luggage bangs annoyingly against my leg as I descend to the gravel below, and I almost wish I hadn't taken it.

But there is something inside I had to bring with me. I'm not sure why, but I knew it had to make this trip as urgently as I did. An unsettled question lingers inside me—and not merely *lingering* but *growing* there for the last thirty-five years. I wonder if what I carry with me, heavy though it is, might help me finally find an answer.

As my feet meet the gravel below the station platform, my eyes are met by a familiar face.

"Good morning, Peter." Pastor Wainwright greets me warmly. He appears genuinely delighted to see me again. "I trust your trip was pleasant?"

Like the train depot, he too has endured the weather of many years. A face which used to be round and rosy is crisscrossed with lines and blotched with age spots. His hair is curly, as I remembered it, but what remains is wispy and translucent, no longer the loamy brown of my childhood. Even my old pastor's kind, honey-brown eyes have lost the twinkle of his youthful mirth. They are watery and drained of their color, like the bark of an old ash tree.

"It was uneventful," I respond, gripping his outstretched hand. "It's good to see you, Pastor."

The old man chuckles, waving away my formality. "I think you're old enough to call me Fred, don't you?"

I smile and shrug but know I won't. Some childhood observances remain too deeply ingrained to forsake, even if I am in my mid-forties. To call him by his first name would constitute an even deeper heresy than diesel-powered trains.

"Thanks for picking me up," I say, as we make our way toward the depot's gravel parking lot. "Seems like everyone else has moved on in one fashion or another."

"Pierre is a very ... *changed* place since your childhood," says Pastor Wainwright. "It's not as alive as it once was. Pardon my choice of words. I didn't mean—well, you know."

I grunt a wry laugh. "Don't worry about it."

We arrive in silence at his 1942 Buick Roadmaster. Unsatisfied only with train depots and old men, Time has also made itself an enemy of this automobile. Though its victims are countless, they are never enough.

Heat radiates off the Roadmaster's black paint as Pastor Wainwright opens the trunk. I deposit my suitcase within, taking care to fit it into a space where it can't slide around. What I packed inside it bears a hefty price tag, and I don't want it damaged.

Once we are both seated in the roasting Buick, Pastor Wainwright inserts the key into the ignition. The engine growls irritably, then roars to life. The old car creaks begrudgingly forward and begins carrying us westward toward downtown Pierre.

We are well on our way when Pastor Wainwright speaks again.

"Is your brother coming?" he asks.

"He is, but not 'til tomorrow. And no, you don't have to bother yourself with picking him up. I can take the Chrysler."

The pastor offers an approving grunt. "That's good. It's good you'll be together. I can't imagine you see each other often, with him in Chicago and you all the way down in Wichita."

"We don't," I admit. "Not as much as we should, anyway."

"Funny how life manages to pull apart the people who should be closest, isn't it? You'll have a few days together now, at any rate."

We round a hilly corner, and St. Matthew's Lutheran Church rolls into view. From its whitewashed steeple to the Bible-themed stained glass, it might be the first thing I've seen since arriving that looks like its old self. All the way down to the hopper windows peeping up from the basement, the faithful building has neither aged a day, nor nipped or tucked its appearance in any perceivable way.

Seeing it ties a knot in my stomach. Maybe it's the Pennsylvania heat, or the fact that I haven't eaten anything in over a day, but I sense a deeper reason for my abrupt sickness.

I wanted to avoid my ghosts on the train. Perhaps all I managed to do was delay them as I dwelt upon Easter Day. A happier day.

But I can avoid them no longer. The time to confront them is upon me.

And the first is at hand.

As we drive around the front of St. Matthew's, the church cemetery pans into sight. Its first inhabitants were buried there well over a century ago. Since then, hundreds more of their friends, descendants, neighbors, and descendants of those neighbors have gone to sleep beside them within the earth.

In two days, one more will join them. But that, I suppose, is a ghost for later.

"Would you mind pulling over? In front of the graveyard?" I ask apologetically. I'm aware that everything Pastor Wainwright does for me is an imposition.

He answers by easing the Buick alongside the grass. In front of the cemetery's wrought-iron gate, he lets the car idle.

"Thanks," I mutter gratefully. "I won't be long. I promise."

His friendly smile makes another of its generous appearances, and he says, "Take all the time you need, Peter. At my age, Tuesdays rarely hold much excitement anyway."

My stroll among the silent graves begins in the shadow of twin elms, the cemetery's oldest trees. Here the headstones are lichen-covered and smooth, so worn by the cycle of seasons that the names and years of their owners have melted away from the hard granite. As I make my way through the grounds, the trees become younger and sparser. Sunlight cascades down upon the fresher headstones here, and I can read these easily as I walk by.

To anyone passing the cemetery, I must appear aimless and ambling, drifting among the graves like a spirit who has just escaped one. In truth, I simply don't know where I'm going. The person I stopped to see is one I haven't visited in thirty-plus years. Like Pierre and Pastor Wainwright, certain memories have faded in the interim.

As often happens when searching for something specific, I nearly walk right past it. For some reason, the headstone looked different in my mind—or, I realize, not the headstone itself, but its environment. In 1918, an adolescent chestnut stood no more than a dozen feet behind this cemetery plot. Now there is only a blighted stump, a grave marker made from the bones of the very tree which once lived here.

I can no longer hold back the tears as I kneel. They flow freely as I read the name, the dates of birth and death, the epitaph at the bottom. Even after the passage of decades, this still feels so terribly wrong. It is a sadistic paradox, a cruel and humorless farce.

How could Death so quickly reap someone so full of life?

I bury my face in my hands and weep, for I have come to the place of my haunting.

Here lies the first of my ghosts.

EIGHT

The Second Wave

SPRING—AND MAMA'S GARDEN—bloomed into its fullest flamboyant array in 1918 just like any other year. Despite the frequent reports of The Flu's rampage around the globe, our isolated world in Pierre remained untouched. Mama was, for the time being at least, good to her word about our immunity.

Soon the wrathful heat of summer could no longer be held at bay. Springtime melted and the flowers wilted, but what care were they of ours? With the heat also came the merciful conclusion of the school year. Even Miss Carrington, our teacher, must have been counting down the seconds until our two-thirty dismissal that day. When Joe Murdoch ran back for his forgotten cap at two thirty-one, he found the door deadbolted shut and heard a woman within weeping tears of joy. Or so he claimed.

Regardless of his tale's truth, the cheer of freedom and summer's unexplored potential washed over us. The undefined stream of days that followed melted together, each into the next like drops of mercury. The cup of life brimmed and overflowed with the discovery of new forestland, the construction of forts and bunkers, blackberry and blueberry picking, and splashing in the lake's cooling waters. We drank chilled tea and lemonade from the icebox, celebrated Pip's fourth birthday, wrangled fireflies in late evening's pale light, and danced to Daddy's daily fiddling.

It was around the middle of summer when Walter and I noticed a change come over Mama. She began sleeping in most mornings, not rising until well after me and my brothers. When she played with us, her fountain of boundless energy was more like an intermittent stream, running high one moment and dry the next.

Poor Pip suffered the most, as he soon found himself in stiff competition for the snacks in our cupboards.

Only after an uncharacteristic visit by our family's physician, Dr. Schumacher, did we finally learn what was going on. We were all gathered around the dinner table when Daddy made the announcement over one of Abigail's famous berry cobblers.

Mama was pregnant. If everything happened according to Dr. Schumacher's supposed timetable, we could expect a new brother or sister sometime around Christmas.

Walter and I were thrilled. Pip was not.

"Will I have to move out of my room?" he asked dejectedly, pushing the cobbler around his plate with his fork. It was the first time I'd ever seen him uninterested in food.

"Not right away," Mama answered. "But now that you're such a big boy, it'll be time to move across the hall anyway."

"Can I keep my toys? Or will the baby get those too?"

"You can keep your toys, of course," Mama assured him. "But if there's anything you've outgrown, you could give it to the baby as a present."

"I think I'll keep them," Pip said curtly. Having given his final word on the matter, he dove into his dessert.

"Is that why we couldn't go out West this summer? To Yellowstone?" Walter asked. While he had never brought up the matter with Daddy, he had expressed to me his disappointment over the trip's tacit cancellation.

Daddy gave him an apologetic grin. "Sorry, Walter. That sort of travel is difficult on a pregnant woman, and I knew you wouldn't want to see those things without Mama. We'll go next summer with the new baby."

That answer was good enough for Walter, because Daddy was right. Walter never would have left Mama behind, not even if it meant seeing every national park from Montana to California. Wherever Mama was, that's where Walter anchored his heart too.

And so, instead of exploring the West, our summer explorations took place closer to home. Despite her pregnancy, Mama still chauffeured us as often as we wanted to the Isle—that's what we had begun calling it—across Lake Acheron. As we charted this new land, we discovered the telltale marks of previous inhabitants. A rotting cabin and outhouse, abandoned beside a natural spring, became a site of archaeological significance to us. There, under Mama's watchful tutelage, we unearthed treasures which might provide clues about those who had called the Isle "home." On the days Hattie joined us, we commenced the building of a treehouse in the arms of a magnificent oak. Undeterred by Walter's vocal protests, nor by our clear ignorance of arboreal architecture, we managed to nail a few shaky planks into the boughs overhead. But construction was slow going—after all, we had to import our building materials by rowboat—and the project never went much further than that.

Although I still felt uneasy around Hattie, the odd tension between me and my best friend subsided and disappeared altogether in those happy months. We played and laughed and talked more than ever, until I eventually became comfortable in my uncomfortableness. And, by contrast, her interactions with Walter only led to an increase in bickering and astringency between them. If I had once been worried about some budding closeness, I now worried their constant quibbling might drive her away entirely. But as July went out and August came in, Hattie's visits to Asphodel Glade continued.

The weeks of summer waned. Mama's belly waxed. And it seemed that the days of the strange Flu would end with our vacation. The articles about it in the paper, which had been daily headlines at summer's beginning, became relegated to sporadic footnotes shoved into the margins. Like an ice cube in the mid-August heat, it appeared the abstruse illness would melt away into the nothingness from which it had sprung last spring.

As always, the end of August corralled us unwillingly back onto the hard slab benches we had escaped in May. A malaise that had nothing to do with The Flu had apparently stricken thirty-two of Pierre's middle-grade children on the same day. Somberly, we all stared forward at Miss Carrington and her portable blackboard, as we inwardly commenced our countdown until the next summer break.

And so, life entered that miserable quagmire of educational drudgery which all young boys experience those first weeks after returning to school. Like the wheels of a train, rotating in repeated motion along their track, Walter and I would roll out of bed—Pip was still blessed with his pre-educational youth—eat breakfast, walk to school, learn, walk home, finish our homework, and perhaps have a little playtime before dinner, chores, and bed. Best we could figure, this year would be no different than its predecessors. The academic train would plow inexorably forward, taking only infrequent stops to refuel before arriving again at its next summer destination—exactly one eternity from now.

Such was our expectation.

But The Flu had different plans.

It was during a post-lunch recess in early September that Miss Carrington caught Jeremiah Lasseter, Pierre Primary's fifth-grade loudmouth, scaring a group of younger students. He had been jabbering to them about another outbreak of

The Flu. According to Jeremiah, this one was so deadly, people would catch it at breakfast and croak before supper.

Miss Carrington promptly set him to work writing lines at the blackboard, but the damage had been done. By the end of the day, the rumor had reached every ear: we would all be pushing up daisies in a few weeks' time. Poor Miss Carrington found her hands quite full soothing a few of the younger students, who had burst into tears over their impending demise. With so much crying and so little learning going on, she eventually decided to address the whole classroom.

"I don't know what you heard or from whom you heard it," she chirped, in tones far too sweet to be authentic, "but let me reassure you that you are in no danger. God is watching out for you, protecting each and every one of us. Besides that, I don't know of a single person in Pierre who has come down with this Flu, and there's no reason to think that will change."

At face value, her words were reassuring. Yet in them, I detected a slight and unsettling tremor. Miss Carrington was a fine teacher, but she was a shit actress. She was clearly hiding something, or at least knew more than she was letting on.

When the clock struck half past two, she dismissed everyone but Jeremiah. She told the rumormonger he would have to wait inside until she could speak with his father.

For my part, I hurried out the door ahead of Walter and Hattie. My bladder had taken on more liquid than the *Titanic*, and I needed to reach the outhouse before anyone else.

"Where ya goin'?" my brother called after me, as I ran around the side of the three-room schoolhouse.

"Take a pee!" I shouted.

"Well, I'm not gonna wait up for you."

"I'll catch up."

Unfortunately, I found the outhouse locked when I yanked on the door. A kid from the upper-grade classroom must have beat me to it.

"Wait your turn!" the girl inside barked.

Anita Morton was both the most popular and most horrible girl in the seventh grade. By the time her scowling face appeared through the open door, she had made me wait a full five minutes. I would have gladly shared some of my thoughts about her, but I could feel my ears starting to leak. I rushed inside, took care of business, and reemerged into the fresh air, much relieved and a couple pounds lighter than when I had entered. A quick glance around the schoolyard told me the other kids had all cleared out.

Walter had also been true to his word. He was gone, and Hattie had seemingly tagged along with him rather than wait on me.

My disappointment was short-lived.

As I made for the front of the schoolhouse, I heard a pair of voices around the corner. One belonged to Miss Carrington. The other was familiar and obviously male, but I couldn't place its owner. Both spoke in low tones and obviously didn't want anyone else to hear.

Still around the corner and out of sight, I held my breath and listened. "You won't be able to hide it for long," said the mystery man. He sounded a touch exasperated but not outright angry. "Tomorrow, maybe the day after, it'll be in all the papers again."

Miss Carrington's voice still carried that quiver as she replied, "I know. But I can't have Jeremiah scaring the younger kids."

Mystery solved. She was talking to Caleb Lasseter. Whereas we walked home from school most days, Caleb picked Jeremiah up on his way home from the mine.

Miss Carrington went on. "He was telling them how they'll be dying in their beds soon. Very inappropriate. It's up to their parents to tell them what's happening."

"Yeah, but now it's happening *here.*"

Iron fingers grabbed my lungs and squeezed. I couldn't breathe. The Flu? Here? Impossible! I shook my head, trying to convince myself they must be talking about something else.

"Regardless, my point stands, and it's *my* classroom," said Miss Carrington with a note of finality. "It's not Jeremiah's job to share it, especially when his only goal is to scare people."

Caleb released an acquiescent sigh and said, "You're right. I'll have a talk with him. Not his place."

"Thank you."

"Welcome. Sorry for coming at you earlier. I guess I'm just ... *scared.* I already lost his mama. If I lost my boy too, I don't know what I'd do."

Throw a party? I telepathically suggested. Not my most sanctified thought.

"I think we're all a little scared," Miss Carrington replied.

"Yeah. Well, I'd best get Jer home. Have a pleasant evening, Anne."

"And you, Mr. Lasseter."

The school door opened and closed. Around the corner, I waited until the sound of footsteps on gravel had grown distant. When I was certain I was safe, I hurried from my hiding spot. I felt a twinge of guilt over my eavesdropping, but what I felt in far greater measure was fear.

At nine years old, I didn't know how to process either the new feelings or the new information. So instead, I ran. As if The Flu itself were bounding after me, baring its snarling teeth, I ran for my life.

I came quickly to Main Street—the school was only two blocks north. Past Jorgensen's Law Office and Mel's Diner and Harold's Meats went the blur of my spindly form. Sheriff Clark, on the telephone inside the police station, glanced at me and then behind me, certain I was being chased. Folks strolling along the storefronts stopped and gawked, yet I ran on, unfazed by their gossipy whispers.

But as I approached Uecker's Pharmacy, I spotted something that finally managed to stop me dead in my tracks. My attention, so consumed a moment ago with The Flu, fell victim at once to a newer and deadlier dread.

Ahead of me, Hattie was walking at my brother's side.

They were holding hands.

I blinked, certain my eyes were playing tricks on me.

But it was no illusion. Hattie and Walter were truly, really, nauseatingly holding hands.

NINE

Fish Tales

I DON'T THINK EVEN THE FLU could have sickened me as much as what I was seeing.

Hattie ... and *Walter?* But he was always putting her down. Belittling her. At times even going out of his way to badger her. How could she hold *his* hand while mine remained empty?

A frothing concoction of rage and betrayal and hopeless inadequacy surged through my viscera. I didn't know if I wanted to scream or cry or punch my brother. Perhaps all three at once?

But before any explosion occurred, those thundering sensations were swept away by something quieter, yet somehow more substantial. To this day, I still have never found the word which adequately describes the paradox which sprang to life inside me that day. I was, at the same time, both numb *and* in tremendous pain. Empty, yet overflowing with bitter gall.

I was paralyzed. But, no—my legs were moving. They were even carrying me forward, toward the waking nightmare.

Walter and Hattie had their backs turned to me. They had no idea I was approaching.

A jealous daze clung like fog to my brain, and I hadn't a clue what I might do. I wondered if this was how Cain had felt before he struck his brother Abel dead. All I had to do was find a big rock and ...

"Peter!" Hattie shrieked, shattering my fratricidal trance. She must have sensed me coming up behind them, because she had thrown a purposeful glance over her shoulder.

As if Hattie's hand had burst spontaneously into flame, Walter threw it away from his own. Whirling about, he glowered at me suspiciously.

"What are you doing? Spying on us?" he demanded.

"Uh—no. Just catching up, like I said," I replied thickly, my tongue sticking to the roof of my desiccated mouth.

Walter's initial surprise faded, and his anger softened. "Oh. Right. Well, come on then."

"Aren't you going home, Hattie?" I asked. "We already passed your street."

"We already stopped there!" she cheerfully chirped. "Didn't you notice my schoolbag was gone?"

"We asked Mrs. Jansen if she could come over," Walter added. "She said it was okay, as long as Hattie's back for supper."

Without another word, Walter shoved his hands into his trouser pockets and led us down Main Street. Hattie stayed by his side, while I fell into my rightful place. Which was, apparently, behind them.

A two-minute silence followed, one which Hattie broke when she announced, "I think we should go back to working on the treehouse today."

"Nah, we can do that another time," said Walter. Despite the previous hand-holding, he refused to meet her eyes.

Hattie, on the other hand, gave him such a glare, she could have drilled a well with it.

"Why not?" she challenged, crossing her arms in a huff.

"I need to practice climbing rocks today," Walter answered matter-of-factly. "There's lots of rocks in Yosemite Park, and I want to be ready for when we visit."

"You can climb dumb old rocks when I'm not there," she countered. "Today I want to build our treehouse."

"*Your* treehouse, not mine," Walter protested. "I never wanted to build it in the first place. I said it was a dumb idea. Remember?"

"It's not a dumb idea!"

"Fine," said Walter. "We don't have to climb rocks. We can go fishing instead. That's something else I need to practice before I go out West next summer."

I almost fell over in disbelief. What was he doing? Had he placed a sizeable bet against himself? He knew as well as I did how much Hattie hated fishing.

But she was stuck on his earlier comment. "Why do you think all my ideas are dumb? Whenever I want to do anything, you never listen. You either tell me it's stupid or we'll play it later. But 'later' never comes."

"Just dug up a stash of worms yesterday," said Walter, as if he were having an entirely different conversation. "Want to use 'em before they dry up."

The introduction of worms, another of Hattie's great dislikes, was too much for her. She planted her heels so firmly in the road, I nearly ran her over.

"You're a real *goop,* you know that, Walter?" She was in full fume. Ire reddened her cheeks, and tears welled in her grass-green eyes.

"What? No one's making you come, you know."

"*You* were the one who asked *me.*"

"I was just trying to be nice."

The first tear cascaded down Hattie's cheek as she cried, "Fine! Then I'll go home!"

"Suit yourself," Walter replied coolly.

Hattie clenched her fists. A shriek of frustration burst through her lips before she said, rather darkly, "Have fun fishing. I hope you drown, you damn *simp.*"

Walter and I watched Hattie storm back the direction we had come. Neither of us had ever heard her curse before, and the shock of it rendered our legs useless.

Only when I was sure Hattie was beyond earshot did I ask, "What did you do that for? You know she hates fishing."

"Yeah. I know." Walter sounded unsure whether he was annoyed or miserable. "Come on. Let's go home."

I wanted to tell him that I had seen their handholding, but I imagined doing so would only draw his foul mood upon myself. Besides, I had an inkling he already knew what I'd witnessed, and that it may have played a role in his nasty treatment of Hattie.

We traveled a long way in silence after that. Only when we had turned off the main road and were passing beneath Asphodel Glade's iron gateway sign, did I finally dare to speak.

"I overheard Miss Carrington talking to Mr. Lasseter after school," I said. "That's why I took so long."

Surprisingly, Walter seemed welcoming of any conversation that would extract him from his own brooding thoughts. He asked, "Did she kick that idiot out of school?"

I laughed. It was weird, but I felt like we had suddenly joined the same team. In her own way, Hattie had rejected us both that afternoon. Or perhaps the old adage is correct, and misery really does love company. The only difference between us was that I was an innocent victim, whereas Walter had pulled the lever to drop the guillotine onto his own neck.

"She didn't expel him," I answered him. "But I did hear them talking about The Flu."

"Flu's old news."

"The way they were talking, it sounded like it's coming back." And, I realized, so was that sickly fear which had gripped my heart whilst eavesdropping. "What if Jeremiah's right? What if it's worse this time?"

"The only time that shitbrain's been right about anything was when he accidentally wandered into the first-grade math class," Walter replied.

"Maybe. But even Mr. Lasseter sounded scared."

"Mama said there's nothing to be scared of. You think she's a liar?"

"Well, no, but—"

"So don't be scared."

Walter had a way of clamping down any opposing thought, or even measured discussion. When it came to his friends or siblings, whatever he said was the final word on the matter—perhaps the *only* word that did matter to him. The most infuriating part about it was, nineteen times out of twenty, he was right.

When we arrived at Asphodel Hall, we found Mama and Pip painting on large sheets of canvas they had spread across the front porch. The lucky little bastard still had one year of educationless bliss remaining before he would join the poor souls in the lower-grade classroom. For the present, he spent his days at the mercy of Mama, who made sure he was tortured aplenty with children's books, games, arts and crafts, snacks, and trips to Schroeder's Grocery.

"Hi, Mama!" Walter called happily as he bounded ahead of me up the porch stairs.

"Hi, Wahwie," she said, standing to give him a squeeze. "How was school today?"

"Boring. Same as always."

When Mama hugged me and asked the same question, I gave a similar response. I said nothing of the conversation I'd overheard.

"Wanna go fishing, Pip?" Walter asked our paint-smeared brother. "Me'n Peter are gonna use those worms we dug up yesterday."

Pip's nose crinkled in disgust. He was an atypical four-year-old boy with absolutely no interest in creepy, crawly, or slimy things.

"Suit yourself," said Walter. Turning to Mama, he asked, "If I catch a really big one, can we eat it tonight?"

Mama laughed gaily. "I don't know how well it'll pair with Abigail's roast, but we could try it!"

Her response set a glow upon Walter such as Hattie never could have done, and he exclaimed, "Come on, Peter!"

"Have fun, but be safe down by the water," cautioned Mama. "And stay close enough to the house that I can call you in when dinner's ready."

"Oh, I'll be back before then," Walter declared, "and with the biggest fish you've ever seen!"

We ditched our schoolbags right there on the front porch. Daddy would have lectured us for not storing them properly in our rooms, but we knew Mama would take care of that for us long before he came home. She was the great enabler—and often the *pusher*—of our boyhood's impulsive irresponsibility. Unlike other women of the time, she existed not to cook and clean, nor to take care of household chores or even to serve her husband. Rosalie Luther lived for her boys and for whatever joys she might impart upon them. When our hearts were full, so was hers.

Down at the lakeshore, Kalamazoo baitcasting rods in hand, Walter and I spaced ourselves a short distance from each other and flicked our lines into the choppy water. Almost as if expecting us, a breeze had kicked up across the surface of the lake to assist us in our fishy endeavors. When there are natural disturbances in the water, line and tackle become difficult for fish to recognize as the deadly snares they are.

Five minutes passed, then ten, but neither of us attracted even a sampling nibble.

"I'm going down the shore," an impatient Walter informed me. "To Weedy Bay."

"Mama said to stay where we could hear her," I reminded him.

"Well, you listen for her, and come get me when it's supper time."

With that, he went crashing off through the shoreline brush.

On went my luckless afternoon of angling. I would cast, watch my cork bobber float lazily into the shallow water, then reel it in and repeat the process. After another twenty minutes, my impatience-and-monotony stew was ready to bubble over. I was about to call it quits and engage in more fruitful enterprise, when I heard Walter bushwhacking a path back from the so-called Weedy Bay. I supposed he'd had enough as well and was ready to spend the precious hours of late afternoon doing something else.

I soon realized he had returned for a different—and far more infuriating—reason. Dangling from the end of Walter's arm, with his index and forefingers punched through its gill to support its weight, was the longest, meatiest large-mouth bass I had ever seen.

Jealousy boiled up again. First he had won Hattie's affections—never mind that he'd also *lost* them—and now Fate was rewarding him with this prized fish? The scales of injustice—no pun intended—were ever tipped in Walter's favor. It was enough to make me throw back my head and scream at the heavens.

I didn't, of course. Instead, I returned my attention to my own bait and tackle, pretending I hadn't noticed him or his stupid fish.

"She's a whopper, isn't she?" Walter exclaimed as he stopped beside me.

I gave the fish a disinterested glance. "Yeah, it's alright."

"*Alright?*" Walter was scandalized. "That's got to be the biggest bass that's ever come out of Lake Acheron!"

"Is not," I argued. "Karty Phelan caught one twice that size last fall."

"You just made that up 'cause you're jealous," said Walter, accompanying his reply with a shove. "Anyway, it doesn't matter what you think. I'm gonna bring it to Mama to cook for dinner. Maybe we can eat a salad too with all the weeds you catch."

Walter at once began his trek toward the house, so he didn't see the rude gesture I flipped his direction. That was probably for the best. If he had, I would've eaten my own bait as punishment.

Seething, I cast my impaled worm back into the lake. The afternoon's events had cemented a sort of resolve inside me. Two minutes ago, I had been ready to give up. Now I was determined to stay out until I could carry home a prize even mightier than Walter's leviathan. Hell, I'd keep fishing until the lake froze over, if that's what it took.

For a while, it did indeed seem I was heading that direction. The shadow of the forest stretched its dark fingers further and further across the shallows, yet my bobber remained about as active as a chunk of driftwood. The minutes dragged into an hour, then longer. An aroma of meat, vegetables, and herbs wafted past me, and I knew Mama would soon call me in for dinner.

Time was running out. Exasperated and fed up, I dug into my compost pail and unearthed every slithering nightcrawler I could find. In a move of sheer desperation, I stabbed each one of those bastards onto my hook. For all I knew, it may have been the largest mass execution in Pennsylvania's history. But I was a boy beyond such Christian values as mercy or humility, and I would have killed a thousand worms if it meant one monster fish to shove in Walter's smug face.

With every fiber of strength in my scrawny muscles, I launched line, bobber, hook, and bait as far into the lake as I could. My annelid cannonball sent up a geyser of water as it hit Acheron's surface and hurtled down into the depths.

Bearing such formidable weight, the bobber struggled to stay afloat. Only a thin nub of cork remained visible above the waterline. I fixed my eyes upon it, watching and waiting.

That was when the call I'd been dreading rang out through the dim light of evening.

"Peter! Dinner!" Mama cried. "Come inside!"

The voices of internal debate spoke up at once. If I ignored her, such direct disobedience meant certain doom whenever Daddy came home. If I pretended I hadn't heard her, this would land me in hot water for a different reason. Mama had explicitly ordered me and Walter to remain within earshot, thus leaving me in violation of her earlier command.

Resistance was useless, and I knew it. Besides, what would I accomplish out here? Walter's bass had apparently eaten all the other fish in the lake.

The day had defeated me. Beaten, I cranked my reel.

My line jerked and tightened so abruptly, I almost dropped the pole. I hadn't caught so much as a weed all afternoon, but here, at the end of it, like the twisting of a barbed fishhook in my wounded pride, came a snag which bent my rod double.

I yanked the pole side to side and up and down, but whatever I was caught on refused either to budge or break. With a sigh, I opened my reel to create some slack. I would bite through my fishing line and be done. Less a hook, yet finished with this awful fishing and this awful day.

But before I could clamp my teeth upon it, the line went taut again. I realized then that I could hear it vibrating, like steel cables humming in a high wind.

My fingers curled and tightened around the pole's cork handle.

This was no snag. My worm bomb had worked.

Fish on!

I dug my heels into the lakeshore's rich earth. Grampa always told me having a firm base was the most important component to fighting a fish successfully, and I had the feeling I was in for the fight of my life. Although I suspected the hook was already well set, I made certain by jerking the pole's tip upward.

The fish—whatever it was—didn't appreciate that little maneuver. To the left it streaked, then to the right, dragging my skinny arms with it. Careful not to let my excitement get the better of me, I cranked my reel gently, coaxing the fish toward the shore. After a minute's wrestling, twenty feet out had been reduced to fifteen. At ten, my fishy foe regained some of its fighting spirit and surged toward deeper waters with such a fury, I thought my line might melt from the friction.

I growled when I saw how much ground I had lost. The stupid fish was further out now than when I had first hooked it!

Part of me wanted to give up. To let the fish win. But that meant letting Walter win too, and I would sooner die than give him such a satisfaction.

So the life-and-death struggle went on. In my imagination, I saw the movie bill: *Peter vs. The Lake Monster.* Again, I drew him into the shallows. Again, he fled for the depths. Back and forth we went, each contender wearing the other down, inch by painful inch.

How long that struggle lasted, I don't know. You have a way of losing track of time during those angling battles. But when I at last began to gain consistent ground, the sun had already sunk into its celestial bed.

Twilight alone remained when, sweat-soaked and aching from head to heels, I at last hauled my catch ashore.

I gasped. While fighting this devil, I had imagined many fish of differing species and size, but nothing could have prepared me for what now lay at my feet.

It was a pike, the meanest fish in the lake. At almost four feet long, it could have gulped down Walter's bass in a single snap of its razor-toothed jaws.

Conquered and prostrate, the pike glared up at me with hateful eyes as I knelt over its vanquished form.

In hindsight, I should have known better. Right away, I should have dragged the fish further inland and appraised my glorious catch there.

But I didn't.

And so, with one trick left up its gills, my adversary gave a wild thrashing of its head, snapped my line, and flopped ten measly inches back into the safety of Acheron's warm waters.

TEN

A Problem of Blood

THERE IS A SAYING WHICH, in the years since my youth, I have learned about fishing: "If you don't have a picture, it didn't happen." It seems fishermen have a preternatural disposition for embellishing the details of their angling achievements. They can transform even the meagerest of catches into monsters that would make Captain Ahab crazy with bloodlust. Inches become feet, feet become yards, and yards become city blocks. Thus, friends and family, who long ago grew skeptical about their beloved anglers' claims, began demanding photographs as proof to back up such outlandish assertions.

If a picture didn't happen, neither did the fish.

When I was nine, I knew none of this. Certainly there was a blip of disappointment when my magnificent pike slid away into the dark waters, but mostly I was elated. I was in such a hurry to share my fish story that I left my pole right there on the banks of Lake Acheron. I knew I was walking into plenty of trouble for being so late to dinner, yet even that keen awareness did nothing to dampen my spirits.

My arrival into the dining room was met with a rare stern glance from Mama. Usually she left that sort of unpleasantness to Daddy. His place at the table, however, was empty. By default, his absence put her on discipline duty.

"Where were you?" she asked, placing her fork upon her mostly empty plate. "I was getting worried."

"I'm sorry," I replied, gasping for air. Half my breath I'd lost running up the hill, and the rest from sheer adrenaline. "But when you called me, I was in the middle of catching a fish—the *biggest* fish I've seen in my life!"

That last part I aimed at Walter, who was currently picking through the bones of his pathetic bass.

"You're lying," he said with an incredulous smirk. "Where is it?"

"I pulled it up on shore, and then it snapped my line and escaped back in the water. It was a huge pike, at least four feet long! Coulda ate your bass for a snack."

"Yeah. An imaginary snack, because that's what imaginary fish eat," he quipped derisively.

Furious tears pooled in my eyes, blurring my vision, and my hands balled into fists. "I'm not a liar. I caught it. It was for real."

I threw an appealing gaze toward Mama, but the look she returned intimated that she also believed I was, at the very least, exaggerating the truth.

"Peter, sweetheart, why don't you sit down?" she spoke in a soothing tone. "It's okay that you were late. I forgive you. Let's just finish our dinner together, okay?"

Tears dripped freely down my cheeks, but I obeyed and collapsed into the chair beside Walter. The food on my plate had grown cold waiting for me. Fat was congealing at the edges of my beef, while the vegetables had taken on a consistency of damp rubber.

Next to me, Walter made a fine show of sucking bits of fish off its translucent bones. After all, he had a prize to show for his efforts, and I had nothing.

I wanted to crawl in a hole and die—or, better, wanted Walter to. A moment later, I recanted my wicked thought, not because of any remorse for my malevolence, but because if he did, statues would surely be erected all over town in his honor.

Mama tried to ask about my day—what I did at school, played at recess—but I barely mustered one-word responses. Meanwhile, I managed only to eat a couple bites of meat and potatoes. My appetite had vanished along with my catch.

"Can I be excused?" I asked after three short minutes. "I'm not hungry, Mama."

Concern was a rare guest upon her dazzling face, but that evening it came for a visit. She eyed me long and hard, like a doctor inspecting a nasty wound and wondering how she might possibly cure it. She must have come up empty-handed, because she nodded and said, "You're excused. Why don't you go upstairs and do your homework?"

Head hanging, I shuffled wearily to Walter's and my room. My schoolbag sat on my bed. Mama had moved it there from the porch, but I was too exhausted to consider doing homework. Instead, I shoved the schoolbag with its unwanted nuisances to the floor and collapsed into the soft warmth of my bed. The afternoon's events revolved through my mind but went nowhere, like wheels spinning uselessly in a mudhole. I didn't want them there, but I seemed unable to push them away.

My spiraling ruminations screeched to a halt only when I heard the bedroom door open. I assumed it was Mama, coming to apologize and talk through what had happened.

Yet again, the Universe gave me the finger.

"What do you want, Walter?" I growled through clenched teeth.

"What do you mean, little brother?" he responded, adopting a veneer of hurt innocence. "Last I checked, this was my room too."

I sat up, glowering. "You know, I don't care if you don't believe me. I *did* catch that fish."

"I believe you," he said, and for a moment I thought he was sincere. "I also believe a *real* goblin stole our sugar and led us to his *real* hideout on the Isle. And I believe that leprechauns ride unicorns to magical lands in the middle of the earth."

Mustering whatever menace I could, I approached him until we were chest to chest.

"Take. It. Back."

He shoved me, and I lurched backward.

"If I take back calling *you* a liar," he reasoned with a sneer, "then that would make *me* a liar. So ... no. I don't think I will." He appraised me, his fuming, weak little brother, and added, "What're you gonna do about it? Cry some more?"

Truth be told, I didn't know what I was going to do about it. Just like when I had seen Hattie holding his hand, I felt frozen in place.

"That's what I thought," he taunted. "I guess I'll leave so you can cry in peace, little baby."

Coward that I was, I couldn't work up the nerve to assault him when he was facing me. But the moment he turned toward the door, I attacked. I flew forward, closing the gap between us, my fist cocked and ready to smash his stupid skull open.

Walter spun to confront me. Taking immediate notice of my incoming punch, he twirled aside and out of harm's way with all the fluid grace of a ballet dancer. His quick thinking left me clobbering nothing but air, and as my momentum carried me around, Walter pressed his foot into my lower back and shoved—*hard*.

The next thing I knew was blood. Gouts of it, from what I could tell. Gushing over my left eye and down my nose, into my mouth and onto the hardwood below.

"God damn you, Walter!" I screamed.

I lay in a collapsed heap at the foot of our shared dresser, hands clamped over my face. Above me, the corner of an open bin was smeared with blood where it had made contact with my eyebrow.

It might have been the first time in my life that I'd seen Walter truly horrified. The color drained from his cheeks, and his mouth hung agape. He stared at me, petrified where he stood. He turned whiter still when we heard footsteps thundering up the stairs.

"Whose filthy mouth—!" Mama hollered as she threw open the door. Never had I seen her so enraged. But the moment she caught sight of my crimson face and shirt, the rising flood of her wrath subsided.

Walter took the stand in his immediate defense. "I didn't mean to! He tried to hit me, and—"

A surprising calm settled over Mama as she cut him off. Softly but firmly, she said, "Walter, go downstairs. Abigail is in the kitchen. Tell her to phone Dr. Schumacher and ask if he'll make a house call this late."

"Okay," he mumbled miserably.

"And Walter," she added, somewhat more sternly, "do *not* come back here when you're finished. Get Pip and yourself ready for bed, and then both of you are to sleep in his room. Do you understand?"

Walter nodded glumly. He had disappointed Mama. As he exited our bedroom, self-loathing painted itself upon his every feature.

Cradling the bump in her stomach and groaning at the effort of it, Mama knelt beside me. Taking Walter's pillow from his bed, she stripped off its case and pressed it against my eyebrow, stemming the free flow of blood. To my surprise, she then stood and walked out, leaving me alone with only pain and fear to keep me company. She returned a minute later with a pile of towels and damp washrags. Using the former, she sponged the blood as best she could from my face, chin, and clothes, and from the floor. With the damp rags, she then scrubbed at the places where blood had already begun drying.

All this she did in silence. It made me queasy to wonder what she was thinking. Certainly she hadn't forgotten the foul language that had sent her running upstairs in the first place. A whole caravan of possible punishments was undoubtedly parading through her head, and she was debating which of them would best fit my crime.

I could almost taste the soap.

When she finally spoke, there was already a pile of blood-stained linens in the corner.

"Keep that held tight against your eye," she instructed, indicating the rag in my hand, "and let's move you to your bed."

I proceeded to lie down on my mattress, but she told me to stay sitting instead.

"It'll bleed less if you keep your cut elevated," she explained. "Dr. Schumacher will have to stitch it, I'm afraid, and he won't be here for a while—if at all tonight."

As if on cue, Abigail entered the room and said, "The doctor will be here as soon as he can." Noticing the pile of towels in the corner, she asked, "Want me to take those downstairs, Missus Luther?"

"Yes, thank you."

Before Abigail left with the armful of bloody rags, I asked her, "Do you think I should eat some ginger? Would that help?"

Abigail appeared confused, as if I had lost too much blood and was now talking nonsense. Then the light of understanding flickered, and she remembered our kitchen conversation from the previous spring.

She chuckled and said, "No, Little Mister Luther, I'm afraid not. It'll work like medicine on sickness *inside* the body, but it can't do much against an open wound like yours."

Abigail left, and Mama peered down at her crimson hands.

"I should wash up. But when I come back, we're going to have a chat about what happened."

She returned a minute later with clean hands and sat beside me. Wrapping a tender arm around my shoulders, she pulled me against herself and began caressing my upper arm with her thumb.

I leaned my head upon her breast and closed my eyes.

"It's going to leave a stain," she said. "Your blood, I mean. I couldn't scrub it out of the wood in time."

"I'm sorry," I whimpered. "At least it'll be on Walter's side."

Mama's arm drooped. She scooted a few inches away and gazed down at me. Lines of worry creased her brow as she asked, "Peter, what's going on with you two?"

"He wouldn't believe me about the fish," I answered.

"Is that really what this is all about? A *fish?*" She shook her head. "No. There's more to it than that. *Why* did it matter so much to you?"

I squirmed uncomfortably. "Walter always has to be better than me at everything. He treats me like I'm a worthless baby."

"*Are* you a worthless baby?"

"No, but—"

"And is he really better than you at *everything?*"

I thought a moment, then said, "Not everything. I'm better at school. And I can read better than him. *And* I really did catch a bigger fish tonight! Even if no one else believes me, I know it happened."

Mama leaned forward and kissed the top of my head. She pulled me close again, cradling me in the crook of her arm as she ran her fingers through my white-blond hair.

"I hope you know you're every bit as special as Walter, and you don't need to prove it. Not with a fish. Not with anything. Okay? And as soon as you stop trying, I think you'll be a lot happier."

Ignoring the fact that Mama still hadn't voiced any belief in my fish story, I snuggled closer to her and breathed deeply. Her scent was sweet and fragrant, imbued with the flowers she loved so much.

Usually I found deep comfort in Mama's words of affirmation. But that night, they were like a bandage covering a deep gash. They weren't altogether useless—a bandage will sop up a bit of blood, after all—but my inner wounds, and the pain they caused, remained. Hattie had still chosen Walter. Walter, whom I did look up to, even if I wouldn't admit it, still treated me like an ulcer in an ass-crack. And, lurking even beneath these, was the bubbling sense of dread brought on by the overheard conversation about The Flu.

The world used to seem so solid and certain. Now it was liquid. Inconstant and unreliable.

This plunge into the murky ocean of uncertainty was confirmed moments later, when the bedroom door burst open.

It was Daddy.

He didn't need to speak a single word. His expression was enough for me to know that something was terribly, horribly wrong.

ELEVEN

First of the Funerals

I HAD FORGOTTEN ABOUT DADDY'S earlier absence at dinner. Now, as he stood in my doorway, I saw on his face a visible manifestation of the fear which had been creeping into my own heart. His normally rich complexion looked pallid and worn. His hair, always so neatly combed, was ruffled and unkempt, and caused me to wonder if he had also been in a fight.

Mama likewise discerned that something was amiss. Standing to attention, she asked, "What is it, John? What's happened?"

Daddy's voice was hollow and distant. "We decided to close down early today."

"What do you mean? Was there an accident? Is everyone alright?"

"Not an accident. Sickness. Dr. Schumacher says it's The Flu, but that it's worse than before. Two of our underground workers got it, and three from the plant. They all have fevers, among other symptoms."

"Who?" Mama inquired. Her brow was furrowed with concern.

"Carl Sanderson and Jacob Stern from the mine. Then the Arndt twins went home from the plant this afternoon. And just before I left the office, Doc called to tell me Caleb Lasseter fell ill this evening. Same thing."

I could hardly believe my ears. Caleb Lasseter? Not six hours ago I had over-heard him talking with Miss Carrington outside the school doors, and he sounded healthy as a horse. How could that change so quickly? It seemed impossible. Surreal.

Mama wrapped her arms around Daddy and kissed him. She flashed him her brightest smile and said, "Everything will be fine. It'll blow over before too long. Like last time."

"Yeah. Probably." Daddy didn't sound convinced.

"Any idea how long you'll be closed?"

"For the time being, tomorrow and through the weekend. We'll let everything air out a bit."

"It's probably a good idea. And it wouldn't hurt for you and Jacob to relax a few days in the meantime. Play your violin. Play with your boys. Play with *me.*"

Daddy's attempted grin was flimsy and false. "That sounds alright, I suppose. A couple days off will be good for everyone. Especially since we decided to pay our workers for whatever time they're missing."

Mama's admiration was deep and genuine as she said, "That's very good of you, my good husband."

Their embrace lingered. Daddy only broke it when he saw the reddening pillowcase pressed against my forehead and realized his home had also witnessed recent turmoil.

"What happened here?" he asked.

"Only a little roughhousing that got out of control," Mama lied. "Dr. Schumacher is on his way over to patch him up. It's nothing a few stitches won't remedy."

I could hardly believe my ears. For a moment it seemed like a fresh betrayal, Mama's covering for Walter. I wanted my villainous brother to pay for what he had done, and if Daddy knew, Walter certainly would have. But my ire cooled when I realized Mama had also failed to mention both my cursing of Walter *and* the fact that I had assaulted him first. If she had, my hide would have ended up redder than the bloody linen on my face, right along with Walter's.

I decided to call it even.

"You boys need to be more careful," Daddy said. He was trying his hardest to scold me, but his words were flat.

"We will," I promised. "Sorry."

Daddy winked and offered me the weariest of smiles, then said, "I'm beat. I think I'll eat something and go to bed."

"Sounds like you need it," said Mama. "And John, please don't worry yourself sick. Everything will be fine in a couple days. I'm sure of it."

And, for the next twenty-four hours, I believed Mama's ironclad assurances to be as irrefutable as they had been in the past. Dr. Schumacher wove four stitches into my left eyebrow. The bleeding turned to sticky ooze and then into a scab. The next day at school, Walter was kinder to me than ever before—grateful, I'm sure, to have escaped a grisly fate at the retributive hands of Daddy. He had no idea it was Mama, not me, to thank for his narrow escape.

When we returned home that afternoon, Daddy informed us that Caleb Lasseter was expected to make a full recovery, and that a couple of his other workers already had. My family spent the evening enjoying a picnic in Asphodel's fragrant orchards. This was followed by freshly baked sugar cookies and a game of croquet. Besides having to go to school, it was such a wonderful day, I almost didn't care that Walter beat me by three strokes.

Even when he caught me that night, stroking the cool fabric of my bibby along my cheek, Walter kept his usual insults to himself. Since the following day was Saturday, I fell into a worriless sleep, wondering how the weekend could possibly outdo such a superb evening.

But the next day brought a drizzly gloom, the kind that keeps even adventurous boys indoors. Daddy fiddled to liven things up in our Castle Home, but it wasn't long before his tunes took on a mournful spirit.

At half past noon, the telephone rang. Daddy answered in his den. The closed door muffled the conversation, but we gleaned enough from his tone to know it wasn't some trivial chat about the weather. He hung up, and minutes of tense silence followed.

The rest of us, including Mama, eventually worked up the courage to enter unbidden. We needed to know what had transpired.

Unable to muster more than a whisper, Daddy said, "Caleb took a turn for the worse. Doc doesn't think he'll make it long."

The physician's prophecy came to pass before midnight.

I never would have thought I might someday feel bad for Jeremiah Lasseter, but at his daddy's funeral that Monday morning, I couldn't help myself. The same kid who'd delighted in making other kids cry was crying himself, tears streaming like someone had pulled the stoppers out of his eyes. In a matter of hours, his world had shattered, and there was no one left to help him sweep up the jagged shards. The tormenter had become the tormented, and I could only imagine what would become of my orphaned schoolmate.

Despite my surge of empathy, I found I couldn't say anything at all to him. I wanted to, but I was unable to think of a single word that might unburden him of even an ounce of his fierce grief. Besides that, I figured enough of the adults were already lavishing their condolences on him. I could talk to him at school the next day, and my compassion would speak louder when it wasn't being drowned out by so many others.

That was why, when I passed by him after the funeral proceedings, I averted my gaze and stared at my feet.

It was the last time I ever saw Jeremiah Lasseter. When we arrived at school the next day, his desk was empty. Cleared out. Immediately, the rumors flew. Joe Murdoch claimed Jeremiah had hopped a westbound train to dig for gold in California. Cassandra Dieter heard he had already gone to—and been kicked out of—an orphanage in Philadelphia.

The truth was far less outrageous. Daddy, whose ears were well-attuned to the news of Pierre, explained that Caleb's estranged but well-to-do brother had taken Jeremiah to live with him in Manhattan. Overnight, he had gone from rural bumpkin to big-city elite. Fate, it seemed, had shown at least a modicum of mercy by elevating the orphaned boy to a loftier social stratum.

But the disappearance of Jeremiah Lasseter wasn't the only big news to occur that Monday. Shortly before our afternoon dismissal, an elderly gentleman wearing a severe and indelible frown stepped into the classroom. I had seen him once before, but I didn't know his name, only that he was a member of the Pierre school board.

Miss Carrington instructed us to give him our attention, then stepped aside.

I could've sworn I heard the old man's jaw creak when he spoke. With an airy voice, he said, "My name is Olaf Kirk. I've been a member of the Pierre Primary School Board for over four decades, but what I am about to share with you is utterly unprecedented during my time here."

The electricity of gossipy whispers buzzed through the classroom.

"Silence, please!" he demanded, raising a stern hand.

We shut up. Not so much out of respect, but because we needed to know what could have dragged this wrinkled bag of bones up from his crypt and into our classroom.

Olaf Kirk went on. "Due to the global events which have recently made their way into our little town, the board feels compelled to take drastic action. For the safety of our students and teachers alike, Pierre Primary School will be closed until further notice."

The hum among the students grew to a roar. This time old Olaf didn't attempt to quiet us. He merely ceded his front-and-center position back to Miss Carrington and left the room.

She tried to regain control, but apparently no longer had any—not "until further notice," anyway. As students packed their belongings, she implored us to bring our books home and keep up with daily lessons, but she would have had more success asking a snake to tap dance. Sure, our freedom had come through unconventional means, but it was still freedom, and we were dead set on milking every second from it.

It was the gift of a second summer. A new lease to maraud about our forest and lakeshore. During our walk home, Walter and I made plans to trap a bear, build a wigwam, kill and skin a couple raccoons to make caps from their hides, draw a map of our Isle, and restore the cabin which stood upon it. With indefinite amounts of time and a hoard of imagination, we would accomplish every goal set before us.

When we arrived home, I was surprised to see Daddy smoking his pipe on the front porch. A tumbler of brownish liquid sat in his other hand, which he eyed earnestly as it sloshed to the rhythm of his ponderous rocking.

"Whatcha doing home, Daddy?" Walter asked. Without waiting for an answer, he added, "Someone from the school board came in today. He told us school's canceled."

Daddy nodded thoughtfully. "I heard that would be happening. And I'm home for a similar reason. Mr. Jansen and I are keeping the mine closed until we can figure out how to deal with this Flu."

"Okay. Well, we're gonna go play," my aloof brother replied, and off we went to make good on his word.

"Before you go, Peter," said Daddy, verbally restraining me as Walter marched inside to drop off his schoolbag, "make sure you're back here by five o'clock. Dr. Schumacher is stopping by to check on your eye and remove your stitches."

"Okay, Daddy!" I replied, hurrying off after my brother.

Such is the way of the young. In our shortsightedness, we neither knew nor cared to know The Flu's devastating impacts on the wider world around us. We were concerned only for the immediate implications upon our tiny kingdom at Asphodel Glade. By our reckoning, it was The Flu which had bequeathed unto us the manifold possibilities of newfound liberty.

And so, despite its accompanying undercurrent of fear, The Flu became something of a hero to the schoolchildren of Pierre, Pennsylvania. It was a savage, revolutionary leader, upending the establishment and placing itself into the seat of supreme authority.

Its first magnanimous decree? "No more school! Be free!"

Like peasants suckered by the candy-coated speech of a demagogue, we rode high on The Flu's promises of an eternal summer.

But its opiates wouldn't remain in our system long. In only two days' time, the one we hailed as our hero would remove its mask.

Then we would finally see the ruthless dictator for what it had been all along.

TWELVE

The Personal Memoirs of A. W. Vandenberg

WEDNESDAY MORNING ARRIVED, bringing with it the first true chill of infant autumn. Gold filigree already embroidered much of summer's emerald store, and the change of seasons would soon alchemize many of those leaves into luminous yellows and vibrant oranges. Others, such as those of the maples, would become steeped in noble blood, bearing a royal red until they fell brown and dead to the earth.

The day began for me and Walter as many chilly fall days do—with great hesitation to emerge from our cozy cocoons. Eventually, the promising aroma of breakfast tore down our walls of resistance, and we rose from our slumber, disheveled and quite un-butterflylike.

We found Mama and Pip already sitting in the dining room. They munched happily on the crispy bacon strips and syrup-slathered pancakes Abigail had prepared. A platter of scrambled eggs and a bowl of fresh fruit—apples and grapes—completed the well-rounded meal.

"Morning, sleepybones-es!" trumpeted Pip, who had learned a new word from our mother while we slept.

Mama wore a goldenrod play dress and had tied two ribbons of similar color into her hair. By the looks of the dirt beneath her fingernails, she had been awake and active for some time, and I wondered what sort of adventures we might have that day.

"I'm glad you finally decided to join us. Hattie is coming soon," Mama informed us, as we sat half-asleep at the table and began eating.

I sensed Walter bristle beside me. He and Hattie hadn't spoken a word since last week's fight.

"We might as well have some fun together with all this time off!" Mama continued after hearing no response from us. In her cryptic way, she added, "I learned something curious about Asphodel Glade yesterday and would like to see whether it's true."

"Will Daddy play with us too?" I asked, noting his empty place at the breakfast table.

Mama frowned and shook her head. "No. He went to work even before I got up."

"Why?" asked Walter. "Isn't everything shut down?"

"Yes, but I think he and Jacob want to figure out how they can open again safely. I do wish he would've taken more than a day off, but I suppose people still have to earn money somehow, even in a world with this Flu."

The fog of sleep was evaporating from Walter's head. He discerned that Mama's clever mind had been busy planning something, and he asked, "So what is it you learned about Asphodel?"

Mama chuckled and wagged a finger. "No answers yet! I want to wait for Hattie. In the meantime, you might want to make yourselves look a little less like ogres and more like princes. After you're done eating, of course."

An hour later, our stomachs were full, hair brushed, and every bit of sleep's residue washed or rubbed away. Clad in long-sleeved shirts and woolen trousers, we were prepared for a cool day outdoors.

The moment I saw Hattie upon the rise of the hill, I ran up the cart path to meet her.

Pip followed close behind, waving a snacking pancake and yelling, "Morning, Hattie!"

Hearing my brother, I was struck by an acute awareness. By running out to greet her, was *I* behaving like a little kid? Since Hattie was six months older than me, maybe that was how she had begun to see me—like a child, as her sister Arlene had for all of us. Maybe that's why she had chosen to give her affections to Walter instead of me.

I slowed to a casual walk and vowed to conduct myself as an adult from that point forward.

"Hi, Pippie!" Hattie exclaimed, returning my brother's greeting. He jumped at her, and she wrapped him in a hug.

Adopting a dash of Walter's trademark indifference, I said, "Hey, Hattie. We've been waiting for you."

She rolled her eyes, annoyed, but not at me, as she said, "Sorry. Mother kept making me change into warmer and warmer things. Said she didn't want to give The Flu any chance."

Hattie did appear a bit overstuffed. Beneath her peacoat wrapping, she appeared more layered than an onion.

I chuckled. If Walter's horrid treatment of her had indeed given me an opening, I wouldn't miss the opportunity to stick my foot in the door.

"Ditch whatever you want in the house," I said. "Mama won't tell on you."

As we walked toward the Castle Home, Hattie offered up the latest "intown" gossip.

"Did you hear Anita Morton got The Flu?" she asked. She kept her voice low so that Pip, hurrying ahead of us, wouldn't hear.

"Can't say I feel sorry for her," I said, envisioning the prissy girl hogging the school outhouse the other day. "But I hope she gets better anyway."

"Sally Steinbrenner too," Hattie added. "And Patrick McCann. I heard he's the sickest one. Fever so high, he doesn't even know what planet he's on."

That last one made me a bit queasy. Patrick was a copper-haired fifth grader only a few months older than Walter. He was respectful to teachers, kind to the younger students, and studious—the antithesis of Jeremiah Lasseter. On some level, what had happened to Jeremiah seemed balanced on Lady Justice's scales. But for Patrick to fall so terribly ill? It could only be a miscarriage of all that was fair and decent.

"Good thing we haven't been in school with them since Monday," I said, "or else we'd probably have it too."

"Mother says everyone's gonna get this one sooner or later. And Father—well, he's right scared of the whole thing. He wouldn't've let me come, but he's at work and Mother decided not to ask him."

I frowned. Life without Hattie would hardly be worth living. I prayed Mrs. Jansen would keep letting her come *and* keep it a secret from her husband.

Mama, descending the front steps to meet us, looked Hattie up and down with distaste. "It must be a thousand degrees beneath all those layers. Go ahead and leave what you want inside. We'll wait out here."

Hattie returned one minute later and twenty pounds lighter.

Mama wasted no time. She pointed at a pair of shovels leaning against the far end of the raised porch. One was caked in newly tilled earth.

"Walter, Peter, each of you grab a shovel," she instructed cheerfully, "and everyone can follow me!"

Asphodel Glade was awash in copious sunshine that morning as we paraded off with Mama, shovels in hand. We exchanged quizzical glances back and forth, wondering *what* and *where* we would be digging. Perhaps Mama had heard about our plans to trap a bear and had drawn up schematics for a deep pit with sharp spikes at the bottom. When she set course for her gardens, I next thought she was tricking us into work. To my relief, we skirted past them without incident and continued toward the southwest corner of our property where field, forest, and water all met.

Mama, aware that the four children in tow were about to pop with anticipation, explained, "We have these shovels because we have to dig up a treasure."

My ears perked up. Digging didn't sound all that fantastic, but who could argue with treasure?

She went on. "About a week ago, Daddy discovered a leather journal stuck behind some of the larger books in his den. It was very old and practically crumbling to pieces. He opened it carefully and saw, handwritten in the front cover, that it contained the personal memoirs of a certain A. W. Vandenberg—that's the grandfather of Ephraim Vandenberg, who sold Asphodel to Daddy.

"Well, your Daddy wasn't much interested beyond that, but he thought I might be, so he showed me the journal. It mostly contained records of business transactions and property accumulations and other boring things like that, but as I came to the end, I found something interesting. Folded between the last two pages was a thin slip of paper. Since the date on top was much more recent than the other entries in the book, I suspect A. W. must have been a very old man when he wrote the mysterious sentences I found on it. It said: 'Where northern shore meets western wood, I have lain my treasures beneath the earth. To those who might someday seek these riches, heed my words: The least of them shall become the greatest to the one who perseveres.'"

"But how can the least be the greatest?" Hattie wondered aloud.

"I guess we'll have to find out for ourselves," replied Mama. She held a hand to her lips and coughed deeply in the dry morning air. "But I do have one other important piece of information to share with you: I already found the place where A. W. hid his treasures. I didn't want to get your hopes up only to find nothing at all, which is why I didn't tell you about it until today. But this morning, I woke up early and searched the grounds. And I found *this*."

She reached down the front of her shirt and withdrew from it a golden pocket watch dangling from a chain.

It didn't look like much of a treasure to me. With the dirt and leaf particles clinging to it, *dingy* and *worthless* seemed like better words to describe it.

"It doesn't work, obviously. He must have been a little cuckoo by this point in his life, or else he would have put it inside a container to protect it. But it does prove that *something* is buried out here, exactly like he said!"

"But how do you know it's his?" Hattie asked. Mama had so swept her into the story, she momentarily forgot it was make-believe.

Mama never overlooked the finer details of her games. That's why she was so masterful in disarming our disbelief. At this point, she handed the watch to Hattie and said, "Look on the back and see for yourself."

Hattie rubbed at its grimy surface and exclaimed, "It's his initials! *A. W. V.!*"

"What do you think we'll find there?" a wide-eyed Pip asked in an awestruck whisper.

"We'll only know when we dig and find out," said Mama. Beckoning toward the ground, she added, "And here we are!"

We had come to the furthest corner of Asphodel's lawns, near the place where woods and lakeshore met. The telltale signs of digging were already present here. Black scars of soil marred the green turf, each one marking a location where Mama had undoubtedly buried some sundry for us to find. One larger hole she had left unfilled, presumably that in which she had "discovered" the pocket watch.

"Want me to start digging?" Walter asked Mama.

She coughed and replied, "That *is* why you have a shovel! You too, Peter."

Walter uncovered the first item, a bronze-bordered hand mirror. Like the pocket watch, it was worn and cracked and in great disrepair, a treasure to nobody any longer. Not to be outdone, I found the next two buried "treasures," a set of silver cufflinks and a plain, silver snuff box, both of which went beside the mirror in our unofficial junk pile.

When Hattie wanted a turn, Pip demanded one also. Together they unearthed a steel flask with faded engraving and a tiny pewter figurine of an elephant. The latter of these Pip hurriedly slipped into his pocket, so that he might add it to the collection of toy animals in his nursery. Still, nothing seemed like treasure, so we kept digging in shifts. Over the next half hour, we exhumed an additional pewter figurine of a hippopotamus—also claimed by Pip—a bronze platter, a dented cigarette tin, and a suspiciously familiar fishing lure.

Worn out by digging and disappointment, we four children sat upon the grass. Mama, meanwhile, crossed her arms and stared thoughtfully down at the pile of artifacts.

"It certainly doesn't look valuable anymore," she said, "even if it used to be. You might be able to swap the pewter figurines and snuff box for a bit of candy at Schroeder's Grocery, but the rest looks like trash. Unless ..."

"Unless what?" asked Walter, his interest piqued again.

"Well, it's just that in A. W.'s letter, he said, 'The least of them shall become greatest.' Any idea what that could mean?"

"Maybe it means we need to find the one that's most worthless," I offered. "Maybe there's a clue on it."

As I looked to Mama for validation, I noticed that a hot flush had risen into her cheeks. Strange, since she hadn't done any digging here since early morning.

"Which one do you think looks like the 'least of them'?" she asked us.

"Definitely the mirror," answered Hattie. "It's all broken and rusty. But I don't see anything on it that looks like a clue."

"Let's just look through all of it," suggested Walter. "There isn't much."

The idea was reasonable enough, so the rest of us followed his lead. It didn't take long to find the hidden clue.

"I got it! I got it!" hollered Pip, who had opened the cigarette tin and was now flapping a piece of paper in our faces.

"Gimme that," Walter ordered. He snatched the soiled paper from our little brother's grubby fingers and scanned it silently. "This doesn't make any sense. It's just a bunch of letters."

Hattie and I peered over his shoulders to read the inscription:

VO DNGVIY KZVF DI XVQZ OMZZ ADIY
OMZVNPZY NOJMZ, WPO RVMIDIB HDIY:
OCZ OMDKGZ-CZVYZY CJPIY WZRVMZ!
XZMWZMPN WDOZN RDOCJPO V XVMZ.

"Like I said," Walter emphasized. "Gibberish."

"No it's not," Hattie replied coolly. "You thought some of Gurgan's riddles were nonsense too, but you were plenty wrong about those. Maybe you just need someone with a better brain nearby to make up for the mush inside your head."

Normally, Mama would have reminded us to use kindness and manners with each other, but today she did not.

"What do you think *this* means?" I asked, pointing to a tiny note near the paper's lower margin. "It says, 'Start where Vandenberg begins.'"

"More gibberish," said Walter, doubling down stubbornly. He seemed intent upon driving the wedge deeper between himself and Hattie.

"Maybe we should go inside," Mama said. Her arms were crossed, and she was trying to rub away her goosebumps. "We can warm up while we think about it. Besides, I can't stop shivering, and I'm sure you could all do with a snack."

Back at the house, Abigail prepared us a platter of sliced apples drizzled with melted peanut butter and chocolate. We sat around the dining room table, crunching and brainstorming.

All of us except Mama. She was there, but she ate nothing and said almost as little. She must have been unable to shake off the cold, because she seemed occupied solely with shivering. One palm she kept flat against her protruding belly, which she caressed ponderously from time to time.

The breakthrough regarding A. W. Vandenberg's nonsensical message belonged to Hattie. Her mouth was full of half-chewed apple when she shouted, "I've got it!"

"What?" I asked excitedly.

"I knew I'd seen a code like this once, but I couldn't remember how to solve it," she began. "It just came to me though! We have to use the opposite letter of the alphabet."

"What do you mean?" Walter asked doubtfully.

"I mean that *A* becomes *Z,* and *B* becomes *Y,*" she explained. "You do that with the whole alphabet. Let me see the paper again. Pip, can you find me a pencil?"

As soon as my baby brother returned with Hattie's requested item, she began working furiously. First, she wrote the entire alphabet in its normal A-to-Z order. Then, below it, she wrote the alphabet backwards.

"Now all we have to do is change each letter to the one below it," she said. Her gaze flashed back and forth between A. W.'s note and her work page. As she went, she translated the code and wrote down each new letter.

But she hadn't been working long when her face fell.

"No," she sighed, dropping the pencil. "I guess I was wrong. Everything's still mixed up."

I shared a dejected glance with her. Although we hated giving up and asking for Mama's help, it seemed to be our only remaining option.

Suddenly, something clicked.

"What if it's not the *opposite?*" I suggested. "What if it's only shifted over a little bit?"

Walter rolled his eyes, but Hattie was curious to hear more.

"How so?" she asked.

"The note says, 'Start where Vandenberg begins,' and *Vandenberg* begins with *V,*" I explained.

Taking the paper and pencil from Hattie, I wrote the alphabet again, but instead of starting with *A,* I began it with *V.* When I came to *Z,* instead of ending it there as usual, I wrapped back to the beginning, continuing with *A* and the letters which followed, all the way through *U*. Below that first line of letters, I wrote the alphabet again, normally this time, carefully matching each letter with the one above. When I was finished, I had created a new decoder. Now *V* became *A, A* became *F,* and so on. Every letter corresponded to whichever one was five spaces to its right in the alphabet.

After three minutes spent deciphering the message, I had come up with something that was far from nonsense—or "gibberish," as Walter put it:

> AT ISLAND PEAK IN TREE CAVE FIND
> TREASURE STORE, BUT WARNING MIND:
> THE TRIPLE-HEADED HOUND BEWARE!
> CERBERUS BITES WITHOUT A CARE.

The clue was clear.

We would find our treasure on the Isle across Lake Acheron.

THIRTEEN

Our Treasure

AS WE HAD DONE SO OFTEN DURING the weeks of late spring and summer, we piled into the rowboat. Mama's arms revolved in their rhythmic motion as she propelled us along, but that morning her every movement seemed strained, as if she were rowing through syrup rather than water.

When we arrived at the Isle, she emitted a cough, sharp and hollow, and said, "I'll stay with the boat. All you have to do is hike to the highest point of the island. That's where you'll find A. W.'s tree cave."

That, too, was strange. Usually she let us work clues out for ourselves.

"Before we go, what's a *Cerberus?*" Walter asked. "Is it dangerous?"

"Oh, very!" Mama replied with forced excitement. "Daddy told me about him once. Apparently, Cerberus is a monstrous, three-headed dog. He usually guards the gates of the Underworld to keep the dead from leaving, so whatever he's guarding here must be invaluable. You'll definitely want to be on guard yourself!"

We had explored our Isle many times over the past months. From east to west, north to south, we had walked every inch of it, and so we knew that the island's peak was at its extreme western end. There the island's gradual rise ended upon a high outcropping of exposed rock, which plunged steeply from there into Acheron's deep waters.

Walter led us along the trails we had previously forged by our constant crisscrossing of the Isle. Pip whistled and skipped and twirled his way along, while the rest of us debated what type of treasure we would discover.

"I think it'll be candy," said Walter.

"Maybe money," suggested Hattie.

"I bet it's something we never expected," I theorized. After all, Mama was queen of the unforeseen delight.

As we passed the old cabin, Walter stopped abruptly.

"Anyone else hear that?" he asked.

We strained our ears but, other than the customary twittering of a few song-birds, detected nothing unusual.

"I don't hear it anymore," Walter admitted. "Let's go."

But a little further along, it was Hattie who stopped and said, "I hear something too! Sounds like screaming—or crying!"

I heard it also. My first worried thought was for Mama, but I quickly realized no human, either male or female, could create such a yowling racket. Besides, the shrill cries weren't behind us. They came from the forest ahead.

"Hurry up!" shouted Walter, breaking into a run up the hill. "We're almost there!"

My older brother was faster than the rest of us, and we soon lost sight of him. Fortunately, the hill's crest—or "ISLAND PEAK," according to the decoded message—wasn't far, and we soon broke from the trees onto bare rock. As we scrambled up the remainder of the slope, we saw Walter on top, motionless and staring.

The oak which stood upon the summit had died long before. How it had grown up from a bed of hard stone was a mystery, yet there it stood, threadbare and pocked with woodpecker holes. A handful of its thick lower branches had withstood years of wind, snow, ice, and chewing insects, but Time had stripped away most of the once-great tree. At its base, where trunk met granite, a hollow had formed, so deep that not even the bright sunshine could penetrate its deepest recesses.

It was, by all appearances, exactly what A. W.'s message called it: a "TREE CAVE."

And, leashed in front of the cave, tugging wildly at the rope which bound it there and whipping its tail with lethal excitement, was a puppy. He most notably did not have three heads, and he certainly didn't appear committed to his role as cave guardian.

"Some Cerberus *you* are," said Walter. He stooped and stroked the yellow fuzz around the puppy's face and ears.

The playful fellow returned the greeting with yips, licks, and razor-sharp nibbles.

Hattie, Pip, and I crowded around to shower our affections on the furball. The furball, in turn, became so overwhelmed with excitement that he peed all over our shoes.

"So … what? We take him back with us?" Hattie asked, once she was all petted out.

Walter chuckled and said, "He's the treasure, dummy. Mama got us a puppy! Besides, you wouldn't just leave him here, would you? Come on. Let's untie him and get back to Mama."

I obeyed Walter's suggestion at once. Mama's knot was sound enough to keep the puppy from escaping, but I had no problem undoing it. The puppy must have sensed the moment he was no longer anchored to the tree, because he tried to bolt as soon as I loosened the knot. I managed to keep him from escaping, though he nearly ripped off my arm in the process.

Straining to thwart his many attempts at freedom, I groaned, "What—should we—call him?"

"Well, the letter called him 'Cerberus,'" said Hattie. "Maybe that's his name."

"Yuck," said Walter. "Sounds like a name Daddy would give. I'm gonna call him 'Yosemite.'"

Hattie's face scrunched up, and she said, "That's a stupid name. Besides, why do you get to name him?"

"Because I found him first," Walter answered. "And because I'm the oldest."

"You wouldn't've ever found him if me and Peter hadn't solved the code," argued Hattie. "I say *we* get to name him."

"He's not even your dog!" cried Walter.

Though I was certainly on Hattie's side of the argument, I also didn't want to see a full-blown escalation without my mother present to serve as referee, so I said, "Maybe Mama named him already. Let's take him back and ask. Besides, he's about to pull my arm off."

Walter scoffed at my lack of endurance and said, "Give him here. I'll take him."

I handed off the rope, then turned to face the tree. Mama had left a pair of bowls at the edge of the dark hollow so the puppy would have food and water while he waited for us. As I bent to retrieve them, a dark shape within the dead tree trunk caught my eye.

"There's something inside!" I yelled to the others.

They gave me their attention as I lowered myself onto my hands and knees and reached inside. My fingers closed around something cold and angular, and I pulled it toward me. As I removed the rectangular object from the darkness and set it upon the bald rock, sunlight glinted off its shiny surface.

"It's a jewelry box!" Hattie exclaimed.

We boys were less than excited. It did indeed appear to be a jewelry box, clawfooted and embroidered with golden-hued metalwork.

Walter's initial disappointment was quickly supplanted with a desire to know what Mama had put inside it. "What are you waiting for?" he shouted. "Open it!"

I undid the delicate clasp and raised the lid.

It was another note, written in A. W. Vandenberg's now-familiar scrawl. I lifted it out and read: "'To those who have bested the Hellhound, my treasure I give: A dime apiece with which to see a moving picture show this Friday at the Castleton theater (and an extra so your mother may go with you).'"

In the bottom of the jewelry box, previously hidden by the note, five shiny dimes lay glinting in the late-morning sun.

"What's a moving-picture show?" Pip asked, mystified. He'd never been the owner of a whole dime before.

"A movie with famous actors and actresses, like Mary Pickford and Charlie Chaplin," Hattie answered.

Pip shrugged. He also knew nothing of actors or actresses.

"Never mind," said Walter. "You'll just have to wait and see what it is when we go on Friday."

"I hope my father lets me," Hattie remarked quietly.

"Why wouldn't he?" Walter asked, a hint of concern slipping past his mask of indifference.

"Like I told Peter before, he's scared of The Flu. He doesn't want me doing anything with anyone until it's all over."

"If Mama put a dime in there for you, she'll make sure you get to go, one way or another," Walter assured her. Despite their sharp squabble about naming the puppy, he now sounded surprisingly sweet. "We'll bust you out if we have to."

As Hattie turned red, I was turning green.

"Let's get back to Mama," I interjected, before either could pursue any further healing of their rift. "She'll get worried if we're gone too long."

Everyone agreed with this plan. Fifty cents and a new puppy richer, we paraded across the Isle to Emerald Hill.

Mama sat at the foot of the slope near the water's edge, staring out across the lake and lost in her thoughts. Much like that long-ago day when we had hunted for Gurgan's treasure, she seemed to be gazing upon things the rest of us couldn't see.

A happy yip from the puppy startled her, and she looked up at us. She scrambled to her feet at once, eager to greet her triumphant children.

That was when her eyes rolled up into her head, and she collapsed upon the grass.

"Mama!" Walter screamed.

He dropped the puppy's leash. Faster than a greased jackrabbit, he sprinted to Mama's side. There, he dropped to his knees, cradled her limp head in his arms, and began to cry.

The rest of us stood, frozen to the earth, fearful and watching.

The puppy's excitement upon seeing Mama was nothing less than explosive. He shoved his muzzle between Walter's and Mama's heads and, as if she were made of ice cream, assaulted her with his pink tongue.

His aggressive love worked faster than smelling salts. Mama's eyelids fluttered, and she raised an arm to shove the exuberant puppy away.

Walter, ecstatic upon realizing Mama was alive, cried even harder. He shamelessly clung to her as she sat up and wrapped her arms around him.

"I think I stood up too fast," she speculated. "Must've made me lightheaded."

For once, I didn't believe Mama. Everything about her felt forced. Off. Like a bad actress trying to put on a good show.

She swayed as Walter helped her to her feet. Her cheeks, which earlier had taken on a faint rouge, were now an angry red. Nor was the color confined only to her cheeks. Her neck and forehead were also burning with heat.

Mama laid her palms on her pregnant stomach, feeling it for movement. She gave a relieved sigh, then stared down, glassy-eyed, at the puppy running laps around her ankles.

"I'm glad you found him," she mumbled. With an almost dreamlike grin upon her lips, she saw Hattie approaching her with the jewelry box. "You found the treasure too. Good. I was afraid you wouldn't look inside the tree after your encounter with my ferocious monster."

"Let's go home, Mama," Walter said worriedly. There was only one treasure he cared about now.

Nobody objected. We were rattled too.

But when Mama tried sitting in her usual rower's position, Walter did object. "No. I'll do it. You can sit and rest and play with the puppy."

"I'll be fine," she countered. "Really. Besides, you've never rowed before."

Walter finally put his diamond-coated stubbornness to good use, saying, "I know how. I've watched you plenty."

Mama didn't argue further. Everyone climbed aboard the rowboat, and I untied us before jumping inside it myself.

I hated feeling in awe of Walter, but that day I did. As if he'd been rowing a hundred years, his arms flowed in the same circular motion he had observed so many times in Mama. Though only ten, he powered us toward the mainland with the strength and skill of a man twice his age. Indeed, he even exceeded Mama.

Whereas she frequently drifted off course and required a navigator to help her adjust, Walter's bearing was steady, and our boat an arrow upon Acheron's waters.

Daddy's mantle clock struck a single chime when we entered Asphodel's empty Great Room. Immediately, Mama made for the sofa and collapsed upon it.

"I'll get you something to drink," Walter told her. "What do you want?"

"Tea would be wonderful, Wahwie," Mama answered weakly. "And water."

My big brother nodded, then hurried to the kitchen to make good his word.

"Me too! Me too! But I want ice in mine!" shouted Pip, who scurried away after him.

The puppy, introduced to an exotic new environment, began his dutiful work of cataloging every scent of every floorboard and piece of furniture in the Great Room. But when the door to Daddy's den opened, he abandoned his quest in pursuit of something far more fascinating: the making of yet another friend. Like a swashbuckling musketeer's blade, the ebullient puppy's tail sliced back and forth through the air as he bounded toward Daddy.

"Daddy, look!" shouted Pip, dashing in from the kitchen. "We found a puppy!"

"Did you ever!" Daddy exclaimed, as the puppy planted two oversized paws on his thigh.

Home from work much earlier than we had expected, Daddy now scratched the dog's thick scruff. In return, his hands received a foamy glaze of slobber. Shooting a meaningful glance at Mama, he added, "And look! He's already an inside-the-house dog."

For once, Mama didn't engage his banter. She simply replied, "Oh. Sorry about that. I wasn't thinking."

Daddy's playfulness was swallowed by instant concern. Leaving the puppy heartbroken behind him, Daddy knelt in front of Mama and asked, "Are you okay? You don't look so good, Freckles."

"I'm fine," she said. "I think I need a hot drink to warm me up, that's all."

Abigail, who had materialized at Mama's side from seemingly nowhere, disagreed. "No, that is not *all*, Missus Luther. You look like you washed your face in beet juice." She pressed a hand against Mama's forehead and rapidly withdrew it. "You're burning with fever! Upstairs with you. Now."

Daddy helped Mama to her feet. Together, with Abigail's hand on Mama's back for extra support, they staggered to the stairs.

Hattie, Pip, and I dumbly watched their laborious climb to the second floor. Whatever bug Mama had caught was overtaking her—and *fast*. Hardly three hours had passed since Hattie's arrival at Asphodel, yet during that short time, Mama had deteriorated from picture of vibrant health to wobbling invalid.

Our puppy tried to follow them, but I grabbed his leash. He whined and thrashed and glared indignantly at me, but I didn't yield. He relaxed only when Hattie squatted beside him and began stroking the length of his back.

"Where'd Mama go?"

I turned around. Walter stood in the kitchen doorway. His mouth hung open, and he held the steaming mug of tea he had prepared for her.

"Upstairs," was my dazed reply. "With Daddy and Abigail."

"Why? What happened?"

"Mama's sick," Pip answered casually, as if everything were as normal as sweat in summer or apples in autumn. He had knelt in front of the puppy and was now trying to teach him how to shake.

"I'll—I'll bring her tea upstairs, then," Walter announced. He was trying to appear brave, but unmistakable fear had filled his every pore.

Keeping the mug steady and level to avoid sloshing any tea over its lip, he made for the stairs.

He stopped mid-step, startled by a trio of staccato *thuds* above us. It sounded like someone had dropped an armload of bowling balls on the upstairs floor.

The reality was far more distressing. I knew it, even before Daddy's uncharacteristic cry of "Dammit!" reached my ears.

The "bowling balls" were Mama. She had collapsed onto her bedroom floor.

Walter dropped the mug, tea and all, and bounded up the stairs two at a time.

Only then did I admit what I'd been trying for the past hour to deny.

The Flu had come. It had invaded our kingdom of Asphodel Glade and claimed its first victim.

Mama. Our sunshine and our very joy.

It had come for our treasure.

FOURTEEN

An Owl in the Night

"WHAT SHOULD WE DO?" HATTIE ASKED, her voice cracking with worry.

"I—I don't know," I replied numbly, still unable to believe how this day of wonder had so quickly mutated into a waking nightmare.

Almost as soon as he disappeared up the stairs, Walter was thundering back down them. Without a word to us, he raced into the den.

We rushed to the door and found him furiously winding the crank on our bulky, wall-mounted telephone. He jammed the earpiece against his head and waited for the operator's voice.

"Dr. Schumacher," he pleaded. "It's an emergency."

A long pause followed. During it, we watched Walter's face transform from panicked to confused to horrified—then back to panicked all over again.

"Well, is there a doctor you *can* connect me to?" he demanded, his impatience bordering on rudeness. "Why didn't you tell me that before? ... Sorry, I didn't mean that ... Please, my Mama is sick ... Okay, thank you."

Hattie and I traded grim glances. We could hear only one side of the conversation and didn't fully understand what was happening. Whatever the case, it certainly sounded as though Dr. Schumacher was unable to come and save the day as he had for me last week.

"Hello, Mr. Heuer," Walter said after another brief silence. "This is Walter Luther ... Would you please check in on my Mama? She's burning with fever ... Yes ... Only a little bit ago, happened real fast ... Thank you ... You know where we live? ... Asphodel Glade, just a couple miles west and then south at the big sign ... Thank you ... Goodbye."

He hung up, and a hopeless groan escaped his lips. His head slumped forward against the telephone box.

"Mr. Heuer is coming to help Mama," Walter informed us.

"Who's that?" I asked. "Where's Dr. Schumacher?"

"Mr. Heuer is his apprentice," Walter said, in answer of the first question. "But Dr. Schumacher can't help us. He's got The Flu himself."

Nausea and revulsion stirred awake within me, as I realized the full implications of Walter's revelation. Dr. Schumacher, who had visited our house less than two days ago to remove my stitches, was bedridden with The Flu. And Mama had sat right next to me during the entire checkup. Though he hadn't yet exhibited any visible symptoms, he'd been breathing invisible germs all over us both. Whatever viruses had entered my system, I'd fought off and overcome—at least so far. In Mama, however, they had nested, multiplied, and spread their infection. Silently at first, until the proper time to reveal themselves had come.

Now their warfare had begun. Activated like sleeper agents, they were fully engaged in their devastating campaign.

The stakes? Mama's very life.

Worse, I knew whose fault it was.

Mine.

If I hadn't taken a swing at Walter, he wouldn't have shoved me into the dresser. I wouldn't have sliced open my eyebrow. Dr. Schumacher wouldn't have come to stitch me up, and his infection would have remained his own. If only I had swallowed my pride and controlled my anger, we would be outside with Mama right now, teaching our puppy new tricks, drinking hot apple cider, and basking in autumn's contemplative weather.

The guilt that settled upon my chest was a slab of granite. Crushing me. Stealing my breath. Suffocating me beneath its weight.

If Mama didn't recover, I would see the person to blame every time I looked in the mirror.

Mr. Heuer arrived that afternoon wearing a gauze mask. He diagnosed Mama with The Flu—no surprises there—but regretfully explained there was little he could do on her behalf. As with any other virus, he told us to keep her hydrated and feed her as normal, even to force these things on her if she refused them. He left a few extra masks in Daddy's care and recommended that those tending to Mama wear them.

Then he was gone, and Mama's life fell into the hands of Daddy and Abigail.

And, as it turned out, Eli's.

That afternoon, after Hattie left to return home, was the first time I ever saw him in Asphodel Hall for a non-maintenance-related reason. With his pronounced limp, he staggered up the stairs carrying a sloshing basin of ice water. Not long after this, he was sent to gather every available towel and washrag he could find. Then it was a tray of hot tea and crackers, balanced steadily in his weather-beaten hands.

As a rule—his, not ours—he didn't speak a word to us, and he avoided eye contact at all costs. But he was *there.* His mere presence was reassuring. Mama was not alone. All of Asphodel Glade was fighting for her! What match could one tiny virus pose against us all?

Nevertheless, a pall settled over the Castle Home. My brothers and I spent little time outdoors, even when Daddy encouraged it. Mostly we hung around our bedrooms, waiting for any updates or news. Pip played with his toys. Walter thumbed through pamphlets and magazines about the natural wonders depicted on his bedside posters. I tried to read L. Frank Baum's *The Wonderful Wizard of Oz* but found myself constantly distracted. Every noise I heard down the hallway drew my focus away from what I was reading, as I sought to glean any possible information about Mama's condition.

We hardly saw Daddy during those days, and when we did, the lighthearted father we had known now brooded beneath tempestuous clouds. He forbade us from entering their bedroom, citing our own safety as the reason. He ate little and slept even less. When Mama was awake, he played his violin to soothe her. When she was asleep or too disoriented with fever even to speak, he read aloud from her favorite authors. If he wasn't in the room with Mama, it meant he was outside, puffing solemnly on his pipe, or catching a few hours of troubled rest on the nest of blankets in the corner of his study. Certainly he had abandoned any notion of spending time at the coal mine. His loyalty was to Mama alone. Even we boys became fatherless, so great was his devotion to her.

Besides Daddy, Abigail, and Eli, the only other person allowed inside the room was Pastor Wainwright. Perhaps he was fearless, or perhaps his dedication to his parishioners outweighed his worries of contracting The Flu. Whatever the case, he visited frequently during Mama's illness, disappearing for long stretches behind the bedroom door. Each time he left, he gathered me and my brothers for a brief prayer before moving on to other clerical business.

I didn't think God was listening. And if he was, he definitely wasn't doing a good job answering.

The days wore on, and as they did, a change came over Walter too. At first, he believed it unthinkable that Mama wouldn't recover. After all, she had assured him on numerous occasions that the Luthers had nothing to worry about. But with the rising of each new sun, he grew exponentially perturbed.

On the fourth day of Mama's illness, Walter dragged the chair from his homework desk and stationed it outside her bedroom door. There he sat, unmoving as a statue for hours on end, like a heartsick dog waiting for its master to come home. Every time Mama hacked her dry, barking cough, Walter would go rigid with his ears perked up and whine pitifully. Only when each fit passed could he relax again. That night, he removed the blanket and pillow from his bed, and did his best to make himself comfortable on the hallway floor outside her door.

On day five, Sunday afternoon, a sleek black car parked in front of our house. A man dressed in a snappy black suit stepped out of the Model L and placed a dark mask over his mouth and nose. From the backseat, he retrieved a hefty leather bag.

I answered the door when he knocked.

"Good day," he said, brisk and businesslike. "I'm Dr. Caraway."

Since I knew nothing of any Dr. Caraway, I stared dumbly up at his gaunt, smooth face.

"Your father is John Luther, yes? He phoned me yesterday afternoon. I've driven all the way from Philadelphia to see your mother. Would you show me to her, please?"

I nodded and led him upstairs. Walter, parked again on his chair, stared suspiciously at the approaching stranger.

Dr. Caraway didn't acknowledge him as he stepped past. He knocked on the door, and Abigail admitted his immediate entrance.

That was the single, brief glimpse I had of Mama during the throes of her sickness. She was unconscious, propped up on a quartet of sweat-sodden pillows. Her hair, greasy and damp, hung over her face and shoulders like ratty curtains. Red blotches—or were they dark purple?—lay scattered about her cheeks, while the rest of her skin was a translucent hue of blue.

Like I said, it was only a glimpse—Abigail hurriedly shut the door behind the good doctor—but it was enough to shake me to my marrow.

Walter and I mashed our ears against the door to listen as best we could. The conversation within sounded like the disembodied voices of a faraway radio, but when we sat motionless, we could hear every word.

"Thanks for coming, Doctor," said Daddy.

"My pleasure. You know my fee?"

I suppose he didn't acquire such a fancy car by swapping his services for baskets of apples or cartons of eggs.

"Yes," Daddy replied. "Abigail, would you get it for him? It's over on the dresser."

Mama entered a coughing spasm, drowning out whatever the doctor said next.

Daddy spoke again. "It's been like this since Wednesday. Sometimes better, sometimes worse. Always bad."

"Eating and drinking?"

"When she's awake," Abigail answered. "Doesn't have much appetite though."

"Any symptoms other than fever and the obvious coughing?"

"Terrible headaches, confusion, dizziness," listed Daddy.

"Any blood from the nose, ears, or mouth?"

"Yes. When she coughs. It's been growing worse each day."

"And the baby—she's pregnant, yes?—has he been active?"

"Last time she was awake, she said she felt him moving."

"I see her skin has a bluish tinge," Dr. Caraway noted. "Common among the severe cases I've seen. And how long have those spots been on her cheeks?"

"Those showed up just this morning," Daddy replied. "Noticed them first thing after I woke up."

"A frequent sign of impending mortality," the doctor said. "Not always. But often."

Walter and I exchanged hopeful glances. Pastor Wainwright used words like *immortal* and *immortality* all the time in church. Those words had to do with living forever, so we figured this similar word—*mortality*—meant Mama would soon take a turn for the better.

"What should we do, Doctor?" Daddy asked, overcome with emotion. After the long battle Mama had already waged, he must have been relieved to hear it.

"No more than you've been doing," Dr. Caraway replied. "I suppose you might also try a bit of quinine. I brought some with me. Mix a little into a hot drink with lemon and some whiskey. It might be the best thing for her now."

Daddy said nothing, so Abigail replied on his behalf. "Thank you, Doctor."

"Well then, I suppose I'll be off. Many other patients to visit."

"I'll show you out," said Abigail.

Walter and I scampered away from the door. As they exited the bedroom, we pretended we hadn't been listening, nor that we had the slightest interest in what had happened behind the door. They went downstairs, and we hurried into our room.

"Did you hear that?" Walter exclaimed, whispering as loud as whispers go. "She has *mortality!* She's gonna be okay!"

"If only she had a real doctor before now, she'd be better already!" I said, equally ecstatic.

"But the doctor did say the spots only mean that *frequently*," Walter remembered, suddenly sober again. "Not *always*."

"Yeah, but it's Mama," I reminded him. "She isn't some old person. She'll be fine."

In a rare reversal of roles, Walter seemed to take courage from my words. He grinned and said, "Yeah. You're right. I'm gonna sneak out to tell Hattie. If Daddy asks where I am, tell him I went fishing, okay?"

Before I could protest or insist that I tag along, Walter was already out the door and on his way.

The abatement of my concern for Mama allowed room for a resurgence of jealousy. I should have been elated that afternoon. Instead, I returned to my former state of melancholy, and was unable to free my thoughts from images of Walter and Hattie together.

Despite the good news he had received, Daddy strangely didn't leave the bedroom to share it with his boys. He remained shut up behind the door, selfishly keeping these positive developments to himself.

At least it meant I wouldn't have to cover for Walter.

My brother returned two hours later, alight with joy and bouncing weightlessly with each step. Abigail fixed us dinner—roasted chicken with potatoes and carrots—but said little as she prepared and served the meal. She instructed us to clean up after ourselves when we were finished, and disappeared upstairs once more.

Evening marched into night. Abigail, not Daddy, was the one who helped Pip get ready for bed. Once she had tucked him in, she told us to do likewise.

Walter fell asleep with his usual ease. By the light of the gibbous moon glowing in my window, I watched his chest rise and fall with the rhythm of his first peaceful slumber in days.

I was my usual self too, fitfully tossing and turning.

A full hour after I had crawled into bed, a denizen of the night added to my sleepless woes. In one of the trees outside my window, a barred owl had taken roost. Like a skipping record, its repeated call pierced through the inky dark: *Who-cooks-for-you! Who-cooks-for-you!* Though I couldn't see the nighttime hunter itself, I imagined it perched upon the nearest branch, staring straight into my window and grinning to itself as its eerie notes warded sleep away from my weary eyes.

Eventually, I could stand it no longer. Clutching my bibby to my nose and mouth, I tiptoed from the room.

Pallid light escaped Mama's room through the gap below her door, painting the upstairs hallway and staircase a gloomy gray. But wait!—as I crept down the topmost steps, I realized a light was also on in the kitchen.

Someone was still awake. I debated retreating, but I knew I would only find more owl-inspired insomnia in my bedroom. Summoning my Cowardly-Lion-sized courage, I proceeded toward the kitchen.

Abigail stood with her belly to the sink, deathly still. She was staring out the kitchen window, peering somewhere into the murky night beyond. In front of her, she held a dishrag and teacup, and she appeared to have frozen mid-wipe.

Upstairs, Mama hacked.

Abigail jumped at the sound. When she turned and saw my small figure standing against the darkness of the doorway, she cried out in alarm.

"Sorry!" I apologized. "I didn't mean to scare you. I couldn't sleep and came down for a drink of water."

"Sweet Jesus, you almost gave me a heart attack, Peter," she replied, gasping and clutching dramatically at her chest. "You ought to warn a person before sneaking up on her like that. Especially on a night like tonight."

"What do you mean?" I asked, stepping fully into the kitchen.

She removed a glass from the cupboard and said, "I mean with that owl a-hootin' outside."

"You heard it too? It's keeping me awake," I told her. "Are you scared of it?"

"They ... spook me a bit," Abigail answered. She filled the glass with water and handed it to me. "They're bad omens, owls are."

"Bad omens? What's an *omen?*"

"Sign that something bad's about to happen."

I was confused. "You mean, the owl's gonna attack?"

Abigail chuckled and considered how best to explain the idea to a boy. Finally, she said, "No, no. The owl isn't gonna *do* anything. But when you see an owl, it's supposed to mean someone'll die soon."

"Oh," I said, beginning to understand. "So do other birds mean other things?"

"Yes, they do, and many of them good. Hummingbirds mean you'll find joy and new blessings soon. Seeing a seagull while you're traveling means you'll have a successful journey. Cardinals are good too. They can bring love, or even messages from loved ones who have died."

I took a drink. "But there are bad ones too?"

"Yes, some," Abigail replied somberly. "Crows mean you'll have bad luck. Ravens and whippoorwills usually mean some kind of disaster too. And owls—well, owls symbolize mortality."

Despite the glass of water I'd just finished, my mouth went dry. I had heard that word, *mortality*, while eavesdropping with Walter. We had assumed it meant Mama was going to live. That everything would be alright.

But we were wrong. Owls, Abigail said, brought death. Mortality.

"Of course," she said, noting my look of grave concern, "those are all just superstitions. Old wives' tales, we call them. Birds are just birds, God's creatures like any other. They don't mean anything more than that."

But I hardly heard her. I handed Abigail my empty glass, mumbled a feeble "goodnight," and made for my room.

Partway up the stairs, I stopped.

The forlorn strains of Daddy's violin had entered into the deathly gloom, breaking the stillness of our home. Each note he played was haunted, tormented, like the anguished cries of a spirit doomed to restless wandering upon the earth. Then his own trembling voice joined with the strings, and the haunting became complete. Slowly, pitifully, he played and sang:

> *"From this valley they say you are going,*
> *I shall miss your bright eyes and sweet smile,*
> *For alas you take with you the sunshine*
> *That has brightened my pathway awhile."*

Daddy didn't make it past "Red River Valley's" first verse before he broke down.

The darkness around me seemed to swell with his unrestrained cries, as he pleaded with heaven itself for his wife's salvation.

I couldn't stand to hear it. I hurried into my bedroom, shut the door, and dove under the protection of my covers.

Outside, the owl continued to call its warning.

Death was near at hand.

With my bibby pressed against my mouth to muffle the noise, I sobbed and sobbed until I finally, mercifully, fell asleep.

FIFTEEN

The Healing Power of Ginger

I WOKE UP THE MORNING of September 23, 1918, to a violent shaking. Startled and gasping, I shot up in bed, smashing my forehead against Walter's ear as I did.

"Ow!" he cried, grabbing the side of his head.

I expected retribution, but in the clearing haze of sleep, I saw that Walter wasn't angry at all.

"Peter, I know what to do!" he triumphantly exclaimed. "I know how to make sure Mama gets better!"

I decided then that I would say nothing of my late-night conversation with Abigail. It was better if Walter didn't know.

Without waiting for my reply, he continued. "Remember what Abigail told you? About ginger?"

I straightened up sharply. How had I not seen this answer, dangling in front of us like low-hanging fruit on a tree? A fountain of hope surged inside me.

"Yeah, I remember. She said it could cure anything."

"So, all we need to do is *get some ginger*," he said, stating the obvious. "Put your clothes on, and let's find Abigail!"

Except for me and Walter, the rest of the house was silent as we dashed down the stairs. It seemed even Mama had found a bit of peace from her constant hacking.

We discovered Abigail asleep in the kitchen, slumped over the little table in the corner. Her face was buried in her crossed arms like a makeshift pillow, and she was snoring lightly. After five days of caring for our entire family, including our sick mother, exhaustion had bested her at last.

I hated to wake her, but our mission couldn't wait.

"Good morning, Abigail," Walter said gently.

She stirred, then lifted her head and rubbed her eyes.

"Oh, Lord Lord Lord," she muttered. Her eyes focused as she came to her senses. "I fell asleep. Oh, I shouldn'ta done that."

My single-minded brother was short on patience. He blurted, "Do we have any ginger here?"

"Ginger? Mmmm, I don't think so," answered Abigail. "Why?"

"You'll see!" Walter replied. He was already leading me by the arm from the kitchen.

"What's the big idea?" I demanded, irritated at his impetuousness.

He fished a handful of coins from his pocket and said, "If we don't have any ginger, we've gotta go to town and buy it ourselves. We'll use the movie money Mama gave us. So put on your shoes, and let's go."

I didn't argue. Soon, we were running up the cart path. Walter likely would have sprinted the whole way to Schroeder's Goods and Grocery, but he slowed to a walk when he noticed me lagging.

"Think we'll become famous?" he asked.

"For what?"

"For finding the cure."

"Maybe," I said with a shrug.

A bit begrudgingly, he said, "I guess we should give Abigail some of the credit. I'm surprised she didn't think of it herself."

"She's been too busy to sit down and think," I suggested.

"Maybe we'll get rich too," Walter said, his imagination leading his mouth. "Then we could quit school! And when Mama's better, we could take her to London and Paris and all those Europe cities she's always talking about."

"And Daddy could sell the mine, and we'd all be together all the time."

I half-expected Walter to mock me, to tell me he wouldn't want to spend every day with a stooge like me.

Instead, he said, "That would be the best life ever."

We walked in silence as Pierre took shape ahead of us.

"I'm sorry about your eye," Walter said, his apology coming from nowhere. "I really didn't mean to."

"It's okay," I mumbled. "Besides, it was my fault. I tried to hit you."

"Yeah, but I was being a real goop that day. Like Hattie said."

I bristled at the mention of her name.

"I *was* being kind of a baby," I admitted.

Walter cast me an amiable smirk. "You're right about that. Good thing Daddy wasn't home then, or else we'd both be dead right now."

On we went, and before long, we found ourselves parading between Main Street's two-story storefronts. Normally after the weekend break, downtown Pierre would have been abustle with folks catching up on business matters, both personal and professional. Not today. Pierre's streets were all but empty. Only a handful of strays remained out and about, and all of them wearing gauze masks. Whenever anyone crossed our path, he or she would glance at us suspiciously and rush past without so much as a word of greeting.

It was eerie. Unsettling. Like taking our first steps on an alien world.

Schroeder's Goods and Grocery was a large market situated one block north of Main Street. The owners, Tom and Katherine, were members of our church and two of Pastor Wainwright's good friends. Mama and Daddy had even invited them to Asphodel once or twice for afternoon dinner and games. Certainly they would be delighted to help us.

But as we approached the store entrance, we discovered that they had added a new feature. In the doorway was a large white sign. Its message was simple and straightforward: *NO MASK, NO ADMITTANCE.*

"What're we gonna do?" I asked Walter. Had we come all this way only to be turned back by a *sign?*

Walter didn't think so. "They'll let us in. We know them! Besides, we're kids. Nobody expects us to wear masks like all the grownups."

As it turned out, Walter was wrong on both counts. The Schroeders neither cared that we were family friends, nor believed that kids were exempt from the mask rule.

"Out!" Katherine Schroeder cried from her station behind the cash register. "Put on masks or don't come in at all."

"But Mama—"

"I don't care who needs what," the belligerent woman hollered. "Neither you nor anybody else is bringing their sickness in here. Not while I'm alive."

Outside, Walter and I sat on the curb, pondering and waiting for the spark of inspiration which would solve our conundrum. The beginnings of defeated tears already stung my eyes, but Walter remained sharp and focused.

A minute later, he confidently stated, "We'll just have to steal it. It's the only way."

"But they won't even let us inside," I argued.

Walter had a plan for that too. "There's a back entrance through the alleyway that goes into the storeroom. Joe Murdoch told me he snuck in once to pinch some licorice, and Mr. Schroeder caught him and whooped him good."

"But what if one of them is in the storeroom? Or what if there isn't any ginger in there at all? We'll have to sneak through the whole store without them seeing us."

"You can create a diversion up front. Then I'll sneak through the back, grab the ginger, and sneak out again."

"I don't know," I said. "What if I can't keep them distracted long enough?"

"Fine," retorted Walter, his temper rising. "*I'll* distract them. You sneak in."

"But stealing is wrong!" I reminded him.

"It ain't stealing if we pay for it," said Walter. He removed a silvery dime from his trousers pocket. "Leave this for them."

I swallowed hard and took the coin.

"I'll give you two minutes to get to the back door," Walter instructed. "Once you hear me making a racket, wait fifteen seconds before sneaking in, that way you're sure Mr. Schroeder's good and distracted too."

I nodded, scared.

Walter must have noticed my skin looking paler than normal, because he clapped me heartily on the shoulder and said, "You'll be okay. And remember, we're doing this for Mama. Now go!"

As fast as my gangly legs could carry me, I sprinted into the narrow alleyway behind the building. When I reached the grocery's back door, I knelt beside it, panting. My heart was playing drums with my ribcage, and I worried I wouldn't be able to hear Walter's distraction.

It wasn't an issue. Through the closed door, I couldn't make out exactly what he was yelling, but his raucous howls could have brought the paralyzed running to see what the commotion was all about.

I held my breath and counted to fifteen, then opened the storeroom door and slid noiselessly through.

"It's like my brain is on fire!" Walter hollered. "There's a thunderstorm in my brain! Someone, help! Please, help!"

Walter was playing his part brilliantly, and it was up to me to do the same. After all, Mama was counting on us even more than he realized.

A second door separated the storeroom from the main grocery floor. I took another deep breath and, crouching low to the floor, slipped through it.

Many times I had entered through the front of the store, but never from the back, and I found myself momentarily disoriented. Everything appeared different from my burglar's angle, and it took a few seconds to get my bearings straight.

"It's spreading! It's spreading!" Walter cried. "I feel it in my throat! Aaaaargh!"

"What do you want me to do?" Mrs. Schroeder screamed at her husband. "Should I call for a doctor?"

"Sheriff, more likely!" Mr. Schroeder bellowed. "He's just bored and trying to cause trouble. That's what happens when they let kids out of school!"

Beneath the horrific uproar of Walter's protesting shrieks, I continued my stealth mission. I wound around racks of baked breads and pastries, past shelves of cereal and canned fruits and vegetables, until I at last arrived at the produce bins. Here, I could no longer remain close to the ground. I had to stand to look inside the various crates and cartons.

As I rose, I risked peeking toward the entrance. Walter, clutching his head, then his throat, then his stomach, swayed and lurched and smashed into things like a drunk in the dark.

If anyone ever handed out acting awards, I'd be sure to submit his name for consideration. He certainly had the store owners' attention. Katherine Schroeder stared at him, the telephone receiver suspended in midair as she watched the bizarre show, while Tom was doing his best to wrangle my brother.

I had to hustle. The Schroeders had kindly labeled the contents of each bin, and my eyes flew from one to the next. Turnips, potatoes, carrots, apples, pears—it seemed as if they stocked an endless supply of everything that *wasn't* ginger root.

But—finally!—there it was. The ginger bin! I still thought they looked like weird potatoes as I grabbed the largest hunk I could find. I started for the storeroom door before realizing I had forgotten something. If I didn't want to call this *theft,* I had to leave the dime.

As I was fishing for the coin in my pocket, I heard Mr. Schroeder yell, "And don't come back 'til I've had a good talk with your parents! Understand?"

My stomach dropped. The diversion was gone. Either Mr. Schroeder had succeeded in wrestling him out the door, or Walter had assumed I would be quicker in my task. Either way, there was no more time to think. I had to act.

Still crouching, I dropped the dime and hurried for the storeroom door. Unfortunately, without any ongoing diversion from Walter, the tinkling of the coin against the polished floorboards drew Mrs. Schroeder's immediate attention. Seeing a second Luther boy standing in the middle of her store must have caught her by surprise, because her split second of hesitation gave me just enough time to run like hell.

The moment his wife raised the alarm, Mr. Schroeder was after me. I burst into the storeroom and streaked toward the alleyway door.

But as I yanked it open, a risky idea popped into my head. Even if I made it into the alleyway, the much faster Mr. Schroeder would still catch me before I reached the street. Then he would search me, find the ginger, and confiscate it. I would likely end up with a few bruises to show for the encounter, but zero ginger.

So instead of opting for the clear alleyway, I took a major gamble and dove behind a pile of empty crates. I sucked in one more breath and froze.

My ruse worked. As soon as he saw the open door, Mr. Schroeder assumed I had run into the alley and did likewise.

I knew it wouldn't take him long to figure out he'd been duped, which meant I had no time to waste. I scrambled from my hiding place and streaked through the doorway—not into the alleyway, but back into the store.

Mrs. Schroeder didn't stand a chance. She sprang up to stop me, but with the front counter between us, I was out the door and free in the fresh air before the imprint of her butt could disappear from her seat cushion.

Walter was nowhere to be found. He must have cleared out as soon as he saw the commotion I raised. It was no matter. At worst, I would meet up with him on the road home.

But with an irate Mrs. Schroeder after me, as well as Mr. Schroeder still at large, I couldn't stay put. She was hollering for her husband, calling for backup as I sprinted west along the road. Across the intersection, I came to another narrow alleyway cut between the buildings. I darted down it. Ahead, leaning against the brick wall, was a high stack of boxes. I dove behind them and, shielded there from searching eyes, sat to catch my breath.

Suddenly and sharply, I cried out. Someone was grabbing my arm!

"Quiet, you ass!" hissed a voice. "It's me."

I had been focused on escaping my pursuers. It never crossed my mind to check whether anyone else might be hiding among the boxes. As luck would have it, Walter had also ducked behind them for safety.

"Don't move and stay quiet," he ordered. "We'll get outta here once the coast is clear."

Ten silent minutes later, we were on the move again, hugging the buildings and peering around every corner as we worked our way safely along the alleyways. Eventually, we reached the backside of Uecker's Pharmacy at the west end of Pierre's downtown district.

"I think we're safe," Walter whispered, peeking out from behind the wall. "Let's go."

I was stepping out and onto the boardwalk when Walter yanked me back behind the corner. A horse and rider had galloped into sight, furiously pursuing the westward road which led to Asphodel.

"That's Pastor Wainwright!" I exclaimed. "He's sure in a hurry somewhere."

"Too bad he doesn't preach that fast," Walter joked, as the galloping horse streaked past. "Come on. Let's go home."

Quicker than we had come, our legs carried us Asphodel-ward. The assurance of our mother's recovery lay quite literally in my hands, and I clutched the ginger root tightly. That misshapen root was our very salvation, and I wouldn't chance it to my pocket, for fear it might somehow slip out as we ran.

When we turned south onto our cart path, we saw that not one, but *two* sets of fresh tracks preceded us there. Both tire and hoof had passed over the lane since our departure from Asphodel one hour earlier.

"Pastor Wainwright must be visiting Mama again," Walter supposed. "But I wonder whose car this is?"

"Maybe that doctor from Philadelphia," I suggested casually. It mattered not. Doctor or no doctor, Mama's cure was coming home with us.

We saw Eli on his front porch as we passed the Lincolns' cottage. Usually he was hard at work throughout the daylight hours, but on this particular morning, he sat motionless in his rocking chair. He gazed at us, and for once I detected no malice or ill will upon his face. He stared almost curiously, as if he were appraising us fairly for the first time.

Over the hill we went. Asphodel Hall, with its sparkling backdrop of lake water, seemed merry in hailing our return home. Pastor Wainwright, who typically stabled his horse during visits, had uncharacteristically tied Hezekiah to one of the porch pillars. The unsupervised animal was currently snacking on tender thistle shoots, which had sprouted next to the porch without Mama's hands present to uproot them.

Also parked in front of the house was a boxy black wagon.

"I guess it isn't Dr. Caraway," Walter noted.

The big-city physician had driven a sleek sedan. This vehicle was wide and angular. It was topped with a high roof, and everything behind the single bench of seats was closed-off cargo space. Three words were painted in white on its side, but we were too far away to make out what they said. The wagon's rear, where one would normally find a trunk or luggage rack, was entirely open to allow for painless loading and unloading. Rolled and tied above this doorless space was a thick tarp, which could serve as a flimsy cover when the vehicle was moving.

Something about it made me uneasy. I had seen one before—I was sure of it—but I couldn't quite place my finger on when or where.

As we drew near, the white words along its side became clear enough to read.

"What's a *coroner?*" asked Walter.

I shrugged. "Some kind of doctor, I think."

We passed in front of the *Camperson's Coroner Services* van and bounded up the porch steps. From inside, we heard our puppy announcing our arrival with his frantic barking.

Walter threw open the front door victoriously. We had returned from our quest as conquerors.

But the scene in the Great Room was not as expected.

For some unknown reason, Pastor Wainwright hadn't gone up to Mama's room. He had chosen instead to sit on one of the downstairs sofas. Likewise, Daddy was not at Mama's side as he had been the past five days. He was beside Pastor Wainwright, his head buried in his large hands as his shoulders bobbed up and down.

Was he laughing?

Our pastor certainly didn't look as if anything funny had happened. His expression was drawn and grave, his eyes unfocused.

Pip and Abigail were there too, seated across from Daddy and Pastor Wainwright. Our baby brother seemed confused as Abigail lightly stroked his shoulders. The dark rivulets of fresh tears streaked her cheeks, and, like Wainwright, her eyes bore a faraway look.

Our puppy barked on, furious, though not at me and Walter. His attention was fixed upon the staircase, where two strange men carried something long and flat. Each stood on one end of a stretcher, straining beneath its weight as they hauled it down the steps.

I realized then that a *coroner* must be a type of ambulance. These men had come to take Mama to the hospital.

But if that were the case, why was her head covered beneath a white sheet? Wouldn't that make it harder for her to breathe?

When the front man reached the bottom step, our dog charged forward, indignant. A wild beast again, he yipped and growled and nipped at the man's ankles. Gently but firmly, the ambulance man tried pushing our puppy away with his foot. Unfortunately, this threw him off balance, and he lurched backward off the step.

When he did, a lifeless arm flopped to the stretcher's side, dangling where the sheet could no longer conceal it.

Up to that point in my short life, I had not yet seen a drowning victim. But the signs of asphyxiation, of a body starved of its oxygen, were similar in at least one respect.

The fingertips. I'll never forget them. Such a dark blue they were almost black. Limp and splayed, at the end of an arm blotched with purple.

Our puppy licked at them, trying in vain to revive those lifeless fingers. To the tune of his pitiful whines, the men hauled the stretcher out the door.

Walter collapsed in a heap. Curled on the floor, my brother let loose such a howl of anguish, even the damned in hell would have pitied him.

And the ginger root, Mama's salvation come too late, slipped through my fingers and tumbled uselessly to the ground.

SIXTEEN

Where She Has Gone

"IT'S OKAY. IT'S OKAY."

Whose voice was that? It was familiar—or not? It was right next to me. Or maybe a million miles away. There was a hand on my shoulder, but in the fog, I couldn't place whose it was.

"Your Mama's suffering is over. She's home. She's with Jesus now."

Pastor Wainwright?

Yes. Pastor Wainwright. Kneeling beside me. Giving me his best, most desperate comforts. Holding Walter's arm, too, and whispering to him.

Then Daddy was there with Philip. Together, we Luther men sobbed, gnashing our teeth and clutching at our stomachs, hoping to tear out the grief inside us. How long this lasted, I don't know. But after our eyes were drained of their tears to match our drained hearts, we picked ourselves up off the floor and looked around.

The whole house was changed. Physically, its features were exactly as they had been a week earlier, but the spirit of every room, of every lamp and portrait and knickknack and piece of furniture, was transfigured. The kitchen, haunted with the cakes and breads Mama would never bake. The dining room walls, echoing with laughter that would grow ever fainter, for Mama would share her mirth with them no more. Her bedroom, sitting empty because Daddy could no longer bear the sight of the place where Mama had taken her final breaths. The nursery, undisturbed by the cries of a baby who would never sleep there.

And the Great Room became the Grief Room, for in it, Walter and I had watched helplessly as our triumph turned to torment.

Everything was the same. Everything was broken.

The rest of that day and most of the next were lost in a haze of mist and confusion. Pip, who didn't fully comprehend what was happening, kept asking when the men with the black wagon would bring Mama home. Each time he did, the knife of our torment stabbed a little deeper.

While Pip *could* not understand, I simply didn't *want* to. I tried losing myself in books, trekking through Oz with Dorothy and Toto, or flying high above the streets of London with Peter Pan. But each character bore Mama's face, and every adventure reminded me of the ones she had invented for us. Before long, the book would lie readerless, and I would be sobbing again.

Walter handled things altogether differently. Following his initial throes of agony in the Great Room, he wrapped himself in a cloak of stoicism. All outward signs of anguish evaporated like morning mist under a summer sun, and his tears became lost to drought. It was unnerving. Out of us all, Walter had been the most attached to Mama, the doting puppy long before an *actual* puppy came into our home. To see him so detached was upsetting, even disorienting for me.

Normally, a family like ours would have expected a revolving door of sympathetic mourners, but in September 1918, that wasn't the case. Afraid of The Flu, many shut themselves inside their homes, barring the doors against their own escape. Even Gramma and Grampa shared their condolences by telephone rather than in person.

But the most surprising omission was that of the Jansen family. Jacob had certainly heard the news, yet Daddy's longtime business partner didn't have the courtesy for even a quick visit. Worse, he hadn't brought Hattie to see us. Mama had been like a third parent to her, and we Luthers a second family. If Hattie was scared of catching The Flu herself, she could have at least offered us a comforting wave through the window. Instead, the little joy she might have provided us remained an undelivered one.

Still, there were some brave souls remaining in the world. Pastor Wainwright, for his part, hardly left Daddy's side. Old Hans Albrecht, the grumpy St. Matthew's usher, dropped by to deliver a bag of potatoes and a ham. A delegation of Daddy's employees, from both the mine and the processing plant, dropped by with two bottles of bourbon, which Daddy would soon put to good use. Even Tom and Katherine Schroeder dropped off three large bins of assorted foodstuffs, and they didn't whisper a single word about their brouhaha with Walter and me at the grocery.

While Daddy sorted through his own grief, it was Abigail who became our rock. Mama's departure had created a vacuum in her roles of emotional support and physical caregiver, and Abigail filled both with neither hesitancy nor complaint. A tireless force awoke within her, some untapped motherly instinct long pent up by the children she never had.

The day after Mama died, it was Abigail—not Daddy—who gathered us to the dining room for supper. Before each of our chairs sat a plate piled high with our favorite meals. For Walter there was fried chicken, mashed potatoes with gravy, and roasted asparagus. A frankfurter sat on Pip's plate alongside a dollop of ketchup, seasoned potato wedges, and a conspicuous lack of vegetables. For me, Abigail had provided a generous cut of beef, tender and well-seasoned, between a wedge of Swiss cheese and a butter-slathered cornbread muffin. She even treated the puppy to a hearty bowl of scraps left over from her dinner preparations.

There was a fourth plate at Daddy's seat. Waiting for him were roasted lamb with mint jelly and potato wedges like Pip's, but he had not come at Abigail's call.

"Sit down, boys," she ordered me and my brothers. "I spent the afternoon fixing your favorites. It's high time you all ate something."

"I'm not hungry," Walter muttered peevishly. He took his seat anyway.

"Listen," Abigail said sternly, "starving yourselves ain't gonna bring your Mama back. The night before she passed, she made me promise to take care of you and your Daddy, and I won't let you make a liar out of me by wasting away to nothing."

"How come you're not making Daddy eat?" Pip asked, his mouth already stuffed with ketchupy potato.

"Because he's a grown man," sighed Abigail. "If he wants to make foolish decisions, that's up to him."

Walter took one miserable bite of mashed potato, then set down his fork and asked, "Abigail, where did Mama go?"

I was only nine, but even I thought it was a strange question. Walter had been in church enough to know "heaven" was the obvious answer. That's just where people went when they died, and we had heard it from Pastor Wainwright's lips a hundred times.

Abigail also knew the obvious, so she said, "Your Mama went to be with God and the angels in heaven."

"But why would God do that? Take her away from us?" Walter asked.

Abigail gave him a sad smile and said, "God must've wanted to make heaven a little more beautiful by adding her to it."

Walter stared dully at the food he was pushing around his plate, unsure of Abigail's response. After a moment, he said, "Then I think God is selfish."

I stopped chewing mid-bite, shocked at Walter's heresy. I had been to Sunday School enough to know what happened to blasphemers in the Bible.

If the question scandalized Abigail, she didn't show it. "Why do you think God is selfish?" she asked.

"Because he knew how much we needed Mama, but he took her for himself," Walter replied. "That sounds pretty selfish to me."

"I know it might *sound* selfish," Abigail said gently. "But we don't see the big picture God does. That makes it hard for us to understand when sad things happen."

Walter was losing his grip on his temper as he replied, "I understand well enough. God took Mama away, but he got it wrong. Mama shouldn't be in heaven. She should be with *me,* and if God doesn't care about that, then I say he's selfish."

"Walter—"

But my brother was past listening. He slammed his fork on the table, stood up, and stormed out the back door. The entire house rattled as he slammed it shut.

I looked at Abigail, and she read the question in my eyes.

"Eat a few more bites, then you can go," she said with a deflated sigh.

I ripped a giant hunk off the cheese wedge and tamped it down with half my muffin before jumping up from my chair.

"Don't you go choking on that, you hear?" Abigail called after me.

I tried to reply, but my mouth was too full.

Outside, the full orchestra of Asphodel's cricket population regaled me as I left the safety of the porch light for the chilly twilight beyond. Not far ahead, among the scattered silhouettes of shortleaf pine and birch, my brother's dark form slalomed down the slope toward the shoreline. The lake was aglow with the last gasps of daylight, and against it I now recognized the shadow of a second person.

It was Daddy. Standing perfectly still. Staring out across Acheron, whose glassy waters stood in sharp contrast to the turmoil in his soul.

I kept my distance as I followed Walter. I had no plans to join them. I wanted to *watch* them. And so, armed with my odd skill for eavesdropping, I approached them, unseen and unheard in the gathering darkness.

By the looks of the empty glass on the ground next to him, Daddy had been there some time. A pipe, no longer smoldering, was held firmly between his clenched teeth. Even when Walter reached his side, he did not break his gaze upon the lake. He simply put an arm around my brother's shoulders and pulled him close.

"I miss your Mama," Daddy said miserably. He wiped a hand across his cheeks.

"Me too," said Walter.

"I don't know what to do. How do we move on without her?"

Walter shrugged and stuffed his hands into his pockets.

Daddy let go of him and bent to grab something from the ground. At first, I couldn't make out what it was. Then he cocked back and whipped the stone, side-armed, across the placid water. The stone skipped once, twice, six times altogether, before it finally disappeared beneath the surface.

Walter followed suit, but his stone delivered only a single hop.

"You have to give your wrist a good, quick snap," Daddy instructed. "That's what gives it the spin it needs to skip."

Side by side, my father and brother unloaded a barrage of spinning, skipping missiles upon Lake Acheron. They went on like that for five minutes, then ten. When they had used up all the suitable stones in one spot, they moved along the shoreline to find more. It was as if they were trying to unload all their rage and grief through those little stones. If only they could sink enough of them into that lake, perhaps they might displace the water high enough to wash away our family's woe.

And yet, even if each of those skipping stones had carried with it a metric ton of their heartache, they would have gone on and on until the shores of Lake Acheron, and our thousand-acre wood, and all of Pennsylvania's vast forestland were nothing more than roots and dirt.

Night's shadow was fast approaching when Daddy threw a final stone. With it, he sent across the waters a howl of frustration and bitterness. His soul was spent. His knees buckled, and he collapsed, sobbing and hopeless.

Walter sat beside him, and together they poured out their exhausted hearts with inexhaustible tears.

"Daddy?" Walter asked when he could cry no more.

"Yes?"

"Where did Mama go?"

There was that question again, the one whose answer never seemed to satisfy him.

Daddy sounded unsatisfied with his own response as he said, "You know where she is. She's in heaven."

"That's what Miss Lincoln told me too," said Walter. "But what *is* heaven?"

"Well," Daddy replied, choosing his words carefully, "heaven is where you live forever in joy and happiness with God and the people you love. And that's where she has gone."

"But aren't *we* the people Mama loves?" countered Walter.

"Yes, but there are others. And someday you and me and your brothers—we'll die too, and when we do, we'll be with Mama again."

Walter's next question shocked me. "Why can't we die *now?*"

Daddy sighed. Walter's interrogation was wearing on him, and his soul was already too aggrieved to go on talking about heaven and Mama.

"Because God still needs us here," Daddy answered, but without an ounce of conviction. "You might not know the reasons why, but he does."

Daddy stood and stared up at the sky, as if only now realizing how dark it had become. "We should go inside while we can still see where we're going."

Walter rose obediently from the ground. "Can I ask one more question?"

Daddy chuckled wearily. "Sure."

"*Where* is heaven?"

Daddy faced the lake fully. Raising a hand, he beckoned toward the darkness beyond and said, "It's out there, someplace. That's where Mama is, arranging the best games you could ever imagine for the day you finally see her again."

"When will that be?"

Daddy shook his head and said, cryptically, "We all have to cross Acheron sometime. When that day comes, she'll be waiting. Come on. Let's go inside."

I stood stiller than a spooked rabbit as they ambled up the hill. They passed by but did not see me pressed against the tree in the dark. Only when they had reached the porch did I finally relinquish my eavesdropping post. Like a hundred moths and other nocturnal insects had already done, I made for the yellow porch light hanging over the back door.

When I slipped inside, I saw that Abigail had removed only Pip's dishware from the table. Three full plates of food remained exactly where she had set them at dinnertime.

I realized two things at once—how hungry I was, and how tired.

My food had grown cold during my spying session. Still, it was delicious. When I had downed every scrap of it, I moved on to Walter's chicken and potatoes, and kept eating until I was satisfied.

Despite refueling, exhaustion's sleepy fingers tightened their grip, and my heavy eyelids drooped. I carried my dinnerware to Abigail in the kitchen and set it beside a mountain of dirty pots and pans.

She was scrubbing furiously at something buried beneath the layer of suds. Grimy perspiration trickled down her face and neck.

"Need any help?" I asked. She had gone to such trouble preparing each Luther boy's favorite meal, and it must have broken her heart to watch half go uneaten.

Without glancing away from her task, she replied, "No, thank you, Little Mister Luther. Kind of you to offer, but I'll manage." She wiped at a sweaty rivulet with her shoulder and added, "Go play with your brothers. Get your mind off things."

She didn't have to tell me twice. Upstairs, I saw the light on in Pip's room, so I poked my head inside. My baby brother was in the middle of the floor, but he had already fallen asleep on a bed of tiny tin zoo animals. Clutched in each of his pudgy fists were the pewter elephant and hippo we had unearthed during our final morning with Mama. Although Pip was struggling to understand his loss, life without Mama was bleeding him dry too.

I decided to let him rest. After closing the door, I glanced from one end of the hallway to the other and realized I wanted nothing to do with what lay inside any of its adjoining rooms. Judging by the light eking through the gap below my bedroom door, I would find Walter inside, brooding and darker than a storm cloud. At the other end of the hallway was Mama and Daddy's room—*only* Daddy's room, I reminded myself—and it held nothing but the hated memories of Mama's final days. If I could help it, no one would catch me dead inside there for the rest of my life.

In the end, I opted for my bedroom. As expected, Walter lay on his mattress, fingers laced behind his head as he stared up at an old water stain in the ceiling.

I crossed to my hemisphere of the room. In doing so, I stepped over the dark blotch in the floor where my fully healthy Mama had sopped up my blood not two weeks ago.

It felt unreal all over again. How could she be gone? For a moment, I wondered if I had perhaps hit my head so hard that everything since had been nothing but an injury-induced nightmare. Maybe I was lying in a hospital somewhere, comatose and lost in my own hallucinatory dreamscape.

A boy can hope.

But even as I wondered it, I knew it wasn't so. The past week's events bore none of the hallmark traits of a Peter Luther dreamworld.

This nightmare was all too real.

And it was taxing. Already it had consumed me emotionally. Now it was feeding on my physical energy too.

I removed my bibby from its hiding place beneath my pillow. With the cool fabric against my cheek, I toppled onto the mattress. Despite the night's early hour, I couldn't stop sleep's sails from billowing and carrying me away. Upon what dreamlike seas it ferried me, I don't remember, only that it bore me deep into them.

So deep, in fact, that I did not awaken when Walter packed his schoolbag. I didn't stir as he tied to his bedframe the long length of rope which had once served as our puppy's leash. On I slept, not waking even when Walter, fully dressed and carrying his schoolbag, opened his window, threw down the rope, and slipped into the night.

Only in the earliest light of morning were my pleasant dreams shattered, as I reentered the nightmare my waking world had become. But I did not dwell long on my grief or its cause. At once, my attention flew to the open window. From it came a sound of rough slithering, like that of a snake through dried leaves.

A scream rose in my throat as two dark arms reached inside. In my sleep-addled state, I was certain they belonged to some giant spider—or worse.

"Shhhh!" hissed the monster. It apparently preferred quieter meals.

In a tangle of sheets, I scrambled from my bed and ran to Walter's. He would protect me. Whatever mythical beast had come to suck our bodies dry and grind our bones to bread, Walter could fight it off. And if not, he might at least sacrifice himself so I could escape.

"It's me, you dummy!" the insulting window-creature whispered.

"Walter?" I said disbelievingly.

Why was he climbing into a second-story window? Especially so early in the morning? And why had he been outside at all?

Walter finished pulling himself through and collapsed onto the floor. Breathing like a marathon runner, he unshouldered the supplies-stocked schoolbag and dropped it beside him. From the bag's open mouth, a tin can rolled out and across the floor, stopping only when it bumped up against my bare feet.

"Beans?" I asked, staring open-mouthed at the can. "Why do you have beans?"

"Thought I might be gone longer," came Walter's vague reply.

"Gone where? What were you doing out there?" I asked, noticing then the rope tied to his bedframe.

"I went to the Isle," Walter answered excitedly.

"In the dark? Why?"

"Last night I was talking to Daddy, and he said Mama was out across the lake. He told me she was waiting for us to get there."

"Okay?"

I didn't understand. Walter sounded crazier than old Mrs. Schwartz from church. I didn't always care for my brother, but I certainly didn't want him taking up residence in the room next to hers at the nuthouse.

"Daddy told me we had to cross Acheron to get to her," Walter explained. "So I did. I took the rowboat to the Isle."

He seized my shoulders and lowered his face squarely before my own. His eyes glowed faintly in the gray light, as tremors of elation passed through his fingers and into my upper body.

What he told me next was miraculous. And impossible.

"I found her, Peter."

My jaw dropped. I searched his eyes for any trace of a lie but found none.

"She's there. Mama's there. She's *alive*."

SEVENTEEN

The Deep Dispositions of Luther Men

WALTER'S SWAY WAS SO PRONOUNCED, I worried he might tip and tumble into the hole himself. The undertakers were already planning to shovel one Luther into the earth—what was one more?

We Luther men stood beneath the shading boughs of a young chestnut that morning, in a line from shortest to tallest. Daddy wore a double-breasted black suit and matching bowler hat, whereas we boys had been forced into our finest and itchiest flannel blazers.

As I gazed at Mama's casket, I wondered what she was wearing. Had the coroners who took her simply left her as she was? Wrapped in the same sweat-stained, shoddy nightclothes she had been wearing when she died? Or had they decided to send her to the Pearly Gates in style? Was she wearing her Sunday best too? Or did they strip everything off altogether, so they could burn the diseased clothes while saving themselves the hassle and expense of dressing her in something else?

And what about the baby? The brother or sister I would never meet? Had they done anything to honor that little life? Or did they treat it like it was no more than another internal organ? A part of Mama's body that would decay along with the rest?

My questions would go unanswered. Out of precaution against further spreading of The Flu, her casket was to remain closed throughout both funeral and committal.

Pastor Wainwright stood between Mama's head and the rectangular hole in the ground, open Bible in hand. Normally his preaching voice was strong and clear, but it carried a tremor that afternoon as he read from John 14:

"Let not your heart be troubled; ye believe in God, believe also in me."

I scoffed. Mama's lifeless body lay across the hole, stuffed into a box where she would be entombed for the rest of time. How couldn't my heart be troubled? How could I quell the flow of my tears, as if the sadness didn't exist?

"In my Father's house are many mansions: if it were not so, I would not have told you."

Mama didn't need a mansion. She had our Castle Home. Wasn't that more than enough?

"I go to prepare a place for you. And if I go and prepare a place for you, I will come again, and receive you unto myself; that where I am, there ye may be also."

I looked again at my unsteady brother. His all-night expedition had left him so drowsy he couldn't keep his eyes open.

"I found her, Peter. She's there."

That's what Walter had said.

"Mama's there. She's alive."

It was nonsense, of course. Mama was in a polished chestnut casket not six feet away. And yet my heart had no choice but to wonder: Could it be true? Could Mama somehow be both here *and* on our Isle? Preparing the best games imaginable for us? Waiting for us to join her, just as Daddy had told Walter? If so, why were we all standing here? Why were we gathered around a box, mourning as though we would never see her again?

I shook my head. It was too fantastic to be true. Daddy had been trying to comfort Walter, and Walter, for his part, was either lying or totally cuckoo.

The reading of John 14 ended, and Pastor Wainwright invited us to fold our hands as he prayed. When every other eye was shut, I opened mine to look around at the handful of mourners who had gathered.

Jacob Jansen was there, standing a careful distance off Daddy's left side. His pathetic attempt to rectify his earlier absence was completely undone by the fact that he had brought none of his family. Even Hattie hadn't taken this final chance to say goodbye to a woman she had known and loved since birth.

Also in attendance that morning were a handful of women who played cards and drank wine with Mama on a semi-regular basis. I didn't know any of their names, but they raised such a racket of misery, they might have moonlighted as professional mourners.

It was Miss Carrington's presence which surprised me most. I hadn't expected to see her until the schools opened again, yet here she was, standing in solidarity with two of her students. If Olaf Kirk and his school board comrades ever decided we could resume classes, I made a mental note to go easy on her—at least for the rest of my fourth-grade year.

Even though Gramma Opal and Grampa Henry hadn't visited when Mama was sick, nor even to grieve with us when she passed, they did come that afternoon to say their final farewells to their youngest daughter. I don't know if they were afraid of the germs or of standing too close to a Lutheran service, but they kept their distance, looking on from beneath an ancient oak. Grampa appeared much older than I remembered, his face grim and sagging as he stared, dead-eyed, at Mama's casket. It was as if the lifeless body inside had stolen his life too.

Gramma was the one who shocked me most. Who would have thought such a bitter old woman capable of tears? Yet there they were, gushing down her cheeks like a waterfall on rock.

And stupid Aunt Louise? Nowhere to be seen.

Pastor Wainwright ended his prayer and closed his Bible. He spoke from memory as he said, "Lord, we commit these bodies to the ground; earth to earth, ashes to ashes, dust to dust, in the sure and certain hope of Rosalie's—and her child's—resurrection unto eternal life."

This was the undertakers' cue. Wearing their eerie gauze masks, they proceeded to lower Mama into the belly of the earth.

For those whose emotions weren't too strained to sing it, Pastor Wainwright led the mourners in a few verses of the Scottish hymn "Abide with Me."

Tears welled and trickled from every eye as we sang.

There was only one exception.

Walter.

He was alert again—the commotion of lowering a bulky casket into the ground made it impossible not to wake up—yet he remained unaffected by the proceedings. Mama had been his world, the desire and delight of his young heart. So where were his tears? He should have wept harder than anyone, but he looked almost *bored* to be there. Inconvenienced, at the very least, as if more pressing issues awaited him.

When the casket was in its place, resting upon the dirt below, Daddy sank to his knees. He scooped dark earth into his hands, then sprinkled it upon that hated lid which hid from him his beloved wife's face.

Barely able to choke out the words, he whispered, "I'll love you always, Freckles."

Walter, wrested back into the moment by Daddy's distress, knelt beside him. With dry eyes of his own, he looked straight into Daddy's glassy ones.

"Everything will be okay," Walter whispered. "You'll see."

Daddy pulled him close, and his whole body convulsed with his sobs.

I turned away. It's hard for a young boy to watch the strongest person in his life reduced to such a state. The fortress where I had long fled for safety lay toppled upon the ground. I felt vulnerable and helpless, for my champion and defender had lost his very spirit.

After a minute's weeping, Daddy composed himself. With Walter's help, he returned to his feet.

It was then that I noticed how scandalized Jacob Jansen appeared. Perhaps he thought such a display of mourning inappropriate for a grown Christian man, or perhaps he thought such behavior would bring a blight upon the business which bore their names. Regardless of the reason, he appraised Daddy with a judgmental—perhaps even suspicious—gaze.

It didn't matter that we were at a funeral. It didn't matter that the funeral was for my own Mama.

I wanted to punch him.

Daddy didn't notice his expression. If he had, the service certainly would have ended in a punch or two.

But there was someone angry enough to confront Mr. Jansen. It happened shortly afterward, when Daddy's business partner began walking away.

"Where's Hattie?" Walter asked, breaking away from the rest of us. He strode forward, purposeful and demanding.

Mr. Jansen wheeled about to meet his approaching inquisitor. Curtly, he answered, "Hattie is at home."

Walter's tone was laced with accusation as he said, "She should have been here. Hattie loved my Mama, and if she could've been here, she would have."

"What exactly are you suggesting?" Mr. Jansen asked sharply.

"That Hattie didn't come because *you* didn't let her," Walter replied. His face was like flint and his voice like steel.

Mr. Jansen swallowed hard. Teeth and jaw were rigid with fury as he spat, "That's right. I didn't let her come. And what's more, she will no longer be allowed at Asphodel Glade. I won't have her breathing your infected air. I will *not* lose my little girl. Do you hear me?"

Walter was full on seething. With crimson face and clenched fists, he appeared ready to take a swing.

Pastor Wainwright intervened at once, stepping between them and shouting, "Peace, both of you!" Turning to Mr. Jansen, he said, "Jacob, do you really think his mother's funeral is the place for this? Go home."

Mr. Jansen glowered at the Lutheran minister. Then, without another word, he spun on his heels and stormed away.

Daddy didn't say a word about the altercation. In his state of emotional desiccation, he simply didn't have the capacity to deal with his son's impudence. Silently, he ushered us to the buckboard wagon, took his place alone on the bench behind Castor and Pollux, and pointed us homeward.

Walter was far from ready to let the matter drop.

"I hate that Jacob Jansen," he fumed.

"Enough, Walter," Daddy said, exhausted.

"I can't believe he didn't let Hattie come," my brother continued, deaf to Daddy's directive. "Of all the low, sleazy things to do—"

"That's *enough,* Walter," Daddy repeated, this time with a stern edge to his voice.

"But doesn't it bother you? How could you let him say something like that?"

Daddy sighed. "Maybe you'll understand when you have your own kids someday. You'll do anything to protect them. Sometimes that leads to misguided decisions."

Walter sat back and crossed his arms, pouting.

Even I felt a touch betrayed by Daddy's flaccid inaction. He should have punched that Reformed ass square in the mouth. Instead, he was treating Walter like the villain for speaking out and standing his ground.

A moment later, Daddy said, "I'm more worried why Abigail and Eli weren't there. She told me last night they'd come. I guess I wasn't holding out much hope for Eli, but I at least thought Abigail would be true to her word."

I hadn't found this strange in the least. All the black folks in town gathered at the Purcell Park pavilion each week for their worship services. As far as I could remember, I'd never seen a single one at St. Matthew's, nor exiting any of Pierre's other churches. The real surprise would have been if one or the other *had* shown up at Mama's funeral.

But Daddy seemed stuck on the subject. "Doesn't seem right. After everything we've done for them—everything your Mama did—just doesn't seem right."

He spoke no more about it, but the further we drove, the more agitated he became.

I didn't understand why at the time, but I've learned enough about human nature since then to realize that Daddy was searching for an outlet. The bitterness, anger, grief—to that point he had been internalizing everything, trying to make some sense of what had happened. Naturally, this left him frustrated. What had happened to Mama was the product of chance and chaos. He never would find any rhyme or reason in it.

All Daddy had left was blame. If he could find the culprit who had brought this sorrow into his world, he might regain a sense of control over his life. Of course, the logical response was to blame The Flu. But the annoying thing about viruses is that you can't hurt them back. They don't respond to enmity or ridicule or cutting words. You can't punish them. Push them around. Find ways to inflict your misery upon them. That's why blaming a virus was so futile.

People, on the other hand? They do feel pain, humiliation, and loss. It's what makes them such satisfying outlets for blame's many manifestations. In the weeks and months to come, as Daddy searched for control amidst the chaos, he would dish around plenty of this irrational and unwarranted blame.

Most of it he would end up serving to himself.

But on the afternoon of Mama's funeral, he set his sights upon the Lincolns. He had to wield the sword of control over *someone*. Who better than the hired help?

The rest of the way to Asphodel, no one spoke, yet the volume seemed to swell with Daddy's smoldering exasperation. That's why none of us Luther boys was surprised when he brought the wagon to a halt in front of the Lincolns' cottage.

"You boys wait here," he said firmly. "I need to have a chat with Abigail and Eli."

I glanced nervously at Walter and Pip. Both wore similar expressions. We all sank a hair lower on the buckboard, worried we might find ourselves singed in the upcoming explosion.

Daddy rapped on the cottage door. No one opened it, so he pounded again, this time hard enough to rattle the windows. Still, no one answered.

He was raising his fist to knock a third time when the curtains fluttered in the window beside the door. Eli's wrathful visage appeared behind the glass.

Or so I thought. But when he spoke, I realized it was not wrath upon his face. It was dread.

"Mr. Luther, you have to leave! Go away!" he pleaded through the window, not with anger but concern.

Daddy's demeanor changed in an instant, his indignation replaced with an anxiousness that mirrored Eli's.

"What's wrong? What's going on?" he asked.

"Abigail's burning with fever. Has been since last night."

My jaw dropped. I had seen her sweating rivers while washing the dinner dishes. I assumed it was because of exhaustion—the last week had consisted of around-the-clock waiting on us Luthers—but the truth was dreadfully worse. In all her caring for Mama, Abigail had contracted The Flu herself.

Upon hearing Eli's revelation, Daddy's bronze skin paled.

"Is there anything I can do?" he asked.

In that moment, Eli discovered where *he* could lay proper blame for his own fear and worry. His eyes narrowed with accusation as he replied, "No. You and your family have already done enough."

With that parting shot, Eli disappeared behind the curtain.

For one numb second, Daddy stared at the window. He had come expecting confrontation. Instead, we all were leaving with a new fear.

Less than an hour after putting Mama in the ground, The Flu had returned to Asphodel Glade.

EIGHTEEN

A Blaze of Cardinals

DADDY HURRIED FROM THE LINCOLNS' cottage and hauled himself aboard the wagon. He flicked the reins, and the horses pulled away. But Daddy wasn't satisfied with our standard riding gait. Faster and faster he coaxed them, until Castor and Pollux had reached a full trot. The wagon bounced violently over rut and stone as my brothers and I held on for dear life. We passed Maisie—escaped from her stall again—but Daddy didn't notice her. He drove desperately onward, like a soul graced with sixty seconds to flee from Hell.

When Pip could stand no more of the reckless pace, he cried out, "Slow down, Daddy!"

He didn't—not right away, at least. Only when we had crested the hill and were coming down the other side, with the infected cottage out of sight, did Daddy finally ease off the equine accelerator.

Our puppy, tied to the porch, began yipping and crying the moment he saw us.

Pip was crying too. With his head buried between his knees, he snuffled softly.

"Sorry about that," Daddy mumbled. "I—I didn't—"

He couldn't finish the thought. He didn't need to. It was obvious that our father, whom I once believed to be fearless in all things, was now terrified of something he couldn't even see. The Flu had driven him to his knees once, and he quaked to hear of its return.

Once Pip had calmed down, Daddy escorted us into the stables. In deep and silent thought, he shut both horses into their stalls.

Finally, he spoke. "I don't want you boys going inside the house. Not for a few days, anyway."

Walter and I exchanged a look of disbelief, and my older brother asked, "Why not?"

"Because I said so," barked Daddy. His expression softened, and he added, "I'm worried it's infected. Abigail's been everywhere in that house. I think we should stay away until the sickness has had time to clear out."

"But where will we sleep?" I asked him anxiously.

"I'll make up some beds in the workshop," said Daddy, jerking his thumb toward the stable-adjacent room.

"But I'm hungry!" moaned Pip. The idea of sleeping so close to stinky animals—and so far from his beloved pantry—was unacceptable to him.

Our father's frustration was mounting. He said, "I'll bring some food from the house. Just think of it like camping in one of your forts."

I frowned, remembering that night last summer. According to my recollections, the fort had been cold and cramped. Rather than snuggling up to my bibby, I had cuddled with about a dozen spiders. If the workshop was anything like that, it meant we were in for a miserable night.

But Daddy seemed resolute. We would have better luck arguing the Pope into Lutheranism than Daddy into changing his mind.

We exited the stable. From his pocket, Daddy removed a gauze mask and wrapped it around his nose and mouth.

I shuddered. Wearing it, he reminded me of the men who had come to carry Mama away.

His voice was muffled beneath the fabric as he said, "I'll be right back. I'm gonna gather up bedding and food for tonight."

When Daddy reached the front porch, he stooped to untie the puppy. The fuzzy missile darted our direction the millisecond he was free. After a quick detour to harass a pair of innocent chickens out for a stroll, he bounded into Walter's waiting arms.

With a gleeful new puppy, azure skies, mild temperatures, and no school, it might have been the perfect day. Yet it was hell. Not only was Mama gone, buried, never to come back, but now Abigail, whom I had known from my first living memories, had fallen into The Flu's clutches. What would we do if she died too? Who would take care of us? Daddy was more than competent to provide income and a generous standard of living, yet I doubted whether he was truly capable of *raising* us. That had been Mama's job. Since Abigail had played the supporting role at Mama's side all these years, it seemed natural that the task of caretaking should fall into her hands.

If we lost her, we would all be lost.

The sickness and dread, which had ebbed and flowed like a tide the last two weeks, rose in my chest once more. I wanted to cry but refused to do so in front of Walter again. His mysterious tearlessness had erected a sort of prideful dam in my own heart, blocking my emotional streams. If he wasn't going to weep anymore, then I needed to match—or even exceed—his indifference.

Daddy's return took longer than expected. After ten minutes, Walter's patience was pushed beyond its bounds.

"I'm gonna go see Mama," he announced out of the blue. "She'll know what to do about Abigail."

I had been lying on the grass, absentmindedly stroking the napping puppy's belly. Now I sat up and stared at him. I was unsure whether he genuinely believed his own claims, or whether he was playing his cruelest prank to date.

The combined experience of all human history weighed heavily toward the latter.

It's where my money was too, so I replied, "Stop being stupid. Mama's gone."

On a normal day, Walter would have roughed me up for speaking to him that way, but on this occasion, he seemed unaffected by my insult.

"Think what you want. It doesn't matter to me. I get to see her whether you believe me or not."

"You're not fooling me," I told him. "But you might fool Pip into thinking Mama's alive, and it'd be really mean to do that."

This heated Walter's blood a few degrees. He scowled and said, "I'm not trying to trick anyone. I'm not lying, Peter."

I realized then that I had a golden opportunity. The chance to rise above the brother who had towered over me my whole life. So often he had provoked and belittled me, using my pride and temper against me. But here I had the chance to give Walter a spoonful of the spiteful medicine he'd been feeding me for years, and I wasn't going to waste it.

"You always were her little mama's boy," I taunted, "and now you can't handle that she's gone."

"Shut up, Peter." Walter's stare brimmed with murder.

"But guess what?" I continued. "She's dead! And you're going cuckoo."

"I said shut up."

"No! Not 'til you admit you're a mean, lying goop."

Next thing I knew, I was flat on the ground, my nose smarting fiercely. The tears, whose passage I'd been denying, burst forth.

Dark against the bright sky, Walter's form hulked over me. The fist which had knocked me down remained poised, ready to strike a second time.

"Walter! Stop it! What do you think you're doing?"

Daddy had exited the house just in time to witness our altercation's climax. In a previous life, Walter would have blanched with fear, but something about the recent days had changed his constitution. His livid gaze shifted from me to Daddy, and it became apparent that he was far from backing down or running.

"He started it!" Walter shouted. "He called me a mama's boy."

Daddy placed the basket he was carrying onto the ground. It seemed that a change had come over him also. Some undefined concoction frothed within him, a blend of frustration and anger and sadness, but mostly of sheer helplessness. He knew he must act, but had no idea what to do or how to do it.

He reminded me in that moment of Pip trying to tie his shoelaces. He so desperately wanted to be like his older brothers, who put on their shoes without anyone's help, yet he had neither the memory nor the coordination to put the steps together. His helplessness and continued failure always produced the same results: frustration and anger, and tears begotten of both.

It was alarming to see that same expression mimicked in Daddy's face. I forgot about my stinging nose and the confrontation with Walter. It was Daddy who worried me now.

At that moment our puppy sneezed and woke himself up. It wasn't much, but the lighthearted moment cut the tension hanging in the air.

"I—here's something to eat," Daddy stuttered. He beckoned toward the basket, which he had filled with a variety of canned fruits and vegetables, along with a tin of crackers and a quarter wheel of cheese. "You'll feel better after eating something."

I couldn't help but notice the brown bottle peeking out from beneath the food. This Daddy grabbed and tucked hastily into his suit pocket.

Suddenly remembering that one of his sons had been knocked to the ground, he asked, "You alright, Peter?"

I nodded, and it was true. Despite his angered assault, Walter had held something back, as evidenced by the lack of blood on my face.

"Good ... that's good," said Daddy, fumbling for words. His gaze drifted again to the basket he had brought, and he winced. It pained him to see the pathetic assortment inside it.

That was when I noticed the sweat beading on his forehead, as well as his belabored breathing. This puzzled me. He hadn't carried the basket far, nor did it contain a particularly heavy load. The cool afternoon air couldn't have caused such perspiration, and he was exhibiting no other signs of sickness.

So why the sweat?

"I know it's not much," said Daddy, nodding at the basket. "I can buy more groceries tomorrow."

He wiped his brow. With a detached and faraway look in his eyes, he stared at the moisture on his fingers.

His next words surprised me as much as Walter's knockout punch—and with even greater force.

"I think I'm gonna ride into the office," he muttered. "I've got a couple things to take care of there."

Pip, who was pouring canned peaches directly into his mouth, found himself suddenly on the verge of tears. He wailed, "Don't leave, Daddy! Stay here with us!"

"I—uh—Walter and Peter will watch you," stammered our father. "You'll be fine with them."

"But when will you come home?" Pip cried.

"I'll be back before dark," my father assured him. "And I'll pick up a proper supper from the diner on my way home."

The promise of better food was enough to appease Pip, who stopped crying immediately.

Walter and I stared in disbelief as Daddy disappeared into the stable and returned on Castor's back. He walked the horse toward us and said, "One thing before I leave: you are *not* to visit Mister and Miss Lincoln. In fact, I don't want you going anywhere near that infected cabin. Understood?"

He didn't wait for an answer. After spurring Castor in a tight circle, he galloped away and was gone.

Walter took immediate advantage of Daddy's absence. The dusty haze Castor kicked up hadn't yet settled, when he said, "I'm going to the Isle."

That was when another sickening realization punched me square in the gut. Daddy was gone, Mama was dead, and the Lincolns were quarantined in their cottage. This meant Walter was the last protector I had at Asphodel Glade—at least until Daddy came home.

"Walter, you can't go," I pleaded. "Not now."

When he spun to face me again, I expected the worst. Instead, he bore an unexpected look of compassion.

"I know you think I'm a mean, lying bully," he said, "but I'm telling the truth. Mama's there. I saw her and hugged her and talked to her last night. It's all *real*."

"If she's there, then why did you come back?"

"I didn't want to. She made me."

I mulled over both his answer and his earnestness. He appeared genuine, but his story sounded more miraculous than Pip volunteering to fast during Lent.

"Walter, she's dead. It's impossible."

"Maybe it is. But if anyone could make the impossible happen, it's Mama. So, are you coming or what?" He wasn't angry, but he *was* out of patience. With or without me, he was going to that island.

Our family had had enough of fracture. Despite the moats of bad blood I had dug in my heart against Walter, I couldn't bear the notion of staying put, with only Pip and the puppy to keep me company.

I sighed with resignation and said, "Fine. Let's go. Come on, Pip."

Pip pumped a cracker-carrying fist into the air and whooped, "Yay! Where're we going?"

"To the Isle," I answered succinctly. I didn't want to give him any false hopes. "We'll play there 'til Daddy gets home."

With Pip and the puppy leading the way, we hurried to the lake's edge. The rowboat, usually stored upside down to avoid collecting rainwater, was already turned upright. Walter had at least gotten that far in his nocturnal adventures.

After shoving us off from shore, my big brother sat in Mama's old seat on the rower's bench. Steadily, he oared us Isleward, where I would expose him as either a liar or a lunatic.

Or where, by the most glorious wonder of heaven, Walter would shame both me and my unbelief.

As we neared the island, I was surprised to see how much of autumn's color was painted on its trees. Scarcely a week had passed since our previous visit. On that day, summer's storehouse of rich green had hardly begun shedding its brilliance, while the conquest of fall's golds, siennas, and vermilions remained weeks away.

Yet this afternoon, the treetops burned with such a deep red, I wondered if they'd been set on fire. Curiously, the color extended beyond the reach of its typical autumn trees: oaks and maples and sumacs. Also sporting this unnatural crimson were the Isle's birches and evergreens. It was as if they had shed their ancient habits overnight, and were trying on something new and provocative.

Our little rowboat glided closer, and I discovered another oddity.

The island was making noise.

I massaged my ears, certain I was hearing things. Perhaps Walter's psychosis was contagious, and I its newest victim.

Any such worries were allayed by Pip, who cried out, "What's that sound?"

That was when I realized something even more: the red in the treetops was *moving*. And not simply wafting back and forth like leaves in the wind. It was swarming. Flitting. Hopping from place to place, sometimes in one direction, then in another, and then back to rest where it had begun.

Meanwhile, the hum grew into a chorus, and then a symphony of musical chirps and twitters. Each one was independent of the others, yet somehow woven together into the symbiotic harmony of a million-piece orchestra.

"They're *birds*," I whispered, awestruck.

"Cardinals," Walter specified.

Although I couldn't see his face, I knew it bore a vindicated smirk.

By the time we arrived at our usual landing place below Emerald Hill, the choir of cardinals had intensified into a deafening uproar. Pip moaned and pressed his hands over his ears, trying but failing to drown out their song. Even the dog, discomfited by the din, whined softly and squeezed himself into the bow's tight point. At least here he couldn't see them.

But there was one important omission: Mama was nowhere in sight.

What *was* Walter playing at? Had he gone crazy after all? Had he delivered us here as a sacrificial meal for some savage breed of flesh-eating bird?

Above the racket, Walter shouted, "Peter, jump out and tie us off!"

Frightened, I did as he asked, though I kept my attention treeward as I anchored us to the rocky shoreline, watching for any sign of an aerial attack. Once the boat was secure, I hauled Pip out and set him beside me. I tried to coax our puppy out as well, but it was clear he wasn't going to budge, and I quickly gave up.

Walter danced deftly toward the prow of the rocking boat and hopped out.

The moment his feet touched dry land, the cardinals fell silent. It wasn't a gradual winding down of their singing. No, it was an abrupt extinguishing of every last voice of every last bird.

Instead of singing, the cardinals watched. Thousands of them. Wherever each one sat, it stayed, motionless upon its bough, as still as a winter's morning.

My skin crawled as I wondered how many beady, birdy eyes were fixed upon me. Yet I found then that I was not afraid as I had been before. I felt exposed and uncomfortable, as if my soul itself lay naked before their divining eyes.

"Where's Mama?" I whispered to Walter. I wanted to put his charade to rest and leave as hurriedly as possible.

"Climb the hill," he answered. "That's where she'll be."

I swallowed hard and nudged Pip forward. At least I could use him as a human shield if things turned south.

The cardinals continued their silent observations as we labored up the high hill. Like judges at the Olympic Games, they seemed to scrutinize and critique our every move, determining perhaps whether we were intruders or authorized guests. Whatever their purpose, they remained stone still, pivoting their bodies only as much as was needed to keep focused upon me and my brothers.

We approached the hill's crest. Beside me, Walter grew giddier with each passing step, his merriment not unlike that of little Pip at Christmastime.

But when we reached the top, we found only empty grass.

Walter strode forward, glancing this way and that, confused and indignant.

"Well? Where is she?" I asked. Though I had known better all along, I still found myself disappointed after Walter's earnest buildup.

"Peter—I swear it—she was here," Walter pleaded. He pointed at the ground. "I sat right there, and she sat next to me. I talked to her for hours last night. You have to believe me!"

I shook my head and revealed what I knew to be the truth. "You must have been sleepwalking. Mama's gone, Walter. I'm sorry."

Defeated, Walter sank to his knees. He looked ready to throw up.

It was pathetic. I couldn't bear to watch him another second.

I draped an arm over my little brother's shoulders and, with a disappointed sigh, said, "Come on, Pippie."

But when we turned to descend the hill, we found our path blocked. Not by birds, nor by any other creature of the island.

Before us stood a person.

NINETEEN

The Cottage Grounds

I SCREAMED. SEIZING PIP'S ARM, I pulled him backward and away from danger. In doing so, we toppled over Walter's kneeling body, and the three of us tumbled to the ground in a writhing mass of limbs.

Scrambling backward on my heels and palms like a crab, I risked a glimpse up at the interloper. Our puppy, who had conquered his fears and left the rowboat's safety, was yipping and bouncing wildly around the stranger's bare feet and naked shins. Above my spirited puppy, I glimpsed flowing fabric, bordered by a hemline of dainty baby's breath, wafting lazily in the easy breeze. From here, my eyes traveled upward to behold a dress of whites and purples, each color melting into the other and out again like garden violets. The dress was tied around the waist with a sunny sash of black-eyed Susans, the blossoms woven craftily together.

I couldn't quite make out the woman's face. In contrast against the bright backdrop of sky, it remained cloaked in shadow. I held my palm upward to block out the sunlight, squinting as I tried to distinguish her features.

The woman, in turn, seized my raised hand.

I froze, not daring even to breathe. I knew that touch.

"Do you believe in me now, Peter?" The voice was one I thought I'd never hear again during my mortal days under this sun.

Distrusting even my own eyes and ears, I whispered, "Mama?"

She pulled me to my feet and stepped back, allowing me to look upon her fully.

There it was—her exquisite face, no longer blanched and blotched but full and radiant once more. And her hair! It wasn't matted with sweat and grease. No, these springy coils of strawberry blond were interwoven with ribbons of lavender and crowned with a wreath of purple-blossomed ivy.

In the end, it was her eyes which convinced me beyond doubt. No charlatan or master of stage makeup could ever have duplicated them. With all the warmth and sweetness of melty chocolate, those brown eyes smiled at me. In them, I saw the undying adoration and fidelity I had known since the day I first opened my own.

She was Mama. The same Mama who birthed me, raised me, and loved me. The same Mama who had died two days earlier.

She was the same, yet somehow different. Her essence remained unaltered, but her substance, the stuff she was made of, had changed. Light itself was knitted into the fabric of her flesh. Skin and hair and eyes pulsed with an energy, an electricity evolved far beyond that of her previous life. Even her clothing shimmered with this seraphic incandescence, which clung to her like dewdrops at the dawn of Creation.

"Mama," I said again, confidently and without suspicion. The fountains and floodgates of jubilation burst forth in my heart, and I leaped into her.

She caught me in her waiting arms and rocked me, cradling me against her breast. She was of heaven, resplendent and sublime, yet still bone and blood and marrow.

"How? How?" I asked. Tears of joyful relief spilled down my cheeks, but I no longer cared whether Walter might see them.

Mama stroked my hair and shushed me like I was a newborn baby. As she held me, her warm touch soothed every ache and bound up every wound my young heart had suffered.

"What matters is not the *how*, but the *what*," she finally replied.

"What do you mean?" I asked, as she knelt and wiped away my tears.

"I mean, *what* are we going to do with this miracle," she answered. "What will make this gift of extra time as special as it could possibly be?"

"Anything," I said. "Anything, as long as it's with you."

She beamed and kissed my forehead as tenderly as if I were a newborn. Her lips lingered there only a moment, but I wouldn't have traded it away even if I were offered all eternity in exchange. During those seconds, Mama and I were the only two beings in the universe, and I savored them like they might be my last.

But the moment ended, and I became aware again of a third and fourth presence—my brothers, standing on either side of me.

Mama's envied gaze shifted to my left, and she cried out, "Hello, my Pippie! Oh, I have missed you, my little pea!"

Understandably confused, Pip hugged her and asked, "What're you doing out here, Mama? Why didn't you come home?"

She brushed his hair from his forehead and kissed him. "I am so sorry, sweetheart, but I cannot go back. I must stay here on the Isle, or else travel Beyond."

"But *why?*"

With a wistful grin, Mama pulled him into a tight hug and said, "Because that is what has been permitted, and I am not allowed any nearer to the Living World. But you may come here and visit me anytime you like. How does that sound?"

Pip seemed skeptical about her strange plan, but he shrugged anyway and said, "Okay, I guess."

Mama moved on to Walter. Cupping his angular face in her hands, she crooned, "My faithful Wahwie. Thank you for bringing your brothers here."

"Peter didn't believe me," Walter tattled.

Mama chuckled. "I know. Is that why you had to knock some sense into him?"

Walter and I glanced at each other, both surprised. How had she known about our fight if she had been on the Isle this whole time?

But she didn't press the issue, and neither did we. She didn't even make us apologize. Instead, she squeezed all three of us against herself and sighed like someone slipping into bed after a hard day's labor.

The onlooking cardinals emitted a low warble, mimicking Mama's sigh. Her serenity was their satisfaction also.

Mama released us and stood abruptly.

"Come!" she exclaimed. "We cannot waste time sitting around like this. I have far too much to show you, and we have far too much to do."

With that sudden announcement, off she marched toward the trees.

The puppy didn't need anyone telling him twice. With his tail whipping back and forth, he skipped along beside her.

"Where are we going?" Walter asked, running until he had caught up.

"To the cottage, of course."

I flashed Walter a look of skepticism. What could our risen-from-the-dead Mama possibly want from a rundown cabin?

The throng of cardinals hopped from treetop to treetop, following us as we tromped familiar paths through the forest. Their song rose to the sky, though it was more subdued than before. Neither their music nor their presence was a source of trepidation for us any longer. With Mama going before us, their myriad trills became a jubilant chorus in our ears and hearts.

Just as the Isle had brought both the birds and Mama, it also delivered a third surprise. When we arrived at what used to be a derelict homestead, we discovered a transformation even more pronounced than the changes in Mama. The great boughs overhead, which once choked out the daylight and cloaked the clearing in shadow, had withdrawn their many arms and fingers to make way for naked sky, so that sunshine now enveloped the glade with its cheering glow.

But the far greater marvel were the grounds themselves. They were no longer weedy and overgrown, but trimmed and manicured, as elegant as those of any palace. Thick hedges bordered the glade on three sides, each bisected by high stone archways which led to the forest beyond. But these hedges were no ordinary walls of greenery, square-cut or rounded on top. Rather, they took the form of a menagerie, a circus of animals from around the world, like life-sized, leafy versions of Pip's zoo toys. Four green elephants reared up on their back legs, one at each end or corner of the hedge, trunks raised in silent salute toward the center of the clearing. Between those pachydermatous corner pieces were images of giraffes and rhinos, polar bears and walruses, gorillas, orangutans, chimpanzees, flamingos, cranes, pythons, crocodiles, tortoises, kangaroos, lions, tigers, gazelles, bison—an eclectic arrangement of creatures from around the world, all of them trimmed into the hedges with such fine detail, we could determine which were merry or timid, alarmed or combative.

The north edge of the clearing, however, had no hedge. Instead, a flowerbed's narrow mound stretched between one topiary elephant and its counterpart across the clearing. In this flowerbed, every season of the year and every corner of the world coexisted as one, for upon its soil bloomed the flowers and grasses of spring and summer and fall, and not only those flora native to eastern Pennsylvania, but from across the entire globe. Blood-red anemones from Jerusalem mingled with canary-yellow orchids of Colombia. Australian desert flame danced side by side in the breeze with Alaskan lupine, composing together a waltz of gold and periwinkle. Every hue and shade was represented among the blooms of that garden, so that one could behold the entire visible spectrum of color in a single glance.

As with the hedges, a stone archway stood in the center of this unnatural flowerbed. Emerald vines climbed up its sides and crowned its keystone with vibrant petals of blue morning-glory. Perhaps a dozen feet in front of this arch, the freshwater spring bubbled up where it always had, only now it was encircled by a wall of pale limestone bricks. Within it, the water pooled, clear and cold. It escaped the well through a wide notch near the top of the brickwork, where it gushed out and down the wall's outer face. This became the headwaters of a lazy stream, one which wound like a ribbon down the slopes of the clearing until it finally disappeared into the forest beyond.

As impressive as these perimeter features may have been, what lay *inside* them most captivated our attention. Beginning at each of the four stone archways, four flagstone paths led inward. They did not, however, run straight to a meeting point in the clearing's center. Instead, they spiraled inward like the arms of a pinwheel, looping partway around the grounds before doubling back toward a single focal point in the middle.

Between the bands of flagstone were bands of lawn, and on that lawn stood fruit trees, each spaced evenly from the others. These were no taller than saplings, yet each appeared otherwise mature in its form and function, for all were bountiful with ripe fruits. As we entered through the stone archway, I also realized no two trees bore the same fruit. Each was unique among the garden, so that there was one plum tree, one apple, one lemon, one peach, one orange, and one apiece of many other varieties I had neither seen nor heard of before.

At the center of it all was the cottage. Not the rotting, ramshackle cabin that once occupied these grounds, but a quaint bungalow built of new and sturdy timbers, and whose proud windows gleamed with the afternoon sun's brilliance. Creeping ivy and blooming vines clambered up its high walls, where they met and mingled upon the eaves of a golden-thatched roof. Standing tall above the rest of the cottage were a pair of chimneys, one at each end, whose variegated stones reminded me of our Castle Home's walls. Smoke rose from the west chimney, and with it the unmistakable aroma of fresh bread, which Mama must have begun baking before coming to find us at Emerald Hill.

It was a scene taken straight from one of Mama's fairy tales.

"Did you do all this?" Walter asked, mystified.

"I did," she replied with a self-satisfied grin. "Do you like it?"

"It's ... amazing," he whispered.

Left of the path was a peach tree. It was little taller than Mama herself, yet its branches sagged with dozens of perfect fruits. Effortlessly, she plucked a peach and handed it to Walter.

"Try it," she said. "You will not be disappointed."

Walter bit in. Its juice dripped down his chin, and his eyes widened with wonder.

"That's the best peach I ever had!" he declared. "It might be the best one in the whole wide world!"

Mama giggled. "Good. I have been working hard on those. And the best part is that they never run out."

To show us what she meant, she leaned toward the bit of broken stem still attached to the branch. When she was close enough to kiss it, she whispered soft words to the tree. I couldn't understand them, but when she stepped back, there was no longer an empty stem where she had plucked the peach. Instead, a growing bud, tender and green, had formed there.

Mama had spoken life into being.

She took in our bewildered faces, smiled bemusedly, and said, "You will see greater things than this. Shall we go inside? I have a surprise waiting."

Along the spiraling pathway we went, winding around the cottage to its backside. Through a wooden door engraved with an image of tangled rosebushes, we entered a surprisingly modest dwelling. While everything outside the cottage was fanciful and grandiose, its inside was cozy, glowing with Mama's warm personality.

The puppy made himself instantly at home, bursting past our legs to begin a hasty exploration of these new surroundings. My brothers took a different approach, soaking everything in as we savored the miracle spread before us.

The cottage had no interior walls and thus no real rooms, yet each area was defined as its own. In the middle portion, where the back door entered, was a modest dining space made up of a stout table, four chairs, and a dinnerware hutch much like ours at home. To the left of this was a spacious kitchen, complete with a full array of hardwood cabinetry and polished countertops. A mother-of-pearl washbasin and hand-pump faucet sat below a crystalline window, so that, while scrubbing dishes, you could also look out into the peaceful garden. Against the kitchen's far wall stood an enormous potbelly stove, with space aplenty to roast, bake, barbecue, and fricassee enough food to feed a circus.

Occupying the right side of the cottage was a sitting room. A pair of easy chairs and sofa, all covered in velvety pink fabric and embroidered with purple lilacs, stood arranged before a modest fireplace tucked into the corner and provided ample options for Mama's guests to relax and enjoy each other's company. Lanterns sat upon small tables at either end of the sofa, but because of the effulgent daylight pouring through the high, arched windows, these remained unlit. The far eastern wall contained another door exiting into the garden area, but the rest of it was lined with book-laden shelves. It seemed that all Mama's favorites, ranging from Arthur Conan Doyle to Calvin Ziegler, had found a new home here. Whereas Daddy liked alphabetizing his book collections, Mama kept hers in death just as she had in life—that is to say, in no particular order at all.

I had, of course, expected none of this. But what I expected least of all stood in the corner below an open window.

It was a bassinet. A light blanket lay draped over the top, shielding whatever lay inside it from the direct sunlight.

The puppy approached the bassinet. He snuffled at it curiously, detecting something foreign yet familiar at the same time.

His exploration was cut short by Mama, who cried out, "No, no! Away from there!"

He gave the cradle a final glance of forced indifference, then moved on to inspect other oddities.

Mama crossed the room to the bassinet. She lifted a corner of the blanket to peer inside, then hastily covered it again.

"Still sleeping," she murmured with a dreamy grin. Then, glancing toward us, she said, "Do be careful not to wake the baby. We have had a long few days."

Before any of us could recover from this new bewilderment, Mama gasped and rushed toward the dining room.

"Oh no!" she wailed. "My cakes! Where did they go?"

Only then did I notice the cake stands. There were at least a dozen, scattered throughout all three rooms of the cottage. Some were on the kitchen counters, others on the dining-room table. A couple smaller ones had even made their way onto the bookshelf's bare spaces.

And all of them were empty.

"I spent the entire morning getting them ready," she groaned miserably. "What could have happened to them?"

"I think I know," Walter answered, pointing at the table.

Amidst the vacant cake stands sat a long strip of yellowed parchment, curled at the corners. Near its bottom, and in a text much larger than the lines of poetry above, was a familiar signature.

Gurgan the Goblin.

TWENTY

The Forest and the Serpent

OUTSIDE THE COTTAGE, WE CROWDED around the parchment scroll. Mama had insisted we return to the gardens, citing their tranquil ambience as a better atmosphere for uncluttering our brains. Our puppy, whom Mama had instructed to remain inside keeping watch over the baby, stood with his fat paws on the windowsill, watching us with envy. The cardinals likewise looked down on us curiously as we read the thieving goblin's message:

> *I warned that our last round would not be the end;*
> *So with my own hands I must now make amends.*
> *You dined of my cake, though it wasn't your right,*
> *Insulting me, mocking me, with every bite.*
> *I'll take my revenge when the twilight doth reign*
> *And see to it you know the meaning of pain.*
> *No crumb will I leave, nor a smidgen of glaze;*
> *No morsel uneaten, no garnish ungrazed.*
> *Your tears then will flow, and your wicked hearts break*
> *When Gurgan the Goblin eats up all your cake.*
> *—Most Dis-affectionately Yours,*
>   *Gurgan the Goblin*

"I wish that recipe had never come to me," murmured Mama. "It has caused far too much trouble."

"What're we gonna do?" Walter asked with concern.

Mama sighed. "There may be nothing *to* do. There are a thousand places Gurgan could hide, and he left no clues for us to follow."

"But I'm huuuungryyy!" wailed Pip.

"Unless ..." Mama trailed off. She gazed at the parchment, deep in thought. "Would he make the same mistake twice? Goblins *are* very stupid, but surely he is less stupid than *that*."

"What do you mean?" asked Walter. "Less stupid than what?"

Mama answered by plucking the parchment off the ground and turning it over. She laughed and set it in front of us again. A crude map of the Isle was drawn on back, and on it, Gurgan had marked the position of Mama's cottage with a thick red *X*. A snaky dotted line led from the cottage to the westernmost point of the island, where he had labeled a rough picture of a cave with the phrase "Hidden Hideaway." Three more crude drawings lay along the dotted line between Mama's cottage and the goblin's secret lair. The first drawing was of trees with a black shadow beneath them, and the words "Forest of Gloom" were printed beside it. The second showed the high walls of a gorge with some winged creature between them. This bore the label "Canyon of Fear." Finally, there was the "Maze of Confounding," which was depicted by the minuscule likeness of a labyrinth.

Each of the three drawings was accompanied by a riddling poem. If our previous adventure with Gurgan was any indication, he had left these as instructions for himself to follow.

"This can't be right," Walter muttered. "Sure, there are woods here, but there's no giant maze, and there definitely isn't a big canyon like this."

"And would you say everything on the Isle is exactly as you remember it?" Mama asked, gesturing somewhat sarcastically at the garden surrounding us.

Walter's cheeks turned pink with embarrassment, and he said nothing.

"If we want to recover our cakes," continued Mama, "it seems we have no choice but to follow his map."

"But couldn't we just make more?" I wondered. I didn't know how much time we had with Mama, and I didn't want to waste it hunting down a goblin.

"We could," Mama said, "but Gurgan will keep coming back again and again. As I once told you, goblins can be quite persistent. If we ever want peace, we must find him and deal with him directly. Perhaps we can put an end to this long quarrel."

There was a mumbling of general agreement among the rest of us.

"Good," said Mama. To our surprise, she handed the map to Pip. "*You* will navigate us."

He accepted the parchment page with awe. No one had ever chosen him for such an important job.

Walter hated when Mama conferred special duties upon someone less skilled than himself. "Better not get us lost, Pip*squeak*," he muttered, using a derisive nickname loathed by my baby brother.

"I trust him," said Mama, before Pip could retaliate. "Even if he does, he has the rest of us to set him right again."

"Aren't you going to get the baby?" I asked, glancing back at the cottage.

Mama shook her head. "No. The baby needs to sleep. Besides, I have the sense we are in for a long and difficult quest. Baby will be better off staying here with your puppy."

With that matter settled, Walter gruffly asked Pip, "Well? Which way?"

Pointing confidently at one of the stone arches and the pathway beyond it, Pip exclaimed, "This way!"

Walter groaned and rolled his eyes.

Mama knelt beside Pip and offered a brief tutorial on the proper way to read a map. When she was finished, Pip pointed at another archway and proudly shouted, "*This* way!"

Again, incorrect. After a third—and somehow fourth—incorrect guess, he at last picked the proper direction.

"Great job, Pippie!" congratulated Mama, as he grabbed her hand and pulled her forward.

Beyond the bestial hedge and stone archway, the westward path sloped downhill from Mama's cottage and into the forest. It began as a wide lane, but the further we descended, the narrower it became.

Narrower ... and *darker*. Although we had explored this part of the Isle before, I didn't remember the leafy canopy blocking out so much of the sunlight as it did now. What had begun as a sunny afternoon turned quickly to twilight. The forms of my brothers and Mama became dark shades around me. In the woods ahead, the darkness seemed only to thicken.

"Maybe we should read Gurgan's poem about the Forest of Gloom," Walter suggested nervously, "before it's too dark to read anything at all."

"Good idea," said Mama. Pip handed her the map, and aloud she read:

> *"The Forest of Gloom turns the day into night,*
> *My heart with deep sorrows to torment and smite.*
> *When all has gone dark, I must dwell on the light."*

"How can we 'dwell on the light' if everything's dark?" Walter wondered. "Doesn't make sense."

"Maybe not right away," Mama partially agreed. "But perhaps it will when we have had time to think about it."

When I looked up and realized all I could see of Mama and Walter was the faint glistening of their eyes, I shuddered. What if we became separated somehow? Would we be able to find our way back to each other? What if, less than an hour after finding her, I lost Mama all over again?

In answer to that final, unspoken question, a voice answered me from the now-complete darkness.

"It may seem like a great loss to you, but it wouldn't be any great loss to *me*."

I froze. The voice belonged to Mama.

"Surely you must realize," she continued, "I always loved you least—*if* what I felt for you could even be called *love*."

Tears stung my eyes but did not blur my vision—there was nothing to see anymore—and I cried out, "Mama?"

"Peter! Over here! Where are you?" Mama called back.

I stopped, confused. She sounded much further away than when she had spoken a moment ago. I tried to press forward through the darkness, but a damp heaviness had settled on my shoulders, and my steps were clumsy and lurching.

Walter spoke to me next, his voice low and near, almost as if he were whispering in my ear. He said, "Go get lost. It'll be much better without you around. I'll have Hattie all to myself."

Yet another new voice, speaking derisively into my other ear, said, "The only reason I spend time with a stupid baby-boy like you is because Mother makes me."

Hattie? But how had *she* come here? I hadn't seen her since the day Mama got sick!

"Peter!" Mama's voice cried again from some unknown distance, and yet, simultaneously, the very same voice spoke right beside me. "Be nice to him. You know he'll cry about it if you aren't. He's always been the crybaby of the family."

From somewhere in the blackness, I heard angry shouting—Walter's voice again, but far off, like one of the two Mamas. And ahead of me there was a snuffling sound. A monster? No, it was a noise I recognized—but why?

I bumped into something, and a small voice cried out in alarm.

"Pip? Is that you?" I asked uncertainly.

"Peter? Wh-what's h-happening?" stuttered my little brother. "Why do you wish I was never born?"

"I never said that!" I replied indignantly.

"Did too! I heard you!"

"It's okay, Peter," spoke Daddy's voice, loud and clear. "Like everyone else, he doesn't care much for you either. You aren't strong or brave like Walter. You're the brother he doesn't need."

The darkness around me was suddenly teeming with voices. Mama and Walter and Hattie, my friends at school, Abigail and Pastor Wainwright and Miss Carrington—everyone in my life had apparently shown up here, in the Forest of Gloom, to celebrate their mutual dislike of Peter Luther.

Even as those phantoms continued to jeer, new ones emerged. I heard the hollow hacking of Mama in the throes of her sickness, and Walter's strangled cry when he realized she had died. I smelled the ginger we had stolen from Schroeder's, and the musty earth at Mama's gravesite. All around me, my senses were under assault, and the weight they laid upon my heart dragged me down, down, down …

I found then that I didn't care if I ever left the Forest of Gloom. There was no one who loved me anyway. I was a burden on everyone, and they would be better off without me.

Beside Pip's crying mass, I sat and covered my ears with my hands. It was no use. The mocking, hateful voices only grew louder. And when I screamed at them to shut up and leave me alone, they merely laughed and insulted me with renewed spite.

Then I felt a hand on my shoulder, and a muffled voice cried out above the din, "Peter! Pip! We found you!"

It was Mama.

"I think I know what the poem means!" she shouted. "*Dwell on the light*—you have to focus only on happy things. Then the light will return."

But I couldn't. Nor could Walter, whom Mama had brought with her. While I cried, he screamed with rage into the darkness. Our sorrows were too loud, the trauma of the last days too deeply imprinted. Any happy thoughts were a million miles away, lost in a light we would never see again.

"Mama, can you see?" asked Pip. He spoke clearly, and I realized he was no longer sobbing.

"No," she moaned. "Even I cannot see in this darkness."

Two very surprising words came then from Pip's mouth: "I can."

"You can?" cried Mama.

"Yes! You told me to think about happy things, and everything's bright now. And I think I smell hot dogs! This way!"

"Grab my hand and show me, Pip!" said Mama. "Walter, Peter, you grab hands too."

Walter's wrathful shouting continued, as if he hadn't heard any of their conversation. After a moment's fumbling in the darkness, I located Walter's wrist and locked my fingers around it.

Mama grasped my other hand.

"Take us away from here, Pippie," she begged. "My happy boy."

Our four-linked human chain began moving together through the gloom. At first, I thought her idea had failed. The darkness remained as opaque as ever, and the voices as loud. But when I looked back, I saw the glint of Walter's eyes behind me. Light, however faint, was returning to the forest. The pitch became a murk, and the murk a twilight. Meanwhile, the voices faded with each step. As the light returned, their power over us dwindled, then died altogether.

Nobody spoke as we followed the sunny forest path. What we had gone through was no trick of imaginative fun designed by Mama. Or perhaps it was, I realized by the look on her face, but one that had spun so out of control, even she hadn't been able to tame it.

Walter broke the silence when he asked, "What *was* that? I wanted to lay down and die."

"It was a forest which somehow made all our sorrows and worries real," Mama answered. "I hope we never have to go back there."

Ahead, the trees continued to thin, letting in more of the afternoon's cheering light. Soon, they gave out altogether, and we found ourselves standing on bare rock, staring down into a deep and winding gorge. A steep path, hewn into the cliff face itself, zigzagged from the rim to the canyon floor below.

"When—*how* did this get here?" asked a bewildered Walter, staring slack-jawed into the gorge.

Mama didn't answer. She unfurled Gurgan's map and pointed to the crude drawing of the canyon with its winged creature at the bottom. After clearing her voice, she read the next riddle:

> "The Serpent who dwells in the Canyon of Fear
> Is harmed not by sword nor by arrow or spear.
> My courage is my only weapon 'round here."

"Mama, what's a serpent?" Pip asked. After his contributions in the Forest of Gloom, he appeared proud and confident.

I couldn't blame him. Without his naïve happiness, we may never have escaped.

"A snake," Mama answered, "or some other long, slithery reptile."

Pip shuddered. He hated creepy, crawling things, and none more than snakes. "Maybe—maybe I don't need cake after all," he whispered.

Mama pulled him close. "I cannot imagine anything being worse than that Forest. We will simply have to find our courage, like Gurgan's riddle says."

The canyon's sheer walls rose on either side as we descended the narrow pathway. They must have been a hundred feet high—or more—when the trail finally leveled off onto the canyon floor. With no way to climb up and over, we were completely hemmed in. We would be forced to reckon with whatever dangers lay ahead, or to retreat the way we had come.

We hadn't been wandering the canyon's snaky curves for long when I heard a low rumbling. At first, I thought it was nothing more than a peal of distant thunder, until I realized I could also *feel* it in my feet.

"What was that?" Walter wondered with a look of concern.

We had only taken a few more steps when we heard—and felt—the rumbling again, and then a third time. There seemed to be a rhythm to it, like the rise and fall of tympani disembodied of their orchestra. Stronger they grew, and stronger still, and each tremulous crescendo augmented with it my fear.

When we rounded the next escarpment, all four of us froze.

We had found our Serpent.

And it was angry.

"Back!" screamed Mama. Before I knew what was happening, she had corralled me and my brothers in her arms and thrown us back behind the rocky prominence.

Not a moment too soon. A great spout of orange flame erupted from beyond the wall of rock, scorching the air and cooking everything in its path. When the fiery jet finally sputtered out, wisps of smoke curled upward from the blackened dust and stones where our feet had stood mere seconds earlier.

Walter voiced what I was too frightened to say. "A—a *dragon?*"

Canyon of Fear, indeed.

I trembled. Whimpered. Cowered behind Mama and my brothers. I expected at any moment that the Serpent would leap over the rocks and swallow us all in one bite.

Mama hurried us to our feet and back the direction we had come. When she felt we had put a safe distance between ourselves and the Serpent, she stopped and studied us gravely.

"Is anybody hurt?" she asked.

We all shook our heads. Rattled, yes, but not hurt.

"Thank heavens," she said with a deep sigh of relief. "Now, about this dragon—"

But Walter's mind was already sharpening after our close call. He interrupted Mama, saying, "It's chained up. I didn't get to look very long, but I did see a big chain around its front leg. I don't think it can get us here."

"I saw that too," Mama corroborated. "We were lucky to escape in time. A second later and you would have been dinner."

I swallowed hard, imagining a full-bellied dragon picking its teeth with one of my bones. Perhaps a return trip through the Forest of Gloom wouldn't be so bad after all.

"How do we get past it?" Walter wondered, staring at his toes and deep in thought. "All I have is my pocketknife."

Mama shook her head. "Even a sword would do us no good. Remember what the riddle said? Normal weapons cannot harm it."

"But how can *courage* be a weapon?" I asked, finally overcoming my shock. "Wouldn't a dragon eat a brave person all the same?"

Walter looked at me sharply. My words had caused some light of revelation to flicker in his eyes.

"Maybe not," he said. "Remember what Mama always says about Gramma?"

"Yeah," I replied. "But I'm not allowed to repeat that word. The last time I did—"

"Not *that*," interrupted Walter, rolling his eyes. "The *other* thing. That she's like a barking dog, and if you show her your teeth, she'll back down."

"So what, you're gonna show the dragon your teeth?" I asked skeptically. "Pretty sure his are bigger."

"Not literally, dummy," said Walter. He was losing his patience with me. "I'll just stand up to it. Show it I'm not afraid, that it can't bully me. Like Mama does to Gramma. Maybe that's what the riddle means: If we show it our courage, we'll be able to walk right past."

"I think you might be right, Wahwie," said Mama proudly. "But Peter is right too. That might be a taller order for a dragon than for Gramma."

"We have to try," Walter argued. "'Courage is my only weapon.' That's what the riddle says. So, come on."

Pip and I remained a safe distance behind Walter and Mama as we crept toward the sharp prominence of the canyon wall. Walter peeked around it first, followed by Mama. When their faces weren't immediately incinerated by dragon's fire, Pip and I also poked our heads around so we could see what we were up against.

The dragon's rust-colored body was long and lithe, a bit like a snake who has had too much to eat. Spiraled horns, each as long as an automobile, protruded from its reptilian skull above slitted yellow eyes. Batlike wings lay flat against its back as it paced lazily away from our hiding place. Just as Walter had claimed, a sturdy shackle constricted its right foreleg. From this, it dragged a heavy chain, secured at the other end around an elephant-sized boulder.

"I almost feel bad for it," Mama whispered, once we had retreated again behind the cliff wall. "Stuck there, all alone."

Mama's sentiment was touching, but I felt worse for us. Now that I'd had a good look at the Serpent, I was more scared than before. How could I possibly show it any bravery?

"Everybody ready?" Walter asked.

I wasn't. Beside me, Pip's quaking body told me he wasn't ready either, but we said nothing.

"Come on, then," ordered Walter.

As one, the four of us stepped out into the open, each of us wearing the bravest face we could muster.

The moment the dragon noticed us, it flailed madly and charged. Intent to murder was evident in its terrible eyes.

For a second time, we dove to safety before the dragon's deadly flames could consume us.

"We can't do it!" I cried out miserably. "We'll never get past."

But Walter was strangely calm.

"Did you see? There's a big pin holding the chain together around the rock. All we have to do is knock the pin loose, and the dragon will be free. I think I can do it."

"Then it'll come eat us!" wailed Pip. Though he loved food, he clearly didn't love the idea of *becoming* food.

"Maybe," said Walter. "But I don't think so. I think once it's free, it'll be happy it can finally leave."

It was clear that his mind was made up.

"Good luck," whispered Mama, giving him a grin and confident wink.

Walter sucked in a deep breath. When he exhaled, he released with it every lingering trace of fear.

Then he stepped around the jutting wall of rock and disappeared.

TWENTY-ONE

Into the Goblin's Lair

AS WALTER STRODE FORWARD to confront the dragon—and, I was certain, his own grisly death—Mama peeked around the corner of the canyon wall to keep an eye on her boy.

I couldn't watch. I could barely summon enough courage to keep my ears unplugged. What happened next was a story I heard but did not see.

Walter wasn't out of sight more than two seconds before the dragon let loose a horrific roar of rage, as if my brother were the one personally responsible for its imprisonment in this canyon. I was certain this battle cry would be followed momentarily by Walter's own shrieks of disemboweled agony.

It wasn't. Instead, Walter raised his own voice, rebuffing the dragon's roar with a stern command.

"Get back," he shouted, "or you'll be sorry!"

To my astonishment, the dragon fell silent. Its chains clanked and rattled, which meant it was still on the move, but if Walter was an imminent meal in the making, he was being awfully quiet about it.

"I'm not here to hurt you," Walter explained, sounding more distant than before. "None of us are. I want to help you."

The dragon responded with another throaty cry, but this time its protest was brief and unconvincing.

"Oh! Yes, Walter! Go, Walter!" whispered Mama, cheering him on like a hopeful spectator whose paycheck was riding on a boxing match.

A loud *clang!* reverberated between the canyon's high walls, then a second and third. These were followed by a hollow metallic *clunk*, and I sensed that something heavy had fallen to the ground.

The dragon emitted another great roar, shaking the canyon walls and rattling the stones at our feet. But this wasn't a cry of aggression or fury. It was lighter, happier, like when a dog is barking at the arrival of a friend rather than an intruder. This was a victory trumpet.

Mama looked prouder than a prize-winning peacock as she turned to me and Pip and exclaimed, "He did it! Walter did it!"

I almost asked, "Did what?", before remembering that Walter's mission hadn't been to slay a dragon but to free one. He must have knocked loose the pin holding the dragon's chain around the rock, thus liberating it from its ball and chain. That was the heavy *thud* I had heard.

I risked a glance around the corner. What I saw astounded me.

Looking like a tin soldier standing in front of a full-grown crocodile, Walter stared up at the Serpent. The Serpent stared back, but only for a moment. It then lifted its face and pointed its nostrils skyward, sucking in deep, full breaths. It spread its wings and, like a bird who has forgotten how to fly, attempted a few timid flaps. Its feet hovered above the ground, and it beat its wings again, this time with renewed confidence. Up into the air it rose, its chain still dangling from the shackle on its leg. Higher it went, and faster, until it was flying freely. It circled and careened and cartwheeled with all the joy of a foal released from its stall.

At the conclusion of its aerial acrobatics routine, the dragon performed a final barrel roll above us, then chose its heading and soared away.

"Walter!" Mama cried, once the dragon had gone. She sprinted toward him and scooped him up in her arms. "Oh, my brave boy! That was incredible!"

He tried to act like it was no great shakes to stare down a dragon, but there was no mistaking the blush of pride in his cheeks.

While I was relieved to know I wouldn't become dinner that day, something else also crept up inside me. Something much more familiar.

Envy. Once again, Walter was the celebrated hero, and I the sniveling coward. It was his pluck and determination and faith that had brought us to the Isle, and now he had delivered us unscathed past the claws of a dragon.

Just *once*, why couldn't he get eaten?

"Were you scared?" Pip asked, staring wide-eyed up at his white knight of a brother.

Walter ruffled Pip's hair and answered, "If I were, do you think I'd be standing here? Okay—well—a little maybe. But I didn't let the dragon see that."

I tuned out the rest of Walter's victory celebration. Soon, we were on our way again. Big brother had seen us safely past the halfway point, but there was still the small matter of a "Maze of Confounding" between us and the cake-thieving goblin. Who knew how much time remained until we fulfilled our quest?

Either the winding path began sloping gently upward, or else the gorge's sheer walls themselves were dropping—it was tough to tell for certain. Whatever the case, when we finally exited the canyon's west end, we did so onto a wide spit of rock which jutted high over the lake. Like the Canyon of Fear, this magnificent promontory simply hadn't existed during our previous explorations of the Isle.

In life, Mama had widened the dimensions of our imaginations. In death, it seemed she had the power to widen the dimensions of reality itself.

Our final obstacle wasn't difficult to find. A lofty wall of uniform bricks spanned the promontory's full width, blocking our way forward. Situated in the wall's exact center, a square opening provided the sole entrance into the labyrinth beyond.

In front of this doorway sat a squat well, pooling with clear water—a welcome sight for our thirsting bodies. Above the well was a narrow, rectangular sign, supported on either end by long poles that disappeared down into the water. The sign's painted white letters read: "Maze of Confounding." Beside the words, a white arrow pointed straight ahead.

"Take a drink while I read the last clue," said Mama.

She didn't have to tell us twice. Cold, delicious water was already sliding across my tongue and down my throat as she read:

> "The Maze of Confounding will baffle and vex,
> Befuddle and muddle, perturb and perplex.
> The one who will solve it first stops and reflects."

"No point wasting any time," said Walter, in his taking-charge sort of voice. "Let's get to it."

So "get to it" we did. On the other side of the square doorway, we found ourselves in a long corridor with towering walls on either side. As we looked from one end of the interior wall to the other, we located a half-dozen gaps, each the beginning of another path leading deeper into the maze. Although I couldn't yet be sure, I had the sinking feeling those splinters would lead to plenty more of their own false tracks and dead ends.

Unless we wanted to be trapped in that maze all day—or longer—we would require a healthy dose of luck.

Too bad we were Dutch German and not Irish.

We wandered down path after path in the afternoon heat, each time running into a dead end—often literally, as some paths ended in a fatal drop to the lake hundreds of feet below. We soon became disoriented, unsure where we were or how we might find our way back to the starting point. I was quite certain we had begun revisiting old paths, but with golden boy Walter leading the way, I was hesitant to voice my suspicions.

The minutes dragged into hours—at least they *felt* like hours, even though the day curiously never seemed to grow any older. Eventually, my patience wore thin. When I noticed Pip absentmindedly scraping a long, white streak along the wall with a stone he had picked up, a bright idea came to me.

"We can mark our paths!" I exclaimed, as we returned to a feeder corridor from yet another dead end. "Pip, give me that rock for a minute."

My baby brother was too tired to protest. He handed me the stone, and with it, I scratched an arrow pointing the direction we had just come. Then, over the arrow, I scratched a large *X*.

"Now we won't keep going down the same paths again and again," I explained. "Sooner or later, we'll *have* to come to the end!"

Perhaps this was the kind of "reflecting" Gurgan had been talking about? Thinking through the confusion to devise a strategy that might simplify the maze?

Mama was the only one of our traveling party who seemed at all excited about my idea. Pip was too hungry and Walter too upstaged to offer more than a grunt of unenthusiastic acceptance.

I didn't care. I diligently marked each used—and failed—path we took, narrowing down our remaining options as we went. I knew my system would work.

Until it didn't. Some time later, we found ourselves back at the maze's entrance. Every path leading away from that main corridor, and every subsequent inner path, had received the mark of the dead-end *X*, yet we had come no further to reaching our goal.

"Great idea, Peter," Walter mumbled. "We must've missed something further in, and now it'll be even *more* confusing with your dumb marks all over the place."

"It was a good idea," Mama whispered to me, but even she sounded unconvinced. "Since we are back at the entrance, we should take another drink from the well and think over the riddle. Perhaps Gurgan was cleverer than I thought, and has fooled us into a dead-end journey."

As I drank from the well, I looked up at the sign. "Maze of Confounding." An arrow pointing upward, indicating the maze ahead.

Or was it?

"What if the real Maze is up there?" I suggested, pointing to the top of the wall.

"Great idea," mocked Walter. "I'll just grow twenty feet and boost you up."

It *did* sound ridiculous, but I wasn't ready to back down yet. Indicating the sign, I said, "The arrow points up. Maybe it doesn't mean *ahead*. Maybe it actually means *up*."

Walter rolled his eyes, but Mama was intrigued by the idea. "How could we climb up there?"

I thought back to the last line of Gurgan's riddle: *The one who will solve it first stops and reflects.* Earlier, I had assumed he meant we had to think hard about a clever solution. But maybe he was using the word *reflect* in a different way?

As I thought, I looked down to scoop up another handful of well water.

And the answer became as clear as the afternoon sky.

"It's a ladder!" I shouted, grabbing the two posts that held up the sign.

Turns out, all we needed to do was *reflect* in the water itself.

Walter, Pip, and Mama crowded around to peer into the pool. Sure enough, when the ripples ceased and its surface was calm, it was easy to recognize that the signpost was in fact the top of a long ladder, most of which lay submerged in the well.

"Great job!" cried Mama, hugging me proudly to her side. "My clever boy."

Begrudgingly, Walter helped me hoist it up. The wood was heavy with water, but still sturdy and strong, as if it hadn't been in the pool too terribly long. We struggled to lean it against the high wall, but in the end, we had a way to the top. Walter, not to be outdone, clambered up it first.

"No problem!" he shouted down when he stood again on solid stone. "The wall is plenty wide for us to walk on. Come on!"

I went up next. My baby brother—with Mama close on his heels, begging him to slow down—scampered eagerly after me. A couple minutes later, all four of us were staring out at a whole new maze.

Up here, there was a second sign. Beside a downward-pointing arrow were the words "Impossible Labyrinth."

That cleared up a thing or two.

"Okay," Mama said with a sigh. "Almost there. I can practically smell the cakes!"

I had thought to slip the marking stone into my pocket before climbing up the ladder. It became useful again in branding the dead-end paths, so that we wouldn't find ourselves retreading the same ground. Although the walls were wide and level, Mama took no chances with the easily distracted Pip—not when there were twenty-foot drops on either side of us. Despite his loud protests, she clutched him close to her chest as we navigated our way from the east end of the maze to the west.

At one point, when Walter and I were too far ahead to be heard, my big brother muttered, "Sorry I made fun of you. About the maze being on top of the wall. It was a good idea."

I shrugged coolly and said, "It's okay. Besides, it did seem a little crazy, even when I said it."

And that was the end of it. But I did decide then that maybe I was glad Walter wasn't eaten by the dragon after all.

It took us another half hour of navigation, but we finally found ourselves on top of the maze's high western wall. From here, our unnaturally long afternoon's destination was visible. On the furthest point of the promontory stood a beehive-shaped mound of rock. Near its base, a dark mouth opened toward us.

Gurgan's cave.

As luck would have it, we didn't need to go back for our ladder. A second one was already there, propped against the labyrinth's outer wall. We climbed down and approached the cavern cautiously, unsure what a goblin might do when he realized he was trapped with no escape. I half-expected him to come flying out at us like a rabid raccoon, ready to fight with savage tooth and nail.

Gathered around the cave's entrance, we peered inside and down a short, poorly lit corridor. The cavern at its far end glowed with a dim, orange light, which caused the shadows within to dance in their places.

"Ready?" Mama whispered.

"Ready," Walter replied confidently.

Boldly, we strode through the passageway and into a torchlit chamber the size of Asphodel's Great Room. In the middle of that cavern, bare but for a single table strewn with assorted cakes, stood Gurgan the Goblin. With fork in hand and bib tied neatly around his neck, he hovered over the cakes, ready to pounce on them.

Because he was facing the cave's rear wall, Gurgan was oblivious to our entrance. Using the goblin's greedy snickers to cover his footsteps, Walter marched straight up behind him, reached down, and seized Gurgan by the scruff of his neck.

The goblin squeaked with surprise. His arms and limbs flailed frantically, as Walter hoisted the leathery creature in front of himself.

Gurgan was a small, ugly thing. His eyes were black and so tiny, it was a wonder he could see at all. A long, tubular nose drooped down over his fat lips. These he had curled into a snarl, revealing jagged teeth and a sickly green tongue. He had very little by way of hair or ears, but very much of fingernails and toenails. The only clothing he wore was a dirty smock, tied around his waist with a ratty leather cord, and an ancient pair of sandals strapped to his grimy feet.

"Put me down this instant!" Gurgan demanded in a mousey voice.

Walter laughed at the pathetic creature squirming for freedom. "*You've* been causing all this trouble for us? But you're so ... tiny!"

It was true. If the goblin had stood back-to-back with Pip, he would have come no higher than my little brother's shoulders.

Gurgan growled at Walter. He apparently didn't appreciate comments about his stature.

"What'll we do with him, Mama?" Walter asked, as Gurgan scratched at and tried to bite his arm.

Before Mama could answer, Gurgan raised a grimy hand and snapped his fingers. At once, every cake on the table behind him vanished.

"You'll never get them now!" the little goblin gloated. "You can't beat me, boy."

"I've beaten plenty bigger'n you," threatened Walter. "So you'd better bring 'em back!"

Mama's voice echoed throughout the chamber. With towering authority, she ordered, "Enough of this, you two. Walter, put him down."

Walter tried to protest. "But Mama—!"

"Do as I say," she snapped, and he fell silent.

Walter gave Gurgan a final sneer, then set him back on his chair. In turn, the goblin glowered at Walter as he smoothed his wrinkled smock.

Mama cleared her throat, and both gave her their attention. She addressed my brother first, saying, "Walter, you use intimidation far too often, especially with those who are smaller than you."

My mouth hung agape. I couldn't believe what I was hearing. Walter was finally receiving the verbal drubbing Mama had been too kind to dish out in life. Years of long-awaited vindication were mine at last!

"It cannot happen anymore," she continued. "Do you understand?"

Walter nodded dumbly.

"Good. As for you, Gurgan ..."

He stared up at Mama with watery black eyes. For someone whose home he had robbed earlier that afternoon, she held a strange command over him.

"How would you like to come to my cottage and share those cakes with us?"

My brothers and I reacted as if Mama had sent a high-voltage jolt of electricity coursing through our bodies. How could she invite this awful creature into her home? Into our lives and our special time with her?

Gurgan looked as surprised as we were. His mouth mimicked that of a beached fish as he fumbled for a response.

Mama went on. "I cannot speak for you, but to me, that sounds better than eating alone. What do you say?"

A slow but gladsome smile spread across the goblin's lips from one stubby ear to the other. Based on the happy tears glistening in his eyes, I think it had been quite a long time since anyone had shared a feast with poor Gurgan—or offered him any company at all. He responded to Mama's invitation not with words, but by snapping his fingers again.

Quick as we could blink, all the cakes had returned.

"Oh, thank you, thank you, Gurgan!" Mama exclaimed, clapping her hands delightedly. "And I *am* sorry for the troubles we have had together. I never intended any offense."

"Consider it forgotten," he replied sheepishly. He appeared genuinely remorseful for stealing from a woman so noble as Mama. "And I must apologize for my assumptions about you. Clearly you are not like the nasty humans I have encountered in the past. I was wrong to judge and treat you so."

Now it was Pip's turn to speak. His empty stomach rumbled as he cried out, "Can we eat 'em? Can we eat 'em?"

I didn't hate the suggestion. It had been a long afternoon.

"Wait one more minute, Pippie," said Mama, and she addressed the goblin again. "Gurgan, could I ask a favor?"

He bowed politely. "Anything, if I am able."

"I was wondering if you could make those cakes disappear again—but this time *to* my cottage. I would hate to make my boys carry them all the way back."

Gurgan grinned. His eyes twinkled with a playful gleam as he said, "Kind lady, I'll do you one better than that!"

Then he snapped his fingers, and everything disappeared into an immediate, crushing darkness.

TWENTY-TWO

The Ways We Love

IT WAS OUR PUPPY'S YOWLING excitement which convinced me I wasn't dead. Sure, everything was dark, and I had never died before, but I was given to believe dead people didn't hear much of anything anymore.

Then Gurgan snapped his fingers a second time and, as suddenly as the curtain of darkness had fallen upon us, it rose again. No longer were we surrounded by the dim, stony walls of Gurgan's hideout, but by the dazzlingly sunlit dining area inside Mama's cozy cottage.

Pip, who had appeared closest to the puppy, found himself the victim of a vicious attack involving much licking, nuzzling, and light nipping. But the excited puppy would have to wait for our attention. In the cave's faint light, Mama's cakes had been little more than dark shapes on a table. Able now to see them clearly, we became transfixed with amazement. Every one of the confections stolen by Gurgan reoccupied its proper tray. Scattered about the cottage, on the tables and counters and bookshelves, were cakes of chocolate and vanilla and of both marbled together, of devil's food and angel's food, of carrot cake and pound cake and red velvet. Each was beautifully iced and decorated, as if done by the hands of angels themselves—which, I reminded myself, wasn't terribly far from the truth.

"*Now* can we eat?" Pip asked impatiently.

Mama grinned. "Take a seat!"

In church and Sunday school, I had heard many times of the heavenly feast we would eternally dine upon when Jesus came again. That afternoon, as my brothers and I tasted the sweet rewards of our labor, we received at least a morsel of that celestial banquet, if not its full dessert course. The Chocolate Explosion Cake of last Easter, which had once whisked me away to sugary paradise, turned bland and tasteless in my memory compared to that afternoon's confectionary spread.

Everyone ate until their bellies were round and ready to pop. Even the puppy enjoyed a slice of Mama's carrot cake when Pip accidentally dropped it onto the floor. Normally such a gluttonous intake of sugar would have soured my stomach, yet I felt as robust and healthy as I did after eating one of Abigail's "well-rounded" meals.

"Well? Was it worth the wait? And the work?" Mama asked, gazing at those around her table.

"I'll say," Walter moaned, as he patted his protruding stomach.

"I have never tasted anything like it," complimented Gurgan. "Not even my Chocolate Explosion Cake. If only we had made nice sooner!"

"I will take that as high praise," Mama said, winking congenially at our enemy-turned-friend.

Gurgan slid his chair back from the table. Standing upon it, he bowed and said, "I'll leave you to spend some time alone with your children. I'd best be on my way while some daylight remains."

I glanced out the cottage windows. Time seemed to flow more slowly here on the Isle than in the world beyond its shores, but it did not stop altogether. Early evening had arrived, casting its long shadows across Mama's resplendent gardens.

"Will you come back?" asked Walter. He had grown rather fond of the creature he'd been ready to thrash not two hours earlier.

Gurgan offered another polite bow. "Whenever you are on this island, speak my name, and I will come. And now, a fine evening to you all."

He hopped onto the floor and strolled leisurely to the front door. When he had snapped his magic fingers to open it, he faced us once more, raised a clawed hand in farewell, and departed.

With a bemused grin, Walter asked, "Why doesn't he just snap his fingers to go home?"

"Like I said," answered Mama, "goblins are not clever creatures, even if it turns out they *can* be quite polite."

The faint sound of rustling drew our attention toward the covered bassinet in the corner. Mama hurried across the cottage. She lifted the corner of the blanket and gazed down into it.

"I suppose I had best send you home now," she told us, replacing the blanket so it fully covered the bassinet again. "Baby and I both need our rest. Dying is a terribly exhausting business."

The three young faces staring back at her fell. We all remembered what was waiting for us at Asphodel. More sickness. Maybe even more death.

"But Mama, why can't we stay here with you?" Walter asked softly. "Why do we have to go back?"

Her response was vague. "Because that is your home, just as this is mine. Besides, your Daddy needs you. What would happen to him if you all disappeared?"

Remembering how Daddy had abandoned us that afternoon, Walter mumbled, "He probably wouldn't even care."

As if she could read our very thoughts, Mama said, "Daddy is trying to understand his own sadness. This is a confusing time for him, like it is for you. Be patient with him. He loves you and would be devastated to lose any one of you—much less all three!"

"He doesn't care about losing Abigail," Walter mumbled bitterly.

Mama's brow wrinkled with concern. "What about Abigail?"

"She's sick," I informed her.

Mama stared blankly at the tabletop. For a few seconds she said nothing and appeared deep in thought. Abruptly, she stood and said, "Come with me."

The puppy once again took the lead as we followed Mama from the cottage and through her enchanted gardens. After our earlier arrival on the Isle, we had walked narrow trails of trampled grass and brush. Now, as we returned, we found the paths widened and paved with flagstones identical to those on the cottage grounds. With Mama reborn upon it, the island was caught in the throes of an evolution. As a caterpillar transforms into a butterfly, the land itself was undergoing a metamorphosis. It was stretching its wings to soar beyond our puny world of imaginative play, carrying us upon its back into realms of the fantastical and miraculous.

So when we reached Emerald Hill, I was mildly surprised to find it the same grassy knoll it always had been. The setting sun cast its kingly rays of burnt gold over Mama as she sat upon the hill's crown. We sat beside her, expecting her to speak words of farewell.

But no words came. Mama stared across the darkening waters of Lake Acheron at the home whose walls she once walked—and now haunted. As she did, an intensity filled her gaze. I realized it was not a look of longing, but of searching. She was seeing and studying Asphodel as though the gulf of water in between were nonexistent.

For a long while she did not speak. When she did, it was a question upon her lips.

"Walter, do you love Abigail?"

"Of course," he answered, taken aback by the question. "We all do."

"So does Daddy," said Mama. "But sometimes, when we are deep in our sadness, we do not make the best choices. We act out of fear and desperation instead of with bravery and love."

"And that's what Daddy's doing?" Walter asked.

Mama sighed. "I know he would do anything to take care of his family. But when a single desire becomes important above all else—even a noble one like protecting you boys—it can forge a trail of bad decisions. Of destruction."

She fell silent and resumed her smoldering stare across the lake.

Again to Walter, she asked, "Do you love Abigail?"

Frustrated, my brother replied, "Yes! You know I do. I already told you so."

"Good. Then you must take care of Abigail the same way you would take care of me."

"But Daddy said—"

"Did you know," Mama interrupted, "that when I was sick and knew I was going to die, I wanted nothing more than to see my boys one last time?"

We shook our heads. The mental image of Mama, fevered and incoherent, or comatose altogether, still sickened me.

"And yet," she went on, "I never asked Daddy or Abigail to bring you to me. My heart ached with love for you, yet it was that same love which stopped me."

"I don't understand," said Walter.

"When you love someone, you must do what is best for them, even if it comes at great cost to yourself. Even if it means your own pain. That was why I never asked for you boys. Because I did not want you to become sick like me."

"Okay," said Walter uncomfortably. "But what does all this have to do with Abigail?"

"You say you love her. Now you must ask yourself what is *best* for her."

Beside Mama, Walter also stared off at distant Asphodel, as the pieces of their conversation locked into their proper places.

He pushed himself suddenly to his feet.

"Come on," he said, looking down at me and Pip. "We have to go back."

We both stood to follow, but Mama seized my arm and said, "Not you, Peter. Not just yet. Walter, take Pip to the rowboat. I have to speak with Peter alone."

Walter cast me a sour look. He resented the fact that Mama hadn't chosen him for a private conversation, while also forgetting his hours-long one the night before. Still, he didn't argue. Taking Pip by the hand, he said, "Come on."

"Bye, Mama! See ya soon!" Pip hollered over his shoulder as they began down the hill. Then, aside to Walter, he said, "I wonder what Daddy's bringing home for dinner."

The puppy lay at Mama's feet, clearly intent upon remaining with the mistress he thought he'd lost. Gently, Mama forced him onto his paws and said, "You too. Go on with them."

After emitting a low groan of protest, the dog did as Mama commanded.

She laughed and patted the long grass beside her. I sat, and Mama draped her arm around me, pulling me closer into her warmth.

"What did you want to talk about?" I asked nervously. Had I disappointed her somehow? Was she ashamed of my cowardice when we had faced the dragon?

"Do you remember last Easter?" she asked. "When we were following Gurgan's clues around Asphodel? And to this island?"

I straightened, a bit surprised. This was going a different direction than I had imagined.

"Yes, I remember. Why?"

"Three of those riddles included items we needed to solve them properly. Do you remember what they were?"

Thinking back, I answered, "A compass and a key. And the oars, and the boat too."

"Good memory," she said. "Without any one of those things, we never would have made it here to the Isle, and we never would have found our missing sugar."

"Yeah, I know." I was confused. Why would Mama want to dredge all that up after so long?

"When we were solving Gurgan's new riddles today, your brothers each brought with them something we needed to overcome the obstacles. It was Pip's innocent happiness that led us safely through the Forest of Gloom, and Walter's courage conquered the Serpent."

I lowered my eyes ashamedly. I knew I hadn't brought anything useful to the table like they did.

But Mama had more to say. "And it was *your* sharp mind that brought us through the Maze of Confounding."

I glanced up and saw Mama beaming down at me. Embarrassed, I shrank back and said, "No, it wasn't. I just got lucky. I saw the ladder when I was getting a drink."

Mama shook her head, rejecting my interpretation of events.

"First of all," she said, "we would still be wandering around that Impossible Labyrinth if you had not thought to mark the dead-end paths. Secondly—and more importantly—you noticed the ladder because you were looking for it."

"What? No, I wasn't."

"Maybe not directly," Mama conceded. "But you were wondering the whole time what it meant to *reflect*. And so, when you were staring into the water, the answer became apparent to you because you had been looking for it all along."

I shrugged. So what if I was the book-smart one? That was nothing compared to Walter's courage and sheer nerve.

Mama still wasn't finished. She said, "In a way, it is your ability to ponder and think about things from different angles which provides the key your brothers need."

That got my attention. Mama thought I was the *key?* And that *they* needed *me?*

"Pip's happiness can lift up the rest of you and provide a sense of levity during the dark times, but it is a naïve happiness. Unbridled optimism can detach a person from reality. It can sometimes even inflict more suffering on the sad and hurting when it is an unsympathetic optimism. Your sharp mind, your ability to read people and situations—these will help to keep his happiness grounded."

"And what about Walter?" I asked, ready to move on to the part of Mama's speech where she held me in higher esteem than my big brother.

"Walter's courage is tremendous," she answered. "He will move things and make them happen. He can do what he knows he must, even when he is afraid. It is, perhaps, the noblest quality a person can have."

I hung my head again. So much for skewering Walter.

"But courage without mindfulness can have disastrous consequences. To act before thinking through the various outcomes can be downright deadly. Yes, Walter has courage—courage that you and Pip both need in your lives. But Walter also needs you beside him, helping him to use that courage wisely."

I nodded, processing Mama's words.

She squeezed me close to her side again. "You boys have so much to give each other. I hope you can see that about yourself, Peter."

"I—I can," I stuttered.

At the boat far below, Walter and Pip stared up at us expectantly.

"You better join your brothers," said Mama, rising gracefully to her feet. She grabbed my hand and pulled me up beside her. "Walter has important work to take care of tonight."

"What is it?" I asked.

"You will have that answer soon enough. Now, off you go."

"Aren't you gonna walk to the boat with me? To say goodbye?"

Mama flashed me a sad smile and said, "No. I am not permitted beyond this hilltop. All my goodbyes must be from here."

I fought back the beginnings of burning tears as I flung myself against Mama's stomach and wrapped my arms around her. She squeezed me fiercely, then placed a tender kiss upon my forehead.

"Come back soon, Peter," she whispered when she let me go.

I hurried to join my brothers. At the bottom of the hill, I undid our mooring and climbed clumsily into the boat.

As Walter began rowing us away from shore, Mama watched from the hilltop. Like the dragon in the Canyon of Fear, she was bound with a shackle, an invisible chain holding her back from the life she yearned for. Sadly, there would be no courageous soul like Walter to release her from this captivity. She would remain in this prison—a beautiful and miraculous one, mind you—but a prison nonetheless.

For Rosalie Luther, there could be no flying away to freedom.

Atop Emerald Hill, Mama appeared no larger than one of Pip's toy figurines as she offered her boys a two-handed wave. Once more, her countenance beamed upon us with a warmth and radiance even the sun could not match.

Then she turned away and disappeared into the trees.

"We can't tell Daddy, you know," Walter said, once Mama was gone.

"Why?" asked Pip. "Doesn't he want to see Mama too?"

"He'll think we're crazy," Walter explained, "telling him we were with Mama only a few hours after her funeral. Plus, he wouldn't like that we took the boat without permission. He might not let us go anymore. Then we'd never get to see Mama."

The peril of losing Mama all over again was enough to pacify Pip. I felt uneasy about hiding our adventure, but I also knew Walter was right. We couldn't risk it.

When we arrived at Asphodel, the sun was nearing the horizon. Daddy was still gone.

Below the porch of our forbidden house, Walter seized me and Pip by our shoulders and said, "If either of you tattle on me for this, I'll kill you."

The threat administered, he marched up the porch steps and into the house. He returned a minute later. In his hand was a knobby chunk of ginger root, the very same one I had dropped after learning Mama was dead. I hadn't seen it since, but Walter must have ferreted it away somewhere, keeping it close in case The Flu returned for someone else he loved.

"What're you doing?" I asked plainly.

"What I should have done before," Walter answered vaguely. "You coming with me, or what?"

He didn't wait for a reply. He marched past me and up the cart path. When he reached the crest of the hill, he kept going, headed straight for the Lincolns' taboo cabin.

Nervously, I watched and listened for any sign of an approaching rider. Daddy had told us to stay away from Abigail and Eli's residence, and he could come galloping home any moment. If he caught us near that cabin, there would be hell to pay for sure.

But Walter didn't hesitate. He went straight up the porch steps and rapped sharply on the door. A businesslike determination had overtaken his every feature, and I wasn't sure even Daddy could have stopped him at that point.

From within the cottage, Eli's gruff voice replied, "Whatever it is, you'll have to take care of it yourself. I'm not leaving my sister."

"I'm coming in, Mr. Lincoln," Walter announced. Before Eli had the chance to respond, he turned the wobbly, tarnished knob and pushed the door open.

I expected to hear yelling, disagreement, and perhaps a few new curse words to add to my burgeoning vocabulary. What I heard instead were muffled voices, made indistinguishable through the door Walter had closed behind himself.

Although I hadn't been inside the Lincolns' cabin often, I knew its layout well enough from my scant visits. Grabbing Pip by the upper arm, I dragged him around back, sticking close to the walls to avoid being seen. We crouched below what I knew to be Abigail's window, aglow in the soft firelight of a kerosine lantern.

"Don't move," I mouthed to Pip. "I'm gonna look inside."

When I did, my heart broke anew. Abigail lay fast asleep, her sallow face glistening with sweat. Her chest rose and fell sharply as she fought for each shallow breath, and her lips twitched with the unspoken words of fever dreams.

Suddenly, Walter materialized in her bedroom doorway, dragging a kitchen chair behind him. This he positioned beside her bed, then sat down on it. Opening his fingers, he stared down at the ginger resting upon his flat palm, appraising it like a gold prospector gawking at his newfound nugget. Then, without a word, he placed it next to the lantern on her nightstand.

I heard him clearly through the thin windowpane as he leaned forward and, with choked voice, said, "I'm sorry for how I—how I talked to you last night."

So much had happened in the interim, I had forgotten all about Walter's dinner-table blowup.

"But I brought you something," he continued, sniffling as he spoke. "We weren't in time to save Mama, but I hope it'll make you better."

Unsure of himself, he reached out to squeeze Abigail's clammy hand.

To his surprise and delight, her fingers tightened around his, and the faintest outline of a smile came to her lips.

I realized then that I was an intruder, looking in on something solemn and sacred. Just as when the prophet Isaiah received a glimpse into heaven's throne room, I was dirty and out of place here, peeping through the window at Walter's tender moment with Abigail.

Crouching, so that my face was again hidden below the window, I whispered, "Come on, Pip. Let's go back and wait for Daddy."

Taking his hand in my own, I hurried him down the hill toward the lonely stable.

TWENTY-THREE

Refugees at the Reverend's

BACK IN THE WORKSHOP, PIP AND I helped ourselves to a sampling of the meager rations Daddy had brought us earlier. It was now fully dark, and Daddy still wasn't home. Just as my imagination began running amok, picturing every horrible accident he must have fallen into, the tramp of hooves brought relief to my anxious heart.

The workshop door opened. Daddy and Walter came through it together.

Pip and I froze. Had Daddy caught him with Abigail? More importantly, where was the food he had promised to bring home with him? Despite the feast of cakes we had eaten, I felt strangely ready for another round of something more substantial.

As if sensing my hunger, Daddy said, "Sorry, boys. Mel's was locked up when I got there. Sign in the window says they're temporarily closed."

His gaze, glassy and unfocused, flitted about the dismal workroom he had chosen for that night's lodging.

"I'm sorry about earlier," he mumbled. "I shouldn't've left. I haven't been taking care of you so well the last few days. Not since Mama—not since she got sick."

He stared at us solemnly, a man considering the difficult but important task ahead of him. "I promise to do better. But I don't know what to do without Mama here."

"It's okay, Daddy," said Pip. "She knows it's hard for you."

Walter shot him a venomous glare.

Fortunately, Daddy heard no more in Pip's words than the unintelligible mutterings of an imaginative four-year-old. He flashed a grim, exhausted grin at his youngest son and said, "Thanks, Pip. Let me start making it up to you by getting you out of this workshop."

"You mean we can go home?" Walter asked hopefully.

"Sorry, no," Daddy answered. "I still think we need to air out the house a few days."

"Then where?" I wondered.

"Pastor Wainwright said we could stay in the parsonage with him."

Walter's face fell. He shook his head and said, "I don't want to stay there. I'd rather stay here in the workshop."

The reason why was obvious. If we were lodging with Pastor Wainwright, we couldn't visit the Isle—or Mama.

"It smells like horses and sweat in here," said Daddy. "It's not fit for anyone to stay overnight, much less three little boys and one very tired Daddy."

"But what about Abigail? And Eli?" Walter argued. "Who's gonna take care of them?"

Daddy gave a heavy sigh. "Tell you what—I'll check in on them every day. I'll even call a doctor tomorrow to pay Abigail a visit. They'll be alright."

Walter was unsatisfied. "They need us here," he said. "We can help them."

Daddy had never looked more tired as he replied, "Please, Walter—*please*—don't be difficult about this. It's only a couple days." In an uncharacteristic display of compromise, he added, "We can even come back during the day if the weather stays decent. Deal?"

At that point in my short life, I wasn't yet familiar with the concept of telepathy. Still, I found myself aiming my thoughts into Walter's brain.

Don't make a big deal of it. Please. Please, don't fight.

He must have heard me. Perhaps the weary lines on Daddy's broken face also sent the message that this was not the time for obstinance. Whatever the case, Walter replied, "Deal. But can we at least bring the dog?"

Our puppy, tuckered out from the day's adventures, raised his head as he lay by the workshop door.

"Of course," Daddy replied. "We certainly can't leave him here all alone—not if we want any chickens left when we come home. I'll go into the house and pack some clothes for you boys. Is there anything else we need?"

"My—" I started speaking but stopped abruptly. More than anything, I wanted my bibby, but I also didn't want to sound like a baby. Instead, I said, "My book. It's on my bed."

"Alright, then," said Daddy, fitting a gauze mask around his face. "I'll be right back."

If a straight line constitutes the shortest distance between two points, Daddy doubled the necessary length of his trip as he lurched from stable to house. We had seen him walk like this before, but only on occasion, and usually during holidays or other celebrations.

"Why's Daddy walking funny? Is he sick?" Pip asked as we stood outside in the nippy night air.

"Not sick," came Walter's clipped response. His disapproving eyes followed Daddy. "Just … don't worry about it."

Daddy returned ten minutes later with a large suitcase. Wordlessly, he walked past us and into the darkened stable, then led out the horses and hitched them to the buckboard wagon.

Picking up my little brother and placing him on top of the luggage, Daddy said, "You can take care of the suitcase."

"Did you bring your violin, Daddy?" I asked, suddenly cognizant of the glaring omission. Daddy never failed to travel with his violin for an overnight trip.

"No," he answered, curtly and without explanation.

"I thought maybe you'd play it for us before bed," I said hopefully.

His response was sharp. "I'm not bringing it, Peter. Now climb up."

Despite the darkness, Castor and Pollux sensed their way through the night along the cart path. From there, the city lights guided us the rest of the way into Pierre. Pastor Wainwright's parsonage was situated on the eastern edge of the church property, which meant passing the cemetery where we had buried Mama mere hours earlier.

I shuddered as we rode past. Staring into the graveyard, with its silhouetted trees and gravestones, I felt as if our afternoon adventure with Mama was already years in the past. The sweat of fever and fits of coughing, the fearful days and dismal hour of her passing—it all became as fresh in my heart as the dirt covering her coffin.

I looked away and did not look back.

Pastor Wainwright's home was much larger than one man needed. When the church had been built decades in the past, the pastor serving then had been father to nine children, and the congregation had cordially furnished him with a home to accommodate his fruitful loins. When our present pastor took the position some years later, he inherited a parsonage with four guest bedrooms built in. He had, on occasion, lent out the space to parishioners in need, but mostly the space stayed empty, collecting dust and silence.

Pastor Wainwright was awaiting our arrival. He threw open the front door and exclaimed, "There they are! My family of refugees. Come in! Come in!"

He ushered us at once into the dining room. Perhaps Daddy had told him about our lack of decent meals, or perhaps he had merely perceived the need himself. Whatever the case, he had taken it upon himself to prepare a simple dinner of pork chops, potatoes, and boiled and buttered carrots. It was nothing special, but it beat the hell out of our earlier rations of crackers and pickles.

By the time dinner was over, nine o'clock had come and gone. Walter, who hadn't slept the night before, was dangerously close to tipping off his chair.

With a smirk, Pastor Wainwright said, "I'll show you to your rooms. God knows you boys could use an early night."

"And that the men could use a stiff bourbon," remarked Daddy.

Upstairs, Walter received his own bedroom. He collapsed onto the bed and was asleep before Daddy could fish his pajamas out of the suitcase.

Pip and I were given a double bed to share. We changed into our sleepwear and nestled beneath the covers, while the puppy curled up on the bare floor next to Pip.

Before he kissed me goodnight, Daddy whispered, "I brought something for you, Peter."

He opened his fist, and I saw my ratty bibby. He handed it to me with an affectionate grin and said, "Thought you might want this. Don't worry, I won't tell Walter."

I nuzzled up against it. "Thanks, Daddy."

He kissed my forehead. "You're welcome. I love you boys. Sleep well."

Exhausted by an abnormally long day, that's exactly what we did.

The next morning, over a breakfast of eggs and leftover pork chops, Daddy informed us he wouldn't be returning to the office for at least a few days. I wasn't positive, but I suspected we had Pastor Wainwright's late-night counsel to thank for the decision.

"After we're done eating," said Daddy, "we'll head into town, pick up some groceries for Abigail and Eli, and go back to Asphodel. We can spend the whole day playing outside together. How does that sound?"

Pip received the news with enthusiasm. He couldn't remember Daddy ever taking off work to stay home and play. As for me and Walter, we put on the best show we could, but our delight was far from genuine. Even staying home with Daddy was light-years from where we wanted to be.

An hour later, we were heading west from Pierre when Daddy abruptly stopped the wagon. He jumped off, ran into the brush beside the road, and puked up his guts.

"I thought you said Daddy wasn't sick," Pip said to Walter, his tone both worried and accusing.

"He's not," Walter replied in hushed tones. "At least not with The Flu."

"Then what?"

"He's making *himself* sick. Like I said yesterday, don't worry about it."

Wiping his mouth on his sleeve, Daddy staggered back to the wagon and climbed aboard.

We continued. Upon our arrival at Asphodel Glade, Daddy set up a magnificent croquet course in our orchard. This we played until a sandwich lunch of pimento and cheese on rye, followed by a surprise of Hershey's chocolate bars for dessert. Afterward, Daddy built a small fire so we could warm ourselves beneath the lakeshore trees. Over this he boiled water for coffee. Previously, my brothers and I were considered too young for such a drink, but when he brewed a pot for himself, he let us each try a swallow.

Pip and I spit it back out.

Walter didn't. He grimaced and coughed, yet managed to swallow it and even asked for more. Impressed, Daddy poured Walter his own mug, from which my big brother proudly slurped the daintiest of sips. With that initial swallow, he had taken a step toward manhood, and was loath to backtrack into childhood again.

But that was the day's only real high point. From there, the afternoon slipped into doldrums. Despite Daddy's sincerest efforts to engage us and bring joy back into our lives, only Pip received these with enthusiasm. For my part, I forced as warm a reception as I could, but it was hollow, and I knew Daddy saw through my insincerity.

Walter, by comparison, was downright disinterested, and he didn't pretend otherwise. While he joined us for tag among the trees, and later for Lasca on the back porch, he was with us only in body. His heart was halfway across Lake Acheron, on the Isle with Mama, and he couldn't help but steal frequent, longing glances in her direction.

These didn't go unnoticed, yet Daddy refrained from saying anything about it at the time.

We returned to the parsonage that evening. We ate roasted chicken, listened to the good reverend share updates about the war in Europe and The Flu's worldwide resurgence, and went to bed early.

I awoke some time later in the dark and unfamiliar room. The clock on the wall informed me it was past midnight, which was why I was surprised to hear voices downstairs. Even at that young age, I was experienced enough to know that conversations held past the witching hour were usually important ones.

The puppy raised his head in alarm as I crept out of bed. I held a finger to my lips and motioned for him to stay put. Silent as the moon sailing across the sky, I opened the bedroom door and tiptoed into the upstairs hallway.

The key to successful eavesdropping is simple: You don't need to be close enough to hear *every* word, because *enough* words will do. That is to say: as long as you can glean enough of the conversation to piece its meaning together, there's no need to move closer and so risk being caught.

Since the top of the staircase was near enough for my purposes, that was where I stopped.

Pastor Wainwright spoke first: "I know you're worried about the boys, John. That's what you do—you worry about your family. But you need to take care of yourself too."

"I'll be fine, Fred," Daddy replied. "I'm sad, of course, but I'll handle it."

"If you say so," said Pastor Wainwright. He sounded unconvinced.

"I *am* concerned about the boys, though. I don't think they're handling things right."

"And what's *right?*"

Daddy sighed. "I don't know. Shouldn't they be sadder? Crying more? *Lieber Gott,* Fred, you were at the funeral. You saw Walter. It was like he didn't care. Like he had somewhere better to be."

"Yes, I remember. I also remember how tired he looked. Could've been that he was up crying all night and already emotionally spent."

"It's not only that," continued Daddy. "I keep catching him staring out at the island where they used to play with her."

"So? That doesn't sound unusual to me."

"Here's the problem: He's not staring at it like he's sad. He's staring at it like he wishes he could be there instead of with his brothers and me. And Peter hides it better, but he's disengaged too. Not sad. *Bored.*"

"And Philip?"

Daddy scoffed. "He's four. He doesn't know what's going on. But I'm not at work and he gets to play with me all day, so he's having the time of his life."

"I know you're concerned, John. That's only natural at a time like this. But I've presided over a lot of funerals in my time as a pastor, and I can say from experience that children deal with loss in very different ways. We all have unique and complex procedures for sorting these things out. Walter and Peter are no different."

There was a pause, before Daddy said, "You're probably right."

"Keep an eye on them, of course, but be careful of holding them to your own definition of mourning. And keep watch over yourself too. You've been through a lot. If you're not careful, you might fool yourself into thinking you're handling things well, when you're actually coming undone. I've seen that happen plenty in my ministry as well."

Somewhat dismissively, Daddy said, "I will. But for now, what I need to handle is my pipe. I'm gonna step outside for a few minutes, then turn in."

"Would you turn off the lights when you do?"

"Of course. Goodnight, Fred."

"Goodnight."

The back door banged shut as Daddy exited.

I was tiptoeing backward along the hallway toward my room, when a commanding voice from below stopped me.

"Come forward, Peter."

I winced. I'd been caught. Sheepishly, I showed myself to Pastor Wainwright.

To my relief, he didn't appear angry. Rather, he wore a wry grin upon his lips as he labored up the steps to meet me. He sat upon the landing, then patted the empty space next to him.

I sat hunched forward with my elbows on my knees.

"I've lived in this house a long time," he said. "Do you think I can't recognize the sound of creaky footsteps when I hear them?"

Embarrassed, I stared at my feet and didn't reply.

He chuckled, but his lighthearted demeanor turned serious as he asked, "How are you doing, Peter?"

I shrugged. "Okay, I guess."

"Only someone with a truly terrible mama would be 'okay' the day after her funeral," Pastor Wainwright replied. "And your Mama was far from terrible."

"Yes, but—well, it's different," I argued. "It's hard to explain."

"Do me a favor and try, would you? Because, I must admit, you and Walter do seem quite okay."

And then, like Daddy had done with his breakfast that morning, I vomited out the whole thing—Walter's midnight expedition, our stealing the rowboat, Mama's cottage, Gurgan, the cakes—all of it. Even Mama's bizarre staring across the lake at Asphodel made it into my rapidly told recollection. When I was finished, I found myself panting for breath, worried what Pastor Wainwright would say next.

But there was no theological dismantling of my fantastic account. He didn't quote Scripture at me or explain why my story was such damnable heresy.

Instead, the wonderful man nodded thoughtfully and said, "Well then, if that's all true, be sure to say hello from me next time you see your Mama."

Then he winked, stood, and said, "Good night, Peter." Humming lightly to himself, he moseyed down the hallway, opened the door at the end of it, and disappeared within.

Before Daddy could return indoors and catch me out of bed, I sped away, quick as the pastor's wink, into the quiet safety of my room.

TWENTY-FOUR

Many Returns

DADDY EMERGED FROM HIS BEDROOM late the following morning, looking worse than the losing boxer after a prizefight. His eyes were red and dry, his hair disheveled. When he sat beside me on the sofa, I caught a whiff of his putrid breath. Immediately, I set aside the book I'd been reading and excused myself to take a pee.

He vomited twice during our drive home that day, the first time right along Main Street before he could dismount the wagon. After both occasions, he apologized and continued as if nothing had happened.

We spent the morning hours at Asphodel learning how to play backyard baseball. Daddy fashioned a makeshift bat from a narrow piece of plywood, and we took turns swatting at a ball and sprinting to the empty gunny sacks we were using as bases.

At lunchtime, Daddy checked in on Abigail and Eli. He returned with happy news: Abigail's fever was subsiding. She had even sat up to drink a bowl of bone broth.

The next morning, Daddy decided it was safe to return home. Although we knew we would feel Mama's emptiness there, it was comforting to know we would sleep in our own beds, surrounded by our own walls and our own belongings.

When we entered the glade, we were met with a sight that brought us even greater joy. Abigail sat in her rocker on the porch. Her eyes were closed, and her face bore a serene expression as she soaked in the sunbeams of an uncharacteristically warm morning. Above her, a pair of hummingbirds sucked happily from the feeder dangling below the cottage eave.

Upon hearing the clackety approach of our wagon, Abigail smiled and raised a hand in greeting. To our astonishment, when Eli limped around the cottage corner with an armful of split logs, he did the same.

In answer to a mystery I had shelved three nights ago, Daddy smirked at Walter and said, "Maybe your visit to Abigail did some good after all."

How Walter had been caught, yet escaped without repercussion, was beyond my comprehension. I made a mental note to ask him about it the next time we were alone—if there ever were a "next time." Daddy's constant presence was suffocating. For the first time in my life, I found myself wishing for his return to the office. After all, his presence meant Mama's loneliness as she awaited our return on the Isle.

"Can we say hello to Abigail?" Pip begged.

Daddy slowed the wagon and nodded. "Sure. But we'll keep our distance. She might be contagious still."

Abigail was glad for the visit. She began recounting for us the various stages of her illness, but when she arrived at the night of Mama's funeral, she stopped abruptly. I could see that she was piecing something together in her mind, something that had become lost and which she was only now rediscovering in the aftermath of her illness.

"I had a dream that evening, I think," she said after a long moment. "I'm sorry if it makes you sad, but now that I've remembered, it's so powerful and vivid in my mind."

"What was it?" Walter asked eagerly.

"I dreamt about you boys and your Mama," she said. "You were all together at a cottage in the woods. There were flowers and fruit trees all around, and your Mama—she was dressed in flowers too. And then a little while later, she was standing on top of a high hill, staring at me across a mile of grass and trees and what seemed like an ocean of water."

Noticing Daddy's grave face, Abigail glanced down at her hands and said, "But that was all. Right after that was when Walter came to visit me. Anyway, I felt I had to share that with you, even if it makes you sad or mad. I loved your Mama dearly, and for some reason, I think she'd have wanted me to tell you."

Abigail leaned her head back against the rocker and closed her eyes. She looked so peaceful, she very well may have fallen asleep.

Silently, we left her and rode the rest of the way to Asphodel Hall. Though the dips and humps of the cart path rattled me as much as ever, I hardly noticed them. I was too lost in my disbelief over Abigail's story. How could Mama's force, or spirit energy—whatever you want to call it—reach across such a wide expanse?

She had even bridged the metaphysical plane between waking world and subconscious, allowing Abigail to gaze upon her face exactly as we had seen it on the Isle.

But as I've thought about it in the years since, I suppose it made sense. In life, Mama always did have a gravity about her, a larger-than-life presence that never went unremembered. She had a way of leaving her imprint on everybody she encountered, like a benevolent virus whose loveliness and cheer infected others so that they were made better through contact with her. Still bearing that same spirit in death—and having broken free of the natural laws which constrained her in life—why *shouldn't* others have sensed her presence? Felt her impact? She was, after all, a mere continuation of who she had always been, though now in a more potent form.

Of course, such deep and discerning thoughts didn't cross my preadolescent mind in 1918. I simply marveled at the miracle of it all, as my brothers and father and I rode on to begin life anew at Asphodel Glade.

During the days that followed, Daddy continued his Sisyphean quest to bring activity and joy into our lives. In addition to more croquet and baseball, he helped us train the puppy to perform a dozen new tricks ranging from "Sit" to "Play Dead." He taught us how to play Kick the Can and even had a whole badminton set delivered from a department store in Allentown. When the weather went foul for a few days, we turned to checkers and hide-and-seek. In the evenings, he read fairy-tale stories to Pip and *National Geographic* articles to me and Walter.

But for all his efforts, the results didn't change. Pip bought what he was selling, while Walter accepted it reluctantly. For my part, I treated it like batty old Mrs. Norman's beet-and-hamburger potluck casserole—with all the faux gratitude I could muster. Truth be told, I felt a bit guilty. Daddy was trying so hard to revive what we had lost in Mama, but he was simply no replacement for the real deal.

After a few days, he realized it too. His efforts became as halfhearted and hollow as our reception of them. Before long, the despondency and frustration he had shown on the day of Mama's funeral began seeping back into his speech and mannerisms.

Yet not all was discouragement and doldrums. That week also saw the gradual return of Abigail to Asphodel Hall. She eased into her work, first by preparing evening dinner, then progressing to breakfast and lunch. She took up cleaning and laundry next. Finally, on the fifth of October, Abigail resumed the full gamut of her pre-sickness caretaking.

I remember the date because it was the same day my father returned to his office. This was strange for two reasons: first, because it was a Saturday; and second, because Luther & Jansen Coal was still boarded up, which meant no real work was happening there.

We happily forgave his absence. After all, it provided us the opportunity we'd been waiting for. The moment Daddy was out the door, Walter shouted, "Get Pip and the dog and meet me at the boat!"

Six minutes later, under the shroud of a chilly morning mist, Walter shoved us onto the water.

"Do you think we'll see Gurgan again?" Pip wondered aloud.

"Probably," Walter answered as he strained against the oars, "but all I really care about is whether there's breakfast."

My rumbling stomach agreed. We had left home before Abigail could fix us anything to eat.

The sun was melting away the last of the fog when we arrived at the Isle. As we disembarked, the host of cardinals greeted us from the treetops with their cheering songs. We expected to find Mama waiting for us upon Emerald Hill, but when we arrived, we discovered only grass and empty silence.

It didn't last long. From somewhere in the forest beyond came a quartet of staccato notes. *Bang-BANG! Bang-BANG!*

"What was that?" Walter wondered, glancing at me quizzically.

Our puppy responded by loping off into the trees and out of sight. I wasn't worried. On a small island like this, it was impossible to stay lost for long.

"Sounded like someone shooting a gun," I said.

"Or a hammer!" suggested Pip.

Another round of rapid *bangs!* disturbed the still morning. Even the cardinals seemed agitated.

Although we knew which paths led to Mama's cottage, we decided instead to follow our ears toward the curious sound. We didn't have to go far. The noise led us eastward until we came to the site of Hattie's abandoned treehouse construction.

Pip's guess was correct. The sound was hammering.

Perched high among the oak's thick limbs was Mama. Wearing her flowering dress and the crown of ivy, she sat upon one of the few planks we had previously hoisted up and secured to the branches. With one hand, she steadied herself on the crude platform. With the other, she wielded her hammer, working to nail a second plank beside the first. A sort of sling, fashioned from the same material as her cottage curtains, crossed her chest diagonally from shoulder to waist. Inside this was a tiny, wriggling bundle.

"Why'd you bring the baby?" Pip called up to her with a note of irritation. Even a dead baby he viewed as a threat to his status.

Mama jumped with surprise. When she spotted us below, she grinned and said, sarcastically, "Good morning to you too, Pip. Do you expect Baby to stay in the bassinet all day long?"

Sulking, Pip shrugged and lowered his eyes.

Walter cared little about Pip's jealous feud. He was more interested in Mama's reasons for hammering boards into a tree so early in the morning. Curiously, he asked, "Whatcha doin' up there?"

"What does it look like?" Mama replied. "Building a treehouse!"

If Mama had been planning to work longer, she abandoned those intentions at once. Setting down her hammer, she stretched a hand into the empty air—or, at least, it *had* been empty. A springy green vine, materializing from seemingly nowhere, now hung before her. This she grabbed with both hands and scooted forward off the branch. As if designed for her exact weight, the vine lowered her gracefully to the forest floor.

"I was expecting you," she said, hugging all three of us together, "though not quite so early. I suppose Abigail did not make you breakfast yet?"

"How'd you know she's better?" Walter asked, mystified at her apparent omniscience.

Mama ran her fingers through his dark tangle of thick hair. "Those upon Acheron—and Beyond—have deeper knowledge and more powerful sight. I can see much further now than I used to. How or why that is, I do not know, only that it is. And do you know what I see now?"

We all shook our heads.

She cracked a wide grin and said, "That my boys need some bacon and eggs in their bellies."

"And juice?" Pip asked hopefully.

"Why do you think I have all those fruit trees?" Mama replied, beaming delightedly at him.

At her cottage, she took only a moment to unload the baby into its covered bassinet, then proceeded to prepare a breakfast smorgasbord. Bacon and eggs, sausage and ham steaks, blinis and pancakes, strawberries and peaches and syrup and cream, as well as both orange and apple juice—everything flowed in a steady stream from kitchen to dining room. Despite the vast array of foods, the preparation and cooking of it took no longer than if Abigail were scrambling a dozen eggs.

We sat around the table, and Mama led us in prayer. But before anyone could touch a morsel, Walter piped up with an idea.

"Let's call Gurgan!"

Immediately, a faint pulse rippled through the air.

"Did I hear my name?" squeaked a small voice.

Pip laughed and jumped onto his chair with unbridled delight. Right before our eyes, between the plate of bacon and a bowl of fruit, the tiny goblin had appeared.

"Hello, Gurgan!" hailed Walter. "Wanna eat breakfast with us?"

"Let's see," said the goblin, thoughtfully stroking his pointed chin as he surveyed the culinary offerings. "Bacon, pancakes—ooo, blinis!—and plenty more. That should be enough for one hungry goblin."

He scampered off the table and onto Pip's chair, which my baby brother was more than happy to share. Mama fetched Gurgan a plate, and we all dove into the feast.

Although there was enough food to stuff a platoon, we ate with all the urgency and vigor of wild dogs fighting for meat scraps on a lean bone. When we were finished, and none could muscle down so much as another strawberry seed, Gurgan generously rescued us from the drudgery of cleanup. He snapped his fingers, and all the leftover food and dirty dishware disappeared into thin air.

"You are quite the handy friend to keep around!" Mama exclaimed, impressed. "I suppose that leaves us free to take care of today's important business."

Despite my bloated belly, I leaned forward with anticipation. To Mama, *business* and *play* were interchangeable terms.

Without any further buildup, she dropped an old journal onto the table. Its weathered cover was forest green, and a thin cord of ecru twine bound it shut. I deduced from the edges of its cracked, brown pages that it was either very old or very poorly cared for.

"I found this journal while gardening the other day," Mama explained. "I cannot be certain, but I believe it belonged to whoever built the old shack that used to occupy these grounds."

"What's in it?" Walter asked.

"Mostly nothing. In fact, all its pages are blank except for two—the two that tell of a great treasure hidden on this island."

We sat up straighter. If she didn't have our attention before, she certainly did now.

Mama continued. "I often wondered why anyone would choose to live here. There is little open land for cultivating and growing crops, and there is no wild game larger than squirrels for hunting. Life would have been difficult, to say the least. But when I found and read this journal, it all made sense."

A shadow of reverent sorrow fell over her.

"It also explains why the old cabin fell into such disrepair."

"Why?" asked Pip. His eyes were bigger than dinner plates.

"I am afraid he—or she—died. Or, rather, was *killed.*"

"Killed by what?" I asked.

"Killed," she whispered perilously, "by the Hellhound."

TWENTY-FIVE

Hellhound

"KILLED BY *WHAT?*" ASKED WALTER, certain he had misheard Mama.

"The Hellhound guarding the treasure," she said. "It appears the writer of this journal made one or two unsuccessful attempts at the treasure, and in doing so, learned enough to record a few details about its location and its terrible guardian. But there is no record either of success or of giving up, which leads me to believe the quest ended in—well—excruciating death."

A brief hush fell over us, before Walter said, "Well? Are we going for it or what?"

After surviving Gurgan's obstacles, things like "excruciating death" were old hat and held little terror for seasoned adventurers like us.

"What do the notes say about the Hellhound?" I asked.

Mama opened the journal to the appropriate page. As she read it, she said, "First, that it is a three-headed dog bigger than an elephant. Second, that it is chained outside a cave on the Isle's south shore. The writer also says he tried to distract it by feeding it a cow, but this ruse failed because the Hellhound's favorite food is human flesh. He also tried to sneak in at night, but apparently the Hellhound does not sleep. He had a narrow escape that time, and only at the cost of his pants seat, which he left in the Hellhound's teeth. But that is where the journal ends."

During Mama's recounting of the journal's contents, Gurgan had been growing visibly nervous. By the time she was finished, he looked downright ill.

"You'll have to excuse me from this—um—*errand*," he said, trying hard to remain calm and courteous. "You see, I have been unfortunate enough to stumble upon the Hellhound's lair, and it is an experience I don't wish to replicate. So, if you'll excuse me ..."

Without another moment's hesitation, the goblin snapped his fingers and disappeared as quickly as he had come.

Gurgan's fear was unnerving. If he had been willing to mess around with dragons, what kind of creature was this Hellhound to strike such terror into him?

"Are you sure you boys are up for this?" Mama asked, noting our pale faces.

Walter and I exchanged a glance, each of us hoping the other would seize the opening to opt out. Neither did. I had earned at least a modicum of Walter's respect at the Maze of Confounding, and I wasn't about to let that slip away because I was afraid of a dog, no matter how many heads it had.

"Let's do it," I said uncertainly.

Walter smirked and nodded his agreement.

"Then it is decided," Mama conceded. "To the Hellhound!"

Made wiser by our last adventure's foolish omission of water, Mama outfitted each of us with a canteen. As we filled them from the sink faucet, she rewrapped and retied the sling around herself. Keeping her back to us so that we still could not see the baby with our own eyes, she placed him—or her—in the sling, nestled snugly against her breast.

Mama turned just in time to see Pip's nose crinkle with disappointment. She opened her mouth to chide him, then thought better of it and said nothing at all.

On our quest to Gurgan's cave a week earlier, we had taken the west path from the garden. When we arrived from Mama's treehouse-in-construction that morning, we had come through the eastern archway. Since the journal mentioned the Hellhound's cave as being on the Isle's south shore, it only made sense to leave through the hedgerow on that end of the garden.

Unlike the other paths on the Isle, this was not paved with level flagstones, for it cut steeply downhill along the barren bottom of a shallow ravine. Exposed roots and stones protruded up from the ground, tripping hazards that kept our attention fixed upon our feet. All the while, the brush on either side of the ravine grew denser and closer, encroaching upon our heads and shoulders.

When I thought we might run out of breathing room altogether, the ravine opened up to the Isle's rocky southern shore. Here the beach was more of a sea wall, where stones and boulders of various sizes had been deposited helter-skelter by retreating glaciers long ago. Acheron's waters, stirred to life by a late-morning breeze, lapped at them rhythmically.

"This looks like a good place to turn an ankle," cautioned Mama. "Watch your step!"

Walter, surveying the shoreline, asked, "Which way?"

Mama pointed eastward. "This way, I think. It looks like the shore widens ahead. If there is a treasure cave and an elephant-sized, three-headed dog guarding it, it must have some space, right?"

We picked our way along the rocks. The going was aggravatingly slow, especially with Pip's insistence that he hop from rock to rock without anyone's help.

Our lethargic pace did afford Mama the time to ask a question, one which had apparently been troubling her.

"Why has Hattie not come with you yet?"

Walter and I shared a glum look. Neither of us wanted to tell Mama what Jacob had said at her funeral.

"Mr. Jansen won't let her go anywhere," Walter finally answered. It wasn't a *total* lie, at least. "He's afraid she'll get sick if she does."

Mama frowned. "I miss her. But I suppose I understand why Mr. Jansen feels that way."

We walked a few minutes in silence before Mama spoke again. "She has often been in my thoughts lately. In fact, sometimes I cannot *stop* thinking about her, even if I try. I no longer dream, because I do not sleep, but if I did, I somehow feel certain my dreams would be of her."

Mama raised her eyes. Not far ahead, the narrow pathway of stones passed alongside a broad shelf of granite. Except for a few choked pines and knobby clumps of moss, the rocky ground there was bare and open. When we reached the gently sloping granite table, the forest trees no longer obstructed our view, and we were enabled to see what had previously been hidden.

Beneath a high, overhanging precipice, gouged deep into the Isle's gray bones, was the obsidian maw of a yawning cave. I figured it to be at least as tall as our Castle Home's gabled rooftop.

Mama kept in front of us, taking cautious steps as she shepherded us behind her outstretched arms. There was no detectable movement within the cave's rocky jaws, only silence and unfathomed darkness.

Mama halted us a safe distance from the opening. Cupping her hands around her mouth, she called out, "Hello? Is anybody—any*thing*—there?"

We didn't wait long for an answer. From within the cave came an immediate rustling of movement. This was followed by a terrible clanking, like that of a Dickensian ghost trudging aimlessly about in its eternal bondage.

It was the glimmer of eyes which we saw first. Eyes the size of wagon wheels, approaching the harsh sunlight like distant fires kindled at twilight.

There were, in total, six of them.

"I think we found our Hellhound," Mama whispered fearfully.

Out from the cavern it stepped, snarling and baring three sets of pointed teeth. Its fur was jet black, unmarred by streaks or spots of any other color. Each lithe face ended in a moist, black, nostril-flaring nose. Nearly everything about the three heads was identical, with one exception. The left head's eyes were cobalt blue, the center head's eyes were coal black, and the right head's eyes were of a loamy brown.

Shackles, much like the one which had bound the dragon, were fastened around each of the Hellhound's individual necks. Thick chains connected these to some sort of anchor lost in the darkness of the cave.

The Hellhound's padded pawsteps were deliberate and menacing in its approach. Low growls rumbled in the throats of the left and right heads, while the middle one gnashed its teeth and snapped at us.

Mama fell back, corralling us behind her as she did.

"Be ready to run," she said. "We do not know what kind of range it has beyond the cave."

But there would be no reason to run—not yet, anyway. The Hellhound was still a safe distance away when its chain grew taut and arrested its advance.

Both to our shock and to our terrible wonder, the middle head opened its mouth. With a rumbling voice as deep as the Isle's foundations, it said, "My, my, what fortune! Fate has dropped not one but *four* tasty snacks into our lap this morning."

The left head, whose tones were higher and more energetic, cried out, "How long has it been since our last treat?"

"Decades, I think," answered the middle. "Not since that treasure hunter. He thought he could outsmart us! Ha!"

"I picked my teeth with his bones, and I'll do the same with yours," said the right head, and its eyes rolled back with nostalgic ecstasy.

"We did not come here to be your treat," declared Mama. "We came for your treasure, Hellhound!"

The middle head narrowed its eyes and sniffed the air. "What did you call us? *Hellhound?* You give us one name, but are we not *three?*"

"Three heads, yes," Mama replied, "but one beast."

With a sneer, the middle head said, "I'll be sure to save you for last, so you can watch as each of your precious children is devoured by a different mouth. And as you see us taunt and chew and savor and swallow, each in his own way, you will never again make the mistake of calling us 'one beast.'"

"My name," said the left head, "is Past."

"I am Future," said the right.

"And I," growled the middle, "am Present, and I will be your death."

As she listened to Present's gruesome threat, a strange, sly grin crossed Mama's lips. Before we could stop her, she marched confidently forward until she stood a hand's breadth beyond the reach of the Hellhound's chain.

"Foolish woman," Present sneered, foamy saliva dripping from his jowls. "Do you think you can tame me? Will you teach me a trick?"

Mama didn't answer. Instead, she took two more steps.

Present grinned and licked his lips. "Perhaps I will eat you first after all! Along with your tenderest child, whom I now see suckling at your breast."

Like a striking cobra, the great head snapped forward. Before Mama could take another breath, its tusk-sized fangs closed around her, ready to crush her, to tear her to pieces.

My brothers and I screamed.

A fourth piercing yelp clove the air, but this cry did not arise from a human throat. It came, rather, from Present. Like a dog who has tried cozying up to an unfriendly cat, the beastly head recoiled, and the Hellhound's whole body stumbled backward.

Mama stood, planted exactly where she had been, unscathed and unhurt.

"What is this? Sorcery?" Present roared with shock and rage.

"You cannot be my death, Hellhound," taunted Mama. "Nor my baby's. You see, we are already dead!"

Recovering from his initial surprise, Present snarled and shouted, "Perhaps not yours, then, but that of your living boys!"

Throughout this entire exchange, the other two heads had maintained their silence. Now, the one on the left—Past, I think—glared sideways at Present with indignation.

"Why do *you* always get to eat first?" he snapped.

Present seemed taken aback by the question. "What do you mean?"

"I mean," said Past, "what gives you that right over *me?*"

Future likewise spoke up, bawling over Present's head, "And what makes *you* think *you* should eat first?"

"I didn't say anything about eating before *you*, you great buffoon," Past retorted. "I was only commenting on Present. But you *always* have to assume the worst about me, don't you!"

"Shut up, both of you," growled Present, losing his temper.

"Don't tell me to shut up," snarled Future, and at the same time Past roared, "Why don't *you* shut up for once? Just because you're in the middle, you think you're the one who gets to do all the talking."

"No," retorted Present. "The reason I do all the talking is because you two are a pair of nincompoops."

At this, Past snapped at Present, as Present head-butted Future, and as Future lunged at Past. Present ducked beneath the pincer attack, so that the other two inadvertently ended up striking each other. This, of course, stirred the ire of each head against his two brothers, so that what resulted was the strangest, most paradoxical wrestling match anyone has witnessed since Jacob's grappling with God in Genesis. By the time all was said and done, Past had a slash over his eye, Future was licking a bloody nose, and Present was covered in the frothy slobber of both the others. Each stared coldly and silently away from the other two, stubbornly refusing to meet their eyes.

"Can I say something?" Mama asked after a moment's peace.

Present huffed petulantly at her, then looked away from her too.

"Please? I might be able to help," she said.

The Hellhound shrugged indifferently, but none of the heads gave an outright refusal, so Mama stepped forward with a question.

"Have you always been this angry at each other?" she asked.

Present snorted and glared at her. "Not always. We used to be like every other normal, three-headed dog."

"What do you mean?"

"We used to run and laugh and play together," interjected Past. "And when our master's family fed us, we would share the food equally."

"So? What happened?" asked Mama.

"One day Present realized he was in the middle," replied Future, "and because he was in the middle, he thought that should make him our leader."

"Yes, but I only did it because Future insisted on fetching all the balls Master threw," argued Present. "He said it was only right because he knew exactly where Master would throw it. You always needed to be the center of attention."

"But Past said his fur was softest and most relaxing to stroke at the end of a hard day, so his head should rest on Master's lap at bedtime," retorted Future, deflecting the accusation.

"We started arguing much more after that," said Present, casting nasty glances at the other two.

"As our anger increased," explained Future, "we became swollen with it. We grew and grew until Master told us he could no longer take care of us."

"You mean, you weren't always this big?" asked Walter, striding bravely forward to stand beside Mama.

Present shook his head. "No. We used to be the size of all the other dogs."

"Of course," said Past, "it was the saddest day of our lives when Master sent us away."

I realized then that something strange was happening. The iron collars clamped around their necks weren't as snug as when the Hellhound had first emerged from the cave. Either the collars were growing larger, or ...

"It was all Present's fault," said Future. "He's the one who accidentally stepped on Miss Master's foot."

"Squashed it into jelly," Past murmured with a tearful remembrance.

"I wouldn't have done it if *you* hadn't bumped into the wall and thrown me off balance," Present growled at Future.

"I wouldn't have bumped into the wall if *you* hadn't jumped at the window when you saw that squirrel outside!"

Past opened his mouth to add some barbs of his own, but Mama shouted them down.

"Please, stop!"

I rubbed my eyes. Surely I was seeing some kind of optical illusion or trick of the light, because the collars again seemed to fit the canine necks perfectly—and were perhaps even tighter than before.

"What we have here," said Mama, "is a case of sibling rivalry run completely amok. The only way to heal this relationship is to talk through your problems with one another."

Cautiously, Pip and I edged nearer to the bizarre therapy session. Were they perhaps playing a trick? Luring us into lowering our guard so they could pounce?

As Mama spoke with the three heads, she helped each to better understand why he was special. Their need to prove themselves over and above the others stemmed from their own insecurities and perceived lack of worth. Since Past, Present, and Future all shared one body in common, it meant they could never escape the low self-esteem they felt in the presence of their brothers.

A curious thing happened as Mama counseled them. The three heads began to shrink. The shackles around their throats loosened as their swollen anger continued to deflate. They shrunk first to the size of an elephant, then a rhinoceros, and a buffalo. Although their iron collars slipped free during this process, not once did they try to eat us.

When the Hellhound was no bigger than a common dairy cow, Mama charged them with a final task.

"You have all wronged each other," she said. "Arguing over who has done worse than the others will only keep the feud alive. If you want the years of anger and discord to be over, each of you must apologize to the others."

Despite all his earlier bravado, Present was the first to speak.

"I've been the most selfish middle head of any dog in history," he muttered ashamedly. "I'm sorry."

"And if I had shared Master's affections with you, we would still be with him today," Past admitted. "I'm sorry too."

"I'm sorry for priding myself on how well I could catch the balls Master threw," said Future. "If we ever find another master, I'll be sure to let you both have as many turns as me."

The Hellhound—that it ever bore such a name seemed silly now—contracted in size one last time, until it was no bigger than our puppy. Playfully wagging their collective tail, the triple-headed dog pounced on Mama, and three pink tongues licked at her lovingly.

"What will you do now?" she asked, when their enthusiasm had subsided.

"Perhaps if we find Master, he would welcome us home again," said Future.

Present nodded his approval and said, "We at least have to try. Now that our love for each other has returned, the only love we're missing is his."

"Then I wish you the best of luck on your journey," said Mama. "But if you find that your master will not have you, or that he has passed on, return here, and you will have a home with me."

Nuzzling his wet nose against Mama's hand, Past said, "Thank you for showing us kindness, even though we didn't deserve it."

"I'm sorry I tried to eat you," added Present. "It won't happen again."

Mama chuckled. She patted each of the three muzzles and said, "Good boys. Off with you now. I am sure you have a long way to travel before dark."

Baying happily, the three-headed dog trotted across the rocky clearing and, with a final, grateful look back at us, disappeared into the trees.

Mama's gaze lingered after them as they left. Once they were gone, she turned to face her own three boys and declared, "Now for our treasure!"

TWENTY-SIX

Truest Treasure

THE HELLHOUND DISPATCHED, we strode intrepidly into the cave's gaping mouth. Once under its shadow, our sight adjusted to the darkness. We saw that the "cave" was, in fact, a deep outcropping which angled sharply inward from the upper lip of the overhang. The Hellhound's iron chains had been attached here, anchored into the rock above the narrow crease where ceiling met floor.

But that was all we saw. The journal's writer, who believed treasure would be found within, had perished for nothing more than rock and iron.

Or so we thought. It was Pip's keen eye which made the crucial discovery.

"A door! There's a door!" he cried out, jumping up and down and pointing excitedly.

Sure enough, a section of the angled ceiling in the rear of the cave had been chiseled away, creating a rectangular recess. At the end of the narrow alcove, and hewn from the same granite which surrounded it, was a polished door. Engraved upon it were five words formed of blocky letters: FIND WITHIN YOUR TRUEST TREASURE.

"I think you earned honors here, Pip," Mama said, once we had gathered before it.

The deep thunder of stone grinding upon stone reverberated throughout the cavern as Pip—with a little help from Mama—forced the door open.

What we saw inside was even more unexpected than dragons, goblins, and three-headed dogs. Both journal and door had spoken of treasures within, but when we stepped into the dim chamber, we didn't find ourselves surrounded by heaps of gold or chests overflowing with precious gems. We were in a small theater, illuminated from above via a skylight in the ceiling. A movie screen almost as wide as the room itself hung upon the chamber's back wall. Facing the screen, in a single row, were four velvet-cushioned chairs.

The scene made me uneasy, and for a moment I struggled to figure out why. Then I remembered. On the same day Mama had fallen ill with The Flu, her treasure hunt had ended with movie theater money. Along with Hattie, we were all supposed to go to the new theater in Castleton. Then Mama died, and any hope of sitting by her side in front of the silver screen was buried along with her. Finding such a theater here, in the belly of a cave, was not only surprising to me. It also dredged up the dread and distress I had come to associate with that terrible morning.

I expected the screen would flare to life momentarily, yet nothing happened.

"This is the treasure?" scoffed Walter, clearly disappointed with the reward for all our efforts.

"It does seem odd," murmured Mama. "But remember, some treasures are far more valuable than silver or gold."

"Can we sit down?" whined Pip. "My feet hurt."

Mama took his hand and guided him to the chairs. Even when they sat, nothing happened. The screen remained dark.

"There are four chairs here," said Mama. "Maybe we all have to sit to make something happen."

With nothing better to do, and with tired legs of our own, Walter and I didn't waste energy arguing. The instant our rears hit the cushions, Mama's theory proved true. The lifeless screen burst into light and motion. Unlike other theaters, this picture was not limited to black and white and in-between shades of gray. No, every vibrant hue of corresponding color filled the frame, mesmerizing us, drawing us in and holding us captive.

What first appeared was a snow-blanketed field. Near its margins, the level line of a forest divided the white world below from an azure, cloudless heaven above. Many of the trees were barren, but the evergreens popped like brilliant emeralds upon the bleak landscape of winter. Although I didn't immediately know why, this opening image carried with it a powerful aura of familiarity. As I watched, the scene panned from right to left, until it settled upon a snowbound cabin whose chimney billowed smoke.

Then it hit me—this was Asphodel Glade. Not Asphodel as it was today, but as it had been two Christmases ago. I remembered it fondly as the day I unwrapped my toy train beneath the tree. And not just any toy train, mind you. This train used a lump of coal beneath a tiny water reservoir to power it along its track with steam. How I had loved it, playing for countless hours, oblivious to the rest of the world beyond its circular track.

I was losing myself in reminiscence when the scene on the screen changed. Now Daddy was there, standing in the middle of the Great Room, bouncing up and down and playing his fiddle as lively as ever. Next to him danced Abigail, who held a sloshing glass of wine as she indulged in the Luther Christmas festivities. Grampa Henry and Gramma Opal were there too, sitting in the background, one clapping along to the beat while the other scowled at the scandal of it all. Yet even as she did, her ankle swung from side to side under the hypnotic rhythm's undeniable seduction.

The vantage point swung around to show me Mama. Her hair was woven through with festive ribbons of berry red and holly green, and around her neck she wore the pendant of citrine which Daddy had given her that very morning. She watched everything through shining eyes and with a captivated grin, blessing our merriment with her deepest affection.

The scene panned to the Christmas tree in the far corner of the room. My new train sat on the floor, the pride and joy of my heart when I opened it. But this scene did not have the train in its focus. Tiny Pip took the limelight for himself as he played with my new toy. I remembered being nervous he might break it, but he looked so happy. As I soaked in his joy, a tranquility settled upon me as well.

The screen went dark briefly before showing me a third scene: mine and Walter's bedroom. I knew without a doubt the viewpoint here was from my very own bed. After all, how many sleepless nights had I stared jealously across the darkened room at Walter, who always rested so soundly? But in this particular scene, Walter's bed was empty. As the movie reel unwound, I saw my bedroom door creak open. Walter slipped through, approaching the screen. In his hand, I recognized my bibby.

Only when he laid it softly next to my movie self, did I fully grasp what I was seeing. These were *my* memories, the memories of an unforgettable Christmas, a day which I might have considered the happiest of my life.

But no—I remembered something more. Buried among all the mirth was an unpleasantness, an angst. At some point during our Nativity festivities, I had misplaced my bibby. Back then, it was always at my side, and I had panicked when I realized it wasn't. Despite the day's Christmas joy, I fell asleep that night heartsick and sobbing. But when I woke the next morning, there it was in my hands, pressed tightly against my nose. My sleepy subconscious must have discarded the memory of Walter setting it beside me, because I had assumed Mama or Daddy had found it and reunited us.

In truth, it had been Walter. He must have snuck away after I fell asleep and searched for it in our dark house. When he found it, he could have done anything he wanted to it. He might have disfigured it as a cruel joke or shown his spite for my "baby" blanket by throwing it out altogether. But he didn't. He gave it back to me and healed my broken heart.

The movie ended abruptly, and I became keenly aware of how uncomfortable I felt. Having my life, my memories, laid bare like an open book before the others left me vulnerable, as if I could keep no part of myself hidden any longer.

The others remained silent too. Mama continued to stare at the screen as if the reel were still running, and tears trickled down her cheeks. Based on her spell-bound smile, I determined that her tears were those born of joy, not sorrow. Somehow, I didn't think the reunion of boy and bibby would elicit such a powerful reaction from her. I wondered then if she was seeing something different—if Walter and Pip were too. What I had watched seemed wrought of my own memories. Perhaps they also had seen a movie uniquely tailored to their individual selves.

The cavern's dull gloom returned upon the film's ending, and a chill began to settle with it.

Mama stood, wiping her cheeks, and said, "I think I found my treasure. Are you all ready to return to the cottage?"

We followed her wordlessly from the cave. The sunlight was blinding after the dark theater, but it didn't take long to realize how much of the day was now gone. During our previous visit with Mama, time seemed almost to stand still, while today was racing along at double speed. By the time we had traipsed along the shore and through the woods to the cottage, so much of the afternoon was past that Mama insisted we head straight home.

"Why can't we stay with you?" moaned Pip, dejected. "Daddy would let us for just one night. I *know* he would. Or we could get him and bring him here!"

Mama smiled sadly and said, "I wish it were so, Pippie. But Daddy's heart is not ready yet."

"Then when?" pressed Walter, striking a rare discordant tone with Mama. "We should all be together, shouldn't we? Isn't that when we were the happiest?"

I wondered again what he—and Mama and Pip—had seen on the movie screen.

"Of course it was," Mama replied. "But it is not that simple. If Daddy were to come here with an unprepared heart, he would see only trees and rocks. He would not find me. I do feel that I will see him in due time, though I do not know how, nor under what circumstances."

"But I thought you could see everything now?" I asked, sniffing a potential dishonesty in this inconsistency. "Just like you saw Abigail when she was sick."

Mama laughed. "I said I can see *further*, not *forever*."

At that moment, our puppy crashed through the underbrush and into the cottage grounds. We had seen neither tail nor whisker of him since his scampering off after our arrival.

"Perfect timing!" Mama exclaimed. "Your Daddy would be asking questions if you returned home without your puppy."

She hugged and kissed us all, then said, "Off with you now! And you had better hurry. I am afraid your early morning departure created some unintended consequences."

We learned what she meant as Walter rowed us toward Asphodel. Leaning against a shoreline birch, and holding a glass of brownish liquid, was Daddy.

When I informed Walter, he glanced over his shoulder and cursed. We were caught.

Daddy didn't move as we disembarked. With our eyes cast submissively groundward, we shuffled across the dry leaves until we stood before him.

"I received an interesting telephone call from Abigail this morning," he began. "She said you were already gone when she came to make breakfast. She figured you'd gone out to play, but after a few hours passed, she started to worry." He sipped his drink. "Can't say I blame her."

"Sorry, Daddy," I mumbled, not daring to meet his eyes.

He continued, pretending he didn't hear me. "I hurried home, of course, but it didn't take long to figure out where you went. I saw the rowboat was gone, and I knew how much you missed playing out on that island."

He sighed and swirled the liquid in his glass. Like an amateur chess player, he pondered his next move with uncertainty.

What followed surprised me. He said, "From now on, I want you to tell me or Abigail before you take the rowboat. We need to know where you are. Understand?"

Enthusiastically, we nodded our assent. Not only was Daddy being gracious about our expedition across the lake. He had even given his permission to continue using the rowboat in the future!

Daddy sauntered unsteadily over to our trusty ship. He laid his fingertips on its blue gunwale, gazing at it admiringly.

"You can row that big thing all by yourself, hey, Walter?" he asked. A glimmer of pride twinkled in his eye.

"I watched Mama enough," Walter replied. "It's really not that hard."

"I have to admit, I'm impressed," said Daddy. He knelt to pick up a long, straight branch which had fallen from a nearby tree.

"Come here," he said. Noting our sudden tension, he chuckled lightly and said, "Don't worry! I'm not gonna whack you with it."

When we were gathered around him, Daddy singled out Walter.

"Kneel in front of your boat, son," he commanded.

Walter did as instructed, though he looked utterly bewildered—and perhaps still a touch fearful.

Like a king using his sword to dub a brand-new knight, Daddy tapped each of Walter's shoulders with the branch and said, "Walter, I name thee Captain of the Ship. I charge thee with caring for her and for all those onboard, as you would your own family. Now, rise and name her what you will."

Walter beamed as he stood and faced the rowboat. He considered the matter for only a moment before announcing, "I'll call her *The Rosalie*. After her last captain."

Daddy's grin faltered, and a momentary shadow darkened his face. All the same, he nodded and said, "A fitting name. I'll order a few life preservers for *The Rosalie* soon, that way I know you're safe out there."

"Do you think you could order some blue paint too? Just like what's on the top of the rowboat?" Walter dared to ask, indicating the coloring of the gunwales.

Daddy raised an eyebrow. "What for? This paint looks fine to me."

"So I can paint her name—the boat's name—on the back," Walter responded.

Daddy grinned and said, "I think that sounds like a fine idea. I'll pick some up from the hardware store in town." He glanced toward the house and said, "Now run on back and wash up. Since you missed lunch, Abigail said she'll set dinner out early."

But as my brothers and I hurried up the hill, I chanced a look back at Daddy.

I was just in time to watch the glass slip from his hand as he crumbled to the ground beside the boat. *The Rosalie.*

There he sat, and he sobbed.

May 18, 1954 – 12:31 p.m.

SOFTLY, I TRACE THE NAME engraved on the headstone.

R ... O ... S ... A ...

That's where I stop. To the people who knew and loved her best, that was her name.

Unless you were fortunate enough to call her "Mama."

"I'm so sorry—sorry for—well, you know." I choke out the words but am unable to finish the thought.

The guilt is decades old. The guilt is as fresh as yesterday.

"And I'm sorry it's been so long since I visited," I continue, finding my voice again. "It was too hard when I was younger, and now I live halfway across the country. But that's no excuse. And if you were here right now, I know you'd tell me to stop talking at you like a crazy person, but ... here I am."

Great speech, I tell myself wryly. *Two days on a train, and that's the best you could come up with? Nice.*

I exhale a heavy sigh. Lowering my eyes from Mama's birth and death dates, I read the inscription below them. I couldn't count the times I heard those sweet words sung upon Mama's lips. They were as much a part of her as the curls in her hair or the freckles on her nose. That was why Daddy made sure they were etched into her headstone.

I close my eyes. From memory, I sing them tenderly:

> *"From this valley they say you are going,*
> *I shall miss your bright eyes and sweet smile,*
> *For alas you take with you the sunshine*
> *That has brightened my pathway awhile."*

When the verse is done, I stand, straight and tall. I find myself strangely invigorated for what still lies ahead of me.

"Goodbye, Mama," I say. "I'd stay longer if I could, but I shouldn't keep Pastor Wainwright waiting. I love you."

I turn away, careful not to let my gaze wander to the marker beside Mama's. There is one ghost in this graveyard I'm not ready to confront.

The one I put here.

"Do what you needed to?" asks Pastor Wainwright with his easy nonchalance, as I slide again into the passenger seat of his Buick.

I nod and reply, "Yes. She's right where I left her."

"And ... you didn't visit anyone else?"

"No. No, I still can't. All these goddamn years—excuse my language—but I still can't."

"Maybe next time," the old pastor says, as he eases the Buick off the grass and onto the road.

We head into town. He is quick to point out every change, be it ever so tiny, that has occurred in Pierre since the days of my youth. But I'm not paying much attention. My thoughts have flown, and there is little use trying to re-cage them.

It's only as we approach the intersection of Main and 4th Street that my consciousness returns to my surroundings. Even then, I likely would have remained oblivious if Pastor Wainwright, stopping at a traffic light, hadn't reached across my face. He is pointing north toward the residences beyond Main Street's business block.

"Any desire to drop in on Hannah Jansen?" he asks. "She's an old bird like me now, but still sharp as a tack. I'm sure she'd love to see you."

"No, that's alright," I reply. With a chuckle, I add, "I've been traveling for something like forty hours. What I need right now is a shower and a nap. Not necessarily in that order."

Pastor Wainwright's mirthful laughter is exactly as I remember it. Despite the hardships he has weathered during his eighty years, he remains as cheerful as a May meadow.

"My old nose isn't what it used to be," he says, "but you are a tad ripe. I'll have to air out the Buick after I drop you off."

I smirk and find myself thankful that some things—and some people—never change in the ways that matter.

The light turns green, and Pastor Wainwright pulls through the intersection. But before my view is blocked by the next segment of storefronts, I glance aside and up 4th Street one more time. The Jansen house stares back. Its blue exterior and white trim are in dire need of paint, and the flowerbeds around its perimeter have deteriorated into overgrown tangles of thistles and unplanned saplings.

Perhaps before I return to Wichita, I'll drop by and help Mrs. Jansen restore her property. At her age, I'm sure it's been tough to keep up with the gardening, especially since Jacob's passing last year.

But as I lower my head and descend again into the pools of memory, I don't dwell upon Hannah, or Jacob, or the dilapidated property, nor upon how I might help her fix up the old place.

I instead think back to October 29, 1918, and the last time I ever stepped foot inside the Jansen house.

TWENTY-SEVEN

Hattie Takes Leave

OUR SUNDAY DINNER OF ROAST DUCK and butternut squash soup created no small amount of dishes. Even though Abigail was back to her full workload, it was obvious her battle with The Flu had sapped much of her strength, and that she hadn't yet fully regained it. Thus, Daddy insisted we clear the table and clean the mounds of dishes which crowded the kitchen sink.

For once, we didn't mind. Seeing Abigail's return to health lifted our spirits and transformed us—at least momentarily—from selfish boys into altruistic young men.

Daddy, whose mood seemed greatly improved by the outstanding dinner, did not help. He instead retreated into his study. When he emerged twenty minutes later, pipe in hand, he was wild-eyed and somber again, and said not a word as he left the house through the back door.

Walter and Pip shuffled off once the dishes were done. But as I dried my hands, my glimpse of Abigail sitting at the little table in the corner prompted me to hang back. Exhausted and lost in thought, she stared out the window at the darkling sky.

"Are you okay?" I asked timidly, for fear I was disturbing her.

"Yes, yes, I'm fine," she answered. "Just ... thinking."

I sat down beside her. "Thinking about what?"

"There's something I can't seem to get rid of," she replied. "Something I don't know I *want* to be rid of. It's that dream about your Mama when I was sick. Remember the one I told you about last week? Anyway, it's almost like she's haunting me or something, because I can't stop thinking about it. Never had a dream so vivid, or one that stuck with me so long. She seemed so alive and real and—oh, Lordy, Peter—was she ever beautiful. Unlike anything I've seen in all my life. And you boys! You boys were so real too. Real as you sitting beside me right now. And, like I said, I can't get her outta my head. Not hardly for a second."

I shifted uncomfortably. I had already spilled the beans about our adventures to Pastor Wainwright. Walter would have killed me for that alone if he ever found out. But here was Abigail, presenting me with a wide-open door to share our miraculous encounters with Mama. How could I say nothing? Besides, what if she had seen Mama for a reason? What if Mama *wanted* Abigail to see and to know? If that were the case, I'd be doing wrong by keeping my mouth shut.

So I didn't. As had happened at my midnight chat with Pastor Wainwright, the words came pouring out before I realized I was spilling them.

"Your dream was real," I whispered, wary that Walter might yet be within earshot.

Abigail's brow furrowed, and she said, "'Course it is. I remember it like it was five minutes ago."

I shook my head. "No, that's not what I mean. I mean, what you saw was *real*. Mama, us—all just like you dreamed."

"That's not funny, Peter," scolded Abigail.

"I'm telling the truth!" I snapped, upset that Abigail could think me capable of lying about something so serious. "We've all seen her—me, Walter, and Pip, anyway. Mama's out on the Isle. The big one in the middle of the lake. She lives there now, and we take the rowboat out to see her."

Abigail realized I was fully convinced of everything I was telling her, and her expression softened. Her features filled with pity as she said, "Oh, Peter. I knew how hard this was on you boys, but I didn't know it was *this* hard."

"What do you mean?"

She sighed, searching for the right words. "Hard to deal with your Mama being gone. Hard to sort through your sadness and pain, especially since your Mama's the person who's supposed to help you through these things."

"You don't believe me," I said, as an idea came to mind, "but I can prove it."

"And how's that?"

Confidently, I stated, "When you saw Mama in your dream, she was wearing a belt made out of yellow flowers, and she had a kind of crown made out of ivy that had purple flowers on it."

Abigail's jaw dropped half an inch, and she blinked with astonishment. I had, of course, told her exactly what she had seen in her dream.

"That's—but—*how?*" she stammered in disbelief.

"I already told you! We were right there with her!" I exclaimed victoriously.

My triumph was short-lived. As quickly as Abigail's doubt fled, it returned. She shook her head and said, "No. No, I must've been talking in my sleep when Walter visited me. He must've heard me talking about your Mama."

"No, I—"

Abigail cut me off by wrapping her arms around me and pulling me into her dinner-scented clothing. I felt her trembling against me as she said, "Your Mama's gone, Peter. Gone, and ain't coming back. By the good Lord's grace, we'll go to her someday, but she won't come back to us. She *can't*. And you'd do well to accept that, even if it makes you sadder than you ever thought possible. Only then can you move on with life."

"But, Abigail, it's *real*. You have to believe me!"

"I believe there's some part of you that thinks it is. Maybe even your whole self. But it just can't be, Peter. It just can't be."

I was at a loss. It seemed there was nothing I could say which might convince her, so nothing is what I said.

"Have you told your Daddy any of this?" she asked, stroking my hair and cheek.

I shook my head and answered, "No. We can't. If we do, he'll think we're crazy or playing a mean trick on Pip. Then he won't let us take the rowboat anymore. Please, *please*, don't tell him."

She studied the deadly seriousness in my face for a moment, then said, "I don't believe it's my place to tell him one thing or another."

"Thank you," I sighed.

She wasn't finished. "But listen to me, Peter. I've been around this world long enough to know that keeping secrets most always leads to problems."

"We'll tell him soon," I assured her. "But Mama says it isn't the right time yet."

Abigail exhaled concernedly and said, "Just promise me you boys'll keep an eye out for each other, alright? And be careful on that boat."

"We will," I promised. "Daddy told us he'd order some life preservers, so we'll be extra safe."

"Good. Now run along. I've got to bring Eli his dinner."

It bothered me that she didn't believe me, even after I had matched my description of Mama precisely with what Abigail had seen in her dream. But as I thought about it more, I decided I couldn't blame her. It wasn't exactly an everyday occurrence for dead loved ones to magically reappear in one of your favorite playgrounds. Besides that, Abigail's lack of faith wouldn't prevent my continued visits to the Isle. My brothers and I still had what we wanted most: time with Mama.

The next morning, it was the only thing on our minds. Walter and I determined that from then on, it would be wise to wait until our stomachs were filled with an Abigail-made breakfast before crossing Lake Acheron. Besides providing the energy needed for our excursions, this also gave us opportunity to fulfill Daddy's sole rowboat-usage condition by informing her of our plans.

Abigail stared at me knowingly when Walter made our request at the breakfast table.

"Be sure to take care of each other," she said, echoing her plea from the previous night. "And if you're gonna be out all day, you'd best bring some ham and cheese sandwiches along for lunch. I'll fix 'em while you boys eat your breakfast."

Before we were finished cramming down our oatmeal and fruit, Abigail had returned with a lidded picnic basket. She placed it on the table beside my plate. Inside were the sandwiches, as promised, along with warm oatmeal cookies wrapped in a towel and an apple apiece for the three of us.

As we grabbed the basket and made for our exit, she said, "If the weather starts looking dicey, you come back straightaway. Understood?"

Walter, still working down his last bite of fruit, mumbled, "Unnerftood."

"*And,*" Abigail added, "be home well before dinner. I think it'll do your Daddy good to find you here when he comes home."

"We will!" I promised, and out the back door we went.

We had barely made it off the porch when a voice stopped us.

"Where're you going?"

I almost dropped the picnic basket. It was Hattie. She was approaching us around the side of the house.

Our puppy seemed to remember her from their first encounter a couple weeks earlier. He set upon her immediately, jumping and licking and giving her the full best-friend treatment.

"We were—uh—going out to the Isle," said Walter. At least for the moment, he decided to keep the reason a secret. Suspiciously, he asked, "What're *you* doing here? Your father said you weren't allowed to see us anymore."

"Yeah, he told me what happened at the funeral," she said, trying to convey her remorse by pushing away the happy puppy. "Sorry."

Walter shrugged. "Not your fault, I guess."

"I fought him as hard as I could," Hattie said, "but he wouldn't budge. I wanted to be there so bad, and I wanted to see you after, but he wouldn't let me."

Walter raised the obvious question. "So why're you here now?"

Hattie grinned mischievously and replied, "Mother and Father left for Pottsville this morning to visit my Aunt Carol. They'll be gone three days, and they left Jacob Junior and Arlene in charge. I guess with everyone scared of The Flu and shut up in their houses, they weren't worried about leaving us alone."

"Aren't you afraid Arlene'll rat you out? Or Jacob?" I asked.

"Nope! I bribed 'em with doing both their chores for two whole weeks, so long as they keep their mouths shut," said Hattie. "Besides, if they squealed at this point, they'd probably get in more trouble than me for taking my bribe."

"That was pretty gutsy," said Walter, impressed. "And I'm glad you came. There's someone who's been anxious to see you."

"Oh yeah?" cooed Hattie, turning red in the cheeks.

I wanted to puke. She thought Walter was talking about himself.

"Mmm-hmm," Walter affirmed stupidly, oblivious to what he was actually affirming. "Really missed you a lot!"

"Well, if I'm being honest, I guess I missed you too," muttered Hattie, scuffing at the dirt with her toe.

Walter raised a confused eyebrow. When he recognized the mix-up, he broke out laughing. "No, that's not what I meant. I meant that *Mama* misses you."

A blush even deeper than the first filled Hattie's cheeks, though this time for a different reason. A budding pique seeped into her tone as she asked, "What are you talking about?"

Led further into oblivion by his zeal to reunite her with Mama, Walter charged on like a stagecoach driver unaware of an upcoming cliff.

"That's where we're going right now," he said. "We've been visiting Mama on the Isle. She lives there now, and last time we saw her, she told us she wished she could see you too! She's gonna be real happy when we bring you along!"

Hattie's eyes were already glassy with smoldering tears as, softly, she asked, "Do you think I'm stupid or something?"

"What? No!" exclaimed Walter, at last realizing how he was coming across. "I'm—*we're*—not making this up! I know she died, and we even had a funeral and everything. But she's there, Hattie. I'm serious. She lives where that old shack was, only now it's a big cottage surrounded by this amazing garden—"

"You're horrible," Hattie interrupted, too disgusted even to raise her voice. "I've seen you play some mean jokes before, but I never thought you'd play them on *me.*"

As Hattie unfurled her wrath against Walter, was there some sliver of satisfaction inside me that enjoyed watching it happen? Absolutely. A sliver and some. But there was a much larger part that wanted her to join us. So instead of aligning myself against my brother, I stepped to his side.

"It's not a joke, Hattie," I told her earnestly. "I didn't believe him at first either. But after Mama's funeral, Pip and I went with him, and it's all true. Every word."

If I thought adding my credence to Walter's claim would sway her, I was wrong.

When Hattie spoke next, it was with clenched jaw and through gritted teeth. "What is wrong with you? It's *your* mother who died."

"Hattie—" Walter pleaded, but he was cut off.

"You stupid asses have said some awful things to me before," seethed Hattie, "but this is the worst. By far."

Fat tears spilled down her cheeks as she backed away from us. Her nostrils flared like those of a Derby-winning steed, and her face became so red and twisted with rage, I thought her head might explode in a bloody geyser.

"Please, Hattie, just listen," I begged. "Come with us and see for yourself."

"Come with you?" she said, backing away further. "No. I'm never going to your stupid island ever again. In fact, I'll never even come to your stupid *house* ever again."

With a huff, she whirled about and began to stomp away. As she left, she cried out over her shoulder, "And if school ever opens again, don't talk to me there either! Got it?"

We were too stunned to respond. Within a minute, Hattie had stormed up the hill and over it and out of sight.

When Walter was certain she wasn't coming back, he finally tore his gaze away from the empty hilltop. Coolly, as if nothing had happened at all, he turned down the embankment toward the lake and said, "Come on. Mama's waiting."

TWENTY-EIGHT

The Other Empty Seat

I COULDN'T STOP SEEING HATTIE'S face during our voyage across Acheron. She had disobeyed Mr. Jansen's firm orders by visiting us. She had even taken on the debt of her siblings' chores as payment for her misdeed. It was unbearable for me to imagine her walking home, sobbing, full of bitter disappointment over what she perceived as our betrayal. And it didn't comfort me one bit that what we had told her was true. Truth or not, it had alienated someone I loved, someone who was sister and friend and even more to me.

We arrived at the Isle to the same sound of hammering we had heard two mornings earlier. We gave chase as our puppy rushed off along the path leading to Mama's treetop construction site. When he reached the base of the tree, he planted his broad paws on the bark and began yipping up toward the branches.

Sure enough, there was Mama, sitting upon a wide platform which now encircled the tree trunk like a flat, wooden doughnut. A dozen or so cardinals kept her company, entertaining her with their merry warbles and fluttering dances.

Upon spotting us below, Mama and bird alike stopped what they were doing, eerily and suddenly.

"Something is wrong," she asserted. "Where is Hattie? She was supposed to come with you. I was certain she would."

Walter shook his head, chagrined, and explained what had happened at Asphodel.

A strange perplexity fell over Mama as he told the tale. When he was finished, she glanced detachedly around the platform she had built, as if struggling to understand where she was or what she was doing. Although she was high in the tree and I on the ground, I detected in her features a hint even of fear. I didn't know why this news of Hattie's wrath affected her so much, but it sent a shiver down my spine nonetheless.

Mama's next words hit me like a sledgehammer.

"I can't play today," she declared, picking up her actual hammer. "I'm sorry you came all the way here, but I have work to finish."

"Can't we help you?" Walter asked, confused and dejected.

"Not with this. Not without Hattie."

"Should we wait at the cottage?" I asked. "You aren't working all day, are you?"

"All day and into the night, I'm afraid. And perhaps for many days and nights beyond. My project is great, and I'm afraid it's more urgent than I realized."

Walter wasn't ready to back down. "But if we could just help—"

"You can't," Mama insisted. "And I don't have the time or even the ability to explain why. I just *know*. So, you can either go to the cottage and play there by yourselves—don't wake Baby if you do—or you can go back to Asphodel."

It seemed pointless to stay at the cottage without Mama's presence filling it, so we returned, disheartened, to the rowboat. A gloom fell upon Walter. As he rowed us silently back to Asphodel Glade, I didn't dare speak a word, nor for the entire remainder of the day.

The next morning after breakfast, we went back to the Isle, certain Mama wouldn't spurn us twice. Again, we followed the sound of hammering to the ancient oak. Today, the circular platform also held an upright portion of a wall around its outer edge.

For the second day in a row, a frazzled yet determined Mama sent us away.

"You'll have to be patient and trust me," was all the answer she gave when Walter tried to argue.

He was so put off by Mama's second denial, he almost refused to go again on Wednesday. When I goaded him into trying anyway—and when we were rejected a third time—he became surlier than a snowman in late February. Never in my life had I seen him so galled at Mama. Not even the time she had marched him to his classmate Peter Sandusky's house to apologize for a practical joke—one involving a full inkwell and peeking butt-crack—could compare with his resentment after that third rejection.

Still, when Daddy came home that afternoon with the blue paint Walter had requested after naming the rowboat, my brother went dutifully to work. In penmanship that would have made Miss Carrington weep tears of joy, he expertly brushed his ship's name in ornate cursive upon its flat stern.

She was officially *The Rosalie*.

Walter's finished project was a salve to his wounded ego. For the remainder of the day, he became a much pleasanter older brother.

But Thursday brought a different kind of bad news.

It had been determined that Pierre's schools would reopen on Monday. Even if Walter managed to bury his anger and return to the Isle, our availability to spend time with Mama would be limited almost exclusively to weekends.

When we returned to Pierre Primary, Miss Carrington handed each of us a gauze mask and instructed us to fit it around our noses and mouths. She informed us that the wearing of such masks would be required until further notice, then proceeded to pick up where our learning had left off weeks earlier.

Uncomfortable, and petulant over the sudden end of what was supposed to be an endless break, most students put forth even less than the half-hearted effort we had given after the summer holiday. Since none but the most scholarly of students had cracked a single textbook during our hiatus, we were essentially starting the academic year all over again.

Upon our return, two noticeable absences loomed over our classroom. The first was the one we had all expected. Jeremiah Lasseter was gone, and we knew it was unlikely we would ever see his face again on this side of paradise—and if New York didn't help him clean up his act, it was also unlikely we would see him on the other side. The second disappearance was that of Sally Steinbrenner's younger brother Thomas. Although our little corner of Pennsylvania had seen a rapid decline in cases, he had contracted The Flu after his sister's recovery from it. Unlike Sally, he hadn't experienced a quick rebound. Rumors were as reliable as ever back in 1918, but the general consensus was that Thomas wasn't long for the world.

Two days later, he was back in his seat, little worse for the wear. That was how The Flu worked. Just as quickly as it could kill you, it might also release its claim on you entirely. It was as undiscriminating as a hooker and as unpredictable as the weather.

If being back in school wasn't bad enough already, it was made unbearable by the fact that Hattie still refused to speak with us. Walter tried only once to patch the tear between them, but when she spurned his kindnesses, he withdrew into himself and refused to extend the olive branch again. I, on the other hand, made daily attempts to engage her. Each time I was met with a cold shoulder, a cruel word, or worse.

Besides the melting of the leaves into deep gold and red, autumn's other major change was the resumption of operations at Luther & Jansen Coal. To make up for lost commerce, Daddy's work hours lengthened beyond their pre-Flu allotment. Each morning, he left before sunrise. Each evening, he returned well after we boys had finished our dinner. With bourbon on his breath, he would help us with our homework, oversee our chores, say bedtime prayers with us, and tuck us in with a quick kiss before retreating into his study. That was where he had chosen to sleep during Mama's sickness, and it was where he remained after her death. In the back corner, between two bookcases, he had set up a cot and transferred bedding from one of the guest rooms upstairs. In his religious fervor to avoid the room where Mama had expired, Daddy even asked Abigail to relocate his clothing to the study, lest he disturb her spirit—or his own.

Daddy's extended work hours were not without their upside, for they returned to us the opportunity stolen by school's reopening. The second the clock struck two-thirty that first Wednesday afternoon, Walter and I hurried home as fast as our legs could carry us. It had taken a full week, but his indignation toward Mama had subsided enough to attempt another excursion to the Isle.

This time there was no sound of hammering when we arrived. We raced to the top of Emerald Hill and discovered Mama waiting for us there.

"You're here!" Pip shouted, throwing himself into her expectant arms. "Are you done with the treehouse? Can we see it?"

I sensed that she was hiding some impenetrable sadness as she replied, "Not just yet. One last addition is required still. You will have to wait for it."

With the weather growing chilly and the days waning short, we spent our precious minutes with Mama at her cottage, both that afternoon and the next. Mama read us short stories from Mark Twain as we ate piping-hot scones. We played checkers. We talked about school and life. When we told her Hattie still wouldn't speak with us, Mama changed the subject to something lighter of heart.

On Friday, the eighteenth of October, Daddy surprised us by beating us home from school. With him he brought a sack of licorice and, for the dog, a pair of wrapped beef bones. These were the spoils from his first grocery store outing since Abigail had recovered, and he appeared prouder of himself—and more lucid—than he had in quite some time.

"I have another surprise coming," he told us, vaguely and with a giddy air, as we tore into the candy on the front porch. "That's why I'm home. It's being delivered here shortly."

Delivered? My imaginative mind could only wonder what "it" might be!

We didn't have to wait long. Fifteen minutes later, a dust cloud rose over the hill. True to Daddy's word, a delivery truck puttered along the potholed cart path, driven by a man with a handlebar mustache. Similar to the coroner's wagon which had hauled Mama away a month earlier, the green truck's rear was a spacious, covered cargo area.

Our disappointment over not being able to visit Mama was put on hold. As we watched the truck pull into the yard and stop, every wonderful possibility of what it might contain filled our curiosity.

The mustachioed man exited the vehicle. He tipped his gray cap but said nothing as he sauntered to the truck's rear. We watched, speechless, as he placed two Schwinn World boy's bicycles on the lawn. Other than their colors—one was red and the other green—they were identical. Beside these the man placed a larger bicycle, all black and presumably for Daddy. Finally, a handsome red tricycle, just the right size for Pip, joined the others.

"Thanks for delivering way out here," said Daddy, handing the man a wad of cash. "There's a little extra for having to deal with all my potholes."

The man tipped his cap again and said, "My pleasure. I hope you enjoy them."

"Can we take 'em for a ride?" I begged, the moment the man was gone.

"What say we take them to Mel's for supper?" suggested Daddy. "They're open for business again. Seems everything's opening back up these days!"

Pip and I applauded the idea, but Walter balked. His initial excitement over the bicycle had already cooled. He now backed away and shook his head.

"We were gonna go out on the boat," he said, "but it'll be too dark for that when we get back."

"It's only one night, Walter," said Daddy. "The boat'll still be there tomorrow."

Walter chewed the matter over in his mind—and literally upon his lip. Whether it was the alluring sheen of the new bike which won him over, or the understanding that a fight with Daddy would get him nowhere, he nodded and said, "Okay. We can go."

We headed to Mel's, and I thought it was the end of the matter.

It wasn't. Later that night, when I was supposed to be in bed, I overheard Daddy conversing with Abigail in hushed tones outside his study door. Walter was sound asleep, so I snuck out alone to listen more closely. As I sat in shadow at the top of the stairs, neither of the two speakers sensed my presence.

"Truth is, Mr. Luther," I heard Abigail say, "they're rowing out there whenever they find a free minute."

"I had a feeling it had something to do with that," Daddy replied. "But *why*? Why are they so obsessed?"

My heart froze. Would Abigail spill to Daddy what I had spilled to her?

"They sense her there, I think," said Abigail. "Missus Luther. And with so many memories made on that island the last few months, who can blame them?"

My father savored another sip of bourbon from his glass, which seemed practically welded to his hand as of late.

"It's not healthy," he said. "They're not dealing with losing her. They're running away from it."

"Or perhaps running *toward* something you can't see. Either way, who's to decide the best way for dealing with grief? Long as they're not hurting themselves, that is."

"I still don't like it," said Daddy, "but the weather's turning colder. Soon I can put the rowboat up for the winter, and with them none the wiser about my real reason. Maybe a few months off will help them get over whatever this is. Until then, I suppose I'll let them have their fun."

"You're their Daddy, so it's your call, of course," replied Abigail. "But if I were you, I'd speak to them directly."

"I'll think about it. Thanks, Abigail. And goodnight."

It was depressing to know Daddy would soon put our visits with Mama on winter's ice, but I didn't dare share with Walter what I knew. He was too head-strong and unpredictable when it came to anything concerning Mama. It would be best to let Daddy break the news whenever the day in question finally came.

We were able to visit Mama only once over the weekend, on Saturday. She had seemed disturbed during our previous visit. Now she was a Titanic wreck. The flowers which crowned her head and sashed her waist were drooping, their gentle petals spoiled brown and curled at the edges. Yet even then she refused to tell us what she feared. She urged us only to pray that it might not be so, that she had misinterpreted whatever it was her special sight had shown her.

When we arrived at school on Monday morning, we at last began piecing to-gether the source of Mama's troubles.

In addition to the empty seat left by Jeremiah Lasseter, a second desk sat vacant.

This time, the missing student was Hattie.

TWENTY-NINE

Parting Words

"HATTIE WASN'T AT SCHOOL TODAY," Walter blurted, the moment Daddy emerged into the Great Room from the chilled darkness outside. "Nobody knows where she is. Did Mr. Jansen say anything at the office?"

Daddy appeared taken aback by Walter's impetuousness, but he quickly regrouped. The knowing gleam of some puzzle solved, at least in part, filled his expression.

"Interesting," he mused, using his shoe to push aside the excited puppy who had come to greet him. "Mr. Jansen also wasn't in the office today. I figured he decided on a day off, so I didn't bother calling. Were Arlene or Jacob Junior there?"

"They're in a different classroom," answered Walter. "Now that I'm thinking about it, I don't remember seeing them outside during recess."

"Are you sure they didn't take a trip somewhere?"

"Well ... no," Walter replied uncomfortably.

Daddy hung his peacoat on the rack beside the door. "I suppose she would have told you boys if she were going out of town, so that's probably not the reason."

"Hattie hasn't talked to us lately," I chirped. "We got in a fight."

Walter glared at me warningly, and I realized I had said too much.

"A fight about what?" asked Daddy, an eyebrow raised in question.

"Nothing—something stupid," I feebly stammered.

"Something stupid? Stupid like what?" pressed Daddy.

"She always wants to build a treehouse," lied Walter, "and when we said we wanted to do something else, she got really mad and left. Hasn't talked to us since."

"You always do what you boys want," said Daddy. "Couldn't you let her have *her* way for once?"

Walter shrugged but said nothing. He wanted the conversation finished as much as I did.

Daddy was apparently ready to move on as well. He said, "I'll call Mr. Jansen tomorrow if he's not back in the office. In the meantime, don't worry. Cases of The Flu have been dropping like flies in summer."

"Okay," Walter and I said in unison.

But we were worried. Mama's strange behavior the past two weeks had set us on knife's edge. Like a night watchman who knows an enemy army is lurking nearby, Walter and I were waiting, expectantly and uneasily, for the cries of doom and destruction to blight our eardrums and rend our world asunder all over again.

It was coming. We both sensed it. And, although we never spoke our convictions out loud to each other, we also knew it had something to do with Hattie.

When school began the next morning, Hattie's absence persisted. At recess, Walter and I kept vigilant for any sign of Arlene or Jacob Junior, but we found no trace of either. The three elder Jansen children had seemingly vanished into thin air. Hearsay had a way of spreading through Pierre like—well, like a disease—yet in our investigations, we heard not even one warped morsel of gossip pertaining to the Jansens.

"I'm going to their house," Walter announced after school, as we mounted our Schwinns outside Pierre Primary. "Come along if you want."

I did. Five minutes later, Walter stood on their covered porch, knocking emphatically on the Jansens' front door. I could have sworn that I saw one of the window curtains flutter, but when nobody answered, I figured it must have been my imagination.

Walter shrugged and said, "Maybe Daddy heard something. Let's go home."

Daddy was already sitting on the porch when our bicycle tires screeched to a halt in front of Asphodel Hall. He appeared deep in thought, and a cold pipe dangled from his lips.

"Was Mr. Jansen at work today?" Walter demanded, without so much as a "hello's" worth of preamble. He didn't bother taking the time to lower his kickstand, and his bicycle clattered onto the lawn as he bounded up the porch steps.

"No, but I did call him," Daddy answered, tacitly forgiving Walter's forwardness. "Turns out they made an unexpected trip to Pottsville to visit his sister."

The aura of tension surrounding Walter fell away immediately. "Oh! I'm glad they're okay. Come on, Peter. Let's get Pip and go to the Isle."

But as we journeyed across Acheron, I found myself disturbed. There were two elements of Daddy's report which didn't pass the smell test. First, it was hardly a week ago that Hattie told us her parents were visiting her aunt in Pottsville. Why would they make such a trip again after only a few days? Secondly, if the Jansens weren't home, how could Daddy have spoken with Jacob? Did he expect us to believe he had tracked down Mr. Jansen's relatives, calling them one by one until he finally located his missing business partner? I was certain my father was hiding something—if not lying altogether—and grew even more distressed than before.

As a lifelong Lutheran, any notion of Purgatory was false and damnable doctrine in my young ears. Nevertheless, for the next two days, I lived in the gnawing Limbo of uncertainty. Every time we brought up Hattie or the treehouse with Mama, she would change the subject, while Daddy kept his lips tightly sealed around either his pipe or a bourbon glass.

On Thursday, it all came to an end.

After riding home from school, Walter and I leaned our bicycles against Asphodel's porch wall—Daddy warned us they would rust if we left them for the dew—and hurried inside to warm up.

Our father was waiting for us. He sat in the Great Room, cross-legged on an easy chair, swirling that ever-present tumbler of bourbon and staring off into nothingness. The wildness of the drink had overtaken him, and to a degree we had not yet seen, as he mumbled inaudibly to himself like a patient in an asylum.

We set down our schoolbags, and his unfocused eyes flitted toward us. He cocked his head as if struggling to recognize his two older sons.

"I'm so sorry," he said, his voice a raspy croak. "I should have told you. I should have been honest. I wanted to protect you. Keep you safe."

Walter stepped toward him cautiously, like someone approaching an injured animal. The beast appeared wounded, but would it still claw and bite?

I saw Abigail in my periphery, standing in the kitchen doorway. Her arms were crossed, and she watched Daddy with deep displeasure. I wondered also if she was there to stand guard, ready to intervene on our behalf if the situation called for it.

"What are you talking about, Daddy?" Walter asked apprehensively. "What should you have told us?"

"Hattie," my father moaned, and he covered his eyes in shame. "It's Hattie."

A look of pure loathing flashed like deadly lightning in Walter's eyes. "What's wrong with her? You said she was in Pottsville."

The drink had subjugated my father's tongue, and he slurred as he spoke. "She's ... not'n Pottsville. Never was. She's at home. Sick. They're all sick. All the Jansens."

"For how long?" I asked.

Panic climbed up my chest. The Reaper's shadow had again fallen over my world, his cold sickle raised and ready to reap. To inflict upon me a far worse pain than the simple harvesting of my own breath.

"Since Sunday," my father moaned.

"When did you find out?" Walter demanded, pitiless in his fury for the puling man who sat before him.

"Two days ago. When I called Jacob. He didn't answer, but I talked to Mrs. Jansen. They're all sick. All of 'em but her."

"You lied to us," hissed Walter, carrying out his interrogation as ruthlessly as a Secret Service agent grilling a would-be assassin. "Why did you lie to us?"

"I didn't want you to worry. I didn't want you to be scared again, like you were for your Mama. I thought Hattie'd be better in a few days, and she could tell you everything herself. And by then it'd be happy news, not sad."

"So why are you telling us now?" I asked, the panic rising into my throat and voice.

"Because Mrs. Jansen called me. 'Bout an hour ago. She doesn't think—Doc Schumacher doesn't think Hattie's gonna make it."

With those words, he buried his head into trembling hands.

Walter and I stood, rendered speechless by the deathblow Daddy had dealt us.

But my brother didn't stay dumb long. Flaring up like a spark upon magnesium, he shouted, "That can't be true! Hattie isn't dying! She can't. You're lying again! You're a liar!"

"I'm sorry," my father wept. "I had to tell you. I needed you to be ready this time. I didn't do that with your Mama, and I should've. I couldn't do it again. This time, you needed to know."

Over the past weeks, my young eyes had witnessed astonishments hitherto unknown during my nine-and-a-half years of existence. I had seen my mother's fingertips, dead and purpled from The Flu's slow suffocation. I had seen cardinals by the thousands, flocking together in the heights of the Isle's great trees. I had seen my mother, dead, and yet alive, standing upright in garments woven of petals and paradise. I had seen fruit trees bud at a whispered word and a goblin gobbling down cake.

But what I saw next astounded me more than all the others combined.

Like a rabid chimpanzee, Walter threw himself at our father. His arms flailed with furor as he pummeled the sobbing man's chest.

"Shut up!" he screamed. "Shut up! You're a liar! A drunk liar! Keep your damn mouth shut!"

There was a time and place, which now seemed half a world away and a hundred years past, in which Daddy would have tucked Walter under his arm, hauled him upstairs, and painted his ass redder than a barn door.

But not here. Not this day. Instead, my father wrapped his arms around Walter's convulsing form and pulled him close. As punishment for the embrace, Walter lifted his attack, beating upon my father's neck and head and face. Still, Daddy didn't let go. Even as the blows rained against him, he wept, despondent, the failure of fathers.

Before I could fully process what was happening, Abigail had descended upon them like a headmistress breaking up a schoolyard scuffle. Shouting herself, she peeled my frenetic brother away from my father. With a strength twice that of a woman her size, she lifted him, kicking and crying and cursing, and hauled him backward. Even when she lowered him again to his feet, she was a human straitjacket holding him in place.

Walter's vicious outburst died down, though not his fury. There was nothing less than murder in both glare and voice as he said, "You should have told me. I could've done something. If I had more time, I could've helped her."

With a hopeless groan, he yanked himself free from Abigail's grasp. I thought he would take a second fly at our father, but he didn't. Instead, he whirled about and stamped out the front door. As he flung it shut behind himself, the whole of Asphodel Hall shuddered.

I couldn't speak. I could only stare. First at Daddy, then at Abigail.

She, too, was dumbstruck.

Blood trickled from my father's lower lip, and his hopeless eyes were bloodshot and puffy from weeping. These he now raised up from the floor until they rested on my own. In his cloudy stare, I recognized what he was seeking.

Forgiveness. Mercy. Love.

Although I was sure he didn't deserve such things, I promised myself I would give him all three. But this was not the time. He had made us wait for the truth. Now I would make him wait for absolution.

I had something far more urgent to do.

Without seeking any word of permission from my father, I followed Walter. As I hurried onto the front porch, I discovered him already charging up the hill on his bicycle.

I didn't hesitate. I knew he wouldn't slow his pace a single inch to let me catch up, so I hurried to my own bicycle and sped after him. The late-afternoon air chilled me, though not as much as my own heart. Compared to the frost settling over my spirit, the winds of late October were a smithy's forging blaze. The ice which had formed inside me at Mama's death, only to be thawed by her reappearance on the Isle, was recrystallizing, as images of Hattie's fevered frame passed in front of my mind's eye like scenes from a Hitchcock horror. As I rode, my imagination's sway became stronger, creating sharp and vivid abominations. The tears blurring my vision couldn't obscure those terrors set before me, nor the dread toward which I rode.

Whatever possessed me, be it angel or demon, I don't know. What I do know is that I caught up to Walter, despite the fact that he himself pedaled like a cyclist about to win the Tour de France.

We didn't stop until we were in front of the Jansen house. Its windows, obscured by thin curtains, were aglow with a soft light.

"What're we gonna do?" I asked desperately. "Mr. Jansen won't let us in. You know he won't."

Walter, as headstrong and unconquerable as always, quietly replied, "Then we'll make him."

Our bikes fell with a racket onto the walkway, and we bounded up the porch steps two at a time. Walter pounded on the front door, then stepped back and stared at it, daring it not to open.

It did. Hannah Jansen's grim face looked down at us. She had certainly seen better days. Dark half-moons sagged beneath her dull, green eyes, and her hair was unwashed and grimy—the results of too many days caring for her ill household.

She opened her mouth to speak, but before she could utter a sound, a second figure swooped around her to glare down at us.

"You shouldn't be here," Mr. Jansen growled. "Go home."

If Mrs. Jansen looked rough, her husband was the embodiment of Pestilence itself. The twin storms of stress and illness had taken their toll as they had lashed against his stony features. In the month since Mama's funeral, his already-gaunt face had become bonier, and his features sharper. He never did bear the bulky frame of a laborer, but as he stood over us, the only word I could think to describe him was *wispy*. Even his beard, which had been thick and well-trimmed from my earliest memories, was bedraggled and patchy, peppered with gray.

I shrank back, cowering at the very sight of him.

But not Walter.

"We came to see Hattie," he announced. "Daddy told us she was sick."

"And how would he know that?" Mr. Jansen demanded.

His wife stepped beside him and said, "Because I called him."

"You *what?*"

"They deserved to know," she insisted, trying in vain to choke back her emotions. "Hattie's been like a sister to them, Jacob."

"But this is *their* fault, Hannah," snapped her husband. "If she hadn't snuck away to visit—"

He never finished his sentence. At that moment, Hannah Jansen, the sub-servient housewife, reared back and smacked her husband across his face.

It truly was an evening of surprises.

"Our house is full of sickness," she said, addressing me and Walter as she stepped in front of her husband, eclipsing him. "But if you will risk it, I think you'd better go and talk to Hattie. While you still can."

"She needs *rest,* Hannah," argued Mr. Jansen, but even his conviction sounded flat. "She *has* to get better."

With pity also for her husband, Mrs. Jansen said, "You know as well as I do that she needs more than rest. She needs a miracle. It's in God's hands now."

She led us through the dark and eerie hallways, silent but for the occasional hack echoing upon the walls. When we arrived at Hattie's bedroom door, we found it already ajar. A thin filament of golden lamplight seeped through the crack to illuminate our faces.

"I'll wait here while you talk to her," whispered Mrs. Jansen, ushering us forward.

Walter swallowed hard. His cheeks, always such a rich bronze, were pale and bloodless, betraying his true fear.

I was scared too—it simply wasn't as visible because my skin was pasty to begin with. The real difference between us, as Walter momentarily reminded me, was not in our skin tone, hair color, or stature.

It was in his courage and my cowardice.

That was why I remained frozen in place while Walter, despite his fear, pushed open the bedroom door and stepped inside.

Arlene Jansen slept soundly in the bed on the right side of the room. Although her hair was matted and greasy, her complexion appeared hale and colorful. She had endured a tough struggle but was finally approaching the finish line in victory.

By contrast, the girl occupying the bed against the opposite wall was the very image of death. Hattie's every breath was a contested battle, raspy and rapid as she fought for air. Sweat crowned her forehead, turning her springy curls into limp, lifeless tassels. Her oxygen-starved lips were pale and blue, and on her cheeks were the same mahogany spots which I had glimpsed upon Mama before her passing.

Only one thing about Hattie Jansen seemed unchanged by The Flu's ravages.

Her eyes. Still the vivid green of Asphodel's lawn after a summer rain.

She was awake. And lucid enough, at least, to track Walter's approach from the door to her bedside.

Lying there was the girl I had known my whole life. The girl I had seen with winter's snowflakes and summer's lake water shimmering in her eyelashes. The girl who'd stood beside me through so many adventures. The girl I called my best friend, and whom my childish heart first loved.

Yet now, in the hour of her direst need, all I could muster was one step—one pitiful step—into her doorway. Dread had so sapped my strength that I could hardly look upon, or even listen to, the scene unfolding between her and my brother.

"Hi, Hattie," Walter said gently. There was a stool beside her bed. He sat upon it and took her damp hand in both of his.

She mustered a weak smile, and her beautiful eyes found him. With love she searched his face, their bitter feud forgotten without a single word of apology.

"I'm sorry you're so sick," Walter said, maintaining a surprising calm in his voice. "I wish I could do something to help."

Hattie's lips moved as faintly as those of someone lost in a dream. A whisper, thin and shaky, hissed through them like air from a pinhole in a tire.

"You can."

Walter leaned forward. "What do you want? I'll do anything."

My tears spilled, unhindered, when Hattie spoke again.

"After I'm gone, will you visit me on the Isle?"

Walter grinned and squeezed her hand. "So *now* you believe me."

"Your Mama—"

But Hattie's words were cut off by a violent fit of her own hacking.

Walter didn't need her to finish the thought. Leaning in even closer, unfazed by the fountain of Flu her coughing spewed over him, he matter-of-factly whispered, "Mama came to you, didn't she."

Hattie nodded weakly. She closed her eyes, and her head sank deeper into the pillow.

"Then," Walter said, teary-eyed but smiling fondly, "I guess that's right where I'll see you."

I don't know how long we remained like that—Hattie in bed, Walter beside her, and I affixed to the doorframe—but Mrs. Jansen eventually brushed my shoulder and said, "You and Walter should probably leave. It isn't safe for you to linger any longer than you already have."

Across the room, my brother heard her gentle words and stood without a fight. One last time, he squeezed Hattie's hand.

"I'll see you soon," he murmured.

My heart quailed as I realized that, on this side of Death's intrusion, I was receiving my final image of Hattie Jansen. This indelible photograph would remain in my memory, both to haunt and inspire me. To bring me, somehow, both hope and gloom together.

Praying she might hear me from across the room, I miserably, weakly whispered, "Bye, Hattie."

Walter grabbed my upper arm and coaxed my petrified form back into the hallway. Mrs. Jansen closed the door behind us.

Still able to hold his head high, Walter muttered, "Let's go home."

And home is right where we were when, shortly after one o'clock that night, Hattie's body, weakened by the onslaught of the virus inside her, surrendered its fight and gave up her spirit.

THIRTY

The Enchantress of the Treehouse

DADDY HAD SCARCELY FINISHED delivering the morbid news about Hattie when Walter rolled out of bed and asked, "Is it okay if we skip school today?"

Our father scratched his chin and considered the question for a moment before saying, "That sounds reasonable. I can't imagine you'd give Miss Carrington much attention anyway."

"Thanks," mumbled Walter.

"Would you ... like me to stay home with you?" Daddy asked hesitantly.

Although neither had spoken of it since, Walter's detonation the previous afternoon still crackled in the air between them.

"You don't have to do that," Walter replied, perhaps a bit abruptly. "I mean— I know you have work, and Mr. Jansen definitely won't be there to run things."

Daddy lowered his dull eyes and said, "No. I suppose not. Do you want to talk about what happened before I go?"

Walter shook his head. "She's gone. I don't know what there is to talk about."

"First your Mama, now your best friend," said Daddy. "It's a lot for two boys to handle, isn't it? I want to make sure you're okay."

I certainly wouldn't have called myself "okay," but I had spent a good hour crying in bed the night before. Somehow in this Flu-doomed world, we were learning to expect sorrow as the new normal. The mere morning after I had stood paralyzed in Hattie's doorway, a sort of deadening had begun circulating through my blood, a desensitization to what once would have constituted a deep trauma. As a result, my reservoir of tears was already evaporating—or perhaps was simply emptying itself more hurriedly than in the months and years past.

"We're fine," Walter assured him.

Daddy grimaced and blinked rapidly to moisten his whiskey-parched eyes, but he wasn't quite ready to retreat. He suggested, "Then maybe we should talk about what happened last night. Between *us*."

Walter sighed and stared stubbornly out the window. "I don't want to."

"That's fine," said Daddy. "You don't have to say anything. But I'm gonna tell you that I'm sorry. I was wrong to lie to you, even if I was trying to spare you more sadness. And when you called me a drunk—well, I'm sorry about that too. I was way out of line. It's not right for a father to let his boys see him like that."

"It's okay," Walter assured him halfheartedly. Abruptly switching topics, he asked, "Can we take *The Rosalie* out after breakfast?"

Daddy frowned, reluctant to answer. More than anything, I think it was guilt for his drunken sob-fest which moved him to say, "That's fine, as long as you take your brothers with you. But we're going to talk more about this when I come home."

As our downcast father left the bedroom, I felt certain his last declaration would never come to fruition. He would, more than likely, drown the guilt of his failure beneath another pint of bourbon instead.

But that was a problem for later. For the present, Walter and I dressed ourselves in woolen trousers and flannel shirts—outside looked plenty cold through our window. After waking Pip and clothing him, we rushed downstairs and plopped ourselves into our dining room chairs.

Abigail emerged from the kitchen with a large platter of eggs and sausage links. Tears streamed down her cheeks as she set them before us.

"I'm so sorry about Hattie," she said with a sniffle. "Though it makes sense, I suppose, that God would want that wonderful little girl by his side too. Right there with your Mama."

Pip, already moving on to his second sausage link, burst into tears. "Hattie *died?*" he wailed.

"Yes," said Walter. "But it's okay. Daddy said Peter and I could skip school today. We're gonna take the boat out to the Isle."

Little Pip was oblivious to the subtext behind Walter's words, and he cried all the harder as he shoveled another forkful of eggs into his mouth.

With a look of suspicious concern, Abigail stared directly at me. "Your Daddy said you'd be taking the day off school. I hope you'll use it to give Hattie a respectful time of mourning."

"We will," Walter assured her. He still knew nothing of my conversation with Abigail. "It's just—well, we were building a treehouse there with her. Now that she's gone, I feel like we really should finish it. In her honor. Don't you, Peter?"

"Yeah," I mumbled feebly, fully aware that Abigail saw right through the charade.

"In that case," she replied, wiping away her tears, "you better get to work. Wouldn't want to dishonor her memory with any other foolishness."

Ashamed of her disappointed gaze, I lowered my eyes and returned to my eating.

We soon found ourselves gliding over the lake for what felt like the hundredth time that month. This morning, however, we did so with a rediscovered sense of newness and anticipation, such as we had experienced during our first visits there with Mama. Although we hadn't yet witnessed Hattie's rebirth upon the Isle, Walter and I had no doubts she was patiently awaiting our arrival. Perhaps she was, even now, sitting beside Mama atop Emerald Hill, watching our approach over Acheron's placid waters.

As I tethered *The Rosalie* to the shoreline, I noticed that the cardinals had multiplied since our last visit. Their corybantic song-and-dance was no longer confined to the treetops alone. They had expanded their realm to roost upon and flutter about all branches high and low, and their frantic lyrics seemed to cry out, *"Come and see! Come and see!"*

But when we arrived atop Emerald Hill, only one figure awaited us.

"Where's Hattie?" cried Walter. "Is she here?"

Mama stared soberly down at us, motionless but for the breeze ruffling her petaled garments. Her features betrayed no hint of emotion, whether good or bad.

"Are you ready to see the treehouse?" she asked evenly.

"Yes! Yes!" we clamored.

"Then lead the way, Wahwie," she instructed.

What we found at Mama's former construction site was, in a word, magnificent. It was also bewildering. You see, Mama had not designed and built a mere treehouse. No, that simply wasn't fantastic enough for her Isle. What Mama had created was more like a tree *palace.*

Its floor was in the shape of a Celtic cross. Four rectangular wings, uniform in size, extended outward from its circular center, as if reaching for the four points of a compass, and each of these wings ended at a spired, columnar tower. In the middle of it all, climbing up and engulfing the main trunk of the great oak, was a barrel-like citadel which dwarfed even the four towers. The battlements of this citadel loomed high above the treetops, and were adorned with parapets and banners of chartreuse, all rippling in the amiable breeze.

How a single tree could support such a structure was far beyond my capacity. From an engineering standpoint, even so much as a butterfly fluttering by should have sent it crashing to the ground, yet the oak's steady limbs didn't so much as sag beneath their burden.

"It's amazing!" I cried. I was so enthralled by the size and workmanship of the treehouse, that for a moment I lost sight of what truly mattered—whether or not Hattie was inside it.

A pristine white spiral staircase wound up the base of the tree. Its handrail was lined with cardinals, all at attention like British royal guardsmen. These avian sentries watched intently as we approached, judging whether we were worthy to pass up the stairs and into the treehouse above.

Pip sprang forward, eager to learn what waited at the top of the staircase, but Mama seized his shoulder and held him back.

"Walter and Peter must go first," she said, following her disappointing words with a quick kiss. "Besides, I have not had a single moment with you to myself. We can follow them up in a while."

My little brother groaned but didn't protest otherwise.

To Walter and me, Mama said, "Before you go up, I should give you fair warning. Inside that treehouse, there lives a great enchantress, as well as a powerful enchantment. Once you meet the Lady of the Tree, you will not easily be able to break free from her. Will you still go?"

Walter smirked and replied, "Whoever she is, I don't think she'll have much power over me. I'm strong enough. What about you, Peter?"

Not to be outshone, I nodded bravely and said, "Let's go."

My bravado was more of words than of action. That's why I was happy to let Walter lead the way as we wound up the staircase, toward the square hole carved in the treehouse's underbelly.

The cardinals stood and stared and did not move as we passed between them.

When our heads rose through the dark opening and into the treehouse's central chamber, we both gasped. As we had discovered during our quest to find Gurgan, the bounds of space within the treehouse were stretched far beyond the physical dimensions of its exterior walls. The central chamber was, by my best guess, fifty feet in diameter. A series of stately windows, wrapped around the room's upper limits, provided ample light for its scattered decorations and lavish furnishings. There were paintings and tapestries, sofas and chairs and reclining couches. A net hammock hung between a pair of freestanding posts, and upon it sat dozens of stuffed animals and dolls, all organized in neat rows. On the other side of the room, two identical bookshelves, curved like the walls they stood against, housed hundreds of thin hardcovers. Though I could not read any of their titles from my vantage point, I was confident they were the sorts which a young girl my own age might find herself reading. Four gas lanterns, currently unlit, hung upon the walls, spaced evenly to provide nighttime light for reading or play. Finally, there were four wooden doors which, when opened, would presumably lead us into the four wings of the treehouse we had seen from below.

Still gawking at the palatial dwelling, Walter stepped onto the polished marble floor—and bumped directly into something tall and thin. It began to tip, but Walter reached out and managed to grab it before it could fall all the way to the floor.

It was an iron stanchion. On top was a wooden sign, engraved with a message. *TREEHOUSE RULES: THE ONLY RULE IS HATTIE'S RULE.*

"She's here!" I cried out, unable to contain my joy.

Walter beamed too as he said, "Yes, but what does the sign mean? 'Hattie's rule'? Makes no sense."

I was beginning to learn there was little which *did* make sense to Walter at first glance. Perhaps he wasn't so infallible after all.

"I'm sure Mama will tell us if we can't figure it out," I assured him. "Now come on. Let's look around."

It didn't take more than a cursory glance at our surroundings to realize Hattie wasn't present in the central citadel. Everything here was still, draped with an unsettling quiet.

"Which door you wanna try first?" Walter asked, surveying our four options.

Technically, there *was* a fifth, but the very idea of it made me queasy. The staircase we had taken up from the ground continued spiraling around the trunk toward the ceiling, where it finally disappeared into a glowing point of sunlight a hundred feet above.

I shrugged in response to Walter's question. Hattie was just as likely to be in one of the four wings as in the next, so I made for the nearest door and opened it. As the layout from below the treehouse suggested, there was a wide hallway on the other side of the door, leading to one of the four towers we had seen. The tower itself was circular and open like the central chamber, but smaller and with a high, pointed ceiling. In the room's direct center stood a round, polished stone table, which in turn was surrounded by high-backed stone chairs. These were covered in plush upholstery, which matched the chartreuse banners we had seen billowing above the treehouse.

Still unable to believe so much could rest upon such a comparatively small tree, I muttered, "It's the dining room."

"And kitchen," said Walter, pointing at a meal workstation complete with counters, oven, icebox, and sink.

"And pantry," I added, gazing at the shelves beyond the icebox. They sagged under the weight of all the various foodstuffs they held. Some of it I recognized—apples, bananas, hams—but most I had never seen before. Or since.

"It doesn't look like she's in here," Walter said. "Let's keep looking."

So, keep looking we did. In the other three towers we found a parlor, an opulent bathroom, and a library—Mama had designed it, after all—but the one thing we *didn't* find was Hattie.

I began to worry that something had gone wrong, that she had somehow lost her way during her journey here. Or perhaps the Powers governing the afterlife had, for some unknown reason, denied her entrance onto the Isle. A sideways glance at Walter told me he was similarly anxious, though neither of us admitted so to the other.

We returned to the central chamber, where Walter said, "I guess there's only one more place to look."

He was staring up the trunk of the great tree.

I gulped. I'd been hoping he wouldn't mention it. Sure, I wanted to see Hattie, and Mama's craftsmanship had proven reliable thus far, but the idea of climbing a hundred feet of untested staircase was as welcome to me as dropping a hornet's nest down my underpants.

"You really think she's up there?" I asked, trying to mask my fear with incredulity.

"It'll be fine, Peter," Walter assured me, simultaneously sensing and dismissing my fear. "But if you're too scared, you can wait down here."

"I'm not scared," I retorted gruffly.

"Good. Then you can go first."

I approached the bottom of the staircase. My heart was quaking, but I refused to let my emotions bleed into my appearance. I shook the banister, testing the structure's soundness. It didn't budge a single millimeter, which meant I was out of outs.

"What're you waiting for?" Walter asked impatiently. "Need me to go first?"

"No! I'm going. Is it a crime to check it first?"

Like a constrictor suffocating its prey, the staircase's spiraling loops tightened as we ascended the ever-narrowing tree trunk. I didn't dare look up for fear of missing a step, losing my footing, and tumbling back down. Fortunately, I had no reason to doubt Mama's handiwork. The staircase remained just as sturdy up high as it had been at ground level.

Onward we climbed, until calves and thighs and butts ached from the effort. At long last, drenched with a chilling sweat, we reached the top.

Looking up from below, I had expected that the staircase would end in the exposed air of the treehouse's battlements. I was mistaken.

Instead, we discovered another room, dome-shaped and as wide as the chamber we'd just exited. It was capped at its zenith with a great circle of glass, through which poured the ample daylight. Along the dome's exterior, more sweeping windows arced from floor to apex, creating great banners of sunbeam and sky.

It was easy to see why we had been fooled into believing the stairs led to open-air battlements. So much light filled this window-draped space that even now I felt out-of-doors, perhaps standing in a pavilion or gazebo. Eight archways led from the dome's interior to a narrow walkway around the battlements outside. I imagined that a stroll upon these towering parapets would let someone gaze upon all of Pennsylvania—perhaps on a clear day, even to the green waters of the Atlantic Ocean far to the east.

Here, within this expansive dome, the top of the great oak at last arrived at its terminus. The tree's uppermost branches stretched their bare but mighty arms into the dome's empty space. Strands of colored bulbs, purple and pink and white, adorned the branches. Even amidst the effulgent sunshine, these fairy lights twinkled brightly. I supposed that in the dark of night, their effect among the oak's branches would have been nothing short of magical.

Yet not quite so magical as the rest of the wonderland now captivating our eyes. As we looked around the rest of the dome, we saw that it was filled with every sort of plaything or pleasantry we might have imagined. There were life-sized rocking horses and dollhouses so roomy we could fit inside them standing up. A row of freestanding shelves held dolls and stuffed animals next to Lincoln Logs and Erector sets, and these next to board games and jigsaw puzzles, marbles and wooden tops and uncountable other knickknacks. Still more sagging shelves supported bins and bins of assorted candies: peppermints and toffees, candy bars and candied fruits, butterscotches and jellybeans, lemon drops and gumdrops.

We had climbed from Paradise below to Eden above. As our feet and eyes wandered further, there were greater sights yet to behold. A wardrobe longer than our bedroom contained everything from cheap playclothes to extravagant ball gowns—all sized, of course, to suit a young girl. Below them were shoes from London and France and Milan, in as many kinds as one might find occasions for them. There were coats of every color and coats of many colors, hats and ribbons to match, and a wall perfectly painted with jewelry—diamonds and rubies and pearls and jades and amethysts, all in settings of gold, silver, or platinum. Beside the wardrobe, an ornate dressing screen stood like a giant accordion. Its wooden panels, overlaid with gold, depicted scenes and characters from the Japanese archipelago, a storyboard of dragons and plum blossoms and pagodas and kimono-wearing men, women, and children.

Yet there was more still! Ping pong and billiards tables. A small pool with a slide. A bar whose taps poured root beer and cola and orange soda and ginger ale. A player piano, currently silent, sandwiched between a colorful kite rack and miniature carriage.

All these items would have been considered treasures for boys and girls our age. While they did kindle a certain sort of wonder in mine and Walter's hearts, none of them were what caused our spirits to leap into full flame that day.

Such an honor belonged to the massive canopy bed occupying the south end of the cupola. At ten feet by ten, it may have been the largest bed ever built. The top of the mattress rose a full yard off the ground and would have been almost unclimbable for a boy my height, if not for the portable set of steps placed at its foot. Four tall posts stood at each corner, and were snaked with climbing, flowering vines. Opaque maroon curtains, each one trimmed with silver, hung between these posts, hiding anyone or anything which may have rested upon the mattress within.

Walter and I stepped timidly forward. Everything inside the magnificent dome was silent. Only the breath of the wind outside disturbed its peace.

"Anybody in there?" Walter called, slipping his fingers around the edge of a curtain. "Hello?"

From within came a sound of rustling and a soft moan—exactly what you would expect from someone whose deep sleep you were disrupting.

Following Walter's lead, I asked, "Hattie? Is that you?"

Still no answer.

Walter looked at me, and I understood the message in his eyes: *Get ready. I'm going to open it.*

I tensed as his fingers gripped the curtain. If Hattie wasn't on the bed, it would mean the completion of my heart's fracturing. Last night's cowardice would forever stain every beautiful memory of Hattie I carried with me.

Until that moment, I didn't realize how much of my heart was riding on this revelation. I was all in.

Walter swallowed hard. I saw then that he was all in too.

He exhaled a deep breath and flung the curtain aside.

THIRTY-ONE

Hattie's Rule

AT THE HEAD OF THE MATTRESS, atop a downy white comforter, sat a dozen pillows in an organized pile. Some were decorative, while others were for sleeping, and all were of various shapes, sizes, and colors. Some were maroon like the curtains, others lawn green or charcoal gray. In the middle of them sat a teddy bear the size of a St. Bernard.

Above these, we saw that the vines creeping up the four bedposts didn't end at the top. Rather, interwoven together, they formed over the bed a full canopy of white, pink, purple, and green. The floral ceiling was so thick, it allowed only pin-pricks of light to filter through and onto the sleeping girl beneath.

Hattie was here. Miraculously, actually *here*.

Once again, our loss was undone.

Walter slid the curtain aside, allowing more light to flood over Hattie's resting face. The cold-gravy coloring of her sickness had fled with her transition into new life, and she once more appeared healthy and strong. Instead of the uncomfortable crinoline her parents always made her wear, a dusky coral dress, light and airy like one of Mama's, lay draped around her resting form.

Hattie's eyelids fluttered against the bold and intrusive sunbeams, unwilling yet to open. With another gentle groan, she turned away from the light and away from us.

"Haaaaaattieeee," Walter called, playfully drawing out her name. "Waaake uuuup, Hattieeeee."

"It's Peter and Walter," I added. "We're here."

All at once, gasping with shock, Hattie shot up. She looked wild, her eyes feral, like those of a caged animal.

"Where am I?" she cried. "What happened?"

Walter scrambled onto the bed. In a display of compassion unlike anything he had shown before, he wrapped his arms around Hattie and hugged her to his side. Leaning his forehead against hers, he whispered, "It's okay. You're on the Isle now. You made it, just like Mama showed you."

"You mean, I'm—I'm—"

Dead was the word she couldn't bring herself to say.

Walter's empathy surprised me further. He shushed her as he stroked her hair and said, "That's right. You're safe now."

Overwhelmed by the news, and brimming with memories of pain and darkness I couldn't begin to imagine, Hattie buried her face in Walter's shoulder and wept.

When she finally broke away from his embrace to appraise her surroundings, she asked, "What is this place?"

"I think the best way to explain it is to show you," answered Walter, and he grabbed her hand. "Come on."

He led her off the bed and toward one of the arches which opened onto the battlements.

I followed them crossly. Holding hands with the dead was still holding hands, and I resented them for it.

Outside, and standing safely behind the parapets, we gazed out at the infinite world spread before us. The Isle's trees, always a canopy, became a quilted patchwork of autumn's fierce colorings when viewed from such a towering height. Further, beyond the island's bounds, Acheron's glistening waters created a broad moat around the magical kingdom and its palace. We spotted quiet Pierre in the distance, and shortly past this, the corrugated iron structures of Luther & Jansen Coal, whose towering smokestack reached skyward like the neck of some hellish beast, belching a trail of dark smoke toward the heavens.

With a twinge of sadness—and perhaps guilt—I remembered that one less man was present there. Jacob Jansen had certainly stayed home that morning with the rest of his bereaved family.

I shuddered to think that Hattie's lifeless body might still be in her bed.

But the living Hattie before me drew my attention away from such morose musings, as she squealed with delight and exclaimed, "It's a treehouse! And not just *any* treehouse. This is the best treehouse there's ever, *ever* been!"

She cast Walter a perplexed look and asked, "But how did you—how *could* you—?"

Walter snickered. "Wasn't us. Mama built it."

"So ... she's really here." Bewildered and still mistrusting her own eyes, Hattie shook her head. "I'm sorry I didn't believe you before."

"It's okay," said Walter. "It's kind of unbelievable until you see it for yourself."

Hattie crossed her arms. Shivering against the cold, she said, "Let's go back inside."

I would have happily agreed to her suggestion, of course. But then something strange happened. Before my brain could send the message to my legs, they began to move obediently, responding like a reflex to Hattie's command. This happened long before any real concept of robots in our world, but if I had known about them then, I would have sworn someone had replaced my legs of flesh with re-motely controlled appendages.

"What the—?" came Walter's startled cry next to me. He appeared as surprised as I was, and I wondered if he too was experiencing this involuntary phenomenon.

Behind us, Hattie asked, "Why're you walking so funny?"

"Because—because I'm trying *not* to walk, but I'm walking anyway!" Walter responded with a hint of panic.

Hattie stopped. She crossed her arms angrily, but Walter and I went right on marching until we were inside. The moment we crossed beneath the archway, we halted.

She plainly thought we were playing more tricks on her, for she said, "What do you mean by that?"

"I don't know," I said. "It was weird, like I didn't have control over my legs!"

Hattie scowled, waiting for further explanation.

"You have to understand something," Walter told her. "The Isle, now that Mama's here—now that *you're* here—isn't like it used to be. It's ... *different.* Magical, or something. I don't know if it's Mama making everything happen or what, but the games we used to play are *real* here."

"It's true," I said. "We even met Gurgan the Goblin."

"Yeah, and fought a dragon, and met a giant three-headed dog," Walter added.

Hattie mulled over these revelations, then said, "I wouldn't have believed you before, but when you're standing in your own treehouse castle after dying, I guess all that other stuff isn't so hard to believe."

"You should see Mama's cottage, and the garden too!" I exclaimed. "That might be the most magical place of all."

Hattie's eyes lit up. In that moment, she looked more lovely to me than ever before.

"Oh, take me there!" she cried.

My legs, controlled by some power outside myself, obeyed. Marching like a soldier, I made for the dome's center and the staircase which wound down from there. In lockstep beside me, Walter paraded forward too.

Hattie followed with a skeptical hue, eyeing us for any sign of trickery. But as we descended through the floor, she saw the treehouse's lower level and gasped.

"All this is mine?" she whispered, awestruck, to no one in particular.

Unable to arrest our own descent, Walter and I continued on, while Hattie lagged behind to gorge her eyes on her marvelous new kingdom.

The going down was much quicker than the going up. Still in our compulsory march, we soon approached the lower level. The sign, which Walter had nearly knocked over upon our initial entrance into the treehouse, now caught my eye again.

Suddenly, our involuntary actions made sense.

"Walter," I said, pointing, "there's only 'one rule' in the treehouse."

Ruefully, he whispered, "Hattie's rule. Damn! We don't have any choice. We have to obey her."

"Mama *did* warn us she was an enchantress," I remembered aloud.

"*And* said we wouldn't be able to break free from it," Walter added.

If Hattie saw and read the sign, she would become aware of all the power she held over us. That was why, as we came to the signpost, Walter reached out and tried to turn it around. Sadly, his legs didn't cooperate with the effort. Still under Hattie's orders, they went right on obeying her command to bring her to Mama's cottage. As a result, his fingers only grazed the signpost, causing it to teeter and tip. This time there was no catching it, and the heavy sign clattered onto the marble floor.

"Stop!" Hattie shouted. The echoing clang had broken her free from her trance, and she realized how far ahead we were. "Wait there for me!"

Resistance was futile. Her command locked our knees in place like rusty gears on a bicycle.

When she reached the sign, Hattie knelt and picked it up.

"'The only rule is Hattie's rule,'" she read. "What does that—?"

Before she finished her question, the light of realization illuminated her face.

"So *that's* why you're acting so weird!" she gleefully shrieked. "And you knew it, too, but you didn't tell me. Shame on you!"

"We didn't realize it 'til just now," Walter told her. There was a pleading sort of tone in his voice as he did.

But Hattie was beyond listening. She rubbed her hands together like a maniacal despot, and her wondering grin was overcome by a wicked one.

"This," she whispered, "is gonna be *fun*."

Walter gulped. "Don't be too mean. Please?"

"I won't," she assured him falsely, before adding, "to *Peter*. But I've got a lot to make up for when it comes to you, Walter. Shall we begin?"

The color drained from Walter's cheeks. Despite their mutual affection, Walter had frequently shown Hattie the polar opposite in his words and actions. I read in his expression that he was presently recounting the endless list of grievances she might hold against him, and tallying the potential cost of her retribution.

Hattie decided to deal with me first. In a patronizing tone, she said, "Dying is terribly hard work. Thirsty work, too. Be a dear, Peter—run back upstairs as fast as you can and fetch me a cola from the soda fountain I saw there. With a straw, mind you."

Neither my own thirst nor my burning muscles did anything to hinder me as I carried out her wish—which, according to her orders, was to be done "as fast as possible." I did slow down during my return to the lower level, but that was only to make sure I wouldn't spill any of the Enchantress's drink.

In the meantime, Hattie had put Walter to a task of his own. Working furiously, his fingers and hands kneaded her bare feet as he provided her with what looked like a world-class massage.

Reclining blissfully on one of the treehouse's many sofas, Hattie reached toward me, and I handed her the cold glass of cola. She slurped obnoxiously from the straw, finishing the drink with a dramatic smacking of her lips.

I tried my best to slink away while free from the influence of a command, but Hattie caught me and scolded, "You can wait there 'til I'm finished."

So, there I waited.

"How much longer do I have to do this?" moaned Walter.

"Until I say so," taunted Hattie. "And no more whining about anything. That goes for both of you."

After she had deemed the massage treatment complete, we proceeded into the dining wing. According to Hattie, "dying also makes a girl quite hungry," so she ordered Walter to construct a turkey and Swiss sandwich for her. Meanwhile, I busied myself deseeding a cluster of grapes so plump, it was a miracle they weren't bursting like tiny juice-bombs. Once Hattie had finished her meal—hand-fed by me and Walter—we returned up the spiral staircase into the dome.

Savoring her delicious power, Hattie gloated, "I could tell you to jump off this roof, and you'd have to do it, wouldn't you, Walter?"

His face went even paler than before. For a second, he almost looked like me.

Hattie chuckled. "Oh, don't worry. I won't do that. You're much more useful alive."

What followed next was a full hour dedicated to our unmitigated humiliation. We dressed in girls' clothing, all the way down to headbands and jewelry. Although I had never played piano in my life, I discovered I suddenly knew how when Hattie commanded me to play "Spaghetti Rag" on the baby grand. Walter was ordered to tap dance to my tune like an Irishman cutting a jig. After this came a game of ping pong that Walter and I had no choice but to let her win. We built an impossibly roomy Lincoln Log cabin for an entire family of dolls, had a two-person contest to see who could drink the most soda while standing on our heads—most of which came burning out our nostrils—and raced around the battlements with our trousers stuffed full of billiard balls.

When Hattie felt our upstairs activities had been tapped dry, she ordered our return to the lower level. In the parlor, which was nothing less than a cathedral of mahogany furniture and silk trappings, we served her piping-hot tea in brittle China teacups, along with biscuits on matching plates. We dabbed the corners of her mouth with napkins, wiped crumbs off her dress, and provided human shade when the sunlight peeped in upon her royal self through one of the tower windows.

Yet even as we obeyed her every word, the once-gleeful smile on her face began to falter. It became clear that she was no longer enjoying herself as she had at first.

When Hattie declared teatime over, an irritated Walter asked, "What next?"

"Nothing," sighed Hattie. "You know, this would be a lot more satisfying if you weren't being *forced* to listen to me."

"Didn't you always get mad at us for *not* listening?" Walter replied.

"Yes. I guess. Maybe it's not as fun because you're not pushing back."

"You mean, you *liked* it when we argued all the time?" Walter asked.

"No, not all the time, but sometimes I think I liked the challenge," Hattie explained. "This was funny for a while, but now it's—well—a little boring."

"So will you stop?" I asked hopefully.

Hattie chewed her lower lip, thinking over my request. Then the impish gleam returned to her eyes, and she said, "Almost. There's one more thing I need from Walter. Something you were too stuck up to give me before. But I know you were actually just *scared* to do it."

"What are you talking about?" he asked, casting me a "this-girl-is-crazy" look.

"Peter," Hattie said, ignoring his question, "you can go back to the other room and wait for us there."

If ever I were going to break free of her enchantment, it would have been then. The claws of jealousy, born of my overactive imagination, tore upward from stomach to throat as I wondered what Hattie might want from my brother—alone—that she never wanted from me. I wanted to preach a sermon on Walter's unworthiness, to list every reason, one by one, why Hattie was an utter idiot for choosing him over me.

And maybe I would have, if it weren't for her previous prohibition against objection. Anyway, my legs were powerless to resist her command, and they carried me hurriedly away into the central chamber.

When Hattie and Walter rejoined me a minute later, my brother wore the expression of a man knocked senseless. His eyes were round and unblinking, stuck in some euphoric catatonia, and his lips were petrified in a blithe half-grin. He appeared lighter than the very air around him, yet at the same time, his knees quivered like those of a man carrying a sack full of stones.

Beaming victoriously, Hattie walked beside him, her fingers locked tightly with his.

They stopped in front of me, and Hattie said, "Peter, I order you not to follow my orders any longer. *Unless* you want to."

I expected to feel something like the cutting of a puppet's strings. Instead, I felt nothing but the licking flames of envy inside me. They had been doused for a time by my deep and many sorrows, but there, in the enchantress's treehouse, the smoldering embers of jealousy reignited.

Given new life, it was only a matter of time before they would consume me.

THIRTY-TWO

A Voice in the Trees

"DID YOU HAVE ENOUGH TIME TO CATCH UP?"

I jumped, so lost in my envious thoughts of Walter and Hattie, I'd forgotten where I was.

Right on cue—but about two minutes late, by my reckoning—Mama and Pip entered the treehouse via the spiral staircase. Earlier, Mama had greeted us alone atop Emerald Hill. She and Pip must have returned to her cottage during the interim, because Baby was now bundled cozily in the sling against her chest.

The nasty scowl Pip gave his tiny sibling disappeared the moment he laid eyes on Hattie. Shrieking delightedly, he charged forward and tackled her onto a blue velvet sofa, squeezing her in the bearest of all bear hugs.

"Where were you? Why didn't you come play with me anymore? How come you're here now?" His salvo of inquiries went on, leaving Hattie without the two seconds of silence necessary to answer them.

Meanwhile, Mama addressed me and Walter. Raising her arms to show off the treehouse, she asked, "What do you think of my work? Was it worth the wait?"

"Definitely!" cried Walter. "I don't think I've ever seen anything so amazing in my whole life."

"Yeah," I said, plastering on a fake smile. "I think it's even better than your cottage."

Mama winked and replied, "To be fair, I only had one day to work on that. I was able to take my time with the treehouse."

Struggling free from Pip, Hattie hurried forward to wrap her arms around Mama.

Closing her eyes and lacing Hattie's curls between her fingers, Mama whispered, "Welcome to our Isle. I think you will find that one or two things have changed since your last visit."

Hattie was too overcome with emotion to speak. Her shoulders bobbed as she cried once more.

Mama sank to her knees, beaming as she squeezed Hattie. "Oh, I have missed you so much. Like my own daughter after a too-long vacation."

"I'm sorry I didn't believe before," cried Hattie. "I could have been here so much sooner."

With shining eyes, Mama said, "Although I am sad over what happened to bring you here, I am glad to see you now, and I look forward to whatever time we will have together on this side of things."

Whatever she meant by that last little bit, I wasn't exactly sure, but it carried an ominous tone. Since my juvenile heart had room for only one major concern at a time, I filed her words away and continued focusing my anxieties on whatever had transpired between Walter and Hattie in the parlor.

Pip provided a temporary but welcome distraction when he shouted, "I want to see more of the treehouse, Hattie! Will you show me?"

Hattie giggled and scooped him up in her arms. "Of course I will! You'll especially love it upstairs, so we'll save that for last."

We spent the next half hour touring the tree palace. As we did, Pip made it his obligation to explore every corner, ask every question, and tinker with every toy or curiosity he discovered. His youthful fascination inflated with each new room, and when we climbed the spiral staircase into the upper dome, that ballooning enthusiasm exploded. Like a kitten in a yarn-and-catnip store, he darted back and forth among the toys and sundries, eating anything he found that was covered in sugar.

"I do think he would like to live here with you, Hattie," Mama noted with an amused grin.

"Would he? *Could* he? Could everybody?" Hattie asked.

Mama realized she had spoken out of turn. Frowning, she answered, "No. I should not have said that. They are free to visit us, but this is our home, not theirs. Each evening, they must return to the Living World."

Hattie gave Mama a sober nod and said, "I understand. But it's a big home to have all to myself. Will you stay here with me?"

"I have my own place, but I think I could spare a night or two. At least until you start feeling more settled here."

Hattie brightened at once and said, "Walter told me you have a beautiful cottage surrounded by a magic garden. Could I see it?"

Never mind that I had been the one to mention the cottage. Not Walter.

The gall I tasted grew ever more bitter.

"Happily!" Mama replied in answer to Hattie's question. "In fact, while Pip and I were waiting for you three to finish your business, we were there preparing a welcome feast for you."

Despite the sourness in my stomach, the word *feast* didn't sound half bad. Although it had only been a couple hours, it felt like a whole day had passed since I'd last eaten. One of Mama's magical feasts was sure to satisfy both tummy and taste buds.

Mama allowed Pip a few more minutes to enjoy the treehouse. She eventually corralled him, and everybody made for the spiral staircase.

I seized my opportunity. Grabbing Walter by the elbow, I held him back a few paces and whispered, "What did Hattie want from you? When she sent me away?"

Even as I made my inquest, I feared the response.

But the one Walter gave incensed me far worse than the one I had dreaded. Jerking his arm from my grasp, he snapped, "Let go of me. And that's none of your business."

Outside, I sulked behind the rest of the group as we followed the flagstone path from treehouse to cottage. Walter's quick dismissal of my question had confirmed the worst. If nothing of significance had transpired between him and Hattie, he wouldn't have hesitated to share it with me. It was his angry dodging that took away any doubt. *Something* had happened. Had she made him finally admit his feelings for her? Kiss her, even?

The abrupt halting of the group ahead shook me free from my brooding. I hurried forward to learn why.

Hattie was staring off into the forest, a curious expression painted upon her face.

"What is it?" Walter asked. "What's wrong?" He too peered into the trees, trying to locate whatever it was Hattie had seen.

"I ... don't know," she whispered breathlessly. "I thought I heard something. Some*one* out there."

"Are you sure? I didn't hear anything," Walter replied skeptically.

Hattie opened her mouth to argue, but Mama cut her off.

"Come along!" she cheerily exclaimed. "Whatever it is, I am sure it can wait. My feast, however, cannot. Unless you want to eat the hot food cold, and the cold food hot!"

Walter obeyed immediately, brushing past Hattie as he went. I stopped next to her, offering my tacit support as I gazed into the trees myself. But the moment I did, she shrugged indifferently and hurried to catch up with the others.

Objectively, the feast Mama served at her cottage was so divine, the Lord himself would have left with a bellyache. There was a whole turkey, beautifully seasoned, along with sausage stuffing and cubed potatoes so soft and rich, they melted in our mouths like the butter that saturated them. We ate tart and tangy cranberry sauce, a salad of mixed greens and almonds and grated parmesan, and buttery green beans adorned with ground peppercorns. All this Mama referred to as a "practice Thanksgiving," but if this were *practice,* it meant the real deal would be as incomprehensible to our taste buds as calculus to a kindergartener.

But on a subjective level, even Mama's ethereal, beyond-this-world culinary masterpieces tasted bland upon my tongue. I had expected that her feast would return some sense of cheer to me. Instead, it brought the opposite. Walter and Hattie sat across the table from me, their affections for each other uninhibited like never before.

After dinner, we retreated to the sitting room to digest. Mama brought each of us a triple scoop of lime sherbet in a polished rosewood bowl, and we worked to fill the pockets of empty space in our stomachs with melty, fruity sugar. My mood improved then, but only because Pip took it upon himself to monopolize Hattie's attention. At least for the moment, she and Walter couldn't continue the unintended torture their eyelash-batting inflicted on me.

I was so preoccupied with keeping tabs on Walter and Hattie, I failed to notice the change that fell over Mama. Only when she spoke did I realize how pensive— even *gloomy*—she seemed.

"I sure do miss your Daddy's music," she said with a sigh. She stood and meandered to one of the north-facing windows, staring in the direction of Asphodel Glade. "He always played his violin after a big meal. I miss Daddy too, of course. But if I could only have his music again, he might not feel so far away."

Hattie responded to Mama with an idea of her own.

"You've made so much else here," she said. "Maybe you could figure out how to make his music too!"

"Believe me, I have tried," Mama replied, shaking her head grimly. "But that is the one thing I cannot do. Every time I have tried, it falls woefully short of the real thing because I cannot fill it with his spirit. And that, I think, is what makes Daddy's violin so special."

Walter straightened up at once. With full resolve, he said, "If you can't have Daddy's music without him, then we'll just have to bring him here."

Mama gave the idea only brief consideration. "I do not think he is ready. I will see him again, but not until the timing is right. Something more must happen still, though I cannot see exactly what that *something* is. Then he will open his eyes. And his heart."

If she had possessed a flair for the dramatic in life, Mama was developing a flair for the cryptic in death.

Her attention shifted to Pip and Hattie. My little brother had fallen asleep against Hattie's shoulder and was snoring quietly. Hattie herself seemed near to nodding off, her eyelids heavy with the effort of fighting off sleep.

"For now, I think it is time we all went back to our homes," Mama said.

Walter began to protest, but Mama held up a silencing hand. "Hattie has been through much more than you boys could realize. She needs her rest. And Pip— well, after all the candy he ate in Hattie's treehouse, I imagine this is nothing more than a sugar crash. Either way, the afternoon is wearing on, and Abigail will be wondering about you."

"I still don't understand why we can't stay here," Walter pouted. "Wouldn't that force Daddy to come to the Isle? And when he saw all this, he'd *have* to believe, wouldn't he?"

"*If* he could see all this," corrected Mama. "But I think he would find nothing more than a broken-down shack, and my three boys would find themselves in tremendous trouble."

"What do you mean? Why wouldn't he see it?" I asked.

"That is difficult to explain," said Mama. "When you three came here, you *wanted* to see me and *believed* you would, even if that belief coexisted with a bit of skepticism."

I shrank away from the knowing glance she gave me.

"But if Daddy came here now," she continued, "it would be without either of those things. He would see only what he expected to see."

"I still don't get it, but okay," Walter conceded. "We won't tell him."

He nudged Hattie, whose rolling eyes snapped to attention. "Mama says it's time to bring you home."

She gazed at him dreamily. "Okay. But I do wish the rest of you could stay with me."

"I will be with you tonight, Hattie," Mama reminded her. "And the time will come when our reunion will be a permanent one."

"When?" Hattie asked hopefully.

Mama didn't immediately respond. Instead, she approached the bassinet and scooped up the baby, invisible within its bundle of blankets.

"With any luck," she answered, "not for a long, long time. But we should leave the cottage now, while it is still light outside."

I myself was growing drowsy in the autumn afternoon's golden glow as we set out along the trail to Hattie's treehouse. I plodded along lazily, scuffing my feet and blinking great, slow blinks like a ruminating cow on a warm afternoon.

Lost in the fog of my own drowsiness, I didn't notice when Hattie stopped abruptly in front of me.

"Hey!" I cried with annoyance as I stumbled into her.

Then I saw her puzzled expression. She was staring off into the trees again.

"What's wrong?" I asked, trying to follow her line of sight with my own.

"Do you think you heard someone again?" Walter asked with a hint of alarm.

"I don't *think* I did," she retorted accusingly. "I *know* I did. It was coming from that way."

She raised a trembling finger, indicating some undefined point in the forest. With a faraway, dreamy tone, she added, "It was ... a girl's voice."

"What did she say?" I asked.

"I'm not sure. But I think she was calling my name."

A shiver ran down my spine, and my skin prickled with goosebumps.

"Come on," Mama said, urging us onward. "Whoever it is, she can wait until tomorrow."

We continued to the treehouse with the hurried pace of someone convinced he's being followed. At the base of the great trunk, we said our goodnights.

But even as I kissed and hugged Mama, I detected a veiled uneasiness in her eyes. I knew then that something had happened on our beloved Isle entirely apart from her control, influence, or knowledge.

Someone from the outside—or some*thing*—had entered in.

THIRTY-THREE

Mama Is Missing

WALTER AND I FIGURED WE COULD milk Hattie's death at least until her funeral. When we asked Daddy on Wednesday evening whether we could have one more day of mourning, he agreed without hesitation. And so, early Thursday, as soon as Castor's sharp *clip-clopping* faded over the hill, we gathered Pip and the puppy and hurried to the boat.

No one was waiting for us on top of Emerald Hill, but by this point we had learned not to expect it as a given. As had become customary, the puppy scampered off into the woods ahead of us, this time in the direction of Mama's cabin.

I set course to follow him, but Walter had a different plan.

"Mama was staying with Hattie last night, remember? Let's go to the treehouse."

As much as I wanted to, it was hard to argue with his logic, so off toward the treehouse we went. Like the fabled Wolf, we huffed and puffed up the winding staircase, but when we reached the immense bedroom at the top, we found it inhabited only by one.

"Good morning!" Hattie called as we fanned out at the top of the stairs. She was sitting at a little table, and in front of her was a steaming bowl of oatmeal.

"Morning," returned Walter. "Where's Mama?"

Hattie shrugged and said, "She got up early this morning and left with the baby. She was being really quiet, but I woke up anyway. I don't know where she went."

"She probably went to the cottage to make breakfast," I supposed.

"And whatever she's making," added Walter, "it's probably a hell of a lot better than that porridge you're eating."

Against this, Hattie raised no arguments. She pushed the bowl aside and followed us back down the cathedral's worth of steps we had climbed moments earlier.

Unlike the previous afternoon, Hattie heard no strange voices as we traversed the flagging between her treehouse and Mama's cottage. But when we arrived upon the grounds, I noticed two things out of order. First, there was no smoke rising from the chimney, which meant Mama wasn't working in the kitchen. Second, our dog wasn't heralding our approach by yapping like a maniac from the interior windowsill, as he had in the past.

Walter opened the door and stepped in ahead of us. We followed, but all was quiet within.

"Mama?" Walter called, glancing this way and that. "Where are you?"

"Check the cradle," I said, pointing to the corner where the baby always seemed to be sleeping.

"Why don't *you?*" Walter snapped.

Rather than let it become another argument, I strode over to the bassinet and looked inside.

No baby. Only a crumpled blanket lay within.

"I wonder where they went," Hattie mused.

The silence was off-putting. We were used to feasts and merriment, stories and songs here. But in the infant light of morning, a heavy loneliness lay draped over the four walls of the cottage, and the illuminated particles of dust wandering around among the sunbeams only accentuated this forlorn feeling.

Without warning, as if a small explosion had happened nearby, the air around us seemed to pulse. Startled, we glanced around the cottage.

It didn't take long to find the cause of the disturbance. The diminutive form of Gurgan the Goblin had appeared, and presently stood upon the dining room table.

Hattie screamed. She hadn't yet seen the flesh-and-blood incarnation of our one-time antagonist.

"It's okay!" Walter assured her, squeezing her hand. "That's Gurgan, just like I told you yesterday. He's here too."

Gurgan gave a rapid, almost frantic bow, and said, "I'll be pleased to make the young miss's acquaintance later. For the moment, I have more pressing business to share with you."

A chord of concern thrummed through my innards. It wasn't like Gurgan to show up uncalled-for. I knew we were in for nothing good.

"It's your mother," he went on, without waiting for a response. "This morning I decided I would fish the south shore. Not five minutes ago, I came across her there, alone and standing in the water. I tried to speak with her, but she wouldn't respond. She simply went right on staring across the lake."

Walter glanced sharply at me, then back at Gurgan.

"Take us there," he ordered.

Gurgan snapped his fingers. The same sudden darkness we had first experienced in his cave consumed us again, but only for a second. Then daylight enveloped us, and we found ourselves on the southern shore, not far from the Hellhound's cave.

Our puppy had beat us there. He was yapping frantically at a figure standing unresponsive in the shallows.

It was Mama. Her back was toward us, and lake water lapped gently at her bare ankles and the hem of her dress. She seemed as oblivious to our arrival as she was to the dog's incessant racket. Except for a few loose strands of hair caught in the chilly breeze, she was utterly catatonic as she stared south across the water. Her body was so rigid, I wondered whether she had stopped breathing altogether.

"Peter, *look*," Walter whispered, pointing.

It took me a moment to realize what it was he wanted me to see—or, rather, *not* see. When I did, my insides fell.

Mama's hands hung at her side, clenched into tight fists. The sling, still tied loosely around her torso, riffled like a lazy flag in the breeze.

Most notably, there was no longer any baby in it.

"Mama!" Pip cried with a tremble in his voice.

But my little brother might as well have been shouting at a statue. Mama didn't so much as flinch.

"Come out of the water, Mama!" I shouted, adding my plea to Pip's. Perhaps his little voice had gotten lost on the breeze.

Still, no response.

Always the "man" of action, Walter kicked off his shoes and socks and waded out into the frigid water. When he reached Mama's side, he peered up at her. As he gingerly took her hand, he spoke a single word, so soft I could hardly hear it.

"Mama."

Exhaling a tremendous sigh, she glanced down at my brother. All at once, she dropped to her knees right there in the shallows, and her body convulsed with unabashed sobs.

"Oh, Walter, Walter," she moaned, pulling him close. Sounding more miserable than I'd ever heard before, she cried, "Gone. Gone. My baby is gone."

"Where?" he asked.

"Where only I can follow," she answered vaguely.

"Is that where you were going? Is that why you were out here?"

Mama shook her head but gave no further answer.

"Will you go after him?" pressed Walter, but Mama became caught up in another violent fit of sobbing and couldn't answer. She clutched him, clung to him, and he clung to her in return.

It was an unnerving and unprecedented role reversal. There, in the water, my strong and fearless mother was playing the part of the wounded child. Walter, meanwhile, had been thrust into the role of comforting parent. His arms became the refuge in which she might safely weep her well of tears.

After a minute of this, Walter said, "Come up out of the water with me."

He steadied her as she rose to her feet. Side by side, they sloshed back to shore. Mama was deathly quiet as they approached us, but her tears did not cease their flowing down her anguished face. Never had I seen her so despondent.

"What happened, Mama?" Pip asked with innocent concern.

She dropped to her knees in front of him and cupped his rosy-cheeked face in her hands. "Nothing for you to worry about, Pippie. All you need to know is that you're my baby again. For now, anyway."

Before Pip could reply, Gurgan's small voice squeaked, "Would you care for me to return you home, dear Rosalie?"

Mama cast the little goblin a sideways glance. She looked exhausted, broken, as she said, "To my cottage."

Home, we all knew, was impossible. Even for Gurgan.

One finger snap later, we again stood within the four walls of the quaint cottage—all except Mama, who still knelt with Pip in her arms. Without bothering to change out of her wet dress, she shuffled to the sofa and collapsed onto it. Within moments, she was snoring lightly. Like a frightened child, she found safe haven from her distress in the oblivion of sleep.

It was Walter whom Gurgan now addressed, as he said, "I believe I have stumbled into a sensitive family situation. I did not mean to meddle, though it *was* fortunate I found her when I did."

"Thanks, Gurgan," Walter replied distractedly. He was staring at Mama, perplexed.

"I'll leave her in your hands, then," continued the goblin. "If you need me, call for me day or night, and I'll be here."

"We will," Walter answered.

A rippling of air accompanied Gurgan's instantaneous departure from the cottage. Then all was still.

I looked around at my brothers, at Hattie, and wondered if I appeared as helpless as they did. Even the incurably carefree Pip seemed drawn to earth by the gravity of what we had witnessed—although this did nothing to curb his incurable appetite, because two seconds later he was digging through the fruit bowl on the dining room table.

"What now?" I asked.

Walter and Hattie both shrugged. They had as many answers as I did.

Figuring what Mama needed more than anything was peace and quiet, we spent the next couple hours outside in the enchanted garden. Pip busied himself with puerile games of imagination, and our puppy joined him. Certainly he was more entertaining than Walter, Hattie, and I, who mostly did nothing. Lounging on the lawn, we grazed on various fruits from Mama's magical orchard and theorized about what might have happened to her and the baby. Since none of us had actually been present, the discussion was fruitless, serving no purpose but to pass the time. Periodically, Walter would peek through the window to check on Mama, but she slept on and on. I began to wonder if she would ever awaken again.

She did. Still out in the garden, we detected the muffled whimpers of her waking through the cottage walls. Hurrying inside, we discovered her bent over the bassinet, staring down at the empty place where her baby would never lie again.

As at the lakeshore, it was Walter who summoned the courage to approach her. He slipped his hand around her own and led her, gently but steadily, away from the bassinet.

"Come on, Mama," he urged her. "Let's go to the treehouse."

I thought his entreaty was a bit abrupt—even rude, considering Mama's obvious grief—until I realized what he was doing. He was less interested in going *to* the treehouse than he was in coaxing Mama *away* from her cottage. Or, more accurately, away from anything which reminded her of the baby—a baby who no longer was.

Mama didn't argue. She nodded her resigned agreement, and off we went with no further discussion.

We were halfway there when Hattie dug her heels into the earth and halted. Like the day before, she stared off into the forest, searching intently.

Walter and I looked too, but all we saw were empty trees.

"Who are you?" Hattie cried out, more with curiosity than with fear. "Was that your voice I heard yesterday?"

I sensed a prickling in my flesh. Whoever Hattie was shouting at was someone I could neither see nor hear.

"What do you want from me?" Hattie asked the Nothing. "Why did you come here?"

Hattie took two quick steps toward the trees, and I realized at once that she was ready to give chase through the woods.

Mama's hand fell upon Hattie's shoulder like an iron clamp, arresting her and holding her in place. With a wild and urgent look in her eyes, she whispered, "Not yet, Hattie. Not until you know. And are ready."

Whatever that meant, I had no idea, but I didn't care for the sound of it.

Hattie began to protest. "But she told me—"

"I know what she told you," Mama interrupted, "because I can hear her too. I'll explain later. But not now. Speaking about these things isn't meant for the ears of the *Living*." As she spoke that last word, she nodded toward me and my brothers.

Hattie studied Mama skeptically, and for one paralyzing second, I thought she might defy my mother. Then her shoulders relaxed, and she nodded her deference.

As the others hurried on toward the treehouse, my curiosity took an upper hand over my fear. I lingered a moment longer, peering into the forest, simultaneously praying that I might, and might not, catch a glimpse of Hattie's visitor.

But all I saw was the rustling of the leaves—and the vigilant eyes of the ever-watchful cardinals high above.

THIRTY-FOUR

What They Saw

IF WE HAD THOUGHT ENTERING the treehouse might summon a deluge of light to wash away the day's gloom, we were wrong. In near silence in the dining wing, we ate cold turkey and cheese sandwiches, hideous hack jobs slapped together by Walter's untrained hands. Still, they were edible, thanks largely to the superb quality of foodstuffs which Mama had magicked into the treehouse pantry and icebox.

I glanced across the table at her puffy eyes as we ate, wondering whether she still possessed the ability to create anything at all. Perhaps her excessive sorrow had stripped away the spirit necessary to forge such wonders. I took another bite of my sandwich and tried not to dwell on such morose musings, but that was like asking a naval officer not to dwell on the hurricane breaking his ship apart. If she had lost the baby, what else could she lose? The cottage? The treehouse? The enchanted gardens? Maybe even herself?

After our sandwiches, we continued our upward climb to Hattie's bedroom dome. Mama somberly busied herself on the floor with Pip and an Erector set, while Hattie and Walter engaged each other in a checkers battle. With nothing better to do, I sat nearby and silently cheered Hattie on toward what looked sure to be a swift victory.

But the victory never came.

Walter had a pair of men remaining on the board when Hattie shot upright, stiff as a girder.

"Did you hear that?" she whispered. Without waiting for a reply, she leaped to her feet and ran toward the open-air battlements.

"I didn't hear anything!" Walter protested. Frustrated, he jumped up to hurry after her, conveniently knocking over the checkerboard in the process. "Hattie, come back!"

"Stop, Walter." Mama's sharp order seemed unsuited to the malaise which had shrouded her since early morning. "Go, play with your brothers. I'll speak with Hattie."

He frowned. He'd been cut out of too many conversations lately, and the seeds of exasperation were germinating inside him. Still, he obeyed, though as soon as Mama's back was turned, he released his pent-up frustration by kicking Pip's Erector construction.

As he flopped angrily onto the lime-green sofa, I stood up.

"What're you doing?" Walter asked irritably.

"I'm gonna go listen," I whispered. "Besides, Mama only told *you* not to go after Hattie. She didn't say anything to me."

That put a crack in his funk. He grinned at my audacity and said, "Okay. But later, you better tell me what you heard."

I dashed toward the archway through which Mama had disappeared, but I didn't exit myself. Careful to remain out of sight, I flattened my back against the wall. Mama's and Hattie's voices sounded distant—they must have taken a short stroll along the battlements—but when I slowed my breathing and focused my ears, I could hear every word.

It was Mama who spoke first.

"Remember, I can see and hear them too," she said. "You and I are the only ones who can look Beyond."

"How long have you been able to?" Hattie asked. "You never said anything about it before."

"Yesterday was the first time," Mama answered. "Well, the first time since right after I died, anyway. But I was as surprised as you to hear that voice yesterday."

"Who are they? And what happened at the lake this morning?"

A long pause followed, before Mama finally said, "I heard a voice calling early this morning while you were still asleep, but it sounded different than the one you heard yesterday. Besides that, it wasn't calling *your* name anymore. The voice was calling for *me.*"

"That's why you left," Hattie replied matter-of-factly.

"Yes. My curiosity got the better of me, and I paid for it dearly."

"The ... *voice* stole your baby?"

"That's not exactly how it happened," said Mama. "I put Baby in the sling, like I always do, and hurried out into the woods. I couldn't see anybody, but I heard the voice, clear as a bell and calling my name. I followed it all the way to the south shore. That's where I saw *her*."

"Saw who?"

"A young woman standing in the water. The moment she saw me, her face lit up, and she beamed like the sun. I started walking out to her, and I asked who she was. She told me her name was ... Henrietta."

"Who's Henrietta?" Hattie asked. The more Mama answered her questions, the more questions she had.

"My little sister. She died when she was very young."

"And she's the one who took the baby? Why would she do something so awful?"

"It's not what you think," said Mama. "Henny actually stopped me from going any further. If she hadn't, I wouldn't be here right now. She told me she was standing in the gap between Here and Beyond, that she had come to see whether I was ready to move on yet."

"And you weren't."

"No."

"But what's 'Here and Beyond'?"

"*Here* is here. *Beyond* is what we will find someday when we cross Over the Waters."

"You mean heaven?" Hattie asked. When she did, there was a thrill in her tone.

"If that's what you want to call it, yes. It's where the rest are. Henrietta, my grandparents, John's *Mutti* and *Vati*. Henrietta told me they were all waiting for me too."

"So? Why didn't you go to them?" Hattie wondered.

"Because," Mama answered gravely, "once I do, I can't return. Neither can you."

"Why?"

"I don't know *why*, exactly. Only that it is so. It was a rare grace which allowed me to stay here in the first place. Perhaps after we do journey Beyond, what we would see is too beautiful and transforming that we would never *want* to come back."

"But how did you lose your baby? *Was* it Henrietta?"

"Yes, it was Henny. But only because I gave Baby to her."

My shock was matched only by Hattie's.

"But ... why would you do that?" she exclaimed, scandalized by Mama's revelation.

Even though I couldn't see her, I knew Mama started crying again after Hattie's questions about her baby.

"She said that, while she understood why I wanted to stay, she didn't think it was fair to keep my baby here on the Isle—or the *Shadowlands,* as Henny called it. That I was holding back my own child from becoming everything one is meant to be when they cross Beyond. And when I saw how beautiful Henny was, the pure rapture of her voice and eyes and presence—how full of *light* she seemed to be—I knew she was right. I couldn't keep Baby imprisoned in a bassinet any longer. I had to let Henrietta escort my child Over the Waters."

"Oh, I'm so sorry, Miss Luther," said Hattie in sympathetic tones.

But Mama wasn't finished. "The only question left was whether or not I would follow them. Oh, God, it was a terrible choice! Either follow my sister and baby or remain here with Walter and Peter and Pip. Whichever decision I made meant a broken heart."

"Why'd you decide to stay?" asked Hattie.

Mama sighed. "I had actually made up my mind to go with them. Then I heard Pip's voice. He sounded like he was a million miles away, but it made me hesitate. Then I heard Peter too, and when I felt the warmth of Walter's hand on my own, I knew my miserable decision was made. I stayed. Someday I will go to them—to Henny and my baby—but they will not return to me."

A moment of silence passed before Hattie said, "I don't know if what you said is true."

"What do you mean?" replied Mama, taken aback by Hattie's distrust. "I remember it like it happened a minute ago."

"Not about your story," Hattie explained, "but when you said whatever you decided would mean a broken heart—I don't know if that was true."

"How so?"

"If you chose to go Beyond, I think you'd find yourself in a place where regrets are impossible. Where broken hearts don't exist. After all, you said yourself that Henrietta was full of joy and light, didn't you?"

"Yes, but I couldn't have all that without my boys. Henny was little when she died. She hadn't formed all the attachments to this life that I have."

There was another moment of quiet, followed by Hattie's voice: "Do you know who that was, calling for me in the woods today?"

"No. Only that her name was Anna. Who is she?"

"That's just it—I don't know," answered Hattie. "I've never seen her in my life, at least not that I can remember. It's obvious why your sister would come for you, but what does Anna want with me?"

"I don't know. It's easy for me to look and see on This Side of things—toward the Living World—but I can't see Beyond any more than I could through a brick wall. Maybe it's because Here is what I have experienced, while Beyond is more like a country I've never been to, or even seen pictures of."

"Whoever she was," said Hattie, "I think she looked a little like you described your sister. Happy. And full of light."

"Are *you* happy, Hattie?" Mama asked abruptly. "Here on the Isle?"

"I was at first," she said. "Before I died, I thought this was what I wanted. But now that I'm here, I don't feel like I really *belong* here."

If my heart could have stopped, it would have. The full implication of her words was like jumping in front of a speeding train.

Hattie wanted to leave.

Softly, sadly, Mama responded. "I understand. We're caught in the middle here, hanging between the unreachable beauties of life on one side and the unknown mysteries on the other. But you are not stuck here, Hattie. You are free to finish your journey between Life and Death whenever you decide the time is right. I stopped you from following this Anna person earlier because I wanted you to have all the information before making a decision you couldn't unmake."

Hattie was a person arguing with her own self as she said, "But I love you. And I love Walter and Peter and Pip. With all my heart, I love them. So how can I want to go somewhere I'll never see them again?"

"I think you know the solution to that problem, just like I do. It's why I gave my baby to Henrietta. You're asking a flawed question. You know you *will* see them again."

"Yes, but how long will it be? How many years will there be in between?"

"For them, it may feel long. For you, it might be the blink of an eye."

"Well," said Hattie, her cadence that of someone ready to wrap up the conversation, "I guess I have time to think about it. I don't have to decide anything today, right? I won't go until I know for sure it's what I want."

"I'd say that sounds wise," said Mama. "Come on. Let's go back to the boys."

I withdrew from my eavesdropping archway and hurried to rejoin Walter and Pip.

"What did they say?" Walter demanded.

"I'll tell you later. Right now they're coming."

The rest of the short afternoon was a troubled one. Hattie hadn't been on the Isle two days, yet there was already a distance widening between her and the rest of us. I worked hard that afternoon to give her extra attention, trying my best to make sure she felt loved and wanted. I asked her to pick the games we played and treated whatever she said as if it were the most profound utterance I'd ever heard. I lavished my compliments upon her, praising her very name.

Yet as the afternoon aged into early evening, I perceived no change. Her smile was weary, like that of someone entertaining company after a long day at work, and her laughter was as hollow as echoes upon a canyon's distant walls. I didn't want Mama or Hattie to suspect me of eavesdropping, so I buried my swelling distress as best I could. But my efforts were hardly necessary. Both were too distracted by their own troubles to pay me much notice.

Walter wasn't so easily fooled. When we were finally aboard *The Rosalie*, and the figures of Mama and Hattie had departed into the trees, he said, "Spill it, Peter. What did you hear?"

"Nothing important," I said. Why I lied, I'm not sure. Perhaps it gave me some false sense of power over him. The more likely reason was that I myself didn't want to believe my own ears. "Hattie told Mama the girl she heard—and saw—is named Anna. But that's all."

"Who's Anna?"

I shrugged. "She doesn't know. Says she never saw her before."

"And that's it?"

"That's it."

"Bullshit," he snapped. "There's more, or else you wouldn't've been acting so weird."

"Well, Mama *did* tell Hattie she saw Henrietta today. That was her younger sister who died, remember? Anyway, that's who Mama gave the baby to."

"Why?"

I shrugged and said, "I didn't really understand it. Something about Henrietta taking the baby to heaven—or *Beyond*, I guess, was the word Mama kept using for it. Anyway, somewhere that's apparently even better than here. But that's it. That's all they talked about."

Walter stopped rowing. Turning to face me, he said, "If I find out you're lying, I'm gonna kill you."

As coolly as I could, I replied, "I'm not lying, so ... fine."

He eyed me suspiciously but said no more. Neither did I.

A crisp rime settled over Asphodel that night, matching the frost that had already settled in my heart. The sleep I did manage to find was fitful, rife with dreams darkened by loneliness and loss.

Among it all was one certainty: sooner or later, our time with Mama and Hattie was coming to an end.

THIRTY-FIVE

Jacob's Confession

IT IS AN ODD THING, AND THE WEAVER of unsettling doubts, to stand at the graveside of someone you know you'll be visiting later. Although your eyes and ears and touch have told you one story, you suddenly find them telling a different tale. The specter of death swallows up the promise of life, and for a few minutes—or a couple hours, if unfortunate enough to attend a service led by Reverend de Vries of First Reformed Church—it is impossible to be certain of anything at all.

Such was the war between my head and my heart as I stood again before an unfilled grave. On this occasion, we huddled together not in St. Matthew's Cemetery, but upon the grounds of Pierre Memorial Gardens. The coffin across the recently dug cavity was little more than half the size of the last one we had seen lowered into the earth. There could be no doubts that the mortal remains of our dearest friend Hattie lay within the pine box, and yet we *did* doubt. We doubted because, just yesterday afternoon, we had played a game of blind man's buff with her in the gigantic dome of her treehouse.

Walter and I thus remained rather dry-eyed during that Friday afternoon's miserable proceedings. Pip cried some, but that was because he was an impressionable child surrounded by fervent weepers. Due to the closed casket, he may not have wholly understood who all that mourning was for.

There was nothing special about Hattie's resting place. Besides a few distant uncles and first cousins once removed, she was the pioneering Jansen laid to rest in those grounds. Unlike Mama, she didn't even have a tree to serve as her grave's landmark or provide shade on summer days.

The rest of the Jansens stood lined up behind Hattie's coffin. None were able to sing even a single syllable of "Nearer, My God, To Thee" when the reverend struck up the hymn's first *a cappella* notes. The darkness was too bleak and their grief too fresh for their voices to do anything but shudder and weep. The five Jansens were staring into *Sheol*, the Hebrew "pit of death." It had claimed their daughter, and from it there could be no escape.

Or so they thought.

"Let's get outta here," Walter muttered, a half-second after the benediction. With any luck, we might still have most of an afternoon at the Isle—and with Hattie—if we hurried home.

Though Walter didn't see it, Daddy glanced down at him. He had heard my brother's crass remark, and it clearly disturbed him.

Gradually, everyone meandered away from the cemetery plot, but Daddy held his ground long after everyone except the Jansens and Reverend de Vries had gone. He seemed determined to elicit some kind of emotion from me and Walter, even if it meant waiting there until next morning's frost settled upon our eyelashes.

It was, ironically, Jacob Jansen who saved us. Contrary to what we previously thought possible, he was spilling silent tears as he approached us around the deep hole.

"I'm so sorry, Jacob," choked Daddy, stifling his own emotions as he extended a firm hand. "If there's anything I can do, you know I'm only a telephone call away."

Mr. Jansen shook his hand. He wiped his eyes and said, "There is something you can do. Please, give me a moment with Walter and Peter. In private."

Daddy's eyes flashed with concern. He remembered how our previous cemetery encounter had gone.

Mr. Jansen held up a knowing hand and said, "It's not what you think. For what it's worth, I'm sorry for what happened at Rosa's funeral. It was beyond misguided. It was pigheaded, as Hannah let me know many, *many* times."

Daddy hesitated but stepped aside all the same.

Mr. Jansen's stare, always hard as flint, was shining and gentle as he addressed us. "Will you walk with me, please?"

Walter lowered his eyes deferentially and nodded.

We went a short distance up the low hill north of Hattie's burial plot. When Mr. Jansen was certain we were out of earshot, he shoved his hands into his pockets and said, "I must apologize to you both."

Despite what he had said a minute earlier, these were still the last words I expected from him. Mr. Jansen was a potent figure, a pillar of Pierre. People asked *his* pardon, not the other way around. Walter and I were finding ourselves in rare company indeed.

"Walter," he continued, "I am deeply ashamed of the way I spoke to you at your mother's funeral. And I was wrong to keep Hattie from coming. I know Rosalie—your Mama—was almost as close to her as her own mother."

"It's okay," Walter muttered.

"No, it wasn't. It was the worst thing I could have done to you. And to Hattie."

I figured more was coming, or else Mr. Jansen wouldn't have invited me along for the conversation. Two seconds later, he proved me right.

"I was also wrong to keep her from you these last weeks. I was scared. I couldn't imagine going through the pain all over again, but—well, here we are."

Walter raised an astute eyebrow. Even I hadn't caught the full implication behind Mr. Jansen's words. "What do you mean, 'all over again'?"

Long-suppressed memories came bubbling up from deep inside Mr. Jansen's soul, and he sagged visibly beneath their weight.

"There's a part of my life that I have shared with very few people around here," he admitted after a brief rumination. "Not even my own children or your father know about it, only Hannah. But before I came to Pierre, back when I was still near Philadelphia, I was married to someone else. Her name was Katharine. I can see her face like it was yesterday. She had golden eyes, a lot like your mother's, and the waviest brown hair. She was kind, full of life—a perfect complement for some-one like me. Less than two years after we were married, we had a daughter, Anna."

Neither of them noticed, but my jaw dropped an inch.

Anna. That was the name of the girl Hattie had seen in the forest.

Mr. Jansen didn't skip a beat in continuing his tale. "She looked so much like her mother. Acted like her too. Although I made a decent salary at the paper mill, we weren't exactly wealthy. Besides that, I was saving everything I could with the hopes of starting my own business someday. That's why we decided to live in a cheap upstairs apartment over old Mrs. Bruner's home. But we were happy there—blissfully so, if you can imagine it of me. I can't remember smiling so much in my entire bachelor life as I did in those two years with Katie and Anna. I couldn't possibly imagine being happier. Then Katie told me she was pregnant again, and I was reminded how poor my imagination truly is."

Mr. Jansen paused. His head sank. Since he had never introduced us to either a Katharine or an Anna, it was easy to deduce his story's gloomy ending.

"I was in the middle of a mountain of paperwork when my supervisor shut my office door and sat across the desk from me," he continued, forcing his way through clouds of grief. "Right away, I knew something was wrong. He told me

Mrs. Bruner's house had caught fire late that morning. The old woman herself had gotten out in time, but Katie and Anna had not. They burned with the house. In only a few minutes, my family—my life—was destroyed."

Walter and I exchanged uncomfortable glances. Why was he telling us this? And why now?

Mr. Jansen went on. "I remained single and alone for nearly a decade afterward. I hardly ate. I slept even less. I counted the days and weeks and months and, eventually, years that I had been without my Katie and my little Anna. But, as they say, life goes on. A couple years after the fire, while doing a bit of teaching at Swarthmore College, I met an ambitious student named John Luther. By then I was infatuated with the infinite possibilities of the coal age, and I convinced your father to help me revitalize a dying anthracite mine right here in Pierre. I eventually met Hannah, and we were married the following year. Then came four more children. Life was, in a way, put back together again.

"I never did let go of Katie and Anna, though. Every cough, every whiff of smoke, every social gathering around a fire, my imagination would get the better of me. I'd hear them screaming. Feel the heat of the flames that ate them. I'd remember standing in front of their graves, side by side, one big and one so tiny. I lived in fear. The fear that I would find myself there again, looking down on the grave of my new wife or one of our children. And I couldn't bear it. That's why I wouldn't let Hattie see you after your mother passed. I couldn't save Katie, and I couldn't save Anna, but I thought I could save my new babies from this sickness, so I shut them away. I wanted to protect them.

"But I couldn't. Maybe there never was any protection from it—from this damned Flu. It sickens whomever it wants, and it reaps whomever it chooses. In the end, all I really did was rob Hattie of her final weeks of life. I kept her from the people she loved and the things she loved doing."

At this point in his narrative, Mr. Jansen could stymie his tears no longer. They flowed in narrow rivulets, dripping off his stubbled chin.

"I'm so afraid," he whispered. In that moment, he appeared not powerful or influential, but human and fragile—as brittle as a snowflake. "Hattie was so angry at me. I wanted to protect her, but she didn't see it that way. I'm so afraid she died resenting me for what I did."

His shoulders began to jerk up and down with unashamed sobs. My whole life, I had thought him like a piece of granite, cold and harsh, but there on that hillside, I found myself feeling heartbroken for the man. Still, I could think of nothing to say, no words which might ease either his sorrow or his guilt.

But Walter did.

"Mr. Jansen," he declared, clearly and boldly, "I can take you to Hattie."

The man's eyes narrowed with indignation. He was incensed to hear such lies in response to his honest and anguished confession.

Walter saw the outburst coming and outmaneuvered it, saying, "I know how it sounds. Even Hattie didn't believe me until right before she died."

Mr. Jansen remained far from convinced, but he held his dander at bay as he listened to Walter's explanation.

"I'm sure she told you about the island we played on with Mama, right?" asked Walter.

"She did," Mr. Jansen tersely replied.

"After Mama died, we went back to that island, and we found her there," Walter explained. "I know how it sounds. It's impossible. But it's *real*. Peter and Pip, they've been there too."

Mr. Jansen crossed his arms. "Even if this is true, what does it have to do with Hattie?"

"Everything!" Walter exclaimed. "Right before she died, she told me she was sorry she didn't believe me about the island. She wanted to know if she could go there too. Two days ago, the morning after she died, we went back to the island. And she's *there*. Hattie is there with Mama. We've all seen her."

I had remained silent throughout the duration of Mr. Jansen's story, as well as Walter's daring revelation. But at this point I said, "He's not lying."

Mr. Jansen maintained his stony glare. I was sure he would call Daddy over to divulge our whole cockamamie tale. But he didn't. Instead, the fire in his eyes died out completely. His whole self seemed to sink again under the weight of his heartache, as he said, "I don't know what it is you've seen out there, but you sound genuine. Besides, what else is there for me to lose?"

Walter grinned impishly, then said, "Just one thing. Daddy doesn't know, and you can't tell him. Not yet anyway."

He proceeded then with a plan that was shockingly well-developed on such short notice. "Daddy won't be surprised if you don't show up at work on Monday. He'll just think you're too sad to come in. Peter and me—we'll cut school. Meet us at Asphodel at nine in the morning, down by the water. Oh, and try not to let anyone see you."

Walter's quick instructions had caught Mr. Jansen by surprise. Finding himself at a loss for words, he stammered, "O-okay. And Hannah can join me?"

"Yes," answered Walter. "But no more, or else the boat'll be too full."

"I understand," said Mr. Jansen. "See you Monday."

As it turned out, Walter and I didn't have to play hooky. On Thursday, Karty Phelan's father had gifted Pierre Primary's teachers a slab of dried beef. Over the weekend, Miss Carrington and her cohorts discovered—through fits of vomiting and diarrhea, if you believed Karty's version of events—the aforementioned beef to be tainted. Normally, a dozen stodgy, bitter, retired schoolteachers would have volunteered to fill in for the sick faculty, but the days of The Flu were different times. With no one to step in front of the classrooms, old Olaf Kirk and his ilk had no choice but to cancel school for all.

And so, at promptly at nine o'clock Monday morning, we met Jacob and Hannah Jansen on the shores of Lake Acheron. Judging by the puffy flesh beneath their eyes, I knew neither had enjoyed much sleep. Yet when they approached us that morning, both appeared buoyant with hope.

We clambered into the rowboat. Despite the looming sorrow, a hum of anticipation crackled through the air. With the funeral on Friday and Daddy's watchful presence hanging around all weekend, my brothers and I were looking forward to our own reunion after a four-day exile.

Walter hadn't been rowing long when Mrs. Jansen asked, "What's that noise? Does anyone else hear it?"

Sitting beside her, his legs bouncing excitedly, Pip replied, "Those are the birds! The *carn-i-dals!* There's millions of 'em!"

"They showed up the same day Mama did," I added.

The nearer we drew, the more their astonishment grew. The cardinals really were outdoing themselves, singing gaily and with deafening vigor. After seeing no one from the Living World but me and my brothers, they seemed excited to entertain a fresh audience.

Mr. Jansen squeezed his wife's hand. Both faces wore bare and unabashed amazement. They had become believers without even laying eyes on their daughter.

When we reached the Isle and began to disembark, I realized how nervous Walter was. By inviting Mr. Jansen to the island, he wasn't merely providing closure between father and daughter. There was also an angle of self-interest in the invitation. He was seeking approval from Mr. Jansen, a validation and respect he had never received during Hattie's life. Now, in her death, he sought it still.

Walter was last off the boat. The moment he stepped ashore, the cardinals abruptly ended their commotion. Only echoes rang in my ears.

Mr. Jansen put an arm around his wife and hugged her close to his side. Together, they stared up at the birds, unnerved by their sudden and eerie silence.

Pip skipped and bounded ahead of us as we led them up Emerald Hill. When Walter realized Mrs. Jansen was struggling to keep pace, he slowed his own. She was weeping profusely, and her unsteady legs seemed ready to collapse beneath her.

Some people think they will eat their grief, and others that they will starve it. Mrs. Jansen, thin enough to shatter in a stiff breeze, was likely a member of the latter camp. I prayed she might finally eat something and regain her strength after meeting with Hattie.

If she met Hattie. I remembered the treetop conversation between her and Mama and felt queasy all over again.

As it turned out, Mrs. Jansen needed no meal. The moment she laid eyes upon her daughter, radiant with the splendor of rebirth and the morning sun, the grieving mother's legs regained such power that she tore away from her husband to charge up the crowning slope. Her bitter tears gave way to fresh ones of rapture and relief, for her darkest darkness had been cast away by the light in her daughter's living eyes.

Mr. Jansen tapped into his own hidden reserves of strength. With a strangled cry, he followed close upon his wife's billowing green hems.

Where they met at the top of Emerald Hill, father and mother and daughter sank to the grassy floor, a single-bodied mass of tears and kisses and laughter.

"Oh, my Hattie! My sweet girl!" Mr. Jansen cried, sobbing and giggling and sighing all at once. "How can this be? How am I holding you right now?"

"I don't know *how* it can be," the smothered girl answered, "only that it is."

"Did it hurt?" Hannah Jansen asked. "Please, tell me it didn't hurt."

"What do you mean?" replied Hattie. "Tell you *what* didn't hurt?"

"Dying," her mother answered. "Besides the hole in my heart where you should be, that's what torments me most—wondering how terrible it was to die."

Hattie clasped her mother's face between her hands. Solemnly, she answered, "That's an answer I can't share with you. All I can say is that it was what it was, that it is over now, and that it never will be again. Not for me, anyway."

Walter and I, witnesses to their splendid reunion, came at last to the hilltop. But we did not stop beside the Jansens.

Mama waited for us at the forest's edge. Pip was already at her side, holding her hand in his own. She beckoned us to come to her, so we did.

"Follow me to my cottage," she said, "and leave them be. This conversation is not meant for your ears."

We offered up no arguments. Dutifully, we obeyed and followed her into the forest.

But I did glance back once more before the Jansens became concealed by the trees. Though I could not hear them, I saw father and daughter sitting side by side. Her head lay against his shoulder, while his fingers caressed her back. All the unpleasantness of the past forgotten, they spoke and stared off into the far horizon.

I was too distracted to remember what we did at Mama's cottage that day. I only remember returning hours later, when Mama informed us it was time to leave.

Parents and daughter were saying their farewells as we approached the top of Emerald Hill. They kissed and embraced, then kissed and embraced again and again, enough to sustain them all the days between that day and eternity.

Once there were no more goodbyes left to say, those returning to the Living World boarded *The Rosalie*, and we pulled away from the Isle.

High atop Emerald Hill, able to come no further, Hattie waved and waved to her parents.

Tears shimmered again in their eyes as they cried out their love, but it was no longer the weeping of despair. These were the tears of hope reborn.

When Hattie was no more than a pixie atop the green knoll, her waving ceased. For a moment, the world stood perfectly still, but for one young daughter's hair and dress adrift on the icy breeze.

Then she turned and disappeared into the forest.

THIRTY-SIX

The Distant Girl

THE NEXT WEEK MARCHED US steadily into the middle of November. In a rare stroke of good luck, the autumn rains sidestepped eastern Pennsylvania, and the weather took a cordial turn toward the warmer. Daddy made us return to school—the tainted beef episode had given us only one extra day of freedom—but every afternoon, Walter and I hurried home on our bicycles, grabbed Pip and the puppy, and spent the day's golden hours on the Isle.

But each time we crossed the lake, I feared we would find it less a resident.

Or worse, I thought, remembering also Mama's grief whenever she thought of the baby she had given up.

To our relief, Mr. and Mrs. Jansen didn't ask us to return. While we were glad for their closure, we didn't want them impinging on our fun. The shortening daylight hours were already doing too much of that for our tastes. With the marking of each calendar day, the sun set a couple minutes earlier. Our adventures soon felt rushed, like a vacation with too many sights to see and not enough time to see them.

Yet we wouldn't have traded away those precious hours for all the Yukon's gold. Despite their brevity, they were the crucible upon which were forged some of my earliest adolescent memories. Not only did Walter and Hattie return to a gracious concealment of their ardor, but Mama also took it upon herself to maximize the shortened moments we had together. We carved a fort from a carriage-sized pumpkin, grown overnight by Mama. We fashioned scarecrows which, when completed, walked and talked like the one in Oz. We played legendary rounds of hide-and-seek in Hattie's expansive treehouse. On a Saturday, we competed in a tournament of "Goblin Games," whose contests and rules were instructed and led by Gurgan himself. And, of course, we delighted in Mama's abundant feasts and desserts.

As with all things, our merriment was not without its raincloud. Whenever we trampled the forest trails between one place and another—and even during many of our outdoor games—Hattie would stop and stare off into the woods, drawn there by a voice or a face which my brothers and I neither saw nor heard. As when we had found Mama standing offshore in the shallows, a sort of trance seemed to grip Hattie, one whose power increased with each instance. These trances were soon eating up so much of our daylight that the rest of us began inventing reasons to stay indoors. Wherever we found ourselves on a given day, we learned to be content there, because *there* was preferable to enduring another half-hour spell of Hattie's catatonia.

Yet even this was not meant to last.

On November 11, 1918, as the world celebrated an armistice that quieted the guns of Europe, Walter and I were celebrating the end of the school day, as well as our return to the Isle after a Daddy-supervised weekend away. A chill, deeper than any in the weeks preceding it, had blanketed Asphodel the night before, ending the long warm streak. It also served as a harsh reminder that winter was on the horizon.

Under Abigail's stern oversight, we bundled up for our customary afternoon voyage. Like three toasted marshmallows in our plump, brown coats, we plowed through Acheron's biting waters toward the Isle.

We were approaching the shore when I realized something was off.

"The cardinals!" I cried out.

"What about 'em?" asked Walter, turning to stare up at the trees.

"There aren't as many as before," I replied. "They're only high up top. Some of 'em must have flown away for the winter."

Walter grunted his indifference as he sidled *The Rosalie* along the shoreline. No one was waiting for us on top of the hill, but two circles of bruised grass hinted that a pair of bottoms had sat there recently.

"Let's go to the treehouse," said Walter. "I bet they're there."

By this time, we knew the forest paths like we knew our own selves, so there could be no mistaking that we had chosen the correct trail. Yet when we arrived at the tree where Hattie's arboreal palace had roosted the past two weeks, we made a dreadful discovery.

"Where is it?" Walter wondered breathlessly.

The great oak, whose branches had held the magnificent treehouse, now bore only scattered and fading leaves.

My gut twisted uneasily.

"Did we take a wrong turn?" Walter asked with alarm, but he knew as well as I that our sense of direction wasn't the problem. "How could it just be ... _gone?_"

Pip's reaction was one of instant tears. There was no place on earth he loved more than that treehouse.

"I don't know," I whispered. "Let's go to Mama's. She'll tell us what happened."

As we sprinted the trail between the vanished treehouse and Mama's cottage, I feared the worst. What if not only one, but _both_ had decided to leave the Isle? Neither Walter nor Pip knew a single whisper of my misgivings, of course. I had withheld the important snippets of Mama and Hattie's rooftop conversation for myself. The vanished treehouse certainly provided enough fodder for their own worries, yet neither realized how likely it was that Hattie had disappeared along with it.

We rounded the final bend in the path, and I exhaled my relief.

"It's still there," I cried, pointing ahead at Mama's cottage, whose chimney spouted plumes of white smoke.

We cut through the orchard to the front door. Bursting inside, we found Mama standing alone at the kitchen counter. In the crook of one arm, she held a large mixing bowl, and in the opposite hand a batter-covered spoon.

"You know," she said dryly, "it's considered _polite_ to knock before entering someone's home."

None of us was in the mood for a lecture. Pip, still snuffling, wrapped himself around Mama's legs.

I scanned the cottage for any sign of Hattie and blanched. One of my worst fears had been realized.

Hattie was gone.

Then a hand—a beautiful hand—popped up to wave at us from the other side of the sofa.

"Hi, everyone," spoke a voice.

"Hattie!" I cried, hurrying to her side as I held my joyful tears at bay. "Your treehouse is gone! I thought you were gone too."

"I know," she replied, sitting up. "I don't need it anymore."

I was about to ply her with further questions, but Mama interrupted. "Gather around the table, everyone. We need to share a few things with you, and they'll sit better with cookies and milk."

By this point we were beyond asking _how_ Mama could turn batter into cookies so instantly. We simply accepted it as one of the Isle's many mysteries and sat to enjoy them.

After Mama placed the plate of still-steaming chocolate chip cookies on the table, she poured each of us a glass of cold milk. When she herself had taken a seat next to Pip, she said, "There are two things I must tell you, and neither will be pleasant. Hattie and I have spent many tears on them already, and I expect I'll see the same from you."

The cookies were downright angelic, but even they couldn't sweeten my stomach as I listened to her ominous introduction.

"Just tell us," Walter murmured miserably. He hadn't touched a cookie, and his head was bowed low to the table.

Mama sighed, struggling to continue. More than anything, she hated causing her boys pain.

"First—and I can't say why I sense this, only that I do—is that we won't see each other again for a long time," she told us. "The cardinals are already leaving the Isle, and I believe there is a sign in this. You won't return here until after spring thaws winter's ice."

Grief-stricken, Walter buried his face in his hands.

Hattie, who likewise hadn't helped herself to a cookie, stared across the table at him. If anything, she appeared more afflicted than he did.

Mama wasn't oblivious to the daggers forged by her words. She swallowed, cleared her throat, and forced herself to go on.

"The second thing—"

But she never managed to share that "second thing" with us, for at that moment, Hattie shoved her chair away from the table. With tears streaming down her cheeks, she bolted through the front door as if running for her very life.

The rest of us weren't far behind.

Although Walter had always been faster than Hattie—or any of us—he was unable to keep up with her that afternoon. Within a few seconds, the trees along the winding forest path had hidden her from sight.

Her conversation with Mama rang again in my ears.

Beyond the Trees. Over the Waters.

Perhaps this was the hour of her departure, of her journey Beyond, and she simply could not bear another farewell. Perhaps I had already seen my last glimpse of Hattie Jansen, sprinting through the woods, emerald dress billowing behind her.

But no. No, she was running north toward Emerald Hill and our rowboat. The voices she had heard, the sister she had seen, the longing gazes—these had been directed toward the southern end of the Isle.

"Hattie!" Walter shouted, pumping his legs furiously in his effort to keep up. "Where are you going? Wait for me! Please!"

Without a care for his fellow pursuers, he charged ahead. Soon, I lost sight of him too.

But the moment I broke through the tree line and onto Emerald Hill, I skidded to a halt. Although my body begged for more oxygen, what I saw there rendered my lungs breathless.

Hattie had collapsed onto her hands and knees, shrieking and howling and gnashing her teeth. With curled and desperate fingers, she stretched out her arm, like someone in a choppy sea grasping at a life ring just out of reach.

At first, I didn't understand. Hattie seemed to be grabbing at wind and nothing more.

The marrow in my bones iced over when I realized what she was reaching for.

The rowboat. Moored against the shoreline below.

She was reaching out, grasping at the land of the Living. She was reaching for her home, for her mother and father and brother and sisters. She was reaching for her bedroom, her dinner table, her dolls and games. She was reaching for her friends at school. For lazy Saturday afternoons and Sunday morning hymns.

Hattie wanted her life back, and if she could only reach out and grab that rowboat, then maybe—*maybe*—she could undo her premature journey into the Valley of the Shadow of Death.

But the words Mama had spoken weeks earlier echoed through my mind: *I am not permitted beyond this hilltop.*

And neither was Hattie.

Thus, neither her banshee's screams, nor a biblical flood of tears, nor a nunnery's worth of prayers, nor an eternity's worth of heartache would bring her even one inch closer to *The Rosalie.*

My big brother watched in silence for the better part of a minute. His own tears splashed upon the ground of that hallowed hilltop as he looked on, wholly helpless to grant Hattie's sole desire—the one which would in turn fulfill all others.

Eventually, he did the only thing he could. He knelt beside her and pulled her close to his side, and together they wept.

I felt a gentle hand on my shoulder and looked up into Mama's shining brown eyes. Although she spoke not a word, I knew her hand was there to hold me in place, lest I try to drive a wedge into Walter and Hattie's mournful communion.

I wept too, for I had come to my bitterest realization.

Here, at the end of Hattie's story, her love still belonged to Walter, and her friendship to me.

When Hattie finally calmed down, Walter lifted her chin. Unashamedly, and uncaring that anyone might be watching, he gave her the willing kiss she had always wanted.

I averted my gaze and cried all the harder.

With a musical chuckle, Hattie said, "That means a little more when I'm not forcing you."

And Walter replied, "They both meant a lot to me."

"Walter, I—I have to—" Her voice succumbed to another heavy sob, and she was unable to finish the thought.

"I know," Walter said, supplying the words Hattie could not. "You have to go now."

She buried her face in his shoulder and nodded.

"And there's nothing I can do to make you stay?" he asked, but his tone suggested he already knew her answer.

This time, Hattie shook her head.

Walter frowned and said, "I'll miss you. We all will. Pip most of all."

His attempt to inject a note of levity was met with a stiff elbow to the ribs, and he chuckled.

Mama released her vice-like grip on my shoulder. As I approached Hattie and dropped to my knees beside her, I tried to stifle my tears but failed. My hopelessness was complete. I couldn't speak. Words swam in my brain, but they didn't make it to my tongue. I sat there like a dumb mannequin, hands pressed against my eyes as I poured out the teeming miseries gushing up from my heart.

Hattie's turn to comfort had come. She leaned her head on my shoulder, pried my fingers from my face, and held my hand.

"You'll be okay, Peter," she assured me. Her next words were like antidote and venom injected as one. They comforted, even as they pierced me. "You were the best friend I ever had. You know that? And even though your Mama said it'll feel like the blink of an eye, I still can't wait 'til you're there with me too."

"I'll never ever forget you, Hattie," I croaked. "I promise."

"I know you won't," she said, and she smiled and kissed my cheek.

Walter, I realized, was now standing. He offered his hand to Hattie and helped her to her feet.

"It's getting late," he observed, staring out at the lake and sky. "You should probably get going."

Yet again, Hattie burst into tears. She threw her arms around his neck and hugged him close one last time.

"I'll be waiting for you too," she whispered, and as she breathed in the scent of his shirt, she finally seemed at peace.

Pip, who had watched all these things from a distance, was at last given Mama's permission to run to Hattie. She stooped to meet his outstretched arms as he threw himself against her with a whimper.

"Don't go!" he cried. "You can't go. I'll miss you too much. Don't break my heart."

Hattie kissed his wild brown hair and said, "My heart is breaking too, and I'll miss you so much. But in the end, we'll both be okay."

She let him go and stood tall once more. As she wrapped her arms around Mama, she spoke not a single word, and not a word was spoken in return.

Somehow, I think they had already said everything they needed.

When they parted, I noticed that our farewell had attracted a guest. She stood back among the first of the trees, a young woman who looked very much like Hattie, if Hattie had been allowed to grow up. She had curly, golden hair and irises as green as the grass we stood upon.

And how she smiled.

To this girl, Hattie spoke the final words I would ever hear from her lips.

"I'm ready, Anna."

Anna didn't say anything as she stretched out her arm and opened her hand. Hattie strode forward, swelling with new confidence, and took the hand in her own.

Once more she looked back. Her shining eyes lingered upon each of us for one brief moment, as she committed to memory this final image of her Luther boys. One which would have to last for untold years, until memory would again be replaced by sight.

Then, squeezing the hand of the sister who had journeyed there so long before her, Hattie melted away into the trees and was gone.

May 18, 1954 – 12:43 p.m.

WHEN I WAS NINE YEARS OLD, I assured Hattie Jansen I would "never ever forget" her. It wasn't the kind of flippant promise a child might make—and perhaps break—on a daily basis, haphazardly and without much consideration. No, it was my ironclad vow to her as she walked out of my life and into the unknown Beyond. I meant every word of it. Every syllable. Every letter, with every fiber of my being. I would have sworn myself to that promise on the Bible, or the Declaration of Independence, or any other document revered by any other people of any other land.

That is why, as Pastor Wainwright's Buick plows past 4th Street, I am so ashamed.

Until two days ago, when I received the telephone call, how long had it been since I'd last thought about Hattie? When was the last time I closed my eyes to imagine her face? Her hair? Her eyes and scent and laughter? Her petulant tempers and gloating victories? Her sweet demeanor with Pip, or her stubborn one with Walter?

These days, it happens only involuntarily when I dream of her. I made her a promise, but I have failed to keep it.

I recognize my infidelity for the betrayal that it is, and it pierces my heart like a barbed arrow. Sadly, there can be no penance made to the dead. All I have are the ashes of remorse and the sackcloth of guilt, so these are what I will wear.

There in Pastor Wainwright's car, I silently make another promise.

I will never ever forget you, Hattie.

Even as I do, I know I'll break it. Forgetting is what naturally happens when the living move on and the dead do not.

Pastor Wainwright must detect the guilty vibes emitted by my quiet musings, because he says, "You were thinking about her, weren't you."

"I was."

Outside my window, I spot the sign for Schroeder's Goods and Grocery. Its faded face hangs above a boarded-up doorway and darkened windows. According to Daddy, the store went out of business a few years back. Hopefully it wasn't a thumb-sized chunk of ginger root that broke their bankroll and forced them to close shop.

Like a reflex, my musings snap back to Hattie. Now that she has taken over my mind, I can't dislodge her so easily.

"You know what's funny, Pastor?" I say, flashing him a wistful grin.

"What's that?"

"Sometimes I can't remember what I had for breakfast, but when I close my eyes, I still see Hattie as clear as I see you now. All the way down to which teeth she was missing when she died."

Pastor Wainwright chuckles dryly. "That's because she probably meant more to you than your bowl of shredded wheat. From what I recall, you two were thick as thieves—and may have even gotten into a bit of thievery once or twice."

I laugh. "Only once for me, but never with Hattie."

He lowers his tone with reverence as he says, "I remember her too, you know. A lovely girl, both inside and out."

Staring out my window at Pierre's drab and outdated buildings, I say, "Can I ask you a personal question? How were you able to stay so—oh, I don't know the word—*unperturbed* during it all?"

"What do you mean?"

"I mean, with all the people dropping dead from The Flu, how were you able to keep yourself so composed? Calm about everything? Even when Mama died, it didn't seem to affect you much. Cool as a cucumber."

The old man frowns and stares at the road.

"I'm sorry," I say, aware of how insensitive the question must have sounded. "I wasn't trying to make you feel bad. And I was never mad at you for it. But for a long time, I really have wondered *how*."

In an instant, his perennially congenial demeanor becomes replaced by a dreadful weariness. His voice is thin, like a January wind sighing through a keyhole, as he says, "If you think those things didn't affect me, you couldn't be more wrong. And if you saw me as this composed sort of man, that's only because you saw what I wanted you to see."

"You mean you weren't?"

"Those were terrible times, Peter," he whispers, faltering beneath the weight of his own memories. "Everything was so uncertain. Life filled a person one day and left him the next. The people around me needed something—or some*one*—constant and steady among all that turbulence. So that's what I became for them."

He wipes at his eyes. Although I saw none in the past, his eyes at present are glossed with tears.

"But if you had seen me alone in my office, or behind the locked doors of my parsonage, you would've seen someone else," he admits. "Someone far less *composed* than you remember. You would have seen that I was, in fact, quite perturbed. You would have seen me weep for all of them, and not just the ones who died. I wept for Caleb *and* Jeremiah Lasseter. For Bill Herman *and* the wife and four little ones he left without a daddy. I wept for Hattie too. You just never saw it. You mourned for the ones you lost who were near and dear to you, but I mourned for all of them."

I stare at my feet, ashamed and dumbstruck. I never considered how Pastor Wainwright himself might have suffered as he committed so many to the ground.

"I'm sorry. I didn't know."

Pathetic, but it's all I can muster in the moment.

The old man grunts and says, "Such is the life of a pastor. I can't complain, really. I knew what I was signing up for. While you're among the grieving, you find a hidden box in your heart and conceal your own grief deep inside it. Then, later, when you're alone, you vent it all to God."

Before I can curb my cynicism, I roll my eyes. "Oh, I've definitely done my share of venting. Never was great at hiding things."

My words have touched a nerve. I can see Pastor Wainwright wading among the wells of thought and memory.

Eventually, he asks, "Do you still think it was real, Peter?"

Although my inner musings have been steeped in Acheron all day, his question still catches me off guard. Despite his vague phrasing of it, I know what he's asking.

"I'm not sure," I respond lamely. "I have too many memories of our time there for it to be made up. But I also know it's impossible. Now that I have kids of my own, I see how powerful their imaginations can be, especially when they're accompanied by extreme emotions."

I wait for a reply but don't get one, so I ask, "What do you think?"

"What I think doesn't matter," he replies. "But if it *was* real? If you were visiting your Mama and Hattie there? I'd thank the Lord every day for such an incredible gift."

I scoff bitterly. His comment has unchained one of my inner beasts, and I retort, "A gift given by someone who takes everything else away? I'm not sure that deserves much thanks."

"Oh? I was unaware you had nothing," Pastor Wainwright replies. "John's talked so much about his beautiful daughter-in-law and wonderful grandchildren. Bragged to the point of annoyance about how you're one of the finest up-and-coming aerospace engineers in the country. Was he lying?"

Because of my tremendous respect for the man, I refrain from scowling outright. Besides, I know he speaks not from a place of malice, but of ignorance. He hasn't faced such sudden and rending losses as I have.

Unwilling to answer his question—or perhaps trying to dodge its implications—I counter, saying, "No offense, Pastor, but I don't think you understand the hell we went through."

"Oh, but I think I do! And better than you've ever realized." He slows for a pair of elderly pedestrians crossing the road. "Did you know I was married as a young man?"

My ears prickle with surprised interest, and I shake my head.

"It's true. Her name was Christine Monroe. A direct descendent of our fifth U.S. president, in fact. I married her five days after graduating from seminary, and the day after I was assigned to St. Matthew's. When we moved into that giant parsonage, we didn't have enough belongings to fill a single room. But that was okay. We were going to fill them all with children and have a big, loud house full of laughter and love and music. She loved music, Christine did. Just like your Daddy.

"Anyway, seven months after we came to Pierre, she was walking along Main Street—routine trip to the grocery—when a spooked horse pulling an out-of-control buggy ran her down. The witnesses who saw it happen told me she must've been dead before she hit the ground."

I feel gutted. Why have I never heard this story before?

You never asked, I answer myself. *You were too absorbed in your own world.*

"Don't worry," Pastor Wainwright assures me. "I'm not looking for pity from you. It was a long time ago. But there are two lessons in it for you, so listen sharp."

I nod abruptly and obediently.

"Here's the first: The entire flow of our world is one of beauties and blessings which enter our lives, then leave us again. I was heartbroken when I lost my Christine. It's been fifty years, and I still can't wait for the day when I will hold her again. But could I really be thankless and angry for the blessing God gave me in her, just because that blessing didn't stay as long as I would have liked? Would you curse the gracious host who sets out a feast, then sends you away when he decides the feast is over? Think it over for yourself, Peter. Will you curse God, who graced your life with Rosa and Hattie, simply because he took them away before you were good and ready?"

I sit in stunned silence. I've heard Pastor Wainwright speak with such forceful conviction before—just not to me.

He goes on. "The second lesson is this: In all of human history, whose pattern is an unbreakable cycle of death, no one has ever reported a story like yours—not that I've heard of, anyway. If you and your brothers did indeed visit with the dead on that island, it means God gave you something he hasn't given to anybody else. So don't deal too hasty a judgment on the same one who gave your Mama and Hattie back, even if it was only for a while."

I have no rebuttal. His gentle but stiff rebuke has left me uncomfortable and exposed.

Fortunately, now that he has said his piece, he seems ready to move on. Turning left off the main road, he mutters, "Here we are."

As we pass through two stone pillars on either side of the lane, I crane my neck to look up at the rust-eaten gateway sign suspended between them. The years have taken such a toll on it, I can hardly make out the two words written in iron there.

Asphodel Glade.

The Buick lurches and bounces across the poorly maintained cart path. I feel like a bobblehead figurine as I am jostled up and down and side to side.

Neither of us speaks until the trees give way and we arrive in the open clearing.

A small cabin, only a stone's throw beyond the Buick's passenger window, draws my immediate attention. It, too, is home to my ghosts.

"You can drop me off here," I tell Pastor Wainwright. "I think I'd like to walk the rest of the way."

He doesn't object. He parks, steps out, and opens the trunk. I retrieve the bulky suitcase and place it on the grass bordering the lane.

As I embrace him, the old man seems less withered than before.

"Thanks for picking me up," I say. "I know we only had a few minutes, but it was great talking to you again."

Despite the saplings of uneasiness his words have planted within me, I truly do mean it.

"My pleasure, Peter," he replies. "I'll see you in a couple days. If not sooner."

I offer him a melancholy grin. "Yes. And I'm sorry. I've relied on you for too many goodbyes already."

"And yet," he says with a quick wink, "there I am for you."

As he wheels his Buick about on Asphodel's lawn, I withdraw my pipe and to-bacco from my jacket pocket. He offers me a brief wave, and I wave back.

Then he is gone, and I'm alone.

I pack and light the pipe, taking care to stamp out the smoldering match after dropping it into the grass. Leaving my suitcase beside the cart path, I cut across the overgrown grass toward the cabin. Its flowerbeds, which once bloomed and buzz-ed with so much life, are tangled and wild, and much is dead. In the midst of this tiny jungle, choked with constricting vines, is a rocking chair without an owner.

Abigail died in 1941, a full decade after her brother.

I step cautiously onto the old porch. As at the train station, I'm worried I might inadvertently punch a foot through a bit of termite handiwork and injure myself. The floorboards creak, but otherwise hold my weight as I approach the cabin's front door.

My hand freezes on the thumb-latch door handle. The cabin's denizens have been dead for some time, yet I cannot shake the feeling that I'd be committing a grievous intrusion by entering.

I let go of the handle and step away from the door. For a moment, I survey the tired face of the old cabin. Just as Eli preferred, the window curtains are drawn shut so that no prying eyes can see what lies behind them.

I suppose some ghosts just want to be left alone.

Once more, I dive down the mineshaft of the past, deep into the bedrock of ancient memories.

Memories of a bitter and frightening Christmas. Memories of a splintered vio-lin and the blaze which consumed it.

Memories of a bold intervention. One that wasn't quite bold enough to stitch together the disaster unraveling at Asphodel Glade.

THIRTY-SEVEN

The Winter of Our Discontent

WE DID NOT RETURN IMMEDIATELY to Asphodel Glade on the afternoon of Hattie's departure. Although Walter was handling the aftermath of those events with a quiet stoicism, Pip and I were beside ourselves. Mama wasn't about to send us home in that state, so she escorted us back to her cottage. There we ate homemade butterscotch candies, and she read to us from *The Adventures of Tom Sawyer*.

There was one other compelling reason for Mama to extend our stay: She wanted to hold on a little longer. If her gut feeling was indeed the reality we faced, not only was this our last day with Hattie. It was also our last day with Mama—at least for the remainder of autumn and the whole of winter.

Walter's inevitable breakdown came when we arrived at Emerald Hill for the third time that day. Losing Hattie was no small matter to him. But to go months without Mama? Unbearable.

She hugged her sobbing eldest son and combed her fingers through his mop of brown hair.

"I know it's sad," she cooed, "and that sometimes you will feel very lonely. But I also know you are strong enough to handle this. And when it feels like I am terribly far away, remember that my eyes aren't so far, and I am keeping watch always."

We embraced as a family and said our goodbyes. Then my brothers and I ambled down the hill to our rowboat.

Twilight's grasp was weakening when we came ashore at Asphodel. Without even leaning *The Rosalie* upside-down against the tree, we shuffled up the hill. With every step, discontent for our destination grew. Anyone who saw us that evening might have supposed we were en route to our own executions.

Entering into the warmth of the dining room did nothing to improve our moods.

"Where have you been?" Daddy barked. He sat alone in front of an empty plate. Three more, all full of Abigail's now-cold dinner, waited at our respective chairs.

"Sorry, Daddy," Walter muttered. "We were playing and lost track of time."

My father took a sip of brown liquor from his glass. "You were out at that island again, weren't you. You boys've been spending too much time there."

"We'll be back earlier next time," Walter replied apologetically. Even he didn't want a fight.

My father spoke like a judge passing both verdict and sentence, as he said, "It'll be good for you to spend some time away. Besides, winter is coming, and the lake is growing colder every day. It's too dangerous to keep crossing it."

Walter squeezed his eyes shut. I deduced by his balled fists that he was struggling to suppress his rising temper.

"Please don't," he begged softly, a prisoner before his righteous king. "We'll be back earlier. I promise."

The gears in my father's booze-addled brain were lurching and grinding, but turned nonetheless. I saw deep sympathy in his eyes, mixed with his own hopelessness, as he took stock of Walter's visible despondency. But he would not be moved this time from the course he had set.

"It'll be okay," he said in a soothing tone. "We'll find plenty of things to do 'round here. Besides, it's only for winter. When things warm up again—"

He stopped mid-sentence. Walter had spoken something between clenched teeth, but whatever he had said was so quiet, no one had heard him.

"What was that?" my father asked. His turn toward tenderness screeched into reverse as he read Walter's fury.

"I said I'll take the boat out anyway."

My unblinking eyes flitted back and forth between them. Daddy and Walter, these two giants of my young life, seemed poised to rattle the very foundations of our home in a terrific battle.

My father rose from his chair, clouds of impending peril darkening his countenance. If I hadn't known any better, I would have sworn the dining room lights dimmed, surrendering their feeble lumens to the gravity of his mounting anger.

"Who do you think you are, speaking to me like that?" he growled. "Or did you forget that *I'm* the head of this house, and that your voice means nothing?"

I expected Walter's immediate surrender. I'd never seen such a transformation overcome my father. Like a bear whose hibernation is disrupted by unsuspecting spelunkers, he appeared ready to set himself upon Walter tooth and claw.

Walter was unfazed. Bitterly, he spat, "I haven't forgotten anything about you. You're the one who wouldn't let me say goodbye to Mama. You're the one who let her die."

My father reeled backward, as if being assaulted by stones rather than words. He recovered momentarily, slamming his fist down onto the table with such rage, I was sure I heard a piece of it splinter.

With jaw set and teeth clenched, he said, "If you so much as touch that boat again, I will burn it to ashes! Do. You. Understand?"

Walter glared but said not a word.

My father took Walter's silence as victory. A modicum of his former gentleness returned as he said, "Good. Not another word about it then. Now, up to your rooms, all of you. I don't want to see or hear you the rest of the night. Is that clear?"

We honored the *hear you* part of his request right away. Silently, we hurried from the dining room and up the stairs.

But before entering my room, I heard Daddy collapse into his chair with a defeated sigh. He may have imposed his will over Walter, but his exasperated groan sounded like that of a loser, not a victor.

"Mr. Luther, your hand," spoke another voice below. Abigail, who had undoubtedly heard the vicious row from the kitchen, sounded both concerned and indignant.

"I'll be fine," Daddy said. "Don't worry about it. If it still hurts in the morning, I'll see Doc Schumacher."

"Let me look at it," Abigail demanded. This was followed moments later by a disapproving cluck of the tongue. "Doesn't look broken, but you'll have a fine bruise. Less than you deserve."

"What's that supposed to mean?"

"Talking to your boys the way you did. Especially Walter."

"Did you hear what he said to me? What—you think he was in the right?"

"I didn't say that. But you're the adult, Mr. Luther. Returning childish anger with childish anger of your own? We've got enough children running around here on the steam of their emotions. Pardon my saying so, but I don't think we need to add another to the mix."

Daddy began to protest, but Abigail cut him off. "You wait there and think a minute while I fetch some ice for your hand."

By the time she returned with the ice, Daddy had cooled some.

"You don't know how worried I am, Abigail," he said. "Yesterday I was talking with Fred about how obsessed they are with this island. He shared that when we were staying with him, Peter told him something strange. Said they were visiting Rosa there."

So much for pastoral confidentiality.

I wondered if Abigail would inform him now of her own knowledge, but she must have thought this imprudent, because she replied, "Like I said before, they're children, and children invent silly games."

"Sounds like more than a silly game to me," said Daddy. "Sounds like they're losing their minds. Going crazy. Cuckoo. However you want to put it."

"I don't know I'd call it 'crazy' so much as desperate. Between losing their Mama and now Hattie, they've got no clue how to handle their new reality."

"So they're detaching themselves from it?"

"Maybe. Everything happened so suddenly. Maybe these visits with her help them feel they're getting the proper time to say goodbye."

"You're starting to sound a lot like Fred," Daddy growled.

With a hint of sass, Abigail replied, "Good. He strikes me as a wise man."

"Whatever you may think about it is irrelevant now, I suppose. I told them they couldn't use the rowboat for the rest of winter. A few months away from that *verdammt* island will give them time to find a new way of coping."

"Careful, Mr. Luther," Abigail warned. "There are coping mechanisms far worse than make-believe games."

A flare of anger surged back into my father's tone. I imagined them both staring at the bourbon glass in his hand as he replied, "Mind your place, Abigail. Your job is to cook and clean and keep this house in order. Raising my boys is *my* job. Understood?"

There was a pause, and I feared what Abigail might say next. She wasn't one to mince words or restrain her opinions. In the past, we Luthers had largely accepted these traits just as we accepted them among ourselves. But lately my father had become unpredictable and rash, acting first and thinking later. If she said the wrong thing now, there was no telling how he might react.

To my relief, her reply was rather meek, albeit slightly wounded. "You're right. I'm sorry I overstepped. Please understand that I care about you and the boys an awful lot. Besides Eli, you're the closest thing I've got to family."

Frustration, whether at Abigail or himself or the whole situation, bubbled up and into my father's voice as he said, "I'm going into my study. After you clean this up, could you bring me a coffee?"

There was no mistaking the passive-aggressive barb in Abigail's reply. "Of course. After all, that's why I'm here, isn't it?"

The next weeks of our lives were like wading through a boggy tundra, slow and joyless and frosty. The accumulated ice between Walter and Daddy neither thawed nor melted a solitary drop. Indeed, if such things could be gauged by empirical units of weight or size, we would have discovered the glacier growing thicker each day. My father spoke little to Walter, and Walter less in return.

All this made for a bleak and thankless Thanksgiving. Besides the fact that the turkey, stuffing, and other trappings tasted like sawdust compared to Mama's "Practice Thanksgiving" feast a few weeks earlier, November 28 also marked our first major holiday without her. A heaviness sat upon her empty chair, stifling any sparse enjoyment we may have found otherwise. We ate hurriedly and with spare conversation. Afterward, my brothers and I helped Abigail clean up, as Daddy smoked his pipe on the back porch and conversed with Pastor Wainwright over a glass of scotch.

Meanwhile, the rest of the world waited with a worried anticipation. Although the embers of The Flu's second wave were dying out, a new question plagued humanity's collective mind: What if each subsequent wave became increasingly deadlier? Was this mankind's reckoning come at last? The final purge of those who scourged the earth with war and genocide and the raping of its resources? Were we a species staring into the face of our Apocalypse? Not one of our making, but certainly one of our deserving?

Under this specter of uncertainty, the confidence of the general populace eroded with increasing rate. Fewer than ever were ill, yet more wore masks each day. Brother sequestered himself from brother, and even husband from wife. Neighbor became suspicious of neighbor, friend of friend, employer of employee, all for fear that a deadly sickness might exist within one which might infect and destroy the other.

It was amid this general spirit of discontent that my relationship with Walter crumbled. Our adventures with Mama had forged a mutual respect and admiration between us. But the kiss between him and Hattie had brought it all to ruin. He had done nothing wrong, of course, and that's precisely what made him so hard to forgive. I soon found myself doing the very things I knew would annoy him most. During our evening homework, I hummed until he snapped and threatened to sock me. I made sure he caught me using his prized pocketknife to sharpen my pencils. Sometimes, when I was sure he was asleep, I would pile extra blankets upon myself, then open the bedroom window to let sub-freezing air fill the room. Every needle I could find, I used it to poke at Walter.

The most egregious way I sought to even the score over Hattie's affection was by purposefully seeking Daddy's. I asked him what books I should read and what he might teach me about the Classics—the culture and languages and stories of ancient Greece and Rome. It was woefully dry, far more boring even than Pastor Wainwright's longest-winded sermons, but my feigned interest was meant to serve a single purpose. As long as it irritated Walter, I would have sat on Daddy's lap and listened to all dozen books in Aurelius' *Meditations*.

Problem was, the time I spent with Daddy didn't seem to irritate him one bit. Naturally, this made me more resentful. Walter wriggled his way under my skin without even trying, while he, despite my most heroic efforts, remained as unflappable as ever. Even in this, Walter proved his superiority over me.

Much of his indifference was due to the problem he was desperately trying to solve. With Christmas just around the corner, his every thought seemed occupied with the Isle and Mama. Despite the exile Daddy had imposed on us, Walter schemed and dreamed how he might achieve a surreptitious return—and the "greatest Christmas surprise ever" for Mama. Many of these musings he shared aloud with me in the dark of our bedroom.

"If the rowboat's being watched, maybe we could sneak over on Eli's canoe? But no, I'm sure someone would catch us lugging that huge thing all the way across the yard. It'd never work."

I listened, but disinterestedly.

"Maybe we could swim there with the life preservers," he suggested next. The flotation devices Daddy ordered had arrived a few days ago.

"No, that wouldn't work either," he sighed. Like a crazy person, he was literally engaged in spoken conversation with no one but himself. "The water's way too cold for that. I'd freeze to death before I got there."

"Yeah, and then I could actually sleep at night instead of listening to you," I called across the room.

He sat up sharply. "What bug crawled up your butt?"

"Can't you just shut up about it?" I shot back. "Daddy told us we can't go, so we can't go."

"Don't be such a jackass," he snapped. "I know your new best friend told us not to, but Mama's all alone out there. Don't you think she should have some company? Especially on Christmas? Or would you rather memorize more stupid lines from *The Odyssey* with Daddy?"

"Didn't you listen to her?" I retorted. "She said we wouldn't come back until the ice was melted off the lake. And the lake is barely starting to freeze over!"

"Then think how surprised she'll be!" Walter exclaimed. "I bet she'll fix us the best Christmas feast in the history of the whole world."

"She won't," I reminded him, "because we're not going."

Walter shrugged and lay back down. "Suit yourself. I'll figure out a way and go by myself."

The next morning, a Saturday, Daddy joined us at the breakfast table. For once, his eyes were not red and foggy. They had reverted to the clear, crystalline blue of days long gone. This could only mean one thing: he had run out of whiskey before imbibing too deeply last night. Either way, it lifted our spirits to have the old Daddy back for a morning, including Walter's.

As we tucked into our eggs and sausages and washed them down with steaming spiced cider, Daddy shared a bit of news.

"Guess who's coming to celebrate Christmas with us," he said between mouthfuls.

"Pastor Wainwright?" Walter answered indifferently.

"Well, yes, he'll be here," said Daddy, "but not only him."

"Gramma and Grampa!" Pip shouted with youthful confidence.

He must have forgotten how afraid they were of The Flu, unwilling even to offer a comforting embrace at Mama's funeral. I imagined them right then, sitting on their easy chairs at opposite ends of their living room, both wearing gauze masks to protect themselves from nobody.

So it came as quite the shock when Daddy replied, "You got it, Philip! They'll leave Castleton as soon as their Christmas service is finished. Should be here for dinner at noon."

This news was enough to stir up some Christmas excitement. It also provided me a source of relief, because Walter certainly wouldn't attempt some foolhardy trip to the Isle with our grandparents here. They had a reputation among the Luther boys for being top-notch gift-givers. A year ago, they had been responsible for Walter's ivory-handled pocketknife. We also had them to thank for our fishing poles and tackle—as well as a wealth of angling knowledge from Grampa.

I could only dream what they might bring this year. Even Gramma was worth suffering in exchange for such gifts.

"But Daddy," piped Pip, awash with sudden concern, "it's only four days 'til Christmas, and we don't have a tree yet! We can't have Christmas without a Christmas tree!"

"By Jove, you're right again," Daddy replied. "Well, it's a Saturday, isn't it? What would you boys say to a stroll through the woods so we can find the perfect tree to put up in the Great Room?"

"Yay!" squealed Pip, clapping his approval.

Walter's and my agreement wasn't quite as enthusiastic, but genuine nonetheless. To spend a morning with our Daddy, hunting down our own Christmas tree, hacking it to the ground with our manly hands—and all this without a drop of liquor in sight—was the greatest gift he could give us that Christmas.

As we headed into the woods, our tools of arboricide in hand, it felt almost like the old Daddy had returned from the dead. His gentle affections brimmed up from wherever Mama's death had buried them. He asked how we were dealing with our loss of Hattie, what school was like without her, and what we hoped Santa might bring us for Christmas. He listened to and looked at us without distraction, as if he were no longer haunted by some shadow of Mama standing behind us.

Two hours later, Daddy and Walter dragged our eleven-foot kill toward Asphodel Hall. The month-long gulf which had separated them shrank—and even seemed to disappear entirely—as they labored together. Daddy asked him which sights he would most like to visit during a hypothetical trip out West, and whether he had heard of the newly established Katmai National Park in Alaska.

All was perfect—that is, until Daddy and Walter heaved the great balsam fir upright in the Great Room. After securing it into the iron Christmas tree stand, Daddy eyed their work satisfactorily and said, "Well done! Now, wasn't that just as much fun as playing on the island?"

His tone had been innocent enough. To this day, I truly believe Daddy merely intended to express how much he was enjoying our morning together.

But that's certainly not how Walter took it. His face reddened, and his fingers curled into fists. Seething, he stormed up the stairs and slammed our bedroom door shut.

Without another word, my father retreated into his study. He reemerged a minute later, bundled for riding.

"I'm going to town for a few things," he murmured, shuffling past us and out the door.

Pip and I watched through the front windows as he made for the stable. Upon Castor's back, he galloped north, over the hill and out of sight.

He returned a half hour later, carrying only one thing: a hefty bottle of bourbon. Silently, he brushed by me and into his study. The door shut. The lock clicked. And we didn't see him again the rest of the day.

THIRTY-EIGHT

Christmas 1918

"NO DECORATIONS ON YOUR TREE? What kind of travesty is this?"

Gramma and Grampa Vos had arrived a half hour earlier, shortly after the mantel clock's noonday chime that Christmas Day. To our surprise, when they pulled up in front of Asphodel Hall, they did so behind the windshield of a polished black Ford. Everyone ran out to greet them, delighted to know we were related to automobile owners. Even Daddy was impressed, and spent twenty minutes in the cold with us as Grampa showcased its every feature.

"Who needs Gramma anymore?" he'd joked. "I have a new love."

Now, next to the roaring hearth, he stared at our Christmas tree, open-mouthed with disbelief over the state of our holiday trappings.

"We cut it down a few days ago," I explained, "but never got around to decorating it."

"Where do you keep them? The ornaments and such?" Grampa asked. "We really must remedy this at once. No objections!"

"Rosa kept them in the attic," Daddy said, his tone flat. He hadn't yet celebrated the holiday with a drink, but last night's liquor still coursed thinly through his veins. "I'll climb up and bring back what I find."

As Daddy left to find decorations, Pip asked the question we had all been thinking. "How come you and Gramma aren't scared of The Flu anymore?"

I noticed the guilty glance Grampa exchanged with his wife, before saying, "It's not that we were *scared*—"

"Mama said you were," interrupted Pip. "Because of Henri—Henri-*ent*—um, her *sister*."

"I suppose we grew tired of hiding away," Grampa answered. "Especially after your Mama passed."

"Then how come you didn't come 'til now?" questioned Pip, grabbing Grampa's hand and hanging from it playfully.

"Because even though we didn't *want* to be scared, I suppose we still *were* scared," Grampa said, scooping Pip into his arms with a laugh. "And because grownups like me and your Gramma can be incredibly stupid sometimes."

"Speak for yourself!" Gramma croaked from her sofa seat. "I wanted to come the moment we heard Rosalie was sick."

"So you've told me," Grampa barked over his shoulder. "Anyway, I *am* sorry we weren't here. We should have been. But we're here now, and we intend to make up for it the best way we know how."

"With presents?" Pip hollered.

"Of course with presents!" roared Grampa, and he threw Pip into the air.

Pastor Wainwright arrived the exact moment Daddy was returning with the box of Christmas ornaments.

"I'll be back with the tree lights in a minute," he huffed, straining as he lowered the heavy box to the floor. Then, to the pastor he had seen two hours earlier at church, he said, "Hello, Fred, and Merry Christmas again."

"Merry Christmas, John! And to you, Henry and Opal!" exclaimed Pastor Wainwright. Seeing Pip's indignation at being left out, he added, "As well as you, Luther boys. No, I didn't forget about you, Philip."

We tore into the box of ornaments, but our decorating party didn't last long. We had relocated only a dozen of the gleaming globes onto the Christmas tree when Abigail's head appeared in the kitchen doorway.

"Christmas dinner's ready when you are!" she cheerily announced.

"You are a true Christmas treasure," Grampa responded kindly, as the kitchen door swung shut behind her.

In the dining room, we encountered an array of dishes placed in a single line along the table's middle. Mashed potatoes and potato medallions, creamed spinach, rolls so light and airy they were liable to start levitating, cornbread dressing, roasted squash, and creamed corn all flanked the meal's centerpiece—the largest Christmas goose I had ever seen.

But there was something even more amazing.

Abigail had set nine places for dinner. Many times in the past, Mama had insisted that Abigail and Eli join us for certain special occasions, and Christmas always one of them. While Abigail accepted such invitations, her brother Eli stubbornly declined each and every one. Over time, it had become tradition to set him a place regardless. Though Mama knew it would remain empty, she never let it be said that she hadn't tried. Setting that ninth place, as Mama herself would have done, was Abigail's way of honoring her memory on this first Christmas without her.

The surprise was that the ninth place was occupied. Eli sat in it, giving each of us a silent nod of greeting as we entered the dining room to join him.

Gramma followed me in. When she spoke, I wondered if she hadn't discovered Daddy's liquor cache, because she said, "Mother of pearl! Look at this feast! Abigail, you *must* sit beside me and teach me how you do it all."

After Grampa overcame his initial shock, he said, "Yes, please do! Though it hardly seems worth it *now,* when we've already got one foot in the grave!"

"It's your foot, not mine," Gramma snapped. "I plan to enjoy thousands of dinners long after you're gone, you old ass."

Everybody, even Pastor Wainwright, enjoyed a hearty laugh at this putdown.

"I'd love to teach you, Missus Vos," Abigail replied with a cordial, albeit slightly guarded, smile.

"Please," said Gramma, brushing her arm, "it's just *Opal* between us now."

Either three Christmas spirits had paid Gramma a visit, or else the pain of losing another daughter had softened her. While she was still no paragon of jollity and cheer, her frost-encased personality had begun to thaw. If this rate of improvement continued, we could expect her to show up next year wearing a velvety red suit and carrying our presents in an overstuffed sack.

With the full party assembled, Pastor Wainwright stood and offered a mealtime prayer longer than some of his sermons. In it, he thanked the Lord for the blessings of family and friends, of incarnation and salvation. He asked God to comfort those mourning lost loved ones, and to bring them healing as they remembered the reason why Jesus came to earth. Finally—and probably only when he remembered the food glaciating in front of him—he asked God to bless our dinner, as if a dead goose and mashed potatoes needed such a benediction before sliding down our gullets.

We passed dishes around the table, serving ourselves as much or as little as we pleased. Daddy placed glass tumblers in front of the men and poured each a healthy dose of bourbon—his own the healthiest among them. Pastor Wainwright, who hadn't yet satisfied his penchant for speaking, offered a toast in memory of those no longer dining with us at Christmas. This he followed with a second, more spirited toast, in which he praised Abigail for her culinary triumph.

Daddy, putting forth his merriest efforts for the holiday, placed a ban thereafter on any further interruptions to our meal. He atoned for this slight by topping off Pastor Wainwright's whiskey—and his own.

When everyone, including the puppy at our feet, had feasted to his or her heart's content, we all pitched in to clean and put away the magnificent mess. The only exceptions were Eli and the dog. When finished, the former limped off as wordlessly as he had come, while the latter lay comatose beneath the table. Even Gramma voiced no complaints about working side by side with "the help"—as she had called Abigail on more than one occasion.

After cleanup came the long-anticipated unwrapping of gifts. Daddy's were first: a teddy bear and slingshot for Pip, ice-fishing equipment for Walter, and leather-bound copies of both *The Iliad* and *The Odyssey* for me.

My jealousy tactics against Walter had backfired, now in more ways than one.

Any trace of disappointment was erased when I unwrapped Gramma and Grampa's gift. From inside the small package, I lifted out a genuine Swiss Army knife. I held it near my nose for an up-close inspection, marveling that I should own a treasure such as this. Firelight glinted off its polished blades. There was a reamer, screwdriver, can opener, and corkscrew, each of which would undoubtedly come in handy when I found myself in a life-or-death survival situation.

In the ever-revolving pattern of my life, my joy was swallowed again by envy. In the long package which Walter unwrapped, he discovered a genuine Daisy BB gun. The accompanying ammo can contained enough lead BBs to exterminate Asphodel's entire squirrel population.

"Wow!" he exclaimed, throwing himself upon Gramma and Grampa with ecstatic gratitude. "Come on, Peter. Let's go shoot icicles off the porch roof!"

"Hold it," said Daddy, grabbing the BB gun's barrel.

For a moment, I thought he was putting the nix on Walter's present.

"No shootin' 'thout puttin' on your coats and gloves," he said thickly, with a grin and wink. "And take Pip with you too, and teach'm how to be responsible when you're shooting."

The joy of executing icicles at point-blank range hardly lasted five minutes, so we ran inside and collected an armload of tin cans from the kitchen trash. These we set in a row along the wide trunk of a tree that had fallen a week earlier. Walter and I alternated shots until the entire can army lay slaughtered on the frozen ground. Walter set them up a second time, and we allowed Pip his obligatory turn behind the stock.

After three more rounds of sharpshooting practice, Walter offered up another bright suggestion. "Let's find a squirrel. I wanna see if I can hit something moving."

Nothing can plaster a smile to a young boy's face quite like the prospect of killing some defenseless critter, so off into the forest we stomped. Even though I'd been jealous of Walter's present, he had been gracious enough to share his gift of lethal projectiles with me. And, with five thousand BBs in hand, it truly was the gift which kept on giving.

While we didn't bag any squirrels—they must have been cozy and safe in their nests—Walter did manage to pop a noisy crow off his bare roost. This didn't kill the bird, who flew away with a cranky squawk, but the direct hit did seem to slake Walter's bloodlust.

"It's getting cold," he said. "Let's go home and drink some cider."

We returned to the Great Room to find a small audience gathered around Daddy. He hadn't played his violin in months, so we were justifiably surprised to discover it presently nestled against his chin. Once upon a time, his skilled fingers could have tuned its four strings in the dark. Now they slipped and fumbled, loosening those which needed tightening and tightening those that needed to be loosened.

Pastor Wainwright sat closest to the front door. Noting our return, he said, "Your Daddy's going to play for us."

"He hasn't played since Mama died," Walter mumbled. Cider forgotten, he stared at Daddy with misgiving.

"Music is good for the soul," replied Pastor Wainwright, picking up on Walter's anxious notes. "Or so they say."

Pip rushed past Daddy and jumped into Grampa's lap—the reward for which was a butterscotch candy—while I made for the pot of steaming cider, set on a small table near the fireplace. As I passed Daddy, I glanced up at him.

Walter's apprehension wasn't unwarranted. Something was off. Daddy looked like a man trying to walk too soon after a horrific injury. The agony in his expression was subtle—so subtle, only Walter had recognized it—but there all the same. The mere handling of the violin traumatized him, yet for the sake of his holiday guests, he was masking the pain as best he could behind the whiskey's false cheer.

But the mask was cracked. Hidden beneath it was a desperate man.

I forgot the cider. There was an empty place beside Grampa and my lap-dwelling brother, so I sat and stared with an uneasy heart.

"If your strings ain't cooperating, you don't need to go on bothering yourself with it," called Abigail. She also appeared concerned. Tense. Like a mother keeping an eye on the unfamiliar dog near her playing child.

"I'm fine, Abigail," my father snapped, speaking in the curt fashion which had become all too familiar as of late. "I almost've got it."

He proved this true moments later, when he drew the bow along its strings and filled the Great Room with a perfect G-D-A-E resonance. Without missing another beat, his fingers and bow began flying together in a rousing rendition of "Joy to the World." This he followed with "Angels We Have Heard on High" and "O Come, All Ye Faithful."

As Daddy played on, my apprehension fled. He seemed to be a changed man— or a restored one. Perhaps it was the reflected firelight, but Daddy's eyes appeared to burn in a way I hadn't seen since Mama's death. Or perhaps the bourbon in his bloodstream had managed to fool even him into believing that life was merry and mirthful once more.

While these factors may have played a hand in his transformation, I believe there was a more substantial reason which lay beneath. It is possible that an ancient love, deeper even than the one he had shared with Mama, lived in Daddy's soul. Had I been more observant and insightful as a boy, I might have recognized sooner music's power over him and in him. When he tuned his violin, he was tuning into balance the notes of his own soul. And as he played, he was bringing every discordance of his spirit into resonant harmony once more.

But too much of what heals a man can also hurt him. Or perhaps it isn't the medicine itself, but the accompanying substances and circumstances which stand in the way of the remedy's good work.

That Christmas evening might have ended in healing, with the gladsome notes of new birth and a promising tomorrow. Instead, it culminated in dreary, wintry darkness.

After "Go Tell It on the Mountain's" lively conclusion, Grampa asked, "Would you play 'In the Bleak Midwinter'? It was Rosa's favorite, ever since she was a little girl."

At once, the subtle anguish returned to Daddy's face.

As the violin's strains reverberated through the Great Room, Walter's eyes met mine from across the room. They flashed with alarm.

Grampa's request had tripped a trigger inside Daddy. A snare, fashioned by loneliness and laid by bourbon, drew tight around his heart. It squeezed and wrung from him every soothing drop of hope the music had applied to his wounded spirit, until he was left remembering only the bleakness of life without Mama.

The first obvious warning sign occurred with the first faltering note on Daddy's strings. He paused, took a deep breath, slid the bow across the violin's face, and moved on. But the beginning of the next verse brought with it a second discordant glitch. This time he played through it, but as he did, he glanced hate-fully down at the violin beneath his chin.

The third mistake was his last. My father groaned his rage and cast the bow aside, where it clattered to the hardwood floor near Gramma's boots. He held the violin in front of himself, his arm fully outstretched, like someone holding a sack of particularly putrid garbage. With purest contempt, he glowered at the violin. Hating it. Loathing it. Not for what it was, but for the ears its notes were powerless to reach.

My father squeezed his instrument around its neck until his bloodless knuckles blanched white. But he couldn't choke the repulsive instrument to death. No, he would have to kill it some other way. And so he raised it—the violin handed down by his own daddy so long ago—high above his head. Then, with the force of a man sledgehammering rocks, he slammed the violin's lower bout against the floor.

"Daddy!" shrieked Pip, horrified, as a hideous *crack!* rent the air.

But my father was beyond hearing. Still grasping the violin's neck, he lifted the object of his destruction and glared at it again. Its bottom half had ruptured from the fingerboard, leaving only jagged splinters between them. The two pieces were now connected only by their strings, so that everything below the violin's neck dangled before him. At once, his hatred for the instrument morphed into horror over what he had done, and then into a surge of self-loathing.

He raised the violin a second time. The strings binding top piece to bottom acted like a flail, adding even more destructive force as he smashed it against the floor.

"John! What the hell do you think you're doing?" Grampa shouted, twisting his body to protect me and Pip from splintering missiles.

My father gave no reply. Amidst more shouting, the violin crashed against the ground a third, fourth, and fifth time. With each subsequent blow, more of it frac-tured and hurtled away from the central mass, until only a serrated fragment of tailpiece remained of the violin's lower half.

Silence, but for the crackling fire and Pip's miserable snuffles, settled over the Great Room.

In the middle of it stood my father. A man I no longer recognized. Apart from his heaving breaths and ice-blue irises flitting from one gawker to the next, he was deathly still.

He shifted his gaze toward the wreckage clasped in his hand. Then, without a word, he strode casually to the blazing fireplace and tossed what remained of his violin into the consuming flames. He watched the varnished bits of wood flare up and blacken as the inferno reduced his oldest and deepest love to ash.

When he finally turned away, tears glistened upon his cheeks. His eyes wandered among the broken bits of violin scattered about the floor, and for a moment, I thought he might collect and burn every toothpick of that debris.

He didn't. Lowering his head, he staggered to his study door and disappeared behind it. The clicking of the lock was an exclamation point on the sentence his outburst had already written:

Our Christmas celebration was over.

THIRTY-NINE

Another Eavesdropped Conversation

"DEAR JESUS," GRAMPA MOANED IN DISBELIEF.

He was the first to speak following my father's violent spectacle, but Abigail was the first to take action.

"Why don't you boys head upstairs," she told us. "The other adults and I need to talk."

We didn't argue. I grabbed Pip's hand and tried coaxing him off the sofa. When he refused to budge from his curled-up position beside Grampa, I picked him up and heaved him high onto my shoulder. Upstairs, I deposited him safely among the scattered toys of his bedroom, yet even these offered him little comfort.

"Why was Daddy so mad at his violin?" Pip asked, staring blankly at the new teddy bear in his hands. "I thought he loved it."

"He did," I answered.

"Then why did he break it?"

"He's just sad we had Christmas without Mama."

"Daddy always tells me he loves me before bed. Is he gonna break me someday too?" Pip wailed.

"No, Daddy wouldn't do that to us. He loves us way more than his violin."

Even as I offered Pip my most reassuring answers, I felt unconvinced. I didn't know what to expect from my father anymore. One moment he was fiddling as merrily as ever. The next, his fiddle was matchsticks.

Pip must have detected my lack of conviction, because he asked, "Will you keep me safe?"

"Sure," I replied. "Nothing's gonna happen to you, okay? Play with your toys. I need to check on something."

I left the room. After all, I had work to do. If the adults were talking, I had to listen. At first, I tried sitting out of sight at the top of the stairs, but the voices were low and too far away. Abigail had undoubtedly led the others into the kitchen, where they could discuss the evening's events a safe distance from my father's study door.

That left me with two options. I could risk sneaking back downstairs and into the dining room, where I would be closer to the kitchen, but I knew this meant a high risk of being caught and sent upstairs. The other option was to enter the dark bedroom at the end of the hallway, situated directly above the kitchen. Against the bedroom's far wall, beneath the large bed, was an iron grate which vented heat into the room. I knew from previous spy missions that if I pressed my ear against the grate, I could hear every word spoken in the kitchen below.

There was only one problem with the second option: The vent was in Mama's bedroom. I hadn't stepped foot inside it since before she had been struck by The Flu. It was a room overcrowded with the ghosts of cozy mornings snuggling beside her in bed, of leaning against her as she held the newborn Philip, of dark corners for hide-and-seek, and of squealing laughter when she found me. It was a room that had overflowed with more happiness than I myself even knew.

Until that September day when it became a vault of unspeakable pain.

But that Christmas night, I knew it was my best hope. Maybe my only hope. So I sucked in a deep breath—and with it, courage—and tiptoed down the hallway. Worried I might overthink my plan if I didn't hurry, I pushed open the door and stepped into the darkness beyond.

To my surprise, the bedroom didn't smell of sweat and bodily odors and wastes. Instead, something almost floral filled this room of death, a scent that had a chemical cleanliness about it. Although my father seemed ready to abandon the room to forgottenness and decay, Abigail had apparently been caring for it without our knowledge. In the murky light, I saw the bed made, the spare blankets folded, and that all was tidy and neat.

I shut the door and crept toward the overstuffed bed. Even one creaking floorboard might alert those below to my presence above, so I took my time crossing the room. When my waist bumped up against the mattress, invisible to my unadjusted eyes, I lowered myself to my belly and army-crawled into the narrow gap between floor and bedframe.

As I slithered underneath the mattress, my left knee knocked something over—a couple somethings, in fact. Whether they were made of metal or glass, I wasn't sure. Whatever they were, they made a tremendous racket as they clanged against the floor and against each other.

What happened next nearly made me the youngest heart attack victim in Pennsylvania history.

From the darkness in front of me, a voice hissed, "Shut up, you stupid ass!"

I tried to scream but was stifled by the firm hand pressed suddenly against my mouth.

"It's me! It's Walter!" the unseen thing assured me.

Despite my relief over hearing my brother's name and not that of some soul-eating demon, adrenaline continued to pulse through my shaking body.

"What're you doing in here?" I asked. "And what did I knock over?"

"The stuff I use to clean the room," said Walter. "And I'm doing the same thing you are—trying to listen downstairs."

"Yeah?" I replied. For the moment, I decided to ignore the revelation about his clandestine cleaning gig. "What've you heard so far?"

"I'll tell you later. Now, shut up or leave so I can hear."

I wriggled up beside him and turned an ear to the grate. The voices of the adults floated up from the kitchen, changed into metallic versions of themselves by their bouncing journey through the ductwork.

Pastor Wainwright was in the middle of speaking.

"... have to tread lightly with this," he cautioned. "John's in a hard place, especially here at Christmas."

Gramma grunted and said, "I don't care where he is. I'm taking those boys with me. I love John—Don't give me that look, I do—but I don't trust him right now. Not when he's like this. Not with the drinking. Who knows what he might do next?"

"We can't take them away, Opal," Grampa countered. "That's called *kidnaping,* you know. But maybe we can extend our stay here."

"And who will mind the store?" Gramma asked irritably.

"Oh, forget the store, would you? These're our grandchildren! I'll call up Tony, and he can—"

"Tony?" Gramma scoffed. "Whatever he didn't rob us of, we'd lose to his ineptitude."

"We lose what we lose."

"Please," said Abigail, butting into their fruitless bickering, "let's not turn this into a discussion about your store. Pastor Wainwright, I see where you're coming from. I do. And no one wants to come down too hard on Mr. Luther or forget how badly he's hurting. But we have to think about the boys first."

"It's a tough time of year for a man who's lost someone close to him," the pastor replied, reinforcing his earlier point. "It can change you into someone even *you* don't recognize. And it isn't so out of the ordinary, drinking a little too much on a day like today."

Abigail was swift in her rebuttal. "Problem is, it's not just today. It's *every* day. Mr. Luther's well beyond a few extra bourbons to help him cope with some kind of Christmas loneliness. Lately he's been at that devil-drink every morning, noon, and night, and he's gonna drink himself to an early grave if he doesn't change course. And if that's where he's headed, I'll be distressed enough over it. But I'll do everything I can to make sure he ain't taking anyone else with him."

"Okay, okay," Pastor Wainwright conceded. "Point taken. So what do *you* think we should do?"

"That's the tough question, isn't it?" said Abigail. "I'm already on thin ice with him. More than once, he's told me to mind my business. If he knows we're up to something, he could send me away with little more than a moment's notice. Or he could round up the boys and take them somewhere else. Then we wouldn't be able to help at all."

"I say we give Sheriff Clark a call," suggested Gramma. "Let *him* sort John out."

"And what good would that do?" rebutted Grampa. "No laws I know of against getting drunk at home."

"We also have to remember that he hasn't done anything to hurt the boys themselves," Pastor Wainwright interjected. "We can't treat him like a criminal for breaking down and smashing a violin."

"Like I said before, it's a tough situation," said Abigail. "That's why I think it's best to make it look like we aren't doing anything at all. For now, at least."

"You can't be serious!" argued Gramma. "We can't do nothing!"

"Lower your voice, please," Abigail responded curtly. "I didn't say we should *do* nothing. I only said to *look like* we're doing nothing. I'll keep an eye on him the whole time."

"No offense, Abigail, but how could you stop him if it came to that?" asked Grampa.

"I'll keep Eli around," she answered. "*He* will."

"Eli?" Grampa sounded more incredulous than before. In my opinion, he had good reason. "Eli's only here because he's got nowhere else to go—John's words, not mine. And you see how he is, pretending those boys don't even exist. Not to mention that awful limp! What makes you think he would—or could—stand up to John?"

Abigail responded to Grampa's question with one of her own.

"Do you know how Eli came by that limp, Mr. Vos?" she asked. "It was all on account of me. I was only ten years old, but I remember it clear as yesterday. Eli and I were running errands in town for the Vandenbergs—they're the ones who owned Asphodel before the Luthers. He'd gone off to the hardware store, and me to see Jolene the seamstress. We were gonna meet up back at Main Street and walk home together. Well, I finished with Jolene first and was waiting on him when a gang of older boys started harassing me. I don't want to sully your ears, so I won't repeat anything they said. Suffice it to say, they had every plan to make a woman out of me that afternoon.

"Anyway, they were trying to drag me off, and everyone else in town was watching. Just *watching* this happen. And then Eli was there, and even though every one of those boys was older than him, he started knocking 'em down like bowling pins. But there were more of them, and only one of Eli. I ran off and hid. I'm not proud of it, but I was a scared little girl. Eventually, the boys ran off. When I came back for Eli, I thought he was dead, bleeding from everywhere, limbs splayed out at odd angles. Took me a full fifteen minutes to find a soul decent enough to help me carry him to the doc's place.

"He survived, obviously. But he's carried that limp ever since. Now, I'm not telling you this only so you'll think a bit better on Eli—though I do hope you will. I told you so you'd know who he really is. I understand how my brother comes across. Believe me, I do. Truth is, though, he's loyal as a dog to the people he loves. He'd do anything for 'em. And ever since Walter came to visit me when I was sick, he's warmed up to those boys quite a lot. Why do you think he showed up at dinner tonight after a decade of his place sitting empty? Told me he was doing it for the boys."

"That's all fine and well," said Grampa, "and I'm perfectly pleased to hear it. But it doesn't answer my other question. Do you think Eli would really be able to stop John?"

"Walking with a limp doesn't mean someone can't also be strong as an ox," Abigail replied. "A lifetime of hard labor will do that to a man. So, like I said, I'll keep Eli close, make sure he's got plenty of jobs to take care of around the house, especially when Mr. Luther's at the bourbon. Then, if it seems like he's about to hurt himself or anyone else, I'll have Eli do whatever he has to. And he will."

"You be sure to call me if anything *does* happen," said Pastor Wainwright, "though I'm confident John would never come to it."

"And us," added Gramma. "The boys'll need to go somewhere safe."

"I'm not convinced it's the best plan," Grampa sighed, "but it'll have to do."

Ever the reverend, Pastor Wainwright concluded their secret meeting by saying, "Let's pray for John and the boys."

As he began his supplications, Walter poked my ribs and motioned for me to slide out from under the bed. I did, and he followed. When we were back on our feet, neither of us spoke. We were still digesting everything we had heard.

Eventually, I asked, "What else did they say? Before I got here?"

Walter shrugged. "Not a whole lot we didn't already know. Daddy's pretty much gone cuckoo, and Abigail and Gramma are worried about how much he's drinking, and what he could do if he flies totally off the handle."

"What're we gonna do?" I asked. Even when our father was beating his violin into a splintered wreck, I didn't feel as frightened or helpless as in that moment.

Walter shook his head and said, "I don't know. We have to keep an eye on him too, I think."

"But what can we do to stop him?"

My older brother thought a moment, then said, "Maybe it's time for us to go back to the Isle. For good."

"Daddy needs us here," I replied. "We can't leave him all alone. Besides, he'd find us there and take us back home. *Plus,* Mama wouldn't let us. We already tried, remember?"

"Maybe she would if she knew how crazy he was," countered Walter. "Anyway, we can't do anything tonight. But think about it."

Finished with our conversation, he tiptoed his way to the bedroom door.

But I had one more question. Remembering the bottles and jars I had knocked over beneath the bed, I asked, "Why have you been cleaning in here?"

Walter stopped. He looked over his shoulder and answered, "In case we figure out how to get Mama home."

Then he slipped into the hallway, leaving me in my dead Mama's bedroom, alone and with a swelling sense of dread.

FORTY

The Spring Thaw

JANUARY AND THE FIRST HALF of February passed in an unmemorable haze of school, homework, and church. Each week seemed to contain the passage of a year as the chill of early winter settled into a freeze, deep, solid, and harsher than any I remembered. During those days of darkness, we longed for the lengthening of the sun, whose return would bring with it our return to the Isle.

The household bourbon budget dropped off for a time—my father likely felt ashamed of his Christmas spectacle—only to resume in full force on January 16. Not only was this his birthday, but it also coincided with the day Congress voted to ratify the Eighteenth Amendment. Although liquor sales wouldn't be banned for another year, my father took it as a personal challenge to hoard all he could before the future drought set in, like some kind of alcoholic Joseph of Egypt.

Although my father showed moderation in his daily liquor consumption, a tension loomed whenever he was present. This time the discomfort hung not only between him and Walter, but between him and all his sons.

Nor was he unaware of our distrust. In his attempts to assuage our concerns, he renewed his efforts to connect with us by spoiling us. He lavished us with gifts and sweets, some from the grocery, others imported from elsewhere in the United States. One day after a heavy snowfall, he returned home with a pair of brand-new toboggans. He loaded us into the buckboard wagon next to them and carted us off to the high hill between Pierre and Castleton, where we spent two hours zipping down the fresh powder. On another occasion in mid-February, during a bitter cold spell, he announced that school had been canceled, and escorted us onto the thick ice which ringed the lake. Together, we figured out how to use the ice-fishing equipment Daddy had gifted Walter at Christmas.

When Walter asked if we might be able to walk to the Isle, my father stiffened, but not from the cold.

"You wouldn't make it," he answered bluntly. "The ice is too thin over the deeper water."

And that was the end of the matter.

It was also the middle of February when Daddy arrived home with a new purchase delivered to his office. In our Great Room, he pried open the box and lifted a violin case up from the packing straw.

"It's German-made, like my old one," he informed us. But when he held the polished violin to his chin and scrawled out a few tinny notes, he frowned and added, "Not quite the *same* as the old one, though. I suppose it'll take some getting used to."

The return of Daddy's music began at last to thaw the frost which Christmas had glazed over our home. He played nightly after supper, regardless of whether my brothers and I were present. He grew accustomed to the new instrument, and before long his bow was sawing music as beautiful as ever. It pained him sometimes, without the presence of his Muse. Yet he pushed through the sorrowful measures, tasting more of its healing joys as he did.

In watching the transformation which overcame Daddy as he played, a strange desire fell upon me. I decided that I, too, wanted to learn the violin.

When I entered his study late one evening to share my desire, I felt a bit like a peasant approaching his emperor. Although a gentler spirit had overtaken him the past weeks, a formidable uncertainty continued to surround him. He wielded tremendous and unpredictable power, one we had witnessed at his former violin's execution. Especially after Walter's and my Christmas eavesdropping, an inextinguishable suspicion lingered. I wondered when and where that wrathful power might flare up again—and whether he might turn it against us.

But my desire conquered my apprehension. It was a Friday evening when I approached his behemoth oaken desk. A glass of bourbon sat nearby, but his eyes appeared bright and lucid as they flitted along the countless lines of ledger before him.

"Daddy?" I squeaked.

He looked up and beamed warmly.

"Hello, Peter. I'm sorry. I know I shouldn't be working on a Friday evening, but we added four new supply regions this week." With a chuckle, he added, "Not that you care about any of that. What can I do for you?"

"I was hoping—well—" I clammed up, unable to verbalize my request.

Perceiving my discomfort, Daddy rounded his desk and knelt in front of me.

"Out with it," he said, squeezing my shoulder. "I won't bite."

"I want to learn how to play the violin," I blurted. "Like you."

He grinned, then adopted an air of faux earnestness and said, "If that's true, I'll give you your first lesson right away. You don't learn how to *play* the violin. You learn the violin itself."

"What do you mean?"

"You learn everything about your instrument, like it's your best friend," he explained. "You learn its shape, its weight, what kind of wood it's made of, where it came from. You learn how the strings feel under your fingers, how the bow rests best in your hand. And as you're learning every little thing about it, you also learn the music of its strings. How they change to become higher or lower under your touch. How they resonate and sing together."

They were, perhaps, the most poetic words my father ever uttered.

I found myself all the more enthralled. "So you'll teach me?"

Daddy laughed sweetly. "Of course I'll teach you. We'll have our second lesson tomorrow night."

Each evening of the following weeks, an unpleasant dissonance filled Asphodel Hall. If the noise I produced was painful to my own ears, they must have been downright hellish for everyone else. Our puppy—more a full-grown dog by this point—ran to the furthest corners of the house whenever I picked up the violin. Soon, he fled any room I entered, even when I wasn't carrying the instrument of his great displeasure.

But those weeks weren't entirely disagreeable for Asphodel's other inhabitants. Degree by degree, the chill of winter yielded its frozen ground to the relative warmth of early spring and its promises of impending life. Snowmelt turned the roads into mud pits, and grassy acres into green sponges which squelched and burped up water when stepped upon.

Lake Acheron's thick banks of ice also began disappearing. Each day after school, Walter would run down to its banks to discover how much more had melted back into liquid water. Like a lapdog gazing up at a table of unreachable food, Walter would stare across the water at the faraway Isle, wondering when his day might come.

By the last week of March, not one week after my tenth birthday, only scattered ice floes remained. Walter's dreaming and scheming of returning to the Isle had increased daily in an inverse proportion to the amount of ice left on the lake. He was a herald ready to burst with a song of triumph, for he knew the final strokes of victory were imminent.

That Tuesday morning on our way to school, he made the big announcement. Our bicycle pedals had scarcely finished their first rotation when he revealed his intentions. "Today's the day."

"The day for what?" I asked.

"The day we go back to the Isle," he explained. "There's hardly any ice left, and Mama must be wondering why we haven't visited yet."

I put up no argument. Despite my jealousy-fueled bitterness toward Walter, I was also ready to see Mama again.

But Daddy had different plans.

"Good afternoon, boys!" he exclaimed as soon as we opened the front door. He was leaning against the wall outside his study door.

Walter and I glanced at each other, I with surprise and he with disappointment. After all, it was only three o'clock. On a normal day, Daddy wasn't due home until five or six.

Why had he come home so early?

Pip burst into view, grinning and hugging Daddy's leg. Unable to contain his enthusiasm, he answered our unspoken question. "Daddy's taking us on a trip! Daddy's taking us on a trip!"

"Where?" Walter asked suspiciously. "And when?"

With Pip clinging to his leg like a monkey to a coconut tree, Daddy clomped forward and said, "You know how we were talking about taking a train out West? To see Yellowstone and Yosemite?"

"Sure, I remember," Walter replied.

"It got me thinking," said Daddy, "maybe it's about time we went. We'll see a whole gaggle of those places from your posters and magazines. And not just Yellowstone and Yosemite. We'll see the Grand Canyon and Zion Canyon, and the giant sequoias, and the redwoods in California, and Lake Tahoe in the high country, and wherever else we want to go."

Walter's response contained less excitement than Daddy had hoped. "For how long?"

Daddy shrugged. "Two months. Maybe three. Mr. Jansen told me he'd take care of the plant for however long we need."

Each word Daddy spoke was another weight added to Walter's sagging face.

"When are we leaving?" he asked.

"That's the best part," said Daddy. "We're leaving on Friday, which means you get to miss the last two months of school! I already booked our train tickets. We're riding first class the whole way."

Make no mistake: I wanted to see Mama. I wanted to enjoy her feasts. I wanted to partake in her grand adventures, especially after she'd had all winter to plot and plan. I wanted to know the warmth of her embrace, and to hear her adoring voice in my ear as she reminded me how much she loved me.

But Daddy was talking about two months without textbooks, blackboards, pencils, or math. Not only that, but all the Luther boys would be together non-stop, adventuring like outlaws around the American West. Perhaps most importantly, I knew it would also give Daddy something to do besides work and drink. Even as a ten-year-old, I realized how much he needed this escape, and I didn't want to bereave him of it.

Walter felt differently.

"I don't want to go," he announced. "I'll stay here with Abigail."

Pip must have sensed a sudden and dangerous tension in my father's leg, because he let go and hurried away.

"Aren't these the places *you've* always wanted to visit?" asked Daddy, confused and aggravated by Walter's dismissal.

"Someday," Walter answered. He headed for the stairs and added, "Just not right now."

Daddy slid sideways, blocking his path. "But—why not? I thought you'd be up for this even more than your brothers!"

"I just don't," Walter replied. He glared up at Daddy with a diamond defiance. "The rest of you can go, but I'm staying here."

"I'm sorry you don't want to go," Daddy said, trying to keep his temper in check. "But I wasn't exactly giving you an option, so you'd better get used to the idea. Besides, I know once we're there, you'll end up having more fun than anyone."

"I won't, 'cause I'm not going."

The insubordination was brazen. Even for Walter.

My father's cheeks turned a bright shade of vermilion, and he began to tremble.

"You will come," he growled, "even if I have to tie you up and drag you onto the *gottverdammt* train myself!"

Like an insolence volcano, Walter was about to spew more, but our father didn't give him the chance.

"Keep your mouth shut!" he roared, seizing Walter's upper arm and pinning him in place. "You think I don't know why you want to stay here? It's that island! That damned island! Ooooh, yes. Pastor Wainwright and I had a nice chat all about it."

Walter shot me a murderous glance.

Daddy closed his eyes and took three deep breaths. His roiling rage lowered to a simmer as he regained control of himself. Then he said, "I know you've convinced your brothers and maybe even yourself that Mama is there. But she's not, Walter. She's not. And I won't let you continue these delusional games any longer. It's not good for you. It's not good for your brothers. So in three days, we're getting onboard that train—*all* of us—and we're not coming home until this madness is out of your system. Have I made myself clear?"

Walter didn't speak. He maintained a seething glower as he nodded a forced assent.

Daddy sighed, relieved that the fight wouldn't have to continue.

"Good," he said. "Now, go upstairs and do your homework, and don't come back down 'til dinner. Pip, you go play quietly somewhere. Understood?"

This time all three of us nodded obediently.

The moment our bedroom door was shut, Walter laid into me.

"Why did you tell Pastor Wainwright?" he snapped.

I sat casually at my writing desk. With that small purchase of time, I devised a lie which I hoped might appease him.

"I didn't want to," I answered, "but back when we were going to the Isle every day, he took me aside after church and said Daddy was worried about us."

"I don't remember him doing that," Walter said suspiciously.

"It was during that potluck, right before Thanksgiving. Remember *that*? Anyway, he asked what we were doing, and I tried to say it was nothing, but he said he didn't believe me. I was worried he'd tell Daddy I was lying, or maybe that we should get rid of the boat, so I told him."

Walter shook his head pitifully and said, "You've got to be the worst, dumbest liar in the world. Dammit, Peter, you messed up everything."

"I didn't mean to. I thought it was my only choice."

Walter groaned and collapsed into his desk chair. "Guess you can't change it now. But you've got to be smarter from now on."

"Yeah. I will."

"Good. Now shut up while I think about what to do."

I didn't fight him. My lies had weaseled me out of a certain beating, and I wasn't about to push my luck.

Not until the next morning, as we were riding to school, did Walter reveal where his evening thoughts had taken him. We were on the cart path, only a short distance into the woods beyond the glade, when he spoke his sudden command.

"Stop, Peter."

I looked over my shoulder. He was no longer riding his Schwinn.

"What's wrong? Forget something?" I asked, jumping off my bicycle.

"No. We aren't going to school. We're going to see Mama."

"Walter, come on. Daddy'll find out for sure."

"Not if we're careful. Besides, what's he gonna do? He's making us take this stupid trip anyway, so we might as well visit Mama before we go."

It was hard to argue with Walter's logic, but I'd always had a harder time deceiving my father than he did. Daddy's forbiddance of any trip to the Isle was clear, and skipping school on top of such blatant disobedience would double the pain of any punishment. Despite Walter's optimism, I figured our chances of pulling it off undetected were infinitesimal. Miss Carrington would call either Daddy's office or our house to report the unexcused absence from school. If that failed to trap us, we also had Abigail and Eli to contend with, both permanent fixtures upon Asphodel's grounds. Even if they didn't spot us directly, they certainly might notice the disappearance of a large rowboat.

I wouldn't know the word *kamikaze* for another couple decades, but I realized a trip to the Isle spelled exactly that—our certain doom.

Yet there were two other contending desires inside me, and both of them stronger than my wish to stay out of trouble. In the first place, I wanted to see Mama. Months had passed already, and the notion of two more was downright depressing. Secondly—and much more importantly—I didn't want Walter to think me a coward.

"Fine," I said. "Let's do it."

Walter beamed with approval. I hated myself for how proud that made me.

"We'll stash the bicycles here," he said, continuing the explanation of his plan, "then sneak through the woods down to the shed. We'll get out the oars and life-preservers, then hurry the rest of the way to the boat."

"What about Pip? How will we get him out of the house without Abigail knowing?"

With genuine regret, Walter said, "We won't. It's too risky. Besides, he's looking forward to this trip with Daddy. He'll be okay without Mama 'til we get back."

The plan formed, we hurried through the budding spring woods. The sun was still low on the horizon, and our forested acres remained submerged in shadow. A shiver set into my bones, and I found myself longing for a heavier jacket. The going was slow across the soggy, uneven forest floor, but after twenty minutes spent skirting the lawn's eastern border, we reached the backside of the old shed.

Walter peeked around the corner toward Asphodel Hall and whispered, "I don't see anyone. Come on."

My heart thumped against my ribs. Our singular stint of thievery at Schroeder's Goods and Grocery notwithstanding, this was my most rebellious hour. Although the former ran afoul of Pennsylvania law, cutting school to see Mama felt like the more criminal act. We would be punished far worse for this transgression than if Tom Schroeder had caught us, and I paled to consider what that might mean.

I shook my head and pushed it from my mind. I needed all my focus and wits about me if we were to have any chance of succeeding without being caught.

Inside the shed, cobwebs trailed from the oars like party streamers. Walter grabbed these while I removed the life-preservers from the nails they hung upon.

But as we turned to leave, we found the open door already occupied. The large silhouette of a man stood in our way.

Assuming the shadow belonged to Daddy, Walter and I cried out in fear and alarm.

Then the shadow spoke. "What're you boys doing?"

I sighed, relieved. It wasn't Daddy. It was Eli.

The relief didn't last long. Daddy or not, we were still caught.

"You're supposed to be on your way to school," Eli stated, his emotionless voice deeper than the roots of the hills.

"We—uh—decided not to go," Walter stammered. "We're leaving in a few days anyway, and we wanted to take the boat out one more time before we left."

Eli said nothing, but his stony gaze told us he was waiting for more.

"Are you gonna squeal on us?" Walter pleaded. I couldn't tell if he was more afraid of the consequences or of someone stopping us from visiting the Isle altogether.

Eli's dark eyes narrowed, but he didn't ponder the question long. A moment later, he stepped aside and answered, "Your family's business is no concern of mine."

Walter heaved a great sigh and said, "Thank you."

Using his free hand, he pulled me along by my upper arm.

Eli's voice stopped us in our tracks a second time. "Ice may be gone," he said, "but that water's still cold enough to kill you in minutes. If I was you, I'd be careful."

"We will," Walter assured him.

Then he yanked on my arm again, and we hurried along to *The Rosalie*.

FORTY-ONE

The Final Voyage of *The Rosalie*

AS WALTER ROWED US STEADILY toward the Isle that morning, I had the distinct sense that a great change had occurred. Yet, as often happens in life, I couldn't quite place my finger on what it was, or even why I felt as I did. But it was *there*. Undefinable, yet undeniable all the same. Some major shift, an altering of our world's fabric, had taken effect, but I was utterly unable to explain it.

Whatever it was, it left me deeply unsettled.

The quiet was eerie as we moored *The Rosalie* against the Isle's rocky shore and hurried up Emerald Hill. When we reached the summit and found it empty, Walter said, "She must not have realized we were coming. Maybe winter was so long, she stopped watching for us."

"Maybe," I said. "We should go to the cottage."

But as we hurried along the forest path, my heart quailed. What if the cottage wasn't there anymore? What if Mama had grown too lonely waiting for our return? What if she had decided to be with her own kind, Beyond the Trees and Over the Waters, as Hattie had done?

Ruminating over such questions, I stared down at my feet. When I did, a happy realization stared back. The stones Mama used to pave the forest trails were still there. Hattie's treehouse had disappeared after her decision to leave the Isle. If Mama had gone away too, I figured all her created works would have vanished with her—although I couldn't guess at what might have kept her from meeting us at Emerald Hill.

Any lingering doubts were cast wholly aside when we rounded the final bend in the path. Mama's cottage and the surrounding gardens stood as they had before our winter hiatus. While spring was slow to arrive in the world beyond the Isle, here life bloomed in full array. Flowers flowered and branches budded. The hedges grew thick and leafy, shaped no longer like zoo animals but in the fashion of a great castle wall. At the four corners where elephants once stood, magnificent turrets of green rose high enough to brush the lowest branches of the trees over-head.

Of everything in the gardens, the most beautiful and wonderful was Mama herself. She stood beneath one of the fruit trees, leaning in to breathe upon its branches just as she had done during our first visit those many months ago. Wher-ever she breathed, vibrant green buds appeared, as if she were blowing away the last of winter's hoary frost.

"Mama!" Walter shouted, and he ran ahead to greet her.

She had little time to turn before he jumped into her arms, weeping tears of mingled joy and sorrow. To see her after winter's eternity filled his heart, even as the despair of another looming absence emptied him.

"Oh! My baby boy!" she exclaimed, shocked to find Walter in her embrace. Glancing up at me, she cried, "Peter! You're here too!"

She welcomed me into her arms also, squishing her two older boys uncom-fortably together.

"But where is Pip?" she asked when she released us.

"He couldn't come today," was Walter's dodgy reply.

Mama was so overcome with joy, she accepted this response without further question. She hugged us again, rocking with us as she said, "I simply cannot believe you are here! But here you are, and I am so thankful for it."

"Why can't you believe it? Did you think we wouldn't come?" Walter asked, a touch offended.

Mama frowned and said, "There is some sort of disturbance in my soul. I can't explain it, but I feel it growing every day. Some darkness of evil or sorrow. It has clouded my eyes so that I can't see as far as I used to."

"What is it?" I asked, remembering my own uneasiness upon arriving at the Isle.

"A cloud in my heart. Like I said, I can't explain *what* it is, only that I am sadder than I can ever remember."

A sudden smile lit up her face, and she said, "But you're here now, and my heart is glad for that. Though you *are* finding me a bit unprepared."

"That's okay," said Walter. "We only need you."

Mama gave us a third hug and said, "Come inside. It may be spring, but you both look like you could use something warm to drink."

Not five minutes later, a steaming mug of hot chocolate rested between my palms. Seated upon the sofa, with Mama between us, we recounted the events of the past few months. When Walter told the tales of Daddy's threat to burn the boat and of the violin's violent demise, Mama wept aloud.

"Oh, John! You loved that violin! What darkness has crept into your heart? What sadness? Oh, I would be there for you in one beat of my heart if I could! But I can't. I can't cross that divide."

After allowing her a moment to regain her composure, Walter continued, saying, "I haven't even told you the worst part. Daddy's making us go on a trip with him."

"And why is that so bad?" she wondered.

"Because we'll be gone for *two months*," moaned Walter. "Maybe three! We don't wanna be away from you that long, especially after we couldn't see you all winter."

"Perhaps that is the darkness hanging over me," Mama mused, although she sounded unconvinced. "Another long stretch without my boys. But I will manage."

"Don't you get lonely here?" I asked.

"Well, yes," Mama answered, "but I have my gardens to manage and games to plan. I'll be okay. Did Daddy say where he's taking you?"

"Out West," said Walter, "to see Yellowstone and a buncha other places."

"Like on your posters!" Mama exclaimed. "You should have more than enough fun."

"I won't," Walter petulantly replied. "Not without you. And not *with* Daddy."

"Why not with Daddy?"

Walter hesitated to answer. He didn't want to cause her further pain.

"Tell me, Walter."

He sighed and said, "Daddy is ... different now. He's changed. On Christmas, after he broke his violin, we spied on Abigail and Gramma and Grampa and Pastor Wainwright, and they said they don't trust him. Gramma even wanted to take us back to Castleton with them. They said he was drinking too much. They're worried he'll hurt us next time."

Mama sat for a minute, tacit and deep in thought. More tears welled in her eyes, though the sadness behind these was more smoldering and less impassioned.

Finally, she said, "Perhaps *that* is the darkness I've been feeling. John, you have lost yourself. How will you be found again without me?"

"There's one more thing," Walter said.

"I'm afraid to hear it, but tell me anyway," Mama moaned.

"Daddy knows about you. Peter told Pastor Wainwright, and he told Daddy. He thinks it's all make-believe and crazy, us coming out here to see you. He said he wouldn't let us anymore."

Mama's expression turned immediately stern. "Then why are you here?"

"Because we wanted to see you before we leave on this stupid trip!" Walter exclaimed. "We even skipped school—"

"You shouldn't have done that," Mama interrupted. "I know you wanted to see me, and God knows I wanted to see you too, but that didn't give you the right to disobey Daddy and sneak out here."

In a tiny voice, Walter asked, "What else were we supposed to do?"

Mama stood. Approaching the window where her baby's bassinet once stood, she gazed into the gardens beyond.

"You must go home," she said abruptly. "Now! The darkness is deepening, and there is only one way I see for the light to dawn again."

"How?" Walter dolefully wondered. "How can it, if we can't be with you?"

"You misunderstand," she replied. "That's not what I'm suggesting. I believe the time has come at last. You must convince Daddy to come here and see for himself."

"I already told you," Walter protested, "he thinks we're crazy!"

"There is a way you might convince him," said Mama.

"How?" Walter and I asked in unison.

"Back when I first moved to Pierre and was working at the flower shop," she said, "a teacher friend of mine, Otto Scherzinger, introduced me to Daddy. It was obvious he was trying to arrange something romantic between us, but at the time, neither of us was very interested. Daddy was focused on work, and I was focused on—well, on not-so-old men. But Otto invited us both to his Christmas party a few months later. That was where Daddy and I fell in love."

"How will that help convince him?" Walter asked.

"That night," Mama continued, ignoring his question, "before I kissed your Daddy for the first time, I said, 'You know, I like you a lot better after a few drinks.' And then I kissed him, and after I kissed him, he told me, 'Then thank God for whiskey and eggnog.' And he kissed me again."

Some light of enthrallment set Mama aglow as she hearkened back to this scene. Despite everything we had shared about Daddy's current state of alcoholic turmoil, he remained the man she loved and cared about more than anything else in the world. She saw past the twisted shadow he had become. She knew her good husband and the gentle father of her children was still there, buried beneath the detritus left by her sudden departure from the world.

Walter must have seen what I did in Mama's expression, because it was with renewed confidence that he said, "Okay. I'll tell him. He'll have to believe us then, right? How else could we know unless you told us?"

But in my heart, I felt a stirring of apprehension. I had used a similar tactic when trying to convince Abigail. I had even shared an exact description of how Mama appeared in her dreams, but it had backfired. Abigail simply devised an alternate—and much more sensible—explanation for my uncanny knowledge.

So why shouldn't Daddy, so strong in his disbelief, do the same?

But Mama and Walter seemed certain of the plan, so I kept my mouth shut.

"Let's hurry back to Emerald Hill," Mama said, making for the door. "Leave your hot chocolate."

A minute later, as we all hurried along the flagstone path, Mama gave us further instructions. "When you arrive at Asphodel, find Abigail. Admit to skipping school and coming here. The criminal who voluntarily confesses is treated more gently. It'll also build your credibility in Daddy's eyes, and we can't have too much of that for the task at hand. Then, when Daddy comes home, waste no time. Tell him you have a message from me and share those exact words: 'I like you a lot better after a few drinks.' A bit ironic, considering what you told me about Daddy's current problem, but he'll see the meaning behind it. I *know* he will. And if he's still unconvinced, tell him that second part too: 'Then thank God for whiskey and eggnog.' Got it?"

"Got it!" repeated Walter. He sounded triumphant already, like the heavily favored Olympian who has underestimated his dark horse opponent.

Atop Emerald Hill, Mama kissed and hugged us farewell, and we hustled away to carry out her instructions. With any luck, we would return later that day—all *four* of the Luther men—to reunite as a complete family.

So rejuvenated was Walter's spirit, he even whistled as we cast off from shore.

It was his whistling which triggered my sudden realization. When we had arrived on the Isle, I couldn't shake the sensation that some great change had taken place, but I'd been unable to define what that was.

Now, thanks to Walter's twittering like a merry bird in early spring, it hit me.

"Walter!" I whispered. "The trees!"

The branches were empty.

"Oh yeah," he said, as if the omission made no difference whatsoever. "I didn't notice before. No cardinals! Well, not *all* of them left. There are still a few, way high up in the trees."

"Where do you think they went?" I asked.

"South, probably. Isn't that what birds do? But who cares, anyway?"

I did. But Walter would pay my concerns no heed, so I let the matter drop and said nothing more.

Faster than ever, Walter navigated *The Rosalie* across the frigid waters of Lake Acheron. Once ashore, we dragged the rowboat onto dry ground. On a normal day, we would have flipped it upside down to keep out dew and rainwater. We would have stored the life-preservers and oars properly in the lakeshore shed, where they would be safe from the elements.

Had we treated our faithful ship with the respect and attention she deserved, everything may have turned out different. Perhaps that morning's voyage across Lake Acheron wouldn't have been her last.

But our task was too pressing, and our redemption too near at hand. Leaving the boat upright, we sprinted up the hill toward the house.

During our return trip across the lake, we had imagined carrying out Mama's plans as precisely as she had assigned them. Confess to Abigail. Relay Mama's message to Daddy. So simple, it seemed foolproof.

Which is why we were so easily caught off our guard.

When we entered the back door, we had expected to find an empty dining room. Instead, three figures were already present, waiting for us around the table: Pastor Wainwright, Philip, and—

"Take a seat," Daddy snarled.

FORTY-TWO

Exile

WALTER WAS QUICK TO RECOVER from his surprise at finding the dining room occupied. Even my father's livid countenance couldn't stifle his eagerness to carry out Mama's instructions. Remembering the pre-kiss line from our parents' long-past Christmas party, Walter shouted, "You know, I like you—"

"Sit down and shut up!" our father snapped. He sprang up from his seat and slammed a clenched fist down on the table, missing by a half-inch his drained glass and the empty bourbon bottle beside it.

A cursory glance at the wall clock told me it wasn't even ten o'clock.

Stubborn Walter was undeterred. Again, he cried out, "You know, I like you a lot better—"

Again, he was cut off.

"I don't care how you feel about me!" my father howled. "Like me, hate me— what does it change when it comes to you?"

"No, Daddy, you have to listen! You have to—"

"I have to do nothing!" he roared. "I am charge of this house, and that means I am in charge of *you*."

Summoning all my courage, I added my voice to Walter's. "But Daddy—"

His glare fell upon me, and he said, "You sit too, Peter. I'm sure your brother roped you into this somehow, but that doesn't mean you're off the hook."

To my eternal shame, I shut up and bowed my submissive head. This small act of cowardice seemed also to crush Walter's spirit. Dejected, he parked himself in one of the vacant chairs and stared across the table at Daddy.

I sat beside him with burning tears.

My father took a handful of deep breaths. In a much calmer tone, he said, "When Eli told Abigail he caught you sneaking around by the shed, she telephoned me at my office. I knew if you were skipping school to visit that island, it meant your problem—your *addiction* to that place—must be worse than I realized. Since I couldn't get through to you last night, I asked Pastor Wainwright to talk some sense into you. Maybe he'll have better luck than I did." He nodded toward the reverend. "Go ahead, Fred."

Pastor Wainwright's concerned gaze did not, at this cue, shift from my father to Walter or me. "I told you I would come and help, John," he said. "Not 'talk some sense' into them, as you say."

"Phrase it however you want," my father replied with a dismissive wave of the hand. "Just ... help."

Pastor Wainwright looked straight at Walter, then at me, and asked, "Boys, do you miss Rosa? Your Mama?"

Walter and I exchanged a glance, as if seeking some agreed-upon reply in each other's thoughts.

"We did," said Walter, answering for us both. "But then we started visiting her on the island, so we didn't *have* to miss her anymore. I mean, it was like torture during the winter when Daddy wouldn't let us go there. But we don't miss her like we did when she died."

"And do you enjoy those visits with her?" Pastor Wainwright asked. "Do you find comfort in them?"

Despite the dark clouds of Daddy's looming retribution, Walter and I grinned and nodded. Pip did the same.

"I didn't think I'd ever be happy again," Walter told him. "Then, that night before her funeral, Daddy told me she was out across the lake. That's what he said. So I went across to the Isle where we used to play with Mama, and that's where I found her, just like Daddy said."

"Walter, you misunderstood me," our father groaned. "I never meant for you to think you could actually *find* her over there. Acheron—it's a river in the Underworld that the dead cross over. It's just Greek mythology. It's not real. All I wanted to do was help you feel better, not start some grand delusion and wind up with a couple boys who skip school to visit your—your—"

"Hold on a minute, John," said Pastor Wainwright, raising a hand to shush him. "Walter, can you keep telling your story? What changed after you found her?"

"It felt like I could live again," Walter said, quietly but confidently. "It was like everything bad and sad was erased. I was happy again."

"And was it the same for you, Peter?"

I nodded emphatically and said, "I didn't believe him at first. But then I went with him, and he was telling the truth. We saw Mama! She lives in this cottage surrounded by a magical garden, and we've had the most amazing adventures with her and Hattie before—"

"Hattie?" my father howled. "*Hattie* was there too? What other dead people live on this island? George Washington? Julius Caesar? Did you have Shakespeare over for milk and cookies?"

As sternly as when he arrived at the fire-and-brimstone portion of a sermon, the generally good-natured Pastor Wainwright snapped, "That'll be enough, John. You called me here to help, and I'll do it far more effectively without you jumping in whenever one of your boys opens his mouth."

"You came to help," my father shot back, "but *are* you? So far, all you've done is indulge these childish fantasies of theirs. These insane coping mechanisms!"

"And if it's truly helping them cope, what's wrong with that?" barked Pastor Wainwright. His own dander rose proportionally to my father's as he came to our defense. "When you see a widow at the cemetery talking to her dead husband, do you explain that her husband's ears no longer work and that he can't hear her? John, your boys were gutted when Rosa died, and now they're not. If it's helping them through their grief, why do you care whether it's real or fake? Can't you simply be thankful they aren't being crushed by their grief anymore? Like *you* are?"

Even Pastor Wainwright's masterful diatribe was no match for my father's bourbon-clouded head or grief-scarred heart.

"You," he hissed, "were supposed to come to Asphodel, sit my boys down, and explain what happens after a person dies. You were supposed to tell them her body went into the ground and her soul went up to heaven. Not some goddamned island! Instead, you stab me in the back and undermine my authority over my own children by condoning this—this—*insanity* ruining our house!"

"The ruin of this house began long before I arrived today," Pastor Wainwright growled. "I was foolish to give you the benefit of the doubt. Abigail tried to warn me, but I didn't listen."

"Abigail?" spat Daddy. "What did Abigail say?"

"I told him you weren't right, Mr. Luther," spoke a voice from the kitchen.

Abigail herself had answered him. She stood in the dining room doorway, her own anger set like stone upon her hard face.

"I told him you were drinking yourself to death, and that I thought you might be a danger to the boys," she said, her relaxed tone ill-suited to her expression.

"How dare you," my father snarled. "You still can't mind your own business."

Suddenly verging on tears, she pleaded, "Please, Mr. Luther, you need help. You need to come back. You've put too much on yourself, trying to be a father *and* mother to these boys, all while going to work and staying there all hours. It ain't healthy. You can't keep it up and grieve properly at the same time. That's why you turned to the bottle. You're not dealing with your pain, just bottling it up 'til it explodes outta you! But we need you here. Your *boys* need you here. Come back, Mr. Luther. Please, come back."

If she thought her impassioned speech might elicit a morsel of sympathy from my father, she was dead wrong. His voice was frightfully even as he replied, "Abigail, you've been at Asphodel Glade your whole life, and you've served this family faithfully for a long time. That's the only reason I'm not throwing you and Eli off my property today. But when the boys and I leave for our trip Friday, it better be the last time I see either of your faces here. Do you understand?"

"Daddy you can't do that! You can't send her away!" Walter screamed, coming to her defense as she had come to ours. "We need her here!"

But Abigail didn't protest. She buried her face in her hands and, as she wept, said, "I'll go, and so will Eli. But please don't hurt your boys, Mr. Luther. They're the only children I ever loved. Please, stop this madness."

Pastor Wainwright, in an effort to restore reason to the atmosphere, spoke calmly as he said, "John, you can't send them off for trying to take care of you. Where will they go? What will they do? Asphodel is their home."

"No, Fred," my father murmured darkly. "It's *my* home. And since you won't speak the truth to *my* children in *my* home, allow me."

He turned to me and Walter. "Let me tell you where Mama is. She's in a coffin, buried in the ground. Worms and maggots and beetles and other disgusting little creatures are chewing away at her eyes, her nose, her mouth."

Pip cried out as he envisioned such hateful things disfiguring his beautiful Mama.

Abigail covered my little brother's ears with her gnarled hands. "Stop it! Look what you're doing to him!"

"Enough, John!" Pastor Wainwright shouted.

But my father's ears were deaf to their pleas.

"Right now, your Mama is lying in a puddle of her own rot, because the liquid that used to be inside her body is seeping out from any crack or hole it can find. Her fingers and toes are turning black, melting away as they're eaten by all the tiny bacteria in her body. And her skin? Her skin is turning gray and withering around her bones. Soon, all that's left will be her dead skeleton. That's where your Mama is now. That's *what* she is now."

My brothers and I whimpered, sobbing at the horror of such a gory image. How was it possible that my beautiful, vibrant mother could have transformed into such a nightmarish monster? But deep in my deepest heart, I knew my father wasn't lying. What he spoke was heresy in our ears, yet also the truth of the grave.

"Please, Mr. Luther," Abigail whispered. "Please, stop."

He did. His description had produced the desired effect, and he saw no more reason to prolong it.

"Abigail, Fred," my father hissed, "get out of my house and don't come back. If you do, I'll call the sheriff over and have you arrested for trespassing."

Appalled, they did not fight him. With deadened hearts and drooping heads, they shuffled into the Great Hall and out the front door.

The clicking of the latch was a crushing declaration to my heart.

We were alone. Alone, against an enemy who bore the likeness of a man I loved.

When they were gone, my father looked down at us. His eyes were lifeless. Dead.

Like our mother.

"Upstairs, all of you," he murmured. "Start setting aside whatever you think you'll need for our trip. I know you don't want to go, but it'll be good for all of us. We can finally move on from Mama. And all this other craziness."

Before he turned away, I risked a glance up at him. Like a man in the late stages of dementia, he appeared utterly confused, stricken with a misery of his own making. A man with nowhere to go and no reason to get there, he stumbled off, leaving us alone in the dining room.

Upstairs, Walter began packing at once. Just not for a trip out West.

"We have to leave him," he declared. "We can't stay anymore."

"Where are you gonna go?" I asked combatively. After everything that had happened, I couldn't bear the thought of Walter spiraling down the rabbit hole of his crazy ideas and their half-cocked executions.

"Where we should have gone a long time ago," he answered. "To the Isle. You and Pip should come too. I know Mama said we couldn't live there, but we can't live here either. Not with Daddy. Not anymore."

Although it meant dealing a great wound to myself, I had to admit that Walter was right. Our father had lost more than Mama. He had become a foreigner to his own self, a man even he could neither recognize nor understand.

"When will we go?" I asked, opening my own dresser drawers to select the clothing I would take.

"Tomorrow night," said Walter. "We'll spend the rest of today packing. Tomorrow, we'll go to school—I'm guessing Daddy will take us himself after we skipped today—and we can even talk like we're getting excited about the trip. Hopefully it'll lower his guard. Then, tomorrow night when we're sure he's asleep, we'll sneak out and go to Mama."

As he grabbed the BB gun from beside his dresser, he added, "And we'll never ever come back."

May 18, 1954 – 1:31 p.m.

SLANTED RAYS OF DUST-SPECKLED SUNLIGHT illuminate the floor beneath the windows. Although Life has not been absent long from this place, it feels as if Death has reigned here a hundred years. The air smells stale, unused, like that of a newly opened box after a decade shut away in a closet.

But my perception is skewed, and I know it. The past has altered what I am experiencing this warm afternoon in the Great Room. Until two days ago, this air was breathed. It was circulated by fans and open windows, and electric bulbs illuminated it.

I close the front door and set my suitcase on the sofa, relieved to be unburdened of its bulk. Thirteen years have passed since I last laid eyes on these walls. These haunted rooms. The occasion then had also been a funeral.

Most of the Great Room's furniture is exactly as I remember. The dark blue armchair on which Pastor Wainwright sat that fateful night of the violin's demise. The loveseat where Mama and Daddy, clad only in a large quilt, fell asleep by accident one night, only to be discovered by Walter early the next morning. The coatrack next to the front door—though sporting an assortment of jackets and hats I don't recognize.

And, on the mantel above the fireplace, the clock my grandfather gave Daddy. I listen for its faithful, familiar ticking, and realize it has gone silent. Fitting, I suppose. Its years of service have come to an end. There is no need for it any longer. It, too, may rest now, along with the many other souls of Asphodel Glade.

With nothing but time on my hands, I wander the house. Although it spent a season as a cozy inn under Abigail's watchful care, I see that the home has undergone a recent restoration. It now appears much as it did during the happier years of my childhood.

Daddy's study, which for a while served as the lower-level master suite, has again become home to hundreds of books. The large desk is new, but it fits nicely where the old one once sat. Against the south wall, beneath the high window, is a twin bed with tangled sheets and an unkempt quilt.

Its last sleeper never returned to tidy it.

I go to the kitchen next and discover that its appliances finally received the upgrade they needed for so long. The cupboards, once bare hardwood, have been painted white with green trimming. A refrigerator hums steadily where the old icebox once stood. The hybrid wood-and-gas stove, which Abigail refused to give up until the day she died, has likewise been replaced by an electric range. The dinnerware hutch is the only fixture in the kitchen which looks the same, unaltered but for the slow, scouring marks of time.

When I round the doorway into the dining room, I find that our magnificent table hasn't moved an inch. I'm not surprised. It would have taken a construction crane to hoist that colossus out of here. The chairs, also solid maple, remain tall in their proper places, vigilantly waiting to serve whosoever might need them.

I cannot linger here. Like dawn's fog over Acheron, a thick tension pervades the dining room's atmosphere, something which sets my innards to trembling. It came and has not departed since the night of my father's bourbon-fueled description of Mama's rotting corpse. As if haunted by the nymph Echo, the room whispers the terrible things he shouted at us. Like a pyrograph burned into the maple tabletop, I see Pastor Wainwright's mouth hanging open in shock. Abigail forcing her hands over Pip's ears. The despairing faces of my brothers.

And yet, as terrible as that night was, the worst was still to come.

I shudder and return to the Great Room, but the demons follow me. Here I see Mama collapsing onto the sofa, flushed with new fever. I hear Walter's howls of agony and watch him drop to the floor as Mama's earthly husk is carried on a stretcher out the front door. A phantom blaze lights up the hearth, and in it I see the blackening remains of my grandfather's violin. I watch my father sink to the floor, numb with shock after hearing the news Sheriff Clark came to deliver.

My pulse has quickened. Grabbing the suitcase in both hands, I hurry upstairs. Here, I squeeze my eyes shut and take a few slow breaths. I remind myself that the past is the past and will myself to be braver. Though today I am a middle-aged man, courage still doesn't come naturally like it did for my big brother. Bravery was a reflex for him, while I must persuade myself to do what is best, when what's best is also difficult.

And it will be difficult indeed, facing and finishing all that I came here to do.

At the furthest end of the dark hallway, a door remains closed. I once was daring enough to risk a journey beyond it, but I won't find the strength to do so during this visit to Asphodel. It would demand too much of me, and I must conserve whatever emotional energy I possess for the more important matters at hand.

So I turn right instead. Into my bedroom.

I nearly drop my suitcase. Gasping, I raise quaking fingers to my lips.

No longer is the room furnished in the generic fashion which inns tend to use for their transitory guests. Mine and Walter's childhood beds have returned, all eight posts fitted precisely into their worn grooves in the floorboards. A similar story rings true for our dressers and homework desks. Walter's old posters, discolored by age and creased from years of storage, hang pinned to the wall over his bed and desk. My collection of books has been restored to their small shelf, and as I read their titles, I remember fondly the stories contained within them.

Everything is arranged as it was in the spring of 1919. Exactly as it was on that dark night near the end of March.

"Daddy," I whisper, awestruck, "you remembered? After all this time?"

But he is not here to answer.

As I step into the room, I stumble over something lying on the floor. It is thin and straight, hooked at one end.

A cane without an owner.

This must be where he fell.

Below it, forever discoloring the floorboards, is a bloodstain. Even the memory of my fight with Walter is no longer hidden beneath a throw rug. It was an important chapter in our history—and the beginning of a painful one—and Asphodel Glade's most recent owner wished it to be told along with the rest.

Exhausted from both travels and memories, I set my suitcase beside my bed and collapse upon the musty blankets covering my mattress.

Lying on my stomach, I slide a hand beneath the pillow.

My eyes shoot open. The fabric between my fingertips belongs neither to the pillowcase nor the bedsheets.

I remove the tangle of cloth from beneath the pillow. For a full minute, I stare in disbelief at what Daddy was storing there.

My bibby. In all its ratty, discolored glory.

I thought he'd thrown it out when I left for college. In truth, he had packed it away, keeping it safe for its eventual return to Asphodel Glade.

Pressing my bibby to my nose, I inhale deeply. The years have dulled its musk, but that familiar scent is still there, still comforting in my sadness.

Within moments, I am asleep.

Hours later, I awaken to the sound of light scratching. Something familiar, lost in the dark recesses of my mind, acts like a trigger on my resting body. I shoot up in my bed, searching frantically for the source of the noise.

It's coming from the window over Walter's bed. The blinds are raised, and the knotted end of their pull cord is scraping against the windowsill, a gentle pendulum set adrift in the currents of the old house.

Or perhaps held in an invisible hand. One revisiting its final moments here.

Burying my face in the solace of my resurrected bibby, I shut my eyes to divert the memory. But it is hopeless. Soon, Walter's window is the only thing I see. Although there is no hand to move it, the dusty glass panes slide upward in their track, opening to our Castle Home's eastern wall. Like the dense gravity well of a black hole, the window's expanding mouth pulls me toward it. Into it. Down.

For the second time today, I weep freely.

Although the window remains closed and unlooked at, I see Walter's face in it, cloaked under darkness, yet bright with determination and hope. For a moment he stares at me, giving me one last chance to be brave. To join him.

Then he slides down, out of sight, and is gone.

FORTY-THREE

A Choice of Betrayals

WHEN THINKING BACK YEARS LATER to certain days, I discover that many are hazy. Distorted. Like an object passing by on the other side of a foggy window. Indeed, some alleged memories are more like a series of cloudy photographs than anything. They make me second-guess myself. I question whether the remembered events truly happened, or if they were merely the product of a vivid dream.

Such were the seven hours I spent at school that Thursday. I'm sure Miss Carrington stood in front of our classroom as always. She must have taught us math, grammar, literature—all the usual works. Jimmy Fleischmann, my desk mate, would have sat beside me, diligently copying down everything he paid attention to—which, in his case, was nothing. I know such things must have happened, because that's how they always happened in those days.

Yet I remember only one thing clearly from school that day: Walter's presence. It was like electricity humming through nearby power lines. I couldn't see him two rows behind me, but all day long I felt him there.

He had formed our plans the night before, and by his oversight, we'd begun carrying them out. Beneath our beds we had stashed a few pairs of clothes and personal items. These we would stuff into our schoolbags when we returned home that afternoon. Walter also made sure to set aside his BB gun. Since Mama would have extra mouths to feed, he figured it might be necessary to hunt small game on the Isle. To throw Daddy off any scent of deception, we had also packed the larger suitcases he provided for us, thus creating every appearance that we planned to accompany him on our family trip.

The plan's final steps would occur when we returned home after school. While I distracted our father, Walter would sneak into the cellar to stockpile various canned and dry goods. Then, late that night, we would whisk Pip from his bed and flee to Mama, giving her no choice but to welcome us into her home.

Where we would be with her forever.

During our after-lunch recess, Walter and I met to review our plans within the thick stand of white pines near the edge of the schoolyard. As the other students scurried off to play ball or gossip, Walter and I squatted and conspired in hushed voices among the trees.

"You remember what to do when we get home?" he asked, scraping a stick absentmindedly among the fallen pine needles.

"Yeah. I'll open the door on Maisie's stall. Once she's out, I'll run inside to tell Daddy she's escaped again. That's when you hurry down to the cellar to steal our emergency rations."

Walter nodded his confirmation. "And after that?"

"We keep packing and acting like everything's normal, then get Pip and sneak out once Daddy's asleep."

"And we go to the island. For good."

"For good," I repeated confidently.

"You know, Peter," my big brother said, "I'm glad you're coming with me. We'll have the greatest adventure of all time."

His words were as unexpected as candy raining from the sky or stumbling over a pot of leprechaun gold, and they sent through me a rare surge of affection for him. In that moment, he ceased being the one who bested me at everything, who bullied me around, who stole Hattie's heart for himself.

He was just Walter. My brother. My friend.

I was touched, but I also had to act cool about it, so I said, "How will we make sure Pip doesn't blow it when we wake him up?"

"I was thinking about that during math," Walter answered.

At least he was thinking about *something* during math.

"You know how heavy a sleeper he is," continued Walter. "If you take both our bags to the boat, I can carry Pip. Then when he wakes up, we'll already be at Mama's cottage."

"Does he have any clothes?"

"Already snuck into his room and packed some along with mine," Walter answered proudly.

He truly had thought of everything.

Our father was already home when we wheeled our bicycles up to the front porch. After yesterday's events, this wasn't unexpected. He viewed us as a flight risk, and rightly so. By beating us back to Asphodel, he was eliminating any chance of escape. Or perhaps he had discovered, after relieving Abigail of her duties, that bringing a four-year-old into the office wasn't so conducive to an effective work environment.

A drink was already growing warm in his hand when he greeted us at the front door. It must have been his first, because his eyes were still sharp and quick.

He forced a smile and said, "How was your last day of school?"

Walter shrugged. "Good, I guess."

Genuine remorse colored my father's tone as he said, "Thanks for packing your suitcases. Look, I'm sorry things got so out of hand yesterday. Especially with you, Walter."

"It's okay," Walter replied, forcing a grin of his own. "We're sorry we skipped school."

Swirling his drink, my father said, "I do hope you can find *some* excitement for this trip. Maybe not today, but soon. I think it'll be good for us all."

"I'll try," said Walter, careful not to overplay his hand. "Can we go upstairs and finish packing?"

My father nodded and stepped aside. As we rushed past, he called out, "By the way, Walter!"

We froze halfway up the stairs.

"I was looking through your luggage and noticed you didn't pack your BB gun. I thought you might want to bring it along. There'll be plenty of critters out West. Maybe you'll be able to bag one or two. We can stuff 'em and bring 'em home."

"I'll look for it," Walter replied. "Thanks."

When we were safe in our bedroom, we whispered through our plan one last time.

"What if Daddy catches me going outside?" I asked.

Without a moment's hesitation, Walter answered, "Tell him you want to pack your fishing pole. The mountain lakes are full of trouts."

"But what if he sees me in the stables? That's not where I keep my pole."

"Dammit, Peter, are you in or not?" Walter shot back irritably. "You might have to think on your feet for once. But if you're really worried about it, you could go down to the shed where our fishing stuff is, then cut up to the stable through the woods where Daddy can't see you."

"Okay, okay, I'm in," I replied.

"Good. Then stop wasting time, and let's get to it."

I steeled my resolve and crept down the staircase. At the bottom, I took a sharp right and sped through the dining room to avoid passing my father's open study door. Once I had reached the back porch undetected, I felt emboldened to sprint directly for the stable.

From here, everything else was easy as pie. I unlatched Maisie's stall door and opened it wide. She always had been a rebel, and I knew she would wander off without a pitying thought for whoever would have to corral her.

Maisie performed precisely as predicted. A minute later, she was enjoying the fresh spring grass in our yard, and I was running back to Asphodel Hall as fast as my scrawny legs would carry me.

"Daddy! Daddy!" I cried out, bursting through the door.

"What is it?" he called back from the study. "Everything alright?"

"Maisie's out in the yard. She must've broken out again."

"*Scheisse*," my father muttered, appearing in the doorway. "Where is she?"

I led him outside. Even as we left, I heard Walter hurrying down the stairs to execute his role in our plan.

Outside, I pointed up the hill toward the Lincolns' cottage—which, I reminded myself, wouldn't be theirs much longer—and said, "She's up there."

Locating the rebellious goat, my father said, "Alright, come on. She's mischievous, but she's smart too. She knows she's not supposed to be out of her stall, and she'll try to run. I'll need your help cornering her."

At recess, Walter's speaking to me like a true friend had filled me with warmth. Now, Daddy's speaking to me like a real man filled me with pride.

And with the pride, misgiving. For the first time since we had formulated our escape plan, the teeth of conflict tore into my heart. A golden opportunity had been laid in my lap. The opportunity at last to escape life beneath Walter's shadow, to achieve my rightful place as the best-loved, most highly honored Luther son. All I had to do was confess the whole sordid scheme. Surely even Walter would never recover from such a blow as this. Besides that, could I really betray my own father? Take off without so much as a goodbye? What kind of son would that make me?

Yet even then, Walter's words echoed in my heart. *I'm glad you're coming with me. We'll have the greatest adventure of all time.* For perhaps the first time ever, he saw me not as a peeve but as a peer. A comrade. A friend. How could I betray him by blowing the lid off our plans? Or even by choosing now to remain behind with our father?

I was caught between Scylla and Charybdis, with no good path forward.

What Daddy said next did nothing to ameliorate my inner wrestling match.

"I know things have been tense around here," he admitted with a tired sigh. "And I know I've been downright unpleasant at times. But you have no idea how much I'm looking forward to this trip. It's almost like—like I can't breathe here anymore. At Asphodel. Not since Mama died. But out there? In California? In Colorado and Utah and Wyoming? I think I might find what I need so I can finally move on. So I can clear my head and start fresh. Figure out who I am without Mama. Without my Rosa."

With this admission, a great burden came rolling visibly off his shoulders. A look of hope overcame him such as I hadn't seen since before Mama fell ill. He seemed to walk lighter, like someone who has finally confessed his guilt in a decades-old crime.

But now the burden was mine, as the voice of guilt spoke into my struggle. My whole life, Daddy had given me all I wanted, never begrudging me a single thing. What kind of miserable son would I be if here, in his direst hour, I denied him what he so badly needed?

If this wasn't disgrace enough for my soul, the Lord still had one more reproach left to give. It began moments after Daddy caught hold of Maisie's collar, when the rumble of an approaching automobile drew my attention north beyond the hill. From some unseen length of our cart path, a faint haze of dust was rising.

Daddy's gait sped to a jog. Reluctantly, the goat at his side kept pace.

"Who is it?" I asked, worried of the answer I might hear. What if Pastor Wainwright or Abigail had called some higher authority to remove us from Daddy's unstable care?

"I'm not certain," he answered, "but I think it's a gift that arrived just in the nick of time."

The car, a black, open-backed Cadillac, had already crested the hill and was judiciously picking its way down our pothole-riddled drive when Daddy rushed Maisie into her stall. He slid the bolt shut and yanked on the swinging door for good measure. Satisfied that the goat couldn't jimmy her way out again, Daddy grabbed my hand and tugged me along.

A man, tall and well-built like Daddy, stood outside the driver's door. He wore a trim, black pinstripe suit, and the ends of his gray mustache had been waxed and curled into sharp points.

"Are you John Luther?" he inquired in a thick European accent.

"I am," Daddy replied. "And that must make you Herr Hauser."

"*Sicherlich*, certainly," the man said, and he offered Daddy a friendly grin. "I am quite sorry for the delay in my delivery. Although the war is ended, it is not so easy to come by the German pieces my work requires."

"I'm sorry, Herr Hauser, but could you give me a moment?" said Daddy. He turned his attention toward me. "Run along inside, Peter. I need to speak with this gentleman, and I don't want to ruin my surprise."

I did as I was told, wondering as I went what sort of surprise could come from such a fancy deliveryman. And on the day before our scheduled departure! Inside the Great Room, I paced from one wall to the other, impatient to learn more. I heard Walter shuffling about upstairs and knew he was also anxious to show off his haul.

I didn't have to wait long. Outside, the Cadillac's engine roared to life, and Daddy burst through the front door. Cradled in his arms like a newborn child was a black instrument case with polished silver trim and matching clasps.

It was a violin.

My heart surged with joy!

My heart sank with guilt.

"I was so thrilled you wanted to learn the violin, I decided to buy one for you," Daddy explained, holding it out for me. "It's German-made, like mine—and like my old one. Now we can play together on our vacation."

"Thanks," I muttered. With overwhelming shame, I received the violin into my arms. I was Absalom, turncoat and traitor to my own father. Even as I plotted against him, he presented me with a handsome gift of his affection.

"You're welcome," he said. "I'm looking forward to the music we'll make together. Now, run it upstairs and put it with your other things."

When Walter saw the gift, he scoffed and said, "He's trying to buy your respect, you know. This is exactly what he did with the bicycles. Anyway, you won't be able to bring it to the Isle. You'll have your hands full with our bags, and it's too risky to make two trips. Sorry."

But I couldn't dismiss the gesture as casually as Walter. My internal battle raged on, so powerful that I hardly tasted our meager dinner of ham sandwiches and applesauce.

Daddy, also enjoying a side of bourbon with his supper, jovially vowed that the fare would be much improved here on out. He had spared no expense for our train tickets and upcoming accommodations. We would eat the finest foods and sleep in the softest beds money could buy in the American West. He had pulled out all the stops, putting forth his absolute best attempt to raise us up from the doldrums of our grief. By the time we returned, he was confident all four of us would have a new lease on life. We would be ready to move forward without Mama—or any delusional visits with the dead.

There, at the dinner table, he made one other declaration. Lifting high his glass of bourbon, he announced, "This here is my last drink. No more."

Following the strange toast to himself, he downed the glass, and a gentle peace settled upon him.

With it, another realization settled upon me.

All Daddy wanted in the whole world was to create a joy-filled life for himself and his boys. Nothing more. Nothing less.

When dinner was finished, he sent us upstairs to double check our suitcases. "I'll be up'n a little while for a final look over," he slurred as we went. He may have imbibed his final glass of bourbon, but it wasn't going to pass through him without first scratching its initials into his liver.

Twenty minutes later, Walter and I joined Daddy in his inspection of Pip's traveling trunk. This part of the process took some time, as Pip had decided it was more important to pack toys than clothes. One by one, Daddy removed each bauble and asked him why he thought he would need it out West. Each time, Pip offered a heartfelt explanation as to its importance. Daddy would then set it aside and replace it with clothing.

Just when it seemed inevitable that Pip would burst into tears over his abandoned treasures, Daddy offered a compromise. "Now that you have enough clothes, you can stuff all that empty space with whatever you want. As much as will fit."

Pip joyfully accepted the terms. As he began the selection of his best and most beloved valuables, Daddy accompanied me and Walter across the hall to inspect our packing.

My heart beat in my throat and pulsed in my ears. I was sure he could smell our betrayal, or that he would discover something amiss, a clue which would tip him off and unravel our insidious plot. Truthfully, I almost hoped for it. Like a global superpower entering a war, Daddy's intervention could put an end to the bitter conflict inside me. I could rest easy, without betraying either father or brother.

But that would have been far too merciful.

"Everything looks good," Daddy announced. "Glad you found your BB gun, Walter."

He winked, then left.

Once Daddy was gone, Walter breathed a heavy sigh of relief and said, "Good. He doesn't suspect anything. We're in the clear."

But I didn't feel so "in the clear." I felt quite in the thick of it.

"We should go to sleep early," Walter continued. "We want to be rested for tonight. I'll set an alarm and muffle it with a blanket, that way we'll hear it, but Daddy won't."

For the millionth time in my life, I envied how effortlessly Walter fell asleep. It didn't matter that we were on the eve of such a life-altering event as running away from home. Within two minutes, he slipped into the rhythmic breathing of sleep, while I was left wide awake with my embattled thoughts.

Darkness, full and deep, settled over eastern Pennsylvania. Yet there would be no slumber for me. In the scarce light of our bedroom, I rolled onto my side. When I did, my gaze fell upon the decoy luggage trunk I had packed—and the sleek new violin case on top of it.

My eyes lingered here, upon this gift of my father's love. In my mind's eye, I saw the pride beaming from his face as he handed it over to me.

That was the moment I knew what I would do.

The battle was over. A victor had emerged.

Silently, I pushed aside my covers and rose from my bed.

FORTY-FOUR

Through the Window and Gone

LONG HAVE I LOOKED BACK, wondering why I did what I did that night. Why I made the choice which set everything ablaze. Like all people whose decisions lead to ruin, I have sought and found every reason to justify myself, to explain why my actions were warranted. At times, I have even convinced myself that to do otherwise would have been a dereliction of my familial duty. It wasn't my fault that my good intentions resulted in the nightmare that occurred.

But in the end, it's all bullshit. A narrative tincture I force-feed myself to keep guilt's poison from spreading through my mind and soul.

The truth, like everything else in my young life, revolved around Walter. It is a strange thing—and, I have learned, a strangely common one—to admire someone and, at the same time, despise him. To seek his approval and his downfall both at once. Despite the recent strengthening of our friendship, I still hadn't let go of my bitterness. The years of Walter's condescension, of outdoing me at every imaginable turn, had worn deep grooves of resentment into my heart. Our few months of intermittent camaraderie may have begun patching those scars, but the healing was far from complete.

The pot of my jealousy may have moved to a lower burner. Yet there it simmered all the same, bubbling slowly but surely higher.

The night my resentment at last boiled over, it was not in the frothing cascade of a rage-fueled tirade or direct assault upon Walter. It was, rather, a single sloshing ripple which bubbled over the side of the pot, an unassuming dribble which might have evaporated and disappeared unnoticed. Yet in this tiny spillover of my animosity, there existed just enough combustible material to blow everything up.

All it had to do was interact with the flame beneath.

After sneaking past Walter's sleeping form, I found my flame smoking his pipe on the back porch. When I opened the door, my father jolted upright in his seat, surprised at the sudden intrusion into his quiet thoughts.

Seeing that it was only me, he looked up with kind eyes. A drunken lilt clung to his tongue as he asked, "What're you doin' up, Peter? Shoulda been asleep a long time ago. But I s'pose that's what I get for not checkin' in on ya."

The dam burst. My tears gushed as I hung my head and, with more shame than I had ever known, spilled our whole plan to him.

Daddy said nothing as I spoke. Even when I was finished, he remained silent.

I risked a glance up at him. At once, I regretted it.

The gentle eyes of my father were gone. They had been replaced by those of a devil.

He placed his pipe on the squat, weatherworn table beside his oak rocker, as daintily as if it were made of gossamer. For a moment, I wondered if I had misread him in the faint light. Then he stood, abruptly and aggressively, a man wasting no time in carrying out his urgent business. He did not immediately storm inside and up the stairs to our bedroom. He instead turned toward the darkness, reaching for the kerosine lantern which hung from a rusty nail on one of the porch roof's support posts. Except for the rare occasions when my father had to sojourn out into the night, the lantern was a seldom-used tool in this era of electric lights.

But tonight, he had need of it. With one of the long matches typically reserved for lighting his pipe, he ignited its wick, then set it on the little table beside his chair.

He didn't invite me inside with him, so I didn't go. Instead, I collapsed onto the porch floor and continued to sob there.

Irate shouts and protesting replies erupted from within the Castle Home's walls. I squeezed my eyes shut and clamped my hands over my ears, but I couldn't drown out the din of wrath and retaliation. Nearer it drew and nearer, until the thudding stomps of angry footfalls rattled me where I knelt.

The porch door banged open like a starter pistol. From my cowering position, I raised my eyes.

Walter stumbled out first, the scruff of his pajamas clenched viselike in Daddy's closed fist.

My brother looked down at me, puling on the porch floor. To this day, I haven't discovered an adequate English word to describe the emotional cocktail I saw in his eyes. Betrayal, hatred, disappointment, disgust, pity—even a dash of love, I think—all swirled together in a single glance. He couldn't long bear my image sullying his sight, but the snapshot of that fleeting second is one which has remained forever embedded in my memory.

With Walter's nightclothes still grasped in one fist, my father used his free hand to snatch the lantern from the table.

"This ends now," he growled.

Horrified, Walter gazed upon the kerosine-fed flame and cried out, "What are you gonna do? Daddy, what are you gonna do?"

"Something I should've done a long time ago," was my father's vague but menacing reply.

I understood at once. The answer wasn't apparent to Walter, but it was to me, and I shouted, "Daddy, no! You can't!"

"Quiet! Both of you!" he roared, as he dragged Walter down the porch steps toward the shore of Lake Acheron.

Again, my father had given me no instructions to follow him, but this time I did exactly that. I bore responsibility for everything about to happen, which meant I also bore the responsibility to stop it—if I could.

"Daddy, don't do this," I pleaded, wrapping my arms around his leg, trying in desperation to slow his wrathful march. "This isn't what I wanted. This isn't why I told you!"

I may as well have begged it of a deaf man. In his rage, he was beyond hearing me, and I beyond stopping him.

Still, my wailed protests continued, rising with Walter's toward the heavens, for we knew divine intervention alone could prevent what was coming. But here, in the darkness of our thousand wooded acres, so far from everything else, it seemed even God was oblivious to the despairing pleas of his children.

I heard the gentle lapping of water upon shoreline when we stopped among the trees. Before us, blaze orange in the glow of the lantern's trembling flame, was *The Rosalie*—rowboat, oars, life-preservers, and all.

I clamped my hands around my father's elbow, struggling to arrest his arm as I groaned my final, desperate appeal. "Please. Don't. Please ... please ... please ..."

He glanced down at me, hesitating. For one short second, I thought that my begging had elicited his sympathy at last. That he would relent and turn from the course he had laid.

I was wrong.

"Mama is dead," he muttered, choking on his own words as he spoke them. "If this is the only way you can move on, so be it."

With that, he raised his arm and spiked the lantern into the boat. There was a shattering of glass and, as kerosine exploded outward from its reservoir to mix with oxygen and flame, an intense flaring of light and heat. Because Walter and I had neglected to turn the rowboat upside down after its last voyage, the bottom of *The Rosalie* acted like a bowl, collecting the kerosine in a small pool.

Where it could burn, and burn, and burn.

Walter sank to his knees, sobbing beside our father and muttering, "I hate you. I'll never forgive this. I hate you forever."

I never did know if those words were spoken to me or to my father. Both, probably.

Like a super-contagion across a nation, the blaze spread rapidly and mercilessly from one end of the rowboat to the other. First the paint curled and blackened. The dry wood held out as long as it could, but this, too, soon charred and cracked. The oars, embossed with a special lacquer to keep them from taking in water, had no trouble taking on flames. Meanwhile, stashed close to the bow, the life-preservers shriveled like oversized raisins as the inferno's heat licked at them, until they melted away and were no more.

Every second of that rowboat bonfire haunts my memory, and in such vivid and agonizing detail, my gut still goes queasy when I think on it. Those hellish flames, which danced in the stygian night and in my father's bedeviled eyes, burned down through the deepest wells of my spirit, into the very bedrock of my soul.

There they smolder still. Only the day of my own death will succeed in dousing them for good.

When all was said and done, there was little left. The rowboat's entire bottom had burnt through, scorching the grass and dirt beneath. Its cornflower blue rails were cracked and blackened when the flames finally began to die.

The only identifying mark which survived was its name. Like a cold taunting of the life that had been, those words, *The Rosalie,* remained as clear as the day Walter first painted them proudly on her stern.

In the dying light, I dared to look up at my father one more time.

He was crying. His dark eyes no longer burned with the terrible madness. They were those of Daddy again.

Those of a perilously broken man.

With his shame, a gentleness had returned to his voice as he whispered, "Get up, Walter. Let's go inside."

Walter didn't obey. He lay on his side, stretched across the ground, mourning the loss of all he had loved.

"What's done is done," my father muttered. "Go inside, or I will carry you myself."

These words managed to force their way past Walter's grief. He propped himself into a seated position and, as he wiped the tears from his cheeks, said, "Don't touch me. Never again."

He rose unsteadily to his feet. Without another word, he stumbled through the darkness toward the lights of Asphodel Hall.

"How could you do it?" I whispered. As I did, I wondered whether I was speaking to my father or to myself. "How *could* you?"

"It's over, Peter," sighed the man standing over me. "Now we can all move on."

He knelt beside me, but when he reached beneath my armpits to hoist me to my feet, I squirmed and pulled away from him.

"Fine," he muttered, a man bereaved of his own self. "You can hate me too."

Then he stood. Turned. Walked away.

I don't remember how long I remained there. On my knees. Fingers like claws, buried in the dirt and leaves. Staring at the smoldering ruins and hating my father—hating myself—for the evil that night had become. It may have been minutes. It may have been hours. Eventually, I rose to my feet and cast the glowing embers of *The Rosalie* a final, reverent look. I wondered then if Mama, with her uncanny vision, had seen and watched from atop Emerald Hill, helpless to stop her husband's madness.

It was a question I knew would never have an answer.

With nowhere else to go, I returned to my bedroom. Whatever wrath of Walter's I might suffer there would be well-deserved, and I tacitly decided to accept it.

He lay in his bed, snuffling and weeping. But he didn't come after me. He didn't acknowledge me at all.

This—seeing my intrepid older brother reduced to such a broken state—was far worse than any physical retribution he might have inflicted upon me.

Sitting softly on my own mattress, I buried my face in my hands and whispered, "Walter, I'm sorry. I didn't know Daddy would do that. I got nervous, that's all."

"Shut up," he hissed. "Just. Shut. Up. After tonight, I never want to see *you* again either. You and Daddy deserve each other."

"Maybe it'll be good for us," I suggested, trying not to take his impassioned condemnation too personally. "Maybe we do need to get over—"

Walter shot up in his bed so violently, the surprise of it shut me up. The same demonic air which had previously overtaken Daddy now seemed to have my big brother in its grasp.

"I will *never* get over Mama," he declared. "Never. And I'm going to be with her anyway. Boat or not."

With that last prophetic remark, he rolled over and yanked the covers above his head.

I sighed and lay down, holding my bibby close to my nose. The evening's hysteria and trauma must have taken a fine toll on me, for when I turned onto my stomach and buried my head in my pillow, I drifted instantly to sleep.

Whatever time it was when I woke up again, I don't know. A noise, some sort of rustling, disturbed my sleep, and I propped myself onto one elbow.

Walter's open window drew my immediate attention. A taut rope, the same one he had used to sneak out the night of his first visit with Mama, clung to the window ledge. One end was tied snugly around the foot of his bed; the other disappeared somewhere in the darkness beyond the walls of our Castle Home.

From the other side of the open window, my big brother stared at me. For one second, his eyes met my own bewildered gaze. In them, I saw that same amalgam of pity, and wrath, and disappointment he had shown me earlier on the porch.

Then he slid down the rope, beyond my sight, and was gone.

FORTY-FIVE

Notes of Salvation

AS A BOY, I HAD SEEN PICTURES of the original Ferris Wheel at the 1893 World's Expo in Chicago, but I wouldn't ride one myself until much later in life. That experience of spinning around and around on the same track, revisiting the same place you found yourself only a minute earlier, was foreign to me in March of 1919. Still, there were times even then when life, like a Ferris wheel, seemed to come full circle, and the haunting specter of some past evisceration became corporeal again in a fresh tragedy.

On September 23, 1918, after a heroic effort to procure a life-saving hunk of ginger, I witnessed Mama's oxygen-starved fingertips hanging limply below her stretcher. And on March 28, 1919, not long after the rest of the world had finished its lunch break, I stared through a flood of tears at my big brother's black-and-blue fingertips, lying on a bed of decaying birch leaves beside his waterlogged body.

Mr. Garnier, our neighbor down the shore, had pulled Walter's body from Acheron's waters that morning. He'd found my brother bobbing offshore, face down in the rocky shallows, his body buoyed by the air trapped in his knapsack.

As far as any outsider could tell, Walter had suffered a tragic accident while fishing or playing near the lake. Only those who lived at or frequented Asphodel Glade knew the truth. Walter, in his determination to be with Mama, had viewed the burning of his boat as nothing more than a hurdle to overcome. Without *The Rosalie* to ferry him across Acheron, he simply decided to swim for it.

I had betrayed him. Abandoned him. Thus I was not at his side to point out the utter foolishness of his desperate plan.

Despite all its many chances to infect him, Death had been unable to claim Walter through The Flu. So it found another way, stealing the warmth from his body and the breath from his lungs in the icy waters of the lake. Acheron, which for a time served as our road to a world of wonder and magic, had fallen under Death's employ. In its new servitude, it claimed the life of my brother.

During the days that followed, I prayed Death might find me too. That I might be buried alongside Walter as restitution for my grave betrayal. Perhaps then I might expunge a mote of my soul's guilt, bleaching that brotherly blood which stained it a fainter shade of red.

But such a mercy was not to be mine. God was not ready to surrender me to that inescapable blackness. Although the days were dark indeed, light and beauty waited in the wings.

We just had to seek and find them.

Five days after Walter's death, and two after laying him to rest beside Mama, the same group which had congregated a week earlier in Asphodel's dining room was gathered there again—minus one, of course. Pastor Wainwright and Pip ate the lunchtime sandwiches Abigail had prepared. She herself sat beside my brother, making certain he chewed his turkey on rye thoroughly before swallowing. Although no official declaration had occurred, she had unfired herself and, through her own tears, resumed taking care of her remaining Luther boys. Had my father tried to send her packing, I imagine she would have administered him a thorough beating, then kept right on doing as she had been.

For our part, neither my father nor I showed any interest in lunch. My food intake was sparse and infrequent, and had been since Friday. For a scrawny child like me, I was in real danger of withering into nothingness, of simply slipping out of existence like a candle's flame on a windy day.

And I would have been quite alright with that.

Abigail was not. She slid the plate of sandwiches across the table and said, "Eat, Peter. That's an order. I can't make your Daddy, but I can make you."

Solely to placate her, I removed a sandwich from the stack and took a mouse-sized nibble.

Unlike Abigail, Pastor Wainwright had no trouble giving my father orders.

"You too, John," he said, picking up a sandwich and dropping it onto my father's empty plate. "You need to keep up your strength."

"What for?" my father murmured, staring at the sandwich like a cow at a new gate. "Rosa's gone. Now Walter's gone too. Because of me."

Pastor Wainwright sighed. "You didn't know what he would do."

"I wasn't myself," Daddy whispered, sliding away both plate and sandwich. "I lost control. Oh, God, I can't believe I burned his boat! How could I do that to him?"

"You can't change it, Mr. Luther," snapped Abigail. "But you had damn well better learn from it."

Every head, even my father's, whipped toward her with surprise. Not once in all our combined years had we heard her curse before.

"You can keep your shock to yourselves. Besides, Eli hears far worse than that every day." Continuing her previous train of thought, she said, "You still have opportunity to do right, Mr. Luther. Not to your wife, and not to Walter, but to the boys sitting at this table with you. And maybe most importantly, to yourself."

"I know you're grieving," said Pastor Wainwright, leaning toward my father, "and you should be. Part of me wonders if you ever allowed yourself to grieve properly after Rosa died. So, mourn however it is you need to mourn. Mourn with your boys too. But if you need some time alone to do it right, there are plenty of people who can take care of Peter and Philip."

"I should've let Henry and Opal take them when they left," my father replied.

He was referring to the offer my grandparents had extended him the day before. After hearing the news of Walter's death, they had raced to Asphodel, fully prepared to steal me and Pip away with them to Castleton—consequences be damned. But after seeing my father's brokenness, their resolve broke also, and they stayed to assist Abigail in caring for us. Before returning home after Walter's funeral, they suggested letting me and Pip live with them a while. Unburdened of caring for us, my father might then find the space required to process his lost loves and mourn them.

"I should've let *anyone* take them from me a long time ago," said Daddy, continuing his train of thought after a moment's pondering. "Then they would've been safe. But I've learned—like you said, Abigail. I can't change what happened. But I *can* change what happens now."

Pastor Wainwright shared a concerned glance with Abigail and asked, "Change what?"

"I can't be with them anymore," my father explained, breaking into a light sob. "I can't be trusted. Not with them. Not with anyone. Someone else has to do it."

I hadn't thought it possible for my spirit to sink any lower, but I was proven wrong once again. Pip and I had lost so much already. Must we lose a father too? And by his own decision?

It seemed Abigail read my mind, for she said, "They need what they've needed all along. They need their Daddy. Their *real* Daddy. Not some hollowed-out, drunken version of him. They need *you*."

"No," he resolutely whispered. "If I've learned anything through this, it's how much better they—everyone—would be without me."

Pastor Wainwright grimaced and said, "None of that talk, John. I won't have it. There are many ways to cope with grief, and you seem dead set on making use of all the worst ones. Not this time. I didn't put a firm foot down before, but I am now."

My father shrugged and said, "What's one more on my soul?"

With sudden understanding, I looked up at him. His dead eyes stared down at the tabletop—or perhaps through it, into the hellfire he thought awaited him—and I read in them the awful truth his words implied.

We were the same, Daddy and me. We were both responsible for Walter's death. I had killed him by revealing our plan. Daddy, in turn, had killed him by torching *The Rosalie*.

Father and son. Two murderers. If Daddy deserved the fate he was suggesting, so did I.

But then, what would happen to Pip? And Gramma and Grampa, who already mourned the loss of so much? What would Abigail and Eli do when Asphodel passed to new owners? Who would call himself Pastor Wainwright's best friend? Where would this spreading of unspeakable pain finally stop? Would the ends of the earth be far enough?

Our dining room fell into silence. All I heard was my own breath—and the ticking of the mantel clock in the Great Room.

After a minute of this verbal stalemate, Pastor Wainwright stood and said, "I have a two o'clock appointment I must honor. Another sick parishioner, I'm afraid. But I'll be back to check in on you. Abigail, would you please walk me to the door?"

I followed them. Though I stood in plain sight, neither seemed to notice me, and if they did, neither minded my hearing them.

In the light of the Great Room, Pastor Wainwright appeared far more exhausted than he had at our table. Deep lines of fatigue and worry creased his forehead as he said, "Keep an eye on John, will you? I wish he were my only parishioner so I could be here all the time, but I can't. There are other sheep, and I must feed them too."

"I understand your position," Abigail assured him. "I'll keep a watchful eye."

"Keep Eli close too," said Pastor Wainwright. "In case John decides to—to follow through."

"Unfortunately, I don't think Eli'll be much help," Abigail muttered spitefully. "He feels he's to blame for his part in last week's trouble—first for telling me he caught the boys taking the rowboat, then because he wasn't around to stop

John from burning it. It'll be a miracle if he speaks a single word to any Luther for the rest of his life."

"Then do your best," sighed Pastor Wainwright. "I'll be back, soon as I can."

He left, and I returned to the dining room.

Pip was alone. Somehow, my father had slipped away undetected.

"Where'd Daddy go?" I asked my little brother—my *only* brother.

Claws of panic tore into me. What if Daddy had gone off to do exactly as he had insinuated?

Pip, whose mouth was too stuffed with sandwich to speak, pointed at the porch windows. There, amidst a thin haze of smoke, was the back of my father's head.

Relief washed over me. Not daring to take my eyes off Daddy, I sat beside Pip.

Abigail entered the dining room behind me. Her voice cracked under the weight of her own grief and frustration, as she pointed to my untouched sandwich and said, "Eat your lunch, Peter. I won't tell you again."

Realizing how much my hunger strike upset her, I bit off a corner of the sandwich. It tasted better than I expected, so I ate another, then another.

Pleased over her little victory, she said, "That's more like it."

When the first sandwich was finished, I helped myself to a second. As I ate, a question popped into my mind. Before I could stop myself, I asked, "What makes God mad enough to send someone to Hell?"

After my part in Walter's death, I was reasonably certain Hell was the direction I was headed.

Abigail froze and stared at me uncertainly. "Why do you wanna know something like that?"

I dropped my sandwich and began to cry. "Walter's gone because of me. I'm the one who squealed and told Daddy our plan. That's pretty bad, isn't it?"

Abigail wrapped her strong arms around me, and I breathed deeply. In her flour-and-butter scent, I discovered a comfort not unlike what I once had found in Mama.

"Lord, Peter," she whispered. I sensed her trembling as she stifled her tears. "We all do bad things, and we all do plenty we regret. But God ain't the one sending people off to Hell. We get there under our own steam."

"How?"

"By being proud of the bad things we do, and by doing them over and over," she replied. "Are you proud of what happened?"

I shook my head.

"Okay then," she said, squeezing my shoulders in her callused hands. "What's more, from what I can tell, you did what you did out of honesty. You didn't want to deceive your Daddy, and there's no sinning in that. But sometimes, even when we do right, sad things happen. It's the way of the world. Has been since the beginning."

I couldn't bear telling Abigail about the great struggle I had undergone the afternoon of the boat bonfire. It was agony even admitting to myself how much of an audience I had given my pride. Sure, some of my reasons for betraying Walter were born out of love for Daddy, but the majority voice inside me had simply sought to build myself up by taking my brother down. To stand proud and tall above him in my father's sight.

And, to some degree, much had been petty revenge. Revenge for the years spent as his doormat. Revenge for Hattie. Revenge for always finishing silver to Walter's gold.

True, I never intended for my father to burn *The Rosalie,* just as I never intended Walter's death through it. But I did intend to secure my own victory at the cost of his defeat. That made me responsible—and not only for what happened to Walter. My father may have been the one to explode that night, but I was the one who lit the fuse.

That made me responsible for his torment too.

"What do I do now?" I whimpered.

Abigail thought a moment, then answered, "God calls us to love. But when we love the dead overly much, it's easy to forget our main job is to love the living."

"What do you mean?"

"What I mean is that you've got a little brother and a Daddy, and they're the ones who need your love. Not your Mama. Not Walter. The Lord Jesus is taking care of them plenty. You love Pip and your Daddy, and you do it as hard as you can."

"How?"

"You think about what's best for them, and you do it."

"But what if I can't help them?" I asked. "What if my best isn't enough?"

"Sometimes it will be, and sometimes it won't," she responded matter-of-factly. "You can't see every end where your choices might lead. But on the whole, the people you live with and love will know they're better off for your presence in their lives, and you'll be able to sleep at night with a clean conscience."

I glanced aside at Pip absentmindedly munching away on another sandwich, and I almost laughed. He wasn't immune to sadness or pain, but as long as he had something to eat, he could get by alright.

It was the man smoking on the porch who needed me most. But how could I help in a time such as this? That was the unanswerable question.

"Thanks, Abigail," I said, mustering a tiny grin.

Rubbing my shoulders affectionately, she said, "I'm not going anywhere, Little Mister Luther."

I hugged her, then slid off my chair and exited onto the porch.

Despite the door opening beside him, my father's faraway gaze remained unchanged. As he puffed pensively on his pipe, I sat beside him. Resting my head against his ribcage, I felt the rhythm of his dead heart beneath me.

He didn't push me away. He didn't pull me close, either. There seemed only to be a colossal indifference to my presence.

This hurt, but it was a wound I deserved. After all, I had brought it down on my own head. I had aspired to become the greater brother, to win love and admiration, to take for myself the place of highest honor.

In the end, my selfish ambitions won me nothing. No more love. No more attention. No extra helping of praise or admiration. It was my pride's foolish desire to take and take, but every time I obeyed its devilish voice, I only lost and lost until my hands sat bloodstained and empty.

I couldn't bear my father's disregarding silence for long. After two or three minutes with him, I returned indoors to find and play with Pip.

He was lying on his bedroom floor, belly down and propped up on his elbows. Arranged in a semicircle in front of him were his toy animals, as if they were his circus menagerie, and he their ringleader.

Missing, I noticed, were the pewter elephant and hippopotamus from Mama's treasure hunt.

For a while, I humored myself with his silly games. As African beasts faced off against Asian, I let myself become lost in his world of make-believe, trading away my bleak reality for Pip's mindless whimsy. Here, for a few blissful moments, I could escape and become a carefree child all over again.

It didn't last long. The moment I heard the back door open, the spell was broken. My father's heavy footsteps pounded across the hollow floor, reverberating throughout the Great Room and up the walls of our house. Though I couldn't see him, his presence possessed such gravity, it captured every ounce of my attention and held me hostage. I tried to carry on with Pip's game, but my thoughts fled far from the gazelle and onager in my hand.

I saw only my father before me. Dead-eyed. Forlorn. As incurable as Mama or Walter—or myself.

Pip filled his room with a string of belligerent animal sounds as he played. Yet even this cacophony of trumpets, bellows, and grunts was drowned out by the roar of the silence downstairs.

Until suddenly, unexpectedly, the silence was not silence anymore.

It had been broken by the mournful hum of a bow upon four strings. The first elongated note was followed momentarily by a second. Then a third.

By the fourth, I recognized the tune Daddy had begun playing on his violin. *Red River Valley.*

He had played it last Easter, and again on the night Mama died.

I rose from the toy-littered floor, listening.

The melody soared, powerful and confident. Daddy's old violin had wept with him many times before its premature death. Now this new violin also knew what it meant to mourn in his hands. The music he played was a conduit to his very soul, and in those notes, there came pouring out from him all his grief and guilt and shame.

Yet not only these. They were there, yes, and in potent measure. But they were not alone.

Mingled with them, subtle yet present, were the nobler things: undying fidelity, the fond remembrance of beauty, and a longing for hope reborn.

Even pain can be lovely, if only given the chance.

I knew I risked breaking the spell cast by his playing, but I dared to approach anyway. Down the stairs I tiptoed, careful to make no noise which might disturb him. When I reached the bottom, I stopped, breathless, beside our dog. He sat at attention, curiously watching the scene unfolding before him. Together, we observed and listened.

As he played, Daddy kept his eyes closed. Not squeezed shut with anguished torment, but like those of someone who has fallen asleep, at peace and unburdened of the day's many cares. Upon entering the third verse, he increased his tempo, so that it sounded less like a funeral dirge and more like a Sunday morning hymn. Line by line, the music grew livelier and louder as his fingers danced upon the violin's dainty neck. Soon "Red River Valley" was no slower than an Irish jig. The friction of the strings frayed many of the bow's horsehairs, which lashed at his face and neck and arms.

Just when I thought he couldn't go any faster without also setting *this* violin on fire, the song came to a sudden stop. The final note still echoed upon the Great Room's walls, when there arose from Daddy's throat a strangled cry to accompany it.

He sank to his knees, and all fell silent. Tears coursed freely, honestly, as he placed both violin and bow gently on the floor beside him.

In the end, it was music which saved my father's life. Not because it healed his incurable wounds, but because it awakened something inside me. They were notes of salvation—and not Daddy's alone, but mine as well—for in them, I found the courage to act boldly.

Just like my big brother had shown me.

My pride-stained choices had taken Walter's life away.

Now my selfless love would give Daddy's back.

FORTY-SIX

The Violinist

"WE HAVE TO GO, DADDY," I announced, walking tall as I strode to my father's sunken form. "You and me and Pip—we have to go to the Isle."

I expected a fight from him. Now, without Walter here to do it for me, I was prepared to fight back. I was less prepared to see him bow his head and give me a faint nod.

Not realizing how hurtful such words might be to one of his living sons, he muttered, "I suppose I have nothing to lose at this point. Maybe if I went earlier, I would've seen whatever it is you find so special about the place. Then maybe—maybe Walter—"

Grief swallowed up his thought, and he didn't finish.

"We'll have to borrow Eli's canoe," I said.

I didn't need to state the obvious reason why.

Eli answered when Daddy knocked on the cabin door. He spoke not a word as he stepped into the sunshine and closed the door behind him.

"I have no right to ask this of you," Daddy awkwardly began, "but I'm hoping you'll let us borrow your canoe."

Those dark, unsearchable eyes bore into my father, and I wondered for a moment whether Eli might hit him. But when they shifted to rest upon me, the stone encasing them crumbled away, and the humanity which had always been there bled through for me.

He didn't say anything. He simply turned away and disappeared to the backside of the cabin.

"I'm sorry," my father said, looking aside at me. "I'll see about borrowing someone else's boat as soon as I can."

But I wasn't paying him much attention. From behind the cabin wall, the curved keel of an upside-down canoe was gliding into sight. A moment later, Eli's knotty arms and torso appeared, his head hidden in the canoe's belly as he balanced the narrow watercraft on his broad shoulders.

I didn't need to read his eyes to know where he was taking it.

Grinning at my father, I said, "Come on."

We followed. When Eli reached the water's edge, he lowered the timeworn canoe so that its front half rested upon the calm shallows, and its back half upon the gravelly shore. Sweat glistened upon his forehead as he brushed his hands across his trousers and stared over the lake.

Then, as casually as if he were commenting on the weather, he said, "Think I might keep it here by the shore a while."

Without waiting for a reply, he turned and limped off in the direction we had come.

When Eli was gone, I told my father, "We only need two more things."

He raised an inquisitive eyebrow, "Pip—but what else?"

"Your violin. I'll wait with the canoe while you get them."

He didn't protest.

As Daddy returned to Asphodel Hall, I gazed across the lake at our Isle and wondered if anyone was looking back. More so, I wondered *who* might be looking back.

When my father emerged from the house a few minutes later, he was followed not only by Pip, but by our dog as well. I'm unsure whether our four-legged family member sensed our return to the Isle, or whether he was captivated by the tricycle tire-sized wheel of cheese clenched in Pip's hand. Either way, he was more excited than I had seen him in months, bounding at my brother's side as his tail thrashed like a bullwhip.

I helped Pip into the foremost bench. The dog clambered into the bow and sat on my brother's feet, claiming the lookout position for himself.

Daddy stored his violin case delicately in the canoe, then picked up the paddle lying lengthwise along its belly. As he lifted it out, I seized it with both hands.

He shot me a quizzical glance.

"I'll row," I declared.

Again, no argument. After helping me thrust the canoe forward into the water, my father climbed in and took an uncomfortable seat upon the carrying yoke.

The paddle felt strange and rough in my hands as I dipped it into the water. Although I had watched Mama and Walter work the rowboat's oars a hundred times, I had never handled them myself. Certainly paddling a canoe was different than rowing a boat—I was only able to work one side at a time—but in all my combined hours of watching *The Rosalie's* oars circulating in and out of the water, I had gained an intuitive understanding of the physics involved in propelling a watercraft.

Of course, I was only ten at the time and recognized none of this. But I did understand how to steer us in a sort of zigzagging course toward the Isle. I paddled on one side until the nose drifted too far from my bearing, then switched to the other side to maintain an equilibrium.

We weren't far from the mainland when I told my father, "Take out your violin."

He glanced at me like I was a crazy person and replied, "Here? Now? What for?"

"You'll see," I said. "Just play."

He sighed, shrugged, and picked up the instrument case at his feet. He set it upon his lap and undid the silver clasps. When he opened the lid, he stared at the violin inside with an almost worshipful reverence. For a moment, his sorrow over Walter was lost, engulfed wholly in his ancient love for music. Music composed of a bow upon four strings.

Daddy handled his violin with the care of an archaeologist examining an artifact from the dawn of civilization. He leaned his face upon the chinrest and, with a sigh, closed his eyes. Like an ice-skater glissading effortlessly over a pond's frozen surface, the bow glided across its four partners in song. As horsehair met string, sound erupted from Daddy's violin, a rich resonance to fill all of Lake Acheron with a beauty it had never known.

Forgotten for a moment, the notes of Daddy's heartache returned at once, haunting his music in a doleful rendition of "My Grandfather's Clock." As his bow slipped and slid across the violin's face, I matched the cadence of my paddling to his tempo.

When the song was finished, he lowered the violin from his chin.

"No!" I cried out in protest. "Don't stop! Keep playing, Daddy!"

Again, he acquiesced, and struck up the somewhat more spirited "Buffalo Gals." Although my aching muscles objected most vociferously, I met his pace, and we skimmed even faster toward the Isle. He went in for something more spiritual next, and the tones of "Amazing Grace" sang upon his strings. This was followed by a livelier "Yellow Rose of Texas," then "Old Joe Clark."

As he played, I felt the light stirring of a breeze at our backs, assisting me as I heaved the canoe forward. Indeed, the steady wind appeared almost by design. I didn't stop paddling, but if I had, I'm certain we would have continued onward regardless. Some invisible hand was pulling us, unwilling to let go, drawing us inexorably and eagerly toward the Isle.

Pip's way-too-big, hand-me-down shirt billowed in the gathering wind as he rocked blithely to the violin's happy rhythm. The forefinger of his cheese-free hand bounced merrily in front of him, a maestro's baton conducting the violin's vigorous measures.

The severed horsehairs dangling from Daddy's bow danced joyfully to the music he made. He himself began to sway, undulating like a leaf in the currents of the wind, his muscles and sinews and ligaments unable to resist the emotions imparted by the violin's resonant chords. Not only his heart, but his mind and soul and spirit—his entire being—fell in tune with the music he played, until there, on Eli's canoe, Daddy became both hypnotist and hypnotized.

Still, he did not stop—*could* not stop—as we approached the island. Even as I beheld not one, but *two* figures emerging from the forest to stand on top of Emerald Hill, Daddy played on. His eyes remained squeezed shut, for he had no need of them. Violin and bow had taken over his senses. They were extensions of him, and he was one being with them. As a trapezist exercises utter control over her arms and legs, bending them to her will to perform amazing feats, my father's violin was an appendage subjugated to his complete mastery.

The result was as magnificent as it was beautiful.

Daddy, with violin and bow in hand, was exactly the man God created him to be.

The violin faltered only once, when he finally opened his eyes and saw his dead wife and dead son looking down on him. A choked burst of laughter arose from deep within his throat, and he at once resumed his playing, as if his music were the magic holding them earthbound. Even when he jumped into the waist-deep shallows, he played on and on, holding the violin aloft above the water. Now there was a line from one song, then from another—a medley of Mama's many favorites. As fast as his arm and fingers could move, he sawed his bow and sloshed toward the shore, weeping and laughing all at once, until suddenly he was no longer in the water and was sprinting up the hill as fast as his mighty legs could carry him.

When he drew near Mama and Walter, he could bear to play no longer. Daddy cast both violin and bow aside, caring nothing for their fate, as he collapsed into the arms of his living wife and living son. And he kissed them, and kissed them again, anointing them with his joyful tears and pealing laughter.

I sidled the canoe along the rocky spit of our traditional mooring. Pip and dog together nearly tipped us as they scurried over the side and onto dry land. I followed on their heels, taking care before I did to secure the canoe to our anchor tree.

Mama and Daddy were still embracing and kissing and caressing—the dog had inserted himself into this lovefest too—when Pip and I arrived at the hilltop. Having peeled himself away from them, Walter was looking on in disgust the way someone can't help but stare at a mutilated animal carcass.

"Oh, Rosa!" Daddy exclaimed. "Oh, my Freckles, it's you! Oh, why didn't I come sooner?"

Even before Daddy could finish speaking his heart, Mama began speaking hers, saying, "I've missed you so much, John! It was torture, knowing you were so close, yet so terribly far away from me."

"I'm so sorry," said Daddy.

And, at the same time, Mama herself said, "I'm so sorry."

"I lost myself after I lost you."

"I couldn't bear losing you and the boys."

"I failed as a father."

"I should've let them move on."

"I couldn't take care of them."

"I should've let *you* move on."

It was then that Daddy realized what Mama was saying. He stopped speaking and recoiled in mild surprise.

Mama continued. She poured out both tears and words as she said, "I loved being a mama too much. That's what's caused all this trouble. I didn't see it before—didn't *want* to see it—but I can't shut my eyes any longer."

"What do you mean?" Daddy asked. "I'm the one who failed."

Mama shook her head. "No. I'm the one who failed *you*. Remember when we went out on the rowboat last spring? Just you and I in the moonlight?"

An impish grin overcame Daddy, and he giggled. "Of course I remember. That one was hard to forget."

I also remembered that sleepless Easter night. I had heard them talking and moaning through my open window.

"Do you remember when I asked why you were unhappy?" Mama continued. "You didn't answer me, but I knew."

"You did? But even I didn't know!"

"You're a fantastic businessman, John. But you and I both know you were born for something else."

"I'm not sure what you mean," Daddy replied, cocking his head to one side.

"Your coal mine made our family good money. It gave us a comfortable life in a beautiful home, and I loved it. All of it. Some days I felt like I was living in a fairy tale, with our big house out in the forest, the sweeping lawns and horses and lake.

I loved our boys and all our games together, the wonder and adventure of Asphodel Glade. But you were never truly happy with your work. You did it because you're a good man, and because you wanted to give me and the boys everything you could. But every day you went into that office, you lost a little more of yourself, and every evening you spent poring over ledgers and paperwork, another piece died."

Daddy hung his head, exposed and ashamed.

"What's worse is that I knew it. I knew you were miserable, and I knew why, but I did nothing about it. I never tried to lead you away. If anything, I pushed you deeper in. I shut my eyes to what you needed because I was too in love with my life at Asphodel and too in love with my boys. I was afraid if I let you pursue your passion—what you were born to do—I would lose too much of what I loved. And I'm so sorry, John, and so heartbroken. Can you ever forgive me?"

Daddy spoke no word of absolution. Instead, he pulled his wife into his arms and kissed her deeply.

As I watched them, an elbow nudged me purposefully in the ribs.

It was Walter.

I'd become so captivated in the brilliance of Daddy's reunion with Mama that I had taken little notice of my resurrected sibling. As I now turned my attention toward him, I saw the same brother with whom I had shared a bedroom the last five years. Yet he was also different. His features were clearer, more defined. His eyes were a bolder brown, his hair fuller and luminous. Although he wore clothing similar to my own, there were no stains on his shirt or pants, nor did they appear capable of such sullying. He seemed more powerful, his presence more substantial, yet he was also lighter in form and more gladsome in spirit.

He was my brother. And he was *more* than my brother.

It was this renewed Walter who jerked his head toward the trees and said, "We should leave them alone. Grab Pip and come with me. I think we should take a walk."

FORTY-SEVEN

The Last of the Cardinals

"WHERE ARE WE GOING?" I ASKED, suddenly fearful of Walter. I knew from my Sunday school stories how Cain had prefaced his fratricide by asking Abel to take a walk.

"You'll see when we get there," came Walter's cryptic reply.

Together with Pip, we wandered the familiar paths to the cottage, which I assumed belonged to Walter now as much as it did Mama. But we didn't stop here, nor rest at all. After crossing through the gardens, Walter led us down the narrow, descending trail toward the south side of the island. When we reached the shore, we turned east, picking our way along the rocks toward the cave where we had encountered the Hellhound.

We didn't enter when we arrived there. Walter merely stopped and stared into the cavern's yawning black mouth.

"Why did you want to come here?" I asked, still unsettled by his unidentified motives.

He replied with a question of his own. "What did you see when we went in there?"

"Same thing you did," I answered. "A movie screen."

"Yeah, but what did you see *on* the screen? When the movie started playing?"

"My own memories, I think. It was Christmas, and we were all in the Great Room. Gramma and Grampa were there too, and Daddy was playing his violin. And then I saw our room, and I saw you bringing me my bibby because I lost it earlier."

A shameful grimace overtook Walter. "You didn't lose it," he said.

"I didn't?"

"No. I hid it from you. I was embarrassed you still carried a blanket every-where. But when I saw how sad it made you, I felt bad and brought it back after all the grownups were asleep."

Awkwardly, I asked, "Why are you telling me now?"

"Because I saw it too," he answered. "But from *my* memory, not yours. Almost everything I saw before that were memories of Mama. Then that little part about your bibby came up on the movie screen. Back then, I didn't understand why. But I see better now. I think I finally figured it out."

"Figured out what?"

Walter grew visibly uncomfortable as he said, "That I should stop treating one of my—you know—*treasures* in life so rotten. I was a terrible big brother, and I'm sorry."

I was speechless. I had no idea how to react to such a candid confession from someone who'd always kept his nobler parts hidden. Never had he shown such vulnerability, nor spoken with such sincerity and tenderheartedness. The only times he had expressed his emotions this openly were when he'd been angry or frustrated.

"It's okay," he told me. "You don't have to say anything. But I wanted you to know."

It is amazing how quickly one apology can beget another. To his great discom-fort, Walter had laid bare his guilt, leaving me to take second place one last time. As had happened so often in our lives, his courage sparked within me a smaller measure of my own, and my confession came pouring out to match his.

"I'm sorry too," I said, hanging my head in remorse. "If you were a terrible big brother, I was an even worse little brother. I was jealous of you. My whole life, I was jealous of you. You were better than me at everything, and I hated it."

"I wouldn't say *everything*," Walter replied with a smirk. It may have been his-tory's thinnest-ever display of humility.

"In the things that mattered to me, you were," I explained, my voice strained with emotion. "So I was always looking for ways to beat you. To be better than you. I think that's why I told Daddy about our plan to run away. And you know what makes it even worse? We were actually sort of friends before the end! And I still—well—*killed* you."

To my great irritation, Walter snickered when my confession ended.

"It's too bad we were such stupid asses," he joked, wry with sarcasm, "other-wise we woulda figured this out *before* I died. Sharing a room might've been a lot more fun."

His tone dropped into a serious range again, and he said, "But I don't want you to go on thinking you killed me, or that it was your fault I died, just like I don't want Daddy to think it was his. It's my own. I wanted to be with Mama so bad, I forgot about everything else—you and Pip and Daddy. Was even too stupid to think how cold the water was and how far I'd have to swim. The rowboat might've burnt up because of you and Daddy, but I'm dead because of me."

Now it was my turn to laugh at the irony. "You know, even now, you're getting what you want."

Walter grinned. "I guess so. It didn't go exactly like I planned, but I do get to be with Mama."

"And," I happily exclaimed, "we'll still have lots more adventures together, just like always!"

But to this, Walter didn't reply. He instead glanced down at Pip, who had waited silently during our heartfelt conversation, and said, "We should get back to Mama's cottage. It'll be ready soon, and Mama won't like it if we're late."

"What'll be ready soon?" I asked.

"You'll see," he replied vaguely. "Come on."

Although Pip protested being carried, I scooped him up in my arms and followed Walter back along the rocky shore. As we climbed the ravine pathway toward the cottage, I detected hints of kitchen herbs and spices wafting on the air. The closer we came, the more pronounced these grew. Before long, we were hiking through an aromasphere which would have turned the finest Parisian chefs green with envy. When the cottage was finally in sight, smoke rolled heavenward from its chimney, bearing with it a fragrance that would have set the Almighty's mouth to watering—as it certainly did mine.

My gaze followed the white plumes as they rose into the boughs of the overhead trees. Here, my eyes came to rest upon a lonely pair of cardinals, who chirruped and danced blithely among the reborn leaves of spring. I wondered why these two had chosen to stay through the winter, and whether their thousands of brothers, sisters, and cousins would soon return to join them. Though I had once found their teeming throngs eerie and unnatural, they had become a source of comfort for me. The cardinals had first shown up when Mama did, and I almost felt them responsible for returning her to us. They were her handmaidens, the servants of her rebirth and eternal renewal among us.

Pip, who also smelled the promise of what lay ahead, couldn't bear my carrying him any longer. He broke free from my arms and dashed up the remainder of the hill. Walter and I hurried behind him. We all reached the cottage door together, and Pip threw it open.

Mama and Daddy, glowing in the warmth of the cottage and their joyful reunion, were waiting for us in the dining area. They sat beside each other, hand in hand, claiming one side of the table as their own. Across from them stood three empty chairs, each begging to be filled. The tabletop itself was buried beneath a feast so miraculous, the real miracle lay in the fact that the table hadn't cracked beneath such a formidable weight.

When Mama rose to greet us, I could have sworn that she shimmered. Everything she wore, from the ribbons and flowers in her hair to the shoes on her feet, was purest white—whiter than the freshest snowfall. A new radiance cloaked her, and she was somehow more beautiful than I could ever remember. When she spoke, her voice rang with rich music, like a bubbling spring of sweet water in a thirsty land.

"Welcome to our reunion feast!" she exclaimed.

But even that word, *feast,* could do no justice to what we shared that April afternoon. There were meats of every imaginable kind: beef tenderloin, ham, leg of lamb, duck, and goose, among others which I'm not convinced exist on our mortal side of Acheron. We ate potatoes of every variety, cooked in a dozen styles ranging from mashed to medallion. There were breads served alongside dishes of savory-herbed butters, and a pile of noodles surrounded by bowls of assorted tomato and garlic and cheese sauces. There were deep pots of soups—butternut squash, broccoli and cheese, and creamy tomato. Fruits of every imaginable kind and of the highest quality, plucked from the garden's enchanted trees, blessed the feast with their bright colors and provided sweet juices for anyone who needed a break from the savory dishes. And it didn't seem to matter what we ate, nor how much of it. No one's stomach became too full to eat more—at least, not until *full* was what one was ready to be.

As the meal wound toward its close, Pip, who had eaten no less than twice his weight, asked, "What about dessert? Where's dessert?"

Mama beamed at him with a smile sweeter than all the cakes, cookies, pies, and frostings of the world combined. She said, "You'll have to wait a while for dessert, Pippie. But when the time has come, it will far exceed anything you have ever known."

Staring in dismay at the carcass of our feast and the dirty dishes which had held it, I asked, "Well? What do we do now?"

Mama laughed and said, "No need to worry about the dishes. They'll be taken care of soon enough without your help."

"Can we play outside?" Pip asked eagerly. "In the garden?"

Mama winked at him, and, for a fleeting moment, I beheld in her eyes all the eternal beauty of the heavens.

"That," she replied, "is precisely what I was about to suggest."

Among the cultivated trees and manicured flowerbeds, we played and lived together as a family once more. Games of tag and hide-and-seek mingled with the mirth of jokes and ringing of laughter, for we were complete at last.

All the while, the shadows lengthened with the aging day, until they covered the grounds like a blanket. The mottled sun behind the forest was near to kissing the horizon when my attention was drawn again into the treetops. Here, the two cardinals had begun raising a clear-throated song toward the heavens. No longer were they frolicking merrily upon their boughs. Instead, each remained perched in its place, staring intently at us as they continued their serenade.

Daddy and Pip stood on either side of me. Together, we watched the cardinals and listened.

Louder they grew, and louder, a pair of birds gifted with the voice of hundreds. Their uttered syllables became imbued with a language which sounded almost human, as if they were speaking in the tongues of worlds unknown to us. Through their warbles and twitters, they told a rich story of love and laughter, of a beautiful flight together.

When their song was finished, the last of the cardinals beat their wings and took off. Upward they rose, higher and higher in a spiraling dance, each inter-twining in harmony with the other. When they appeared as little more than two errant red flecks dripped upon the sky's blue canvas, they completed their dance and swooped away to the south and were gone.

FORTY-EIGHT

Moving On

WHEN DADDY, PIP, AND I LOWERED our gaze from the cardinals' flight down to level earth, we discovered that Walter and Mama were no longer with us. They stood beside each other at the northern border of the garden and stared intently our direction.

Our puppy, who had enjoyed himself as much as anyone that afternoon, whined and licked at their feet.

"Whatcha doin' over there?" I asked.

Mama's smile faltered, and she said, "Evening has come. We must return to Emerald Hill."

Daddy shot me a questioning glance.

"That's what we call the big green hill by the water," I explained.

"Oh! I forgot my violin there!" he cried out, remembering the instrument he had cast aside. Sheepishly, he added, "Hope I didn't break another one."

Mama reached for Daddy's hand. With her free arm, she scooped Pip off the ground. He wrapped his arms around her neck, nuzzling it sleepily.

As they started off for Emerald Hill, Walter and I followed, shoulder to shoulder. Despite our joyous afternoon together, an inexplicable pall fell over our company. Nobody spoke a word as we traversed the flagstone path through the trees. Even the puppy, always so eager to bound ahead of everybody, lagged behind with drooping ears and tail.

When we reached the hilltop, Daddy let go of Mama's hand and hurried to the discarded violin. After a brief inspection, he lifted it triumphantly and announced, "It's okay! Nothing broken, so far as I can tell."

"I am glad to hear that," Mama replied, "because I very much wanted to hear you play one last time."

My heart stopped.

"What do you mean, 'one last time'?" said Daddy. "I'll be here tomorrow, and the next day, and the next, and every day between now and whenever I take my own final breath."

Without waiting for Mama's response, I seized Walter's arm and added my own assurance. "Yeah, we'll be back tomorrow. We aren't going out West anymore."

Mama and Walter exchanged a mournful but knowing glance. For the first time, my brother's courage failed him. He hung his head and turned away, unable to say what needed to be said.

So Mama became courage for them both. There was no mistaking the pain in her expression as she said, "If you come back after this evening, you will no longer find us here."

"What?" cried Daddy, his voice breaking. "Rosa, no! I just found you again. You can't leave!"

Mama cupped his face in her hands. She stared through his eyes, clear and blue as a winter sky, down into the wells of his soul. Then she lifted herself onto her tiptoes and placed a long, tender kiss upon his lips.

"I wish to God that you could stay with me, and I with you," she whispered. Tears spilled as she caressed his whiskery cheek. "But I cannot keep clinging to my life at Asphodel. I cannot cause any more damage. The toll of my holding on has been a deadly one, and I will not risk losing more."

Daddy wrapped her in his arms and moaned, "I can't live without you, Freckles. I can't. So ... you can't go."

"But John, do you not see?" said Mama. "That is exactly why we *must* go. Walter and I have to let go, so you can move on. The only way you *can* live is without me."

Daddy wept freely as he asked, "But when will you come back? Will we ever see you again?"

"Yes," she whispered. "Someday. You will come to us and find us where we are, Beyond the Trees and Over the Waters. But we will not return to you."

"Then let me die with you," Daddy spat bitterly.

"John Luther!" snapped Mama. "It is not your time yet, and to wish that it were so is to spit upon the best fruits of our life together. My time to care for Peter and Philip is over; yours has come."

"But I can't!" protested Daddy. "I've tried so hard, but I can't do it. I can't take care of *anybody*. All I've done is hurt and kill."

"That," Mama declared, "is because there is someone you forgot to look after first—*yourself*. In my selfishness, I kept you from taking care of yourself so long, you have forgotten what that means, or how to do it."

"Then show me the way," Daddy whimpered. "Before you go, show me the way. I can't find it on my own."

Mama grabbed his hands, waiting for him to calm down, before she said, "Everything you have done, you did because you thought it was best for *us*. Every decision you made was the one you thought would be best for me and our boys. And do not misunderstand me—there is a nobility in that kind of selflessness. Your dedication to your family is one of the things I love most about you. But sometimes you must also make decisions that take care of *you*. That do what is best for *you*. The father Peter and Pip need is not one who focuses only on them, who must always make the perfect decision for them. Who could live up to that kind of pressure? It would drive anybody mad! Take care of *yourself*, John. Give yourself what you need to thrive. Because in your thriving, you will become the best father you can possibly be for our children."

"But I have no idea what I need!" Daddy replied, exasperated.

Mama kissed his cheek. "Yes, you do. You have known all along, but again and again, your sense of duty has suppressed the answer rising in your heart."

Daddy stared at her with a blank expression, unable to fit the pieces together.

Mama's lips brushed his nose as she whispered, "You do not need to come up with the answer this second. I am confident you will before long."

She then turned her attention away from Daddy and gathered Pip into her arms.

Tears glistened as he said, "You're going away again, aren't you."

"I am, Pippie," she whispered, squeezing him as she began to weep anew.

"But we didn't have dessert yet," he protested, his lower lip trembling. "You said we would have dessert."

"So I did," replied Mama, "and so we will. And when we finally do, it will be so much better than anything I could have given you here."

"You promise?"

"I promise," she said.

My baby brother reached into his trousers pocket, fishing for something inside. When his grubby hand emerged, it held the pewter figurines of the elephant and hippopotamus. His eyes flickered back and forth between them. Then he picked out the elephant and handed it to Mama.

"Will you give this to the baby for me?" he asked, as she plucked it curiously from his hand. "And I'll keep the hippo. Then we both have one!"

"Oh, Pip!" Mama cried, hugging him again. "I love you so much, my sweet boy. I was blessed to have you in my life, even if only a little while."

"I love you too, Mama," he replied, before giving her a loud kiss straight on the lips.

Mama hugged him close once more, then set him down.

Next, she knelt in front of me. With those unforgettable golden eyes, she studied me and said, "I cannot believe how tall you are. You have grown so much this past year. Now you must grow even more. You must be the big brother, and that is a big responsibility. Are you ready for it?"

I glanced aside at Walter, deferring to his opinion.

Already he was grinning back at me. "Peter can handle it," he assured Mama. "After all, I'm the one who trained him."

Unable to help myself even in those somber moments, I rolled my eyes at his cocky swagger and answered, "I think I am."

"Then take good care of Pip and Daddy for me, okay?" she choked, overcome again by the flooding emotions. "Without Walter around, you will need to be more than just clever. You must also be *brave* for them. Can you do this?"

I nodded, then flung myself into her and cried fiercely, intent upon holding her for as long as I might be allowed.

When Mama forced our parting, she stood, and we both gave our attention to the farewell happening between Daddy and Walter. Even now, an awkward separation hung in the air between them, and neither moved toward the other to close it.

Daddy's features bore the deep furrows of shame as he muttered, "I'm so sorry for everything that happened between us. I messed up. Badly."

"I made a lot of dumb choices too," said Walter. "We both did."

In an instant, the wall between them came crumbling down. Daddy and Walter both stepped forward, and father embraced son as son embraced father.

"I'm so grateful I was able to see you one last time," Daddy whispered hoarsely. "This incredible island saved my life, Walter. And that's what I'm most sorry for. I'm sorry I doubted you. Sorry I didn't believe in this amazing place."

With his cheek pressed against Daddy's chest, Walter smiled and said, "It's okay. You came in the end. That's all that matters."

Daddy kissed the top of his son's head for the last time, then let him go.

Walter hugged Pip next and said, "Keep eating all your food, okay? Then you'll grow big and strong, and you'll be able to lick Peter any day of the week, just like me."

Pip took umbrage at this remark. Indignantly, he declared, "I can already take him—no problem!"

"Then maybe some Germans," Walter replied with a chuckle. He ruffled Pip's hair and hugged him again.

Lastly, Walter came to me. I was still sobbing from my farewell with Mama, and I cried all the harder when he punched my shoulder.

"I can't wait 'til we can share a room together again," he said. Adding a dash of levity to the heartache engulfing us, he added, "But maybe get rid of the bibby before then. It's embarrassing."

His joke did nothing to console me. Feebly, I replied, "We were supposed to have more adventures together. You can't go!"

Walter gazed at me with a serene sort of confidence. As he did, a flowering of courage bloomed deep inside me, and my shameless weeping ceased. I found in that moment that I was no longer frightened of life without him and Mama. It was as if Walter was emptying the best of himself into me, so that I might depart the Isle not as one brother and son, but as two.

He squeezed my shoulder, thus imbuing me with another surge of confidence. "Our adventures are far from over," he said. "And the best ones are still coming. I can't imagine what's waiting for us Over the Waters, but I'll know soon enough. And, after a little longer, you'll know too. We'll never *stop* knowing those adventures, and we'll never have to say goodbye to them again."

"Or each other?" I asked, snuffling.

"Or each other."

Then I hugged my brother for the first time in my remembering life.

And for the last.

"Bye, Walter."

"See you soon, Peter."

"Say hello to Hattie for me?" I asked.

"When I find her, I will," he promised.

I let go of him. Wiping my sleeve across my cheeks, I backed away.

In those final moments before sunset, we all stood beneath the darkening shadows of the trees, yet some kind of luminous sheen had settled over both Mama and Walter. Caught somewhere between flesh and spirit, their forms rippled and shimmered before my very eyes.

Mama herself seemed taken aback by this phenomenon. Her eyes widened, and with an anxious urgency she flung herself into Daddy's arms. She pulled his mouth toward hers and deeply, yearningly, fiercely kissed him for as long as she dared. When she finally pulled away from him, she stooped to hug me and Pip together.

After blessing our cheeks and foreheads with their final kisses from her lips, she cried, "I love you, my beautiful boys! And you, John—your voice will echo inside me with every beat of my heart. I love you! I love you! And I will be counting down every moment of eternity until we meet again."

Forcing a brave smile through his own tears, Daddy said, "So will I. I'll love you always, Freckles."

Walter and Mama now stood apart from the rest of us, their backs to the trees. Reaching up, my brother clasped my mother's hand in his own. With each passing second, the aura of shimmering air grew brighter around them, and brighter still. Their features were becoming less defined and yet, somehow, more perfectly so.

"Your violin, John! Pick it up!" Mama pleaded, and when she did, her voice seemed changed into something very much like music itself. "Pick up your violin and play me home."

He did. Closing his eyes and pressing the violin against his chin, he drew bow across string, and the opening strains of "Red River Valley" rolled across the hilltop.

Daddy's voice joined in melody, and he sang: *"From this valley they say you are going—"*

Mama looked sideways at Walter. She lifted his hand to her lips and kissed it.

"Ready, Wahwie?"

He nodded. With Mama at his side, he could have been facing anything, yet still given the same answer: "Ready."

"—I shall miss your bright eyes and sweet smile—"

They turned toward the trees. With aching heart, I knew I would never again see their faces on this side of Acheron.

"—But I thank you for giving your sunshine—"

Hand in hand, Mama and Walter reached the first of the forest pines and stopped there. Behind them were the Living World and the first loves they had known.

Before them, those of the next.

"—That has brightened my pathway awhile."

Then, like those who have seen some long-lost friend on the road ahead, Mama and Walter broke into a run and became swallowed up by the trees, disappearing far beyond where my sight could ever reach.

Gently, I grabbed Daddy's elbow and whispered, "They're gone."

He didn't break down as I had expected, and when I looked up, I didn't see looking back the eyes of a man broken beyond repair. Yes, they did glisten with the outpourings of his sorrow, yet behind the tears, I saw the fires of life and hope and purpose, kindled anew.

Still holding the violin bow, Daddy draped his arm around me and pulled me close. I, in turn, reached out to Pip, hugging him to my side. We stood in silence, staring at the place where Mama and Walter had disappeared, hoping even then to glimpse some flicker of movement among the trees.

But there would be none, and we knew it.

Finally, with no other recourse left, Daddy sighed and said, "Let's go home."

Down the hill we went, somber and in single file. When we reached the canoe, I stooped to untie it from its mooring.

Daddy sat in back and picked up the paddle.

That was when I noticed there was one among our party who hadn't descended Emerald Hill with us. Our dog sat atop it, silhouetted against the sky, staring at the tree line and faithfully awaiting his mistress's return.

"Come on, puppy!" I called out to him. "It's time to go."

With a final whine, the obedient animal came bounding down the hill.

Daddy flashed me a weary smirk.

"I think," he said, "it's high time we gave that dog a name."

FORTY-NINE

Farewell to Asphodel

THE NEXT WEEKS WERE STRANGE ones at Asphodel. Daddy spent the vast majority of each day at home with us, leaving from time to time only to run some errand in Pierre or swing by the mine. One Tuesday morning, an unfamiliar man dropped by the house. He wore a dark, trim suit, and spent three hours behind the closed door of Daddy's study. The following Friday, he showed up again. On this occasion, Daddy also ushered Abigail and Eli into his study, and all four spent the better part of an afternoon speaking in muffled voices.

When I worked up the courage to ask Daddy what he was up to, he merely winked and said, "You'll find out soon enough."

Three days later, a different well-dressed gentleman came by. He carried with him a leather valise so polished it shone. Again behind a closed study door, Daddy regaled him with a veritable violin *concerto* lasting well over an hour.

But it wasn't until Jacob Jansen showed up at our front door one week later that I began solving some of the mystery.

"Good morning, Peter," he said briskly and with a congenial tip of his hat.

I stepped aside to let him in. This was the first I had seen of him since chauffeuring him to the Isle. I expected the miraculous encounter with his deceased daughter might have changed him into an entirely different person, but he remained as serious and businesslike as ever—though perhaps not so brusque as before.

"Good morning," I replied, closing the door behind him.

"I came by to see your father," he informed me, as he removed his bowler and hung it on the hat rack. "I'll show myself into his study, thank you."

Once he had closed the study door behind himself, I crammed my ear against it to glean whatever information I could. Their conversation was as winding as a mountain road, roaming from business to side notes to personal matters—even a couple jokes—but by the end of the long gab session, one thing was clear: Daddy was selling his stake in their mining enterprise.

After Mr. Jansen left, I played dumb about his visit, but when Daddy caught me lurking in the Great Room, he flashed a knowing grin and said, "Get your brother and bring him here. I suppose it's time I shared what's going on with you boys."

Inside his study, Daddy drummed his fingertips nervously on the desk as we waited for Pip. My little brother had insisted on first procuring a snack for himself, and I didn't need Sherlock Holmes to detect that Daddy was anxious to reveal his goings-on of the past weeks.

When Pip sat beside me with a handful of chocolate sandwich cookies, Daddy leaned forward and said, "I know you've been wondering what I've been up to this last month. I kept it a secret 'til now because I wanted to be sure everything was set in stone."

He sighed, hesitant to continue. It was clear he was worried how Pip and I would react.

"Just tell us!" I begged. My heart was ready to pop out of my chest in a pulpy mess. If Daddy didn't reveal himself immediately, he would have another dead son on his hands.

He took a deep breath, closed his eyes, and made the announcement as quickly as he could.

"We're leaving Asphodel Glade," he said.

Pip and I exchanged looks of surprise.

"I sold my portion of Luther & Jansen Coal," Daddy continued. "To the Jansens, actually. The three of us are moving to Philadelphia."

"What will we do there?" I asked, too surprised by the news to betray much reaction, either positive or negative.

"I'll be doing what I love," said Daddy. "I'll be playing violin for the Philadelphia Orchestra—well, only as a stand-in at first. Turns out they don't give away the full-time spots to any old person who walks in off the street. To support us in the meantime, I also bought your *Opa's* old pharmacy, the one I practically grew up in, and I'll spend part of my time managing that. It'll be nice to see the old place open for business again."

Daddy stood. He walked around the desk to crouch in front of me and Pip. Grabbing each of us by a shoulder, he said, "And as I do all that, I'll be taking care of the two most important people in my life. My boys."

Pip, who possessed a penchant for overlooking the subtext, asked his next question through a mouthful of cookie. "What'll me and Peter do?"

"Oh, you'll do lots of things," Daddy answered. "You'll go to school during the day, and you'll do your homework at night. You'll help me at the pharmacy. You'll go to church and Sunday school and learn your Bible stories. You'll make friends and play with them. Sometimes you might even let me in on some of your games. I suppose you'll do just about everything a boy your age is supposed to do, Pip."

"But who's gonna take care of the Castle Home?" I asked with concern. I would soon leave the only home I had ever known, and the sorrow of it was creeping in on me.

"I think it's only fitting," said Daddy, "for that honor to go to Asphodel's oldest residents. Technically, it'll still belong to us, but I've given control of it over to Abigail and Eli. They'll stay here like always, taking care of it and using it however they see fit."

"But will we ever come back?" I asked. Tears swam before my vision, but I didn't want to cry. I'd wasted too much of the past months in tears, and I suspected Daddy's decisions were meant to be happy ones for us.

He grabbed my hands in his own and squeezed them.

"Of course we'll come back," he assured me. "We'll visit as much as we can. But there are too many ghosts and too much guilt for me to stay here. I hope you can understand."

I did. Although I was too choked up to speak, I put flesh to my mind by hugging him tightly.

My Daddy had come back. I would have given up a thousand Asphodels to keep him here.

When I regained control of my emotions, I asked, "When are we leaving?"

"Soon," he answered. "But we won't be going to Philadelphia right away. First we'll take that trip out West I promised you. We'll go to all those places Walter wanted to see, and afterward, we'll come back here and tell him all about it."

With a tranquil and contented grin, he added, "Besides, what I need more than anything is some quality time with my boys."

I WISH I COULD REPORT THAT LIFE beyond the shadows of Asphodel Glade was perfect. That our years were filled with nothing but sunshine and prosperity. That when we left Lake Acheron, we left with it all our haunted memories and bitter traumas.

But that's not what happened, because that's not how life works.

There were still countless bouts of grief and tears for Daddy and Pip and me. Some days, especially on Mama's and Walter's birthdays and deathdays, the pain was so fierce, I thought for sure it would bury me. Even though much healing had occurred during that final trip to the Isle, it didn't mean the three of us were immune to strains and rifts in our relationships with each other—many of them born of buried anger and guilt over the events of late 1918 and early 1919.

Nor did it mean that Daddy, just because he had decided upon sobriety, was forever afterward immune to the bottle's beckoning whispers. No, despite the promise he made and remade a hundred times over, he did periodically drink himself into oblivion during our first few years in Philadelphia. It was only when he discovered twelve-year-old Pip drunk as a skunk one night that he finally rid our home—and himself—of the booze for good. He simply refused from that time onward to imprint such an image upon his boys. And so, it was done.

Our puppy, Mama's final living gift to us, joined us in moving to Philadelphia. After much debate, we came to a consensus in naming him "Yosemite," just as Walter had wanted when we first found the dog tied up at the tree cave. For over a decade, he proved to be a good and faithful companion, until the day he slipped peacefully away in his sleep to join Mama, Walter, and Hattie on the far side of Acheron.

Like every other kid who moves away from home, Pip and I attended new schools. We made new friends and enjoyed new, big-city experiences. Before long, Philadelphia began to feel more like home, and Asphodel Glade like some long vacation we remembered in our dreams and daydreams.

But when school let out each year, for one week at the beginning of summer break, we would return to our Castle Home. Each time, I would borrow Eli's canoe. I would paddle out to the island where so much had happened in such a short span of my childhood. I would climb Emerald Hill and walk the forest paths. I would meander to the place where Hattie's treehouse had sat perched aloft in the trees. I would return to the hallowed grounds where Mama's vast gardens and idyllic cottage once stood.

But each year, the trails became more overgrown until the underbrush retook them entirely. The old oak's arms, which had once held a palace, remained bare but for their creeping green mosses. And Mama's magical home became nothing more than a memory, uprooted and reclaimed by the broken-down shack which had previously occupied the untamed clearing.

After my first year at the University of Pennsylvania, I finally put my yearly ritual to rest.

I figured it was time. The dead had moved on. Even Castor and Pollux, the strong stallions of my youth, had made their journey Beyond. Whatever magic once inhabited the Isle across Lake Acheron—if it had really been there at all— could summon them to my side no more.

And so, I moved on too. I graduated *summa cum laude* and became a Boeing airplane engineer. That meant relocating to Wichita, Kansas, where I met a nurse named Jolene who helped sew my fingers back together after a crazy blender accident. Within that same calendar year, she became my wife. Two, four, and six years after we tied the knot came our three wonderful children.

Gregory, Charlie ... and Walter. All boys. Beautiful, unique, flawed boys.

On the night of May 16, 1954, I peeked into their respective bedrooms to whisper a quiet "goodbye" as they slept. I needed that last look to tide me over until they, along with Jolene, could join me at Asphodel Hall.

This happened less than an hour after I had received the telephone call from Pastor Wainwright.

He told me there had been a massive heart attack.

He told me John Luther, my Daddy, was dead.

May 18, 1954 – 4:19 p.m.

THE SWEET SMOKE OF SMOLDERING tobacco rises into my nostrils. With pipestem secure between my clenched teeth, I stroke the arms of the oaken rocker thoughtfully. Years of heavy use have left them with smooth, elbow-polished grooves. A layer of bright, decades-old timber, long hidden beneath the chair's weather-beaten exterior, has risen to the surface.

As I begin to rock, the floorboards beneath me complain with rhythmic creaks and groans. Asphodel Hall's back porch reached its age of expected retirement and replacement a good many years ago, yet here it remains, unchanged but for the patient havoc Time has wreaked upon it.

The only thing that's changed is the man sitting in the chair.

Beside me, upon a squat table which Time has also shown no mercy, rests a ceramic ashtray. Two days ago, another man used it. Even now, it holds in its shallow basin the spent remains of his tobacco.

Next to the ashtray lies a pipe, cold and lonely. It is sad and strange to think that Daddy will never light it again.

I pick up the pipe, examining it. With my index finger, I trace its curved stem and carved rosewood bowl. When I lift it to my nose, the unmistakable scent of Prince Albert greets me like an old friend. For a moment, I consider stashing the pipe in my breast pocket and keeping it as a memento of my father. Perhaps, from time to time, I could even smoke it in his remembrance.

I shake my head and return the pipe to the table. It belongs here, just as Daddy did. Just as a part of him always had. We may have moved to the City of Brotherly Love in 1919, but in many ways, Daddy's heart never left Asphodel Glade.

That was why, in 1939, after arthritis ended his second career playing third chair in the Philadelphia Orchestra, he came back here. Back home.

Abigail still lived here then. For ten years, she and Eli had earned a moderate income by turning the roomy home into a tidy bed-and-breakfast. After her brother's sudden death due to a massive stroke, Abigail hadn't been able to maintain the business by herself and ultimately closed Asphodel's doors to the public.

For a time, the estate fell into disrepair.

They were Daddy's hands which restored Asphodel Hall to its former glory. But he didn't stop there. When he was finished with the house, he set his sights upon Abigail's cottage, for it was her wish to live out the remainder of her days right where she had started them. Next came the tangled grounds. Inch by inch, his arthritic hands beat the invading brush back beyond its ancient borders, taming the glade until it appeared as it had in my youth.

Of course, there was much Daddy's hands couldn't do on their own. Working side by side with his, whenever they could be spared, were those of the once-banished Pastor Wainwright. Their friendship, which had lain dormant for two decades, bloomed anew as the pair of widowers toiled together—and, yes, also shared the occasional glass of beer or whiskey.

"Fred and I have seen each other every day for fifteen years now," Daddy told me when he last visited Wichita. "He's the brother I never had."

It strikes me how hard all this must be for the old pastor himself. The grief of losing Walter almost killed me, and he'd only been my brother for ten years. I make a mental note to swing by the parsonage this evening so I can check in on Pastor Wainwright. He's taken care of others his entire life. It's about time someone returned the favor.

The embers in my pipe fade, then die. I knock the tobacco's spent remains into the ashtray, where they mingle with Daddy's. After stowing the pipe in my breast pocket, I rock forward and heave myself up from the deep chair. My many hours on the train have convinced me that a stretch of the legs is in order, and there are few places on earth better suited to such a task than Asphodel Glade. Besides my itch for exercise, I haven't been here since Abigail's funeral a decade ago, and I want to see what, if anything, has changed.

I stroll along, looking up and down Asphodel Hall's exterior. Daddy has done beautiful work to revitalize it. Where once there were missing stones or cracks compromising the mortar's integrity, he supplied the reinforcements necessary to make those walls sound again. The dead husks of ancient vines, which crept up the home's east face, have been hacked down and disposed of. Shutters painted a bright lavender—Mama's favorite color—have since replaced the sagging brown ones, and bright panes of new glass gleam where age-fogged windows once stood. There are some touch-ups and unfinished projects that still need doing, but on the whole, Asphodel Glade seems ready—perhaps even eager—to hold new life within its walls.

Until now, I haven't thought much about what we should do with the house. As I see it, there are three options: sell it, keep it as a vacation home, or move in. The first option sickens me, while the second would be a disservice to such a beautiful home, leaving it largely unused. And option three? Well, that would mean one hell of a commute to work.

But my engineering degree could have a thousand applications beyond Boeing, and a functional coal mine *does* still exist in the outskirts of town ...

I shake my head, knocking loose such crazy thoughts. Besides, it's no good unraveling any of those threads this afternoon. Sergeant Major Philip Luther will arrive tomorrow morning. Although he lost an arm fighting in Italy, my baby brother would still lick me good if I made any decisions without him.

This reminds me: I need to make a trip to the grocery store. Pippie will be ravenous after the long trip from Chicago.

Continuing my survey of Asphodel, I round the corner to the west end of the house. Here, my heart sinks. It has every time I've laid eyes upon this plot of ground since I was ten years old.

Here is where Mama's magnificent gardens once bloomed, bearing with them the fragrant beauty of abundant life. Now it is a bleak parcel of earth and grasses and a scattering of twisted bushes. That something so wondrous should be erased from existence is nothing short of revolting, a blasphemous heresy of its own.

Immediately, I recognize the old resentments, oozing upward from the dark holes where I buried them.

But then something grabs my attention, and the sweetness of it overcomes the rising bitterness.

Against the home's western wall is a pile of compost. Beside it, propped against the wall, is an assortment of gardening tools. A few are unused, still wearing their price tags. There is a garden rake, a long-handled hoe, a spade, and a pickaxe for particularly stubborn soil. In the belly of a rusted-out wheelbarrow sit dainty envelopes filled with various seeds. Each contains within its dry husk the potential for limitless beauty.

Daddy was planning to resurrect Mama's garden. He had even finished planning and compiling everything for his next project—perhaps his most important one of all. Sadly, he didn't live to see his restorative vision flower and bear fruit.

Death never did alter its agenda for our plans. As it had done to Mama and Hattie and Walter, to Eli and Abigail, to Gramma and Grampa, to Katherine and

Anna and Jacob Jansen, Death heedlessly cut down Daddy, along with his tender aspirations to quicken this lifeless plot of earth.

But I'm still here. Even if no one else helps, I can till and toil and plant and sweat and bleed to carry out Daddy's vision. Regardless of what Pip and I decide concerning Asphodel's fate, that can be my final tribute to him.

And to Mama, I suppose.

But first, there is another tribute I must make.

I finish my lap around the house, then return indoors to my bedroom. Here, I kneel on the floor and undo the clasps on my suitcase. After shoving the top layer of clothes to its margins, I reach inside and lift out a well-loved, hard-shelled case. Nicks and dents, the badges of many years of heavy use, decorate the black Keratol finish. Its silver trim is no longer bright and polished, for Time has stolen away its luster, leaving it dingy and dull.

Fortunately, it is not the container that matters, but what it contains.

I open the lid and give the object within a cursory glance to confirm that nothing was damaged during its journey from Wichita. Everything appears in order, so I shut the case and re-latch it. Because the brittle leather handle appears untrustworthy, I tuck the entire thing under my arm as I carry it downstairs.

When I was outside earlier, I meandered leisurely as I reminisced. Not now. Now I march with purpose, for I know exactly where I am going.

Through the wizened trees ahead are the waters of Lake Acheron. Its infinite and ever-changing liquid mirrors gleam beneath the midafternoon sun, each one a beacon calling me forth.

I heed their summons, hurrying down the gentle slope and through the lakeshore trees.

At the water's edge, I stop and peer across the water. My heartbeat quickens. Soon, I will find myself vindicated—or made into a fool.

Everything rests upon the Isle. Defiantly, it stares at me across the lake's shimmering surface, daring me to approach, to seek its answers to my ancient questions.

As I skirt the shoreline, I expect to find Eli's old canoe.

What I find instead is a ghost, butter-yellow and with bright-blue trim.

I tremble as I approach the rowboat. It is *The Rosalie,* resurrected to live anew after all these years.

But once I am standing over it, I discover a different name painted upon its stern. Contrary to all initial appearances, this is not *The Rosalie.*

It is called *Walter's Joy.*

My heart swells, and I am pained all over again to remember how much I love and will miss Daddy. He could be as hard as a frostbit legionnaire one moment, and in the next, softer and sweeter than whipped cream.

I flip the rowboat so that it is right-side up, then stow the black case carefully in the bow. With a running shove, I launch the boat from shore and leap inside.

The oars, rough and cracked, fit naturally in my callused hands. Back, butt, legs, shoulders, and arms all work together in fluid motion as I dip, pull, raise, and push the oars in their elliptical orbit. Although my adventures with Walter happened two World Wars ago, they are his movements I see and mimic. His muscle memory has become mine, and I row as precisely and confidently toward our Isle as he once did.

I make berth alongside the same rocky spit we used as kids, then climb ashore carrying my precious cargo. The scintillating birch leaves wave their merry greeting as a pine-fresh breeze caresses my face lovingly.

Twenty years gone, and I am back again. I am Odysseus. I have returned to my Ithaca.

The long grasses of Emerald Hill swish about my ankles as I climb it. Buttercups and Virginia bluebells serve as temporary pulpits for sermons hummed by the buzzing bees. Butterflies and wispy moths and hopping things flee my path as I tread upon their hillside residence. Telepathically, I assure them this won't become a daily occurrence as it was for their ancestors in 1918.

I don't know exactly what I was hoping to find on top of Emerald Hill, but I deflate like a cleated football when I arrive at its summit. This had been the location of so many impossible reunions. To stand here, alone, without even a solitary cardinal to offer its greetings, is plumb demoralizing.

Then again, what was I expecting?

The black case tucked under my arm suddenly feels clumsy and foolish, so I set it onto the soft grass. I will return for it later and take it home unused. It's a shame, really. After all, I lugged it halfway across the United States with me.

But the empty hilltop has already given its answer. A peaceful place to walk and think is all this Isle has left to give me.

As I enter the trees, I pass the thick wall of pink-blossomed mountain laurel where "Gurgan" hid our stolen sugar. Further into the pathless forest, I walk beneath the old oak which held Hattie's treehouse in its mighty arms. Beyond this, upon the Isle's lofty eastern peak, is the dead tree where we found our faithful Yosemite. When I reach the rocky south shore, I pass the cave of the three-headed Hellhound. It appears much smaller than I remembered.

Finally, I ascend the ravine toward the clearing where Mama's enchanted cottage once stood.

All that stands here today is an old cabin, twenty years rottener than when I last saw it. Even the spring beside it has dried up, another of the many victims stolen by Time.

I return to the hilltop and sit beside the black case, disheartened. Spread before me are the waters of a modest lake—which long ago seemed bigger than the sea. Beyond it lie the forested acres of Asphodel Glade. Once upon a time, this was a vast jungle to be explored and tamed by three young boys. Now, they are only trees. Old, loyal, beautiful trees—but trees all the same.

And in the midst of them, stately and strong, stands Asphodel Hall. Our Castle Home. A place where adventures were conceived and born, and where they ended again after the day's conquests. A place of goblin riddles and chocolate cakes. A place of Christmas wonder and holiday feasts and violin concerts. A place of boundless joy and infinite sadness, of memories treasured and memories hated. A place of love and laughter, of tears and rage and every other mask Passion might wear, which, when woven together, created an exquisite tapestry not only of life, but of life *together*.

Neither lake, nor forest, nor glade, nor house are what they used to be. But they are beautiful and—thanks to my father—brim with rediscovered potential.

For someone else, they might become again what they once were for me.

The serenity of acceptance settles over me, and the great emptiness is one I no longer find disturbing.

Perhaps I will do what I came for, after all.

I pop the latches of the black case sitting beside me. Tenderly, adoringly, I lift out Daddy's violin. After his departure from the Philadelphia Orchestra, he kept it for a while, fiddling from time to time as he was able. But when the arthritis grew too debilitating even for casual playing, he relinquished it into my care.

"An instrument is born to make music," he told me as he handed it over. "Just like me."

Daddy always played with his eyes closed. Without the distraction of sight, he claimed he could feel the music flowing from his heart into his arms and fingers, and from there across string and into resonance chamber, before returning at last to his ears and heart. In this way was created a circular motion, from spirit to music and music to spirit, like the oars of a rowboat flowing in and out of the water.

With violin in one hand and bow in the other, I close my eyes in honor of the man who taught me, who raised me, and who loved me, imperfectly but always.

There is only one fitting piece to play, and in moments, the mournful tune of "Red River Valley" resonates upon my violin's strings. The best way to pay tribute to Daddy is by honoring the one he loved above all.

I'm halfway through the stanza when I realize I'm not alone. Somewhere in the trees behind me, a birdsong has joined in. Note for note, its tune matches that of my violin.

It's a sound I would recognize anywhere. The voice of a cardinal, singing along with the melody on my strings.

When the verse is finished, I lower my bow, turn toward the forest, and open my eyes.

Sure enough, dancing merrily upon the low branch of a shortleaf pine, is a single blaze-red cardinal.

When he realizes I am no longer playing, he stops and cocks his head. He stares at me quizzically, as if wondering why I have taken the song away.

Then, as quickly as he came, the cardinal beats his wings and flutters off into the forest.

With renewed disappointment, I hang my head and look at the violin clutched in my hand. The afternoon has dragged on toward evening, and I suppose it is time I headed back across the lake.

After all, I have received the answer to my question. I am certain now that everything I experienced all those years ago was mere fantasy, one born of great tragedy and our childish attempts to cope with it. A delusion which served a healing purpose, and nothing more.

But before I can turn around to pack away the violin and row back to Asphodel Glade, my heart leaps into my throat. I stand, paralyzed in place.

Behind me, whispering through the long grasses which crown Emerald Hill, are soft footsteps.

In a moment, they are joined by a gentle voice I have loved.

"Hello, Peter."

DENALI MAJESTO spent his earlier years in the private business sector, yet he never felt quite at home in what he was doing. After an early retirement from the world of business, Majesto dedicated his life to the three activities he treasures most: loving his family, exploring the globe, and writing. He has since written a small library's worth of stories, which he has begun unveiling to the world—one story at a time. Through both his writing and the tireless work of his ambassadors, it is Majesto's wish that he might entertain and bring hope to the lives of countless others.

To learn more about the man behind the stories, or to view his free content, please visit www.DenaliMajesto.com.

DEAD *doesn't have to mean* **GONE.**

TWENTY
years
AGO...

... in a time earlier than I can remember, my father, a respected travel writer and photographer, passed away. But one Christmas—also the night of my twenty-first birthday—a letter from my deceased parent falls unexpectedly into my hands, sending me in the dead of winter on a global scavenger hunt. As I collect more of his letters at each location, I begin piecing together the story of a dying father's love for his little girl. In my encounters with new friends, unexpected dangers, and surprising revelations, I discover not only who my dad was, but who I am and what my life is meant to be.

AVAILABLE IN E-BOOK AND PRINT

LEARN MORE AT:
DENALIMAJESTO.COM

HIS STORIES ~ OUR LIBRARY

www.DenaliMajesto.com

www.ingramcontent.com/pod-product-compliance
Lightning Source LLC
Chambersburg PA
CBHW020016120726
47903CB00004B/1305